I0583287

DESPERATE SOULS

THE JOSEPH CHRONICLES
BOOK 1

WILL MARLER

To my grandson Christian, whose curiosity amazes me.

PROLOGUE

Northwest Pakistan

The dirt squirmed between ten-year-old Joseph Freeman's fingers. Warm. Soft. Like bread before it bakes. Not like the dirt in America that Papa often talked about. This dirt was different. It was home dirt. The dirt of the Christian mission where Joseph had lived since forever. The best dirt in all of Pakistan, Papa always said.

"Plant it deep, beta," Mama whispered in Urdu from beside him, warming his insides like a blanket on a cool evening.

His hands moved fast—dig, drop, cover. The garden was their special place, where safety smelled like cardamom, jasmine, and the sharp green snap of mint.

Crouching over the seedlings, Mama would say that faith in Jesus was like these baby plants—starting tiny and weak but growing strong to do what God intended. Pushing through the topsoil if helped with water, sun, and patience. "Faith can change everything," she had told him almost every day.

He wanted to be like his mother and father. So Joseph

breathed in the garden air, hoping his faith would grow bigger and stronger.

Mama's hands froze. She tilted her head, like she was trying to hear something far away. The mission went quiet. No birds. No voices. Not even Papa's baritone hymn from the white stone schoolhouse. Just a weird buzzing in Joseph's head. Like something bad was about to happen. Something terrifying.

The first rumble came seconds later. Not thunder. Not wind—but engines. Rolling down from the Hindu Kush mountains like a promise of violence. A cold knot formed inside Joseph's belly. He'd heard his parents whispering about such threats, about missions being attacked, but those had been distant worries—until now.

Joseph stopped planting. Dust clouds rose over the wall. Seconds later, three trucks came into view. White ones. They had green and white flags and were coming fast. Too fast. Right toward the mission gate.

"Lyla, get the boy inside. Quickly." The tremor in Papa's voice sent ice down Joseph's spine.

Three hundred meters north, the lead truck burst through the mission's metal gate tearing it from its rusted hinges.

Mama screamed.

Joseph's heart thudded.

"Hurry," cried his father. "Just like we practiced."

Just like we practiced? They'd rehearsed this, yes—running to the classroom, the hidden tunnel—but always as a game. And always when school was open. All that pretend wasn't pretend anymore. School was closed. And Papa was serious.

The trucks roared into the courtyard, crushing his mother's prized marigolds that had spread over the field like a paradise. Angry voices chanted in Pashto. "Death to the infidels."

He didn't understand why they shouted what they shouted—but the hatred in the men's voices was unmistakable, as if they hated him and his parents for just being there.

Pulling him into the classroom, Mama's fingers dug into Joseph's arm, the garden's spicy scents lost in the stench of diesel exhaust.

"Hassan," his father called to his assistant. Papa rushed from the schoolroom window to where Hassan stood near the supply cabinet. "TLP militants."

Hassan's dark face turned pale. "Lord help us. They burned the mission in Peshawar last spring. They vowed to cleanse Pakistan of all Christians and Jews."

Mama hurried him to the bookcase and the trapdoor underneath. Papa gripped Hassan's shoulder. "Take my son to Lyla's sister in Islamabad. Sarah knows what to do."

Islamabad? Joseph couldn't leave—this was home. His parents. His friends. The garden. The place where he belonged. "Papa, no—" His desperate voice faltered.

"Beta." His father knelt beside him, moisture glistening in his green eyes, the same color as Joseph's. He struggled to breathe. The man who'd taught him to be brave was crying. The foundation of Joseph's world, crumbling. Papa's hands clasped Joseph's face. "You go with Hassan now. No arguments."

With her lips finding Joseph's forehead, Mama's warm tears rolled across his skin. She pulled her silver cross from over her head, and placed it over his. "Stay faithful to our Lord, my love. Remember your gift. Your purpose." She paused to breathe in. "Use it where God takes you."

Squeezing the cross tight, the metal bit into Joseph's

palm. He had to hold onto this moment. To stop time from moving forward. *This can't be goodbye forever. It can't be.*

Truck brakes screeched outside. Heavy boots crunched on the gravel walkway.

"Go." Papa yanked the bookcase open, revealing a trapdoor. "Now."

His mother's hands shook as she kissed Joseph. A memory flashed—her singing hymns while making bread in their kitchen, her fingers white and powdery—then vanished as Hassan dragged him down wooden steps into musky air.

"I love you," his father choked out as the trapdoor slammed shut, then the scraping sound of the bookcase pulled over them.

Darkness swallowed them. A thunderous crack from the classroom—the sound of wood splintering.

Joseph's breath came in sharp, painful gasps. The tunnel's cold air tasted of mildew. His mother's cross in his palm was the only warmth in this underground world. His only connection to what he was losing above.

Hassan yanked Joseph into the blackness, one hand gripping his wrist, the other trailing along the rough tunnel wall. Muffled gunshots thumped overhead, vibrating through the stone ceiling.

A high-pitched scream. Mama—cut off suddenly.

Bile flooded the back of Joseph's throat. *No. No. No.* His mind rejected what his heart already knew. That sound— his mother's voice—silenced forever. His legs refused to move, anchored by grief too heavy to bear.

"Keep moving," Hassan whispered. "Don't stop."

Forcing his feet forward, Joseph walked, then ran, then ran faster. His feet clapped against the stone floor. His lungs burned. Left foot, right foot, don't trip, don't slow down.

The walls felt more narrow, scraping his shoulder when he stumbled. The air tasted like wet dirt and something old, like the basement at the chapel. They ran for what seemed like several minutes. His knees wobbled. The light grew dimmer.

Then the passage widened, splitting into the three separate tunnels, each disappearing into a separate darkness.

Hassan hesitated for the first time, his breath ragged. He scanned the openings, fingers brushing the rough walls as if searching for something. Then he grabbed Joseph's wrist and pulled him through the leftmost option.

"This way," he said in an urgent tone.

Joseph stumbled after him as Hassan kicked a stack of loose rocks into the center opening. The stones clattered into the shadows, their echoes racing down the middle tunnel—a perfect decoy for their pursuers.

"That'll buy us time," Hassan muttered. "Come on."

They plunged into the narrow passage, their footsteps cracking as they moved deeper into the oppressive dark. Behind them, voices bellowed in Pashto. Their pursuers must have reached the fork. Then angry voices followed by muted footfalls rushing down the wrong tunnel.

Hassan exhaled sharply, gripping Joseph's shoulder. "We keep going. Fast."

They ran deeper into the labyrinth, pine smell and fresh air growing stronger with every step. Hassan turned a sharp corner, pulling Joseph along behind him.

"Faster now," Hassan urged. "We're almost there."

The tunnel began to slope upward. Joseph's legs burned with the upward climb, but the need to escape drove him forward. Hassan's grip on his arm tightened as they scrambled up the incline.

"Just a little further," Hassan whispered.

Behind them, the angry voices grew louder. The militants had discovered their deception. Boots pounded against stone, the sound echoing through the tunnel like thunder.

Joseph's felt for his mother's cross, his silent prayers a desperate rhythm matching his racing heartbeat. *Please, God. Please help us.*

The tunnel narrowed, then suddenly opened to reveal a small wooden door. Hassan pushed against it, and with a groan of protest, it swung outward. Sunlight—bright and blinding after the darkness—poured in.

They emerged into a small clearing surrounded by pines. Two pack mules waited in the shadows, just as Papa had arranged. Hassan lifted Joseph onto the first mule, then mounted the second. They kicked the animals into motion, climbing up into the wilderness of the Hindu Kush hills.

Joseph twisted in his saddle for one last look. The mission stood against the rising landscape—the garden where he'd worked with Mama, the classroom where Papa had taught God's Word. Smoke curled from the windows now. His throat burned with unshed tears and the taste of the fumes. Everything he knew—the parents he loved—gone in minutes. The life he was meant to have, vanished.

"My cousin has a farm," Hassan said softly. "Three days' ride into the mountains. We'll be safe there until I can get you to Islamabad."

Joseph had only visited the city twice. His mother's sister lived there—his *khalat* Sarah. Joseph's future was now uncertain. Terrifying.

He turned away from the mission to face the rising trail. The mules picked up their pace, carrying Joseph away from everything he'd ever known. His fingers traced the outline of his mother's cross, her final words echoing in his mind.

Remember your gift. Your purpose. Take it with you where God brings you.

What gift? What purpose could matter now that his parents were gone? His mother's words were a mystery, one he couldn't begin to unravel through the fog of his grief.

His tears fell freely, warm against his cheeks. He looked back one last time. The only home he'd ever known disappeared behind the crest of the hill.

He clutched his mother's cross. Where would this tragedy take him. Where would he use his gift?

A flame of purpose settled in the darkness of his grief. Whatever came next—wherever this journey led—he would carry this day with him forever.

———

THE MULES WALKED ALL NIGHT, climbing up the mountain path. Hassan seemed to know the way without even thinking. Joseph could see the stars now—so many of them, like the tiny white lights Papa decorated the mission with at Christmas, only billions more.

His whole body hurt from riding so long. Every time he closed his eyes, he saw the mission on fire. Heard his mother scream.

When they finally stopped in a small clearing with pine trees all around, Hassan helped Joseph off the mule, kept looking around, like he was making sure the militants hadn't followed.

He made a tiny fire, just big enough to keep them warm. Joseph sat with his back against a tree, staring at the flames, squeezing Mama's cross in his hand so tight it hurt.

"Try to sleep," Hassan said, handing him some dried meat. "We have a long ride tomorrow."

Joseph shook his head. "I can't."

Hassan sat down next to him. "Your father was a good man. Your mother too. They loved you more than anything."

"I know." The words felt too small for how much it hurt inside.

They didn't talk for a long time, just listened to the fire crackling. Then Joseph whispered, "I'm going back someday."

Hassan looked at him fast. "What?"

"To the mission." Joseph looked up from the fire toward where his home was, somewhere far away in the dark. "I'm gonna build it again. All of it."

Hassan frowned. "Joseph, that's not—"

"I have to." The words came out louder than he meant them to. "Everything they built, everything they taught us— I can't let it just...end. I can't let those bad men take it away forever."

"Those men control that area now," Hassan said softly. "They won't let—"

"I don't care." Joseph squeezed the cross harder. "Papa always told me faith can move mountains. Well, I have faith. Someday, I'm going back. I'll fix the walls, plant Mama's garden again. I'll teach kids like Papa did."

Hassan looked at him in the firelight. "That's impossible, Joseph. You're just a kid."

"I won't always be a kid." Joseph looked right at Hassan, feeling something strong and hard growing inside where everything else felt broken. "I don't know how I'll do it. I don't know when. But I promise, Hassan—I'm going back. And I'm going to build it all again."

Hassan was quiet for a long time as if he didn't believe Joseph, looking at him the way grown-ups looked at kids when they said silly things. But Joseph didn't care. The bad men had burned down his home and murdered Mama and Papa. They took everything away. But they couldn't take away all the things Papa taught him, all the prayers Mama prayed with him.

"Your father would say that with God, nothing is impossible," Hassan finally said quietly.

Joseph nodded, feeling a tear roll down his face. "Then that's what I'll believe."

The fire popped and crackled, sending little sparks flying up toward the stars like tiny prayers. Joseph watched them rise and disappear into the darkness, but instead of feeling alone, he felt something new growing inside him. Like the kind of seed Mama had taught him to plant deep in the soil, to water and tend even when it seemed like it might never grow.

A seed of a promise.

He would go back someday. And rebuild the mission.

PART 1

ONE

Biloxi, Mississippi

Afternoon sunlight streamed through the high windows
of Grace Thompson's dance studio, casting a gold hue
across the polished hardwood floor. The bite of rosin and a
whisper of sweet perfume mingled with the faintest hint of
sweat from the day's earlier classes. Chopin resonated from
the sound system speakers in the corners, its notes reverber-
ating off the mirrored walls and floating up to the vaulted
ceiling.

Grace stood at the barre, her slender reflection multi-
plied in the surrounding mirrors. Her auburn bun pulled at
her scalp, not a single hair daring to escape. Her pale skin
contrasted with the black leotard that revealed toned arms
and the defined muscles of a lifetime dancer. At twenty-
four, her face retained a teenage quality despite the intensity burning in her hazel-grey eyes.

She drew a measured breath, feeling the cool air fill her
lungs as she extended her spine, elongating through her
fingertips. This sanctuary, this domain, belonged to her—a

place where all motion held purpose, where imperfection found no home.

"Watch carefully," she called to her student Emma. "Notice how each movement connects to the next."

Grace took three preparatory steps, gathering momentum. Her body was oddly heavy today, but she pushed the thought aside. *Focus.* Her muscles remembered these progressions—she had performed them flawlessly since she was Emma's age. She launched into a *grand jeté*. For a moment, her limbs betrayed her—a strange hesitation she had never experienced before. *Push through it.* She forced her legs into the familiar split while her joints protested. For that suspended second, gravity released its hold.

Landing softly through her arches, Grace immediately pivoted into a controlled *soutenu* turn, using the momentum from her leap to fuel the rotation. Her working leg wrapped around, pulling into a tight fifth position as she completed the full revolution.

"Feel the connection between elements," she instructed, flowing seamlessly into a *sissonne fermée*. She pushed off both feet, scissored her legs before closing them, absorbing the impact of her landing through pliant knees. The music crescendoed as Grace prepared for the finale.

Just get through this combination.

She ignored the unusual tingling in her fingers, stepped into fourth position, executed a *relevé*, and launched into *fouetté* turns—normally her signature strength. The first two rotations were flawless. On the third turn, her knees buckled mid-rotation. The studio tilted violently around her. *No, no, no—not now, not here.* Her heart raced as the floor rushed up to her. She caught herself, converting the stumble into an improvised pivot before Emma could notice. In nineteen years of dancing, her body had never betrayed her like the past two months. And today, worse than yesterday. Worse than ever before. A cold wave of fear overwhelmed her, quickly replaced by determination.

Emma gasped. "Miss Grace, are you alright?"

"Just adjusting my form," Grace said smoothly. She forced her breathing to remain even despite the heavy weight settling inside her. "Always teaching moments, right?"

The late afternoon sun streamed through the studio's tall windows, warming her shoulders as she leaned her palm against the mirror to steady herself. She caught sight of her reflection—was she paler than usual?

Maybe just dehydrated. Maybe.

She'd barely squeezed in time for water between her meeting with the wedding planner and the afternoon classes.

"Watch the alignment on that *développé*, Emma." Grace straightened, wincing inwardly as her joints protested. The pain was sharper today, different from normal dance soreness. *Probably just overworked from the showcase rehearsals,* she reasoned, unwilling to consider alternatives three months before her marriage. "Up through the core, like a string pulling you toward the ceiling."

Emma frowned, adjusting her position. "Like this?"

"Almost. Think of your spine lengthening—yes, exactly like that. Now hold it."

Emma's reflection nodded, her face pinched with concentration. Chopin filled the sun-warmed studio, but the melody seemed to warp and stretch, the counts slipping from Grace's meticulous timing. Her temples throbbed, making it difficult to focus.

What is happening to me?

"Again. Five, six, seven, eight." The room tilted. Grace

gripped the barre, turning it into a deliberate teaching moment, hoping Emma hadn't noticed the tremor in her hand. "Notice how I'm using this for balance during the preparation." A bead of sweat rolled down her spine despite the studio's cooler temperature setting.

Emma wobbled on her third fouetté turn. Grace moved to spot her, but her arms were like lead weights. The room spun faster, black spots dancing at the edges of her vision.

I can't drop her. I can't let anyone see me like this.

"Let's break this down." Grace's voice remained steady through sheer force of will, though panic squeezed her breath away like a coiling serpent. "Walk me through your preparation."

Emma lowered her arms. "Start in fifth position, plié, then push through."

"Good. And where are your eyes focused?"

Emma straightened. "Spot the mirror, then whip my head around."

Three more combinations to teach, then the florist appointment. *I can make it. I have to make it.* The wedding invitations needed her approval by Friday, and Andrew's mother expected final numbers for the reception. Grace ran her life on precision—in dance, in business, in planning her future with Andrew. She allowed no room for weakness. "Watch my demonstration one more time."

Emma's mother would arrive any minute. Grace marked the next sequence, negotiating each movement with her increasingly uncooperative body. The steps she'd performed for fifteen years—the foundation of her identity, her livelihood—felt foreign now, as if she piloted someone else's limbs. "Your turn." Grace flattened her back against the mirror, disguising her need for support as casual observation. The cool glass seeped through her leotard as she fought to remain upright. "Full sequence, beginning to end."

Emma positioned herself. Grace struggled to focus on her student's form. The music warped, notes stretching and contracting. Her lungs struggled with an invisible weight. *Just get through this class. Then call Dr. Lawson.* The thought surprised her. She hadn't seen the doctor since she sprained her ankle eighteen months ago.

"Miss Grace? Are you okay?" Emma rushed forward. "Should I get some water?"

"No, stay in position," Grace commanded, her teacher's voice steady despite everything.

Footsteps in the hallway. Emma's mother.

Grace straightened, ignoring the black spots dancing in her vision.

No one can see me like this. I can't lose students. Can't skip another wedding appointment. Can't worry Andrew. Just fifteen more minutes of composure.

"Emma, honey—" Ms. Chen cut through the fog. "Oh. Grace, you're white as a sheet."

"Just my allergies." The lie came automatically, though she'd never had allergies in her life. She touched her cheek —typically rosy, now pale—and forced a reassuring smile as she let go of the barre. "Emma, wonderful work today. We'll pick up here on Thursday."

She maintained perfect posture until they left, then collapsed onto the wooden bench by her dance bag. This was the third class she'd ended early this week. Something was wrong—something beyond stress or dehydration. The realization terrified her. Her hand shook uncontrollably as she pulled out her phone.

"Merit Healthcare, how may I help you?"

"Grace Thompson. I need—" She touched her forehead, surprised by the heat radiating from her skin. "I need to see Dr. Lawson as soon as possible, please."

The receptionist's voice softened. "Of course. What seems to be the concern?"

"I'm probably just overworked—I'm getting married in three months, planning a showcase for my dancers, and running my studio. I just want to make sure I'm not pushing too hard."

"Any specific symptoms?"

Grace cast a quick look at the mirror. Her reflection revealed a rigid posture even while sitting. Fear flickered in her eyes.

What if I'm sick? What if I can't teach for an extended period? What if...

"Fatigue, likely from the wedding preparations. Some dizziness." She left out the joint pain, the fever, and the way her body betrayed her during the simplest combinations. "Nothing serious."

The receptionist paused. "How long have you been experiencing these symptoms?"

"Just a few weeks," Grace lied, ignoring the voice reminding her it had been nearly two months since she first noticed the unusual fatigue. "Just a quick checkup. I'm sure it's just stress."

She ended the call and gathered her things. The lights glimmered off the hardwood floor—or maybe that was just her vision again. Her fingers fumbled with the zipper of her bag, another small betrayal from her usually precise body. *Nothing serious. Nothing that will interfere with the wedding or the showcase or the studio expansion.*

But as she struggled to lift the bag—normally light as air —doubt crept in. *What if this wasn't just exhaustion?* She reached for the light switch, leaning into the wall to steady herself. A powdery smudge of rosin marked the paint where her hand had landed. Out of place. She stared at it, too drained to wipe it away. It clung there like something unwanted left behind. The first flaw in a sanctuary she'd always believed was hers, and hers alone.

THE NEXT AFTERNOON, Grace's hip ached as she shifted in the cushioned chair in Merit Health clinic's waiting room twenty minutes past her appointment time. She was on hold with her accountant after having to cancel their meeting. And at this rate, she'd have to miss a new student's lesson—and good luck explaining that to the girl's mother without raising concerns. She should be at work right now, finalizing the upcoming month's schedule. Melissa finally came back on the phone.

"The venue deposit's due Friday, Melissa." Grace massaged her temple where the room's bright lights drilled into her skull. "And can we move those quarterly projections to next week? I've got three private lessons after this quick check-up."

The local news droned from the TV. A weather report predicted another scorcher. Grace shifted in her chair as her knee twinged.

"Oh, and the roses for the wedding will be superb, Melissa. I found this amazing florist in Ocean Springs." Grace flipped through her planner, each tab color-coded and organized. "You should see what she did with the sample arrangements."

Melissa's laugh crackled through the phone. "And how does the future CEO of Gulf Coast Trust feel about the flower budget?"

"Andrew trusts me with the wedding details. As long as they don't interfere with his five-year career trajectory." The corners of her mouth tightened. "Though he did remind me this morning that we need to wrap up the planning by next month. Something about a major client portfolio review coming up before the ceremony."

Grace frowned wondering if she should share the following bit of information. But, hey, Melissa was her business accountant.

"Oh, and the prenup arrived yesterday." Grace kept her voice bright, but her stomach knotted at the reference of that thick envelope. "Seventy-eight pages of asset protection and contingency clauses. Andrew says it's standard for someone on his career path."

"That's...thorough."

"He's just being practical. You should hear him talk about his ten-year plan—Senior VP in two years, the time of year that works best for having kids, even which golf club membership will help him network with the right people." A rush of frustration surged through her. "Everything's perfectly scheduled."

"Well good luck with that," Melissa said with a slightly sour tone. "I gotta run. Having coffee with a client."

Grace disconnected and checked the time on her phone. Twenty-eight minutes late now. She scrolled through her phone calendar, mentally rearranging her afternoon, when a woman in flowery green scrubs appeared by the doorway.

"Grace Thompson?"

She stood, her hips unnaturally stiff.

"Follow me please," the lady said, checking her tablet. "How are you feeling today?"

"Fine, just a routine check-up," Grace replied, gathering her purse. "Running a bit behind schedule though."

"Aren't we all?" The nurse's smile appeared practiced but was kind. "Let's get your vitals first."

Grace followed the nurse down a hallway lined with motivational posters about heart health and flu prevention. The examination room was small but efficient, with the familiar crinkle of paper covering the exam table.

"Go ahead and have a seat right here," the nurse said, patting the table. She wrapped the blood pressure cuff around Grace's upper arm, the velcro scratching as it secured. "Just relax your arm for me."

The cuff tightened, squeezing until Grace felt her pulse thrumming against the pressure. The nurse frowned slightly at the digital readout.

"Let's take your temperature and get your weight as well."

Grace stepped onto the scale, watching the numbers settle lower than she'd expected. The thermometer beeped after a few seconds under her tongue.

"Dr. Lawson will be with you in just a few minutes," the nurse said, making notes on her tablet.

After the nurse left, Grace sat in the sudden quiet, surrounded by a mixture of citrus disinfectant cutting through someone's morning coffee. She checked her phone twice before a soft knock interrupted her scrolling.

Dr. Lawson entered with a warm smile, her reading glasses catching the overhead light as she glanced up from Grace's file. Her brown shoulder-length hair with lighter highlights, swayed against her white coat collar as she settled into the rolling chair.

"Good morning, Grace. Haven's seen you since you wrenched your ankle. Any lingering problems?"

"None at all. At least not with my ankle."

She pulled up Grace's chart on the computer, scrolling through recent lab results. "Your blood pressure's elevated," she noted, glancing between the screen and the nurse's notes. "The first reading was 148 over 94, and the second was 145 over 92. Have you been feeling stressed lately, or noticed any changes in your routine?"

"I rushed here from the studio," Grace explained smoothly.

"Any joint pain since your last visit?" Dr. Lawson's fingers pinched Grace's knees, then ankles.

The right knee screamed. Both wrists ached from yesterday's advanced class. Her shoulders had barely loosened since morning. "Nothing significant. Probably from demonstrating new choreography." Thirty-two minutes late now.

"How many classes are you teaching per week?" Dr. Lawson asked, making notes.

"Just my usual schedule. Though we did add a few students this month."

"And the fatigue you mentioned to the nurse?"

"Wedding planning." Grace forced a laugh to match her bright tone, already reaching for her purse. "Plus expanding the studio. You know how it is."

"I'd like to run some blood work."

"Is that really necessary?" Grace asked, her professional smile firmly in place. "I mean, I'm just tired from being busy."

"Better to rule things out," Dr. Lawson said gently. "Nadine will be right in."

"Can we do that next time?" The room tilted as Grace stood. She clinched her fists, willing her hands steady. "I've got a student waiting."

"It won't take but a second," Dr. Lawson assured as she moved to the door. "Nadine will be in shortly to draw a sample. We'll run a complete panel. Should have results in a few days."

A new student's first lesson. Then vendor calls. Then a bank meeting. She had a schedule to keep, and that didn't free time for a blood test. But she waited another ten minutes for the nurse to take blood.

As Grace rose to leave, she glanced at the vial of her blood resting on the metal tray—deep crimson against sterile white—harboring secrets that caused Grace to worry. Her image captured by the glass cabinet door revealed a woman outwardly composed, yet beneath her crisp blouse, pain throbbed where no injury occurred.

TWO

Adjacent Wing at Merit Health Center

Nine months of prayers had led to this moment, and here she was, all six pounds four ounces of God's beautiful answer. Nathan Carter steadied his hands on the hospital bed rail as the nurse carried his newborn daughter, Lily, to them in a pink striped blanket wrapped tightly around her tiny frame. Hannah reached out, her face glowing despite the hours of labor. Nathan's heart swelled at his wife's excitement about being a mother.

"Ready to meet your daughter?" The maternity nurse's gentleness matched the hushed atmosphere of the room. "She's been quite the angel in the nursery," she added with a warm smile. "Hardly made a peep."

Unable to speak past the lump in his throat, Nathan nodded. He'd prayed for this moment since the day he got married—prayed for a family built on faith and God's love. Now, watching his newborn daughter settle into his wife's arms, those prayers had been beautifully, perfectly answered.

Hannah cradled Lily. Her hands trembled—that

familiar diabetes tremor that always preceded a crash. "Look at those little fingers," she whispered, touching each digit. "Ten tiny miracles."

"Just like her mama," Nathan replied softly, his voice thick with emotion.

Mom's White Diamonds perfume filled the room before her voice did. "There's my grand baby." She swept in, arms extended. "Oh, Hannah, sweetheart, you look radiant. How are you feeling?"

Rachel slipped in behind her, phone raised and already snapping pictures. "Hey, big brother." Rachel's grin stretched wider as she circled the bed, but her eyes darted to Hannah's hands. His sister had spent enough nights during Hannah's pregnancy crashes to know the signs. "First-time daddy suits you," she teased gently. "Even if you look like you might pass out."

"She's gorgeous." Mom leaned over. "Just like her mama," she added, dabbing at her eyes. "The Lord has truly blessed us today. Your father would have been so proud, Nathan."

Hannah's smile wavered. "Would someone mind grabbing my juice? In my bag?"

"I've got it," Rachel said while moving, having done this a hundred times through all nine months of Hannah's pregnancy. "Top pocket, right?" She reached for the familiar spot. Nathan's stomach clenched as Hannah sipped apple juice one-handed, never taking her eyes off Lily. He should be past this by now—the flash of fear every time her sugar dropped. But watching her hold their daughter, those old worries crept in through the cracks of his joy.

"Seven pounds?" Mom's hands clasped under her chin in a way that meant she held back from snatching up her granddaughter.

Color bloomed back into Hannah's cheeks with each sip. "Just right for a dancer."

"Already planning her future in ballet?" he said with a supportive smile rather than just laughter. "Let's get you back to full strength first."

"It's never too early," Hannah replied with a soft smile. "Besides, with Nathan's genes, she's bound to have rhythm."

His shoulders unknotted. This was their moment—diabetes or not. "Just beautiful," he managed, and meant it.

Rachel raised her phone to eye level. "One more picture with everyone. Nathan, get in there. Mom, lean in closer. Hannah, tilt the baby just a bit—there, that's it."

Perching on the edge of the bed, Nathan slid an arm behind Hannah's shoulders. The warmth of her body against his side, Lily's soft breathing, his mother's quiet prayers of thanksgiving—this was everything he'd dreamed of. His own little flock.

Hannah's fingers brushed his arm. "Your hands are shaking worse than mine," she whispered.

But they weren't. Her fingers still trembled against his skin, even after the juice. A familiar coldness crept into his gut, but he pushed it away. *Not now. Not today.* He placed a kiss on Hannah's temple, breathing in the faint sweetness of her hair, and smiled for Rachel's camera.

Mom's gaze clung to Hannah's hands, her lips speaking silent words that transcended mere gratitude—a desperate prayer that Nathan recognized all too well.

The urge to gather Hannah and Lily, to somehow shield them both, overwhelmed him. Taking his mother's lead, he formulated his own prayer. *God, don't let this moment be as fleeting as it feels.*

NATHAN SHOULD HAVE BEEN BASKING in the joy of holding his newborn daughter, but he couldn't tear his eyes away from Hannah's shaky hands as she reached for her water glass. The sheen of sweat glistened on her too-pale face. His heart raced with familiar worry.

Across from him, Hannah nestled in the hospital bed, her tired smile radiating as she gazed at their daughter. This was the moment they had longed for— their beautiful, faith-filled family off to a great start. Nathan's heart swelled as he drank in his wife's glow, her eyes sparkling with joy despite the tiredness etched on her face from the exhausting chore of delivering their Lily.

Dr. Rachel Montgomery entered the room holding a clipboard and a concerned expression. "How are we feeling today, Hannah?" Her tone was not entirely gentle.

Hannah scowled. Her love/hate meter with Dr. Montgomery was clearly teetering in the red. "Fine," she muttered.

"Your latest blood work shows concerning levels. Your creatinine is elevated, indicating possible kidney stress, and your blood pressure readings have been erratic. With your diabetes, these are red flags we can't ignore."

Nathan relaxed his smile slightly as he listened intently, the joy of the moment punctured by the familiar knot of worry in his stomach. He wanted nothing more than to set aside all fear and simply enjoy this beautiful moment with his wife and daughter, but Dr. Montgomery's words carried a heavy weight.

As he watched Hannah dismiss the doctor's warnings with a wave of her hand, his pulse quickened. Could she truly brush off the risks? He wanted to be in this moment, to cherish it fully, yet the specter of uncertainty loomed large —what if something went wrong? He stifled his fears, forcing a smile back to his face, determined to hold onto this dream. But as the doctor continued speaking, Nathan couldn't shake the feeling that their happiness was so fragile.

Dr. Montgomery adjusted her glasses and glanced at Hannah's chart, her brow furrowing with concern. "We're also seeing signs of diabetic retinopathy in your last eye exam. These blood vessel changes in your eyes, combined with your post-pregnancy hormonal shifts, create the perfect storm for complications."

Hannah waved her hand dismissively, rolling her eyes. "Doctor, I've dealt with these 'red flags' my entire life. Every time my numbers are slightly off, everyone acts like it's a crisis. I bounced back from ketoacidosis when I was sixteen, didn't I? This is just another bump in the road."

She reached for her water glass, missing it slightly before correcting her grip. "See? I'm fine. Just tired from giving birth. Stop making Nathan worry over nothing."

Nathan turned uncomfortably in his chair. Worry swept over him. He leaned forward, his heart racing. "What's wrong, Doc? I mean, we just had Lily and—"

Dr. Montgomery raised a hand to calm him. "I may be overprotective, Nathan. I've been her doctor since she was twelve. But diabetes can be unpredictable, especially postpartum. Hormonal changes can significantly affect glucose levels."

Hannah leaned back against her pillows, as if trying to maintain a sense of control. "I feel fine, really. I'm taking my insulin and monitoring my blood sugar. I can handle this."

"But what if your levels spike again?" Nathan interjected gently, his voice trembling with concern. "I just want you safe, Hannah. You need to take this seriously."

Dr. Montgomery's expression softened but remained

firm. "Hannah, we recommend more frequent check-ups to keep a close watch on your health. Your latest A1C levels are higher than I'd like, which can complicate things."

A chill sank into Nathan's bones at the word "complicate." It echoed in his mind, amplifying the dread bubbling within him. He looked to Hannah, searching her face for any sign of concern. "Doesn't that worry you at all?"

"I've managed this disease since childhood, Nathan," Hannah replied, shaking her head defiantly. "This is just another part of the journey, and I know what I'm doing." She flashed a reassuring smile.

Nathan nodded, but something constricted in his gut as her fingers trembled slightly—a telltale sign she was working harder than she admitted to maintain control. He'd seen this before—the determined set of her jaw, the too-bright smile, the tension feathering around her eyes. A mask. One he'd learned to see through back in middle school, long before she'd mastered hiding pain behind practiced bravado.

His arms tightened around Lily as last year's memory slammed into him. The sharp scent of antiseptic. The frantic beeping of machines. Hannah, pale and motionless in that hospital bed, after insisting for weeks that she was "just tired." His pulse kicked hard against his ribs. She was doing it again. He shifted his weight, hesitating. If he pushed, she'd brush him off. If he let it go... His jaw clenched. How much was she hiding this time?

"Hannah, are you experiencing any symptoms that concern you?" Dr. Montgomery asked with intent eyes from the foot of Hannah's bed.

"I've been feeling a bit more fatigued than usual, but I assumed that was just the after effects of labor," Hannah responded. Her honest tone was admirable, but Nathan couldn't shake the disquiet brewing inside him.

Dr. Montgomery looked at Nathan, then back at Hannah. "While fatigue post-delivery is common, it's essential to consider the implications of your diabetes. We need to ensure that there aren't underlying issues that could jeopardize both your health and that of Lily."

Nathan's throat tightened at the mention of their daughter. He wasn't sure if he could bear to think about anything happening to Hannah *and* Lily.

"I can arrange for a dietitian to review your meal plan if you feel that would help," Dr. Montgomery offered. "It's vital to maintain balanced nutrition, especially now."

Hannah nodded, "Yes, that sounds helpful. I want to do everything right." Her gaze jumped to Lily, who was starting to squirm in Nathan's arms. "The only thing I truly care about is being there for her. Not just for her first months, but for every milestone."

"We'll do this together," Nathan said, his tone filled with conviction. "Let's set reminders for your medications and monitor everything diligently. We can make a new routine, a family routine." He glanced down at Lily. "One that keeps us all together, every step of the way."

Hannah beamed at him, the warmth of her love radiating through the room even in the face of uncertainty. "Thank you, Nathan." It was as if a shared understanding passed between them, a silent vow to navigate their future as a united front.

Nathan's pulse quickened at Lily cooing softly in his arms, blissfully unaware of the discussion. He took a steadying breath. "I just want to take care of you and Lily."

"Don't you worry. I've been looking forward to being a mom my whole life," she said with thick emotion.

Nathan relaxed and began rocking his daughter. "I hope so. Because I can't be a dad without you."

Silence enveloped the room. Dreams of a loving family seemed so fragile—like glass on the verge of shattering. He bowed his head and silently pleaded with God for wisdom and strength. What if Hannah was taken from him? He'd never survive that heartbreak. He fought through his bitter emotions to break free from this depression. Hannah was right. Her diabetes wasn't going to control them or their happiness.

A nurse's rubber-soled shoes squeaked as she entered. "Time to check those vitals, Hannah."

"I have to pee first," Hannah said as she pushed herself up from her pillow.

Nathan's fingers tightened on Lily. Something was wrong with Hannah's movements—too jerky, too fast. His mouth opened to warn her, but it was too late. Hannah swayed. Her hand shot out to grab the bed rail, missing once before catching it, but knocking over the water glass that shattered on the tile floor. He couldn't catch her without risking Lily, couldn't protect them both at once.

"I'm fine," Hannah snapped. The sharpness in her voice couldn't mask how ghost-white her face had gone. "Just stood up too fast. You all need to stop hovering."

The glass fragments scattered across the floor seemed to mock Nathan's earlier prayers. How many more signs did they need that something was terribly wrong?

Dr. Montgomery stepped forward, but Hannah straightened herself, forcing a bright smile. The smile twisted his gut because he knew she used it to hide her fear.

"See? Perfectly steady now," Hannah said. "This is exactly what I mean about overreacting."

Rachel, who had been watching from the corner of the room, stepped forward. "I've got my prayer circle at the church focused on your healing, Hannah. Pastor Jim preached just this past Sunday that with sufficient faith, miracles can happen every day."

Dr. Montgomery's posture stiffened visibly. She clicked her pen with more force, her professional demeanor cracking.

"With all due respect," she said, her tone making it clear she owed none, "prayer circles won't regulate insulin levels or repair damaged kidney function. Hannah needs strict adherence to medical protocols, not false hope."

Hannah's eyes flashed. "My faith isn't 'false hope,' Doctor."

"I've been practicing medicine for fifteen years," Dr. Montgomery continued, gathering Hannah's chart against her torso. "And I've yet to see a single case where prayer outperformed proper medical treatment. Science is the only reliable path forward here."

Nathan noticed how she emphasized "reliable," as if their faith was somehow childish or naive. "We can do both," he offered diplomatically, bouncing Lily gently in his arms.

Dr. Montgomery's tight smile didn't reach her eyes. "Of course. Pray all you want. But don't let it interfere with following sound medical advice. I've seen too many patients decline proven treatments in favor of... *alternative* approaches." Her tone made the word 'alternative' sound like 'stupid.'

The room fell into an uncomfortable silence. Hannah's lips formed a thin line as her eyes locked onto the doctor, her hands gripping the bed rail so tightly her knuckles whitened.

Rachel shifted her weight from one foot to the other, hesitant to challenge a medical professional. The only sound was the soft, rhythmic beeping of the monitors and Lily's occasional coo.

Then Dr. Montgomery cleared her throat and made a note on her clipboard, the scratch of her pen against paper unnervingly loud in the tense quiet.

But Nathan couldn't miss how Hannah's hands trembled as she smoothed her hospital gown. The nurse exchanged a worried glance with him, and his stomach plummeted.

Lily squirmed in his arms, and he held her tighter, watching his wife's trembling fingers from across the room. Two feet of space between them might as well have been an ocean, and the possibility of their daughter growing up without a mother crushed the air from his lungs.

THREE

Grace wandered into the waiting area inside Merit Healthcare at ten in the morning, the sterile smell of antiseptic hitting her like a punch. She scanned the room, making quick assessments of the patients scattered about, each encased in their own thoughts—or worries. But not her. It was just a follow-up appointment to learn why she was so fatigued. Get a prescription or make slight lifestyle adjustments, then get back to the studio in time for a private lesson.

Of course, she was run down. The past few weeks had been a whirlwind of long teaching hours and the stress of planning her wedding. The chaos would settle once she returned from her honeymoon. Taking a seat, she rubbed her temples. The plastic chair was cool against her legs, making her shiver slightly despite the warm morning. "It's fine," she whispered under her breath, clenching her hands on her lap. She had a wedding to plan, a studio to run, and a future to prepare for—exhaustion was simply part of the ride, right?

A woman emerged from the examination room, tears

rolling down her pale cheeks. An unease twisted inside Grace at the thought of what news this poor woman had learned. Grace shook her head as she tried to shake off her concern. "Stay positive," she muttered to herself. "It has nothing to do with you."

"Grace Thompson?" The smiling nurse's voice sliced through Grace's thoughts.

"Right here," she said, standing on instinct.

A small flutter of nerves danced in her stomach, but she buried it beneath a positive outlook. She was just running an errand—get in, get out, get back to the studio within the hour.

The nurse led her down the hallway. Grace's thoughts drifted to her dance studio—the rhythm of the music, her students' laughter. She was too young to worry about her future getting thrown off course.

"Blood pressure first," the nurse said, wrapping the cuff around Grace's arm. "Try to relax."

"I'm fine, really," Grace said. "Just tired from planning my wedding."

"When's the big day?"

"Three months." Grace managed a smile. "Seems both too close and too far."

Dr. Sarah Lawson entered the examination room with measured steps, her usually brisk movements weighted with purpose. She settled into her chair, opened Grace's file, and began clicking her pen—once, twice, three times. Click. Click. Click. "The results from your blood work showed some concerning markers," Dr. Lawson said, meeting Grace's eyes directly. "Your ANA test came back positive."

Grace wrinkled her brow. The term meant nothing to her. "What's ANA?"

"Antinuclear antibodies."

"What exactly does that mean?"

"Think of it like friendly fire," Dr. Lawson explained. "Your immune system is mistaking healthy cells for invaders."

Grace straightened her spine automatically, the way she did when correcting posture in her youngest students. "But there must be some mistake. Could it be a false positive? I read somewhere that stress can affect test results." She smoothed her hands over her leggings, erasing invisible wrinkles. "I'm planning my wedding and have a summer showcase coming up."

"We ran the panel twice to be certain," Dr. Lawson said gently. Her shoulders tensed as she leaned forward. "Along with your symptoms—the fatigue, joint pain, and breathing difficulties—it suggests an autoimmune condition."

"But that can't be right." Grace's dancer instinct to correct a misstep kicked in. "I just pushed too hard last month. Too many back-to-back classes. I need to adjust my schedule, that's all."

The room seemed to shift beneath Grace's chair. She gripped the armrests for balance. "Auto...immune?"

"Your immune system is attacking healthy cells in your body." Dr. Lawson's voice softened, but her words landed like rocks pelting Grace's body.

"But that's..." Grace shook her head, trying to clear the fog creeping into her mind. "I just need rest. The wedding planning, the studio—"

"Grace." Dr. Lawson set down her pen and folded her hands on the desk. "The symptoms you've been experiencing aren't just from overwork."

The realization settled like a weight on her shoulders—shoulders that had maintained precise alignment through thousands of arabesques. "What about my showcase next month? I have to demonstrate the variations for my advanced class."

"With proper treatment—"

"I can't reschedule," Grace said with the sharp tone reserved for students not focusing. "We've been preparing all season. The theater is booked."

Dr. Lawson's expression softened. "I'm not saying you can't dance, Grace. But we need to address what's happening with your body. With proper treatment and management—"

"Management?" Grace said. "You're talking like this is permanent."

"It's a chronic condition," Dr. Lawson said. "But many people with autoimmune conditions lead full, active lives."

"Active? I teach ballet. I need my body to work flawlessly."

"Let's focus on one step at a time," Dr. Lawson said. "First, we need to get you started on medication." Grace's stomach lurched. Her grip faltered as she clutched the armrests.

"I'm quite certain you have Systemic Lupus Erythematosus." Dr. Lawson paused, her eyes softening with practiced compassion. "Lupus."

The word hung between them, heavy with implications Grace wasn't ready to face. Her ears rang with the sound of her own pulse, drowning out the beginning of Dr. Lawson's explanation. Wedding plans, dance routines, and future dreams began to fade like old photographs.

"I know this is overwhelming," Dr. Lawson continued, "but we must discuss treatment options."

The harsh reality began to sink in. Grace allowed herself to ask, "What does this mean for my future? For my dancing?"

"With proper care and management, many people with lupus lead active lives."

"Active is one thing. Professional dance instruction is another." Grace's tried to keep her voice steady. "I need precision. Impeccable control of every muscle."

Dr. Lawson reached for her prescription pad. "We'll create a customized plan for your specific needs, Grace. I'm referring you to Dr. Winters—she's a renowned rheumatologist who works in this facility."

"A specialist? How extensive is this going to be?" The thought of coordinating multiple medical appointments alongside Grace's teaching schedule and wedding preparations sent a tremor through her torso—like pushing through too many fouettés without proper breathing.

"We'll build your support team gradually," Dr. Lawson assured her. "For now, focus on starting these medications and getting rest."

Grace stumbled out of the clinic, Dr. Lawson's information packet clutched in her trembling hands. Her phone buzzed—a reminder for a private lesson in twenty minutes. The screen blurred as she stared at Andrew's name above his number in her recent calls. Her finger hovered. He needed to know. Everyone needed to know. But right now, she couldn't form the words. Couldn't explain it because she didn't understand it herself. Instead, she closed the notification for the lesson and straightened her shoulders. She could hold it together for one more hour. She had to. Because the moment she stopped moving, the moment she said it out loud, the moment she told one soul, her carefully constructed future would shatter like crystal on marble—leaving her life in a mess of broken pieces. She slipped her phone back into her purse, burying Dr. Lawson's packet beneath it. Today, she was still Grace Thompson, ballet dancer and instructor. Tomorrow...well, tomorrow she'd just have to figure out her next step.

Her world had narrowed to two devastating dilemmas—when would she tell Andrew? How would he react? She maintained her exemplary posture, ingrained through decades of ballet discipline. But the manila folder in her purse might as well have been radioactive, its contents threatening to burn through everything she'd built.

The engagement ring on her finger caught the light, sending splintered rainbows across her knuckles—beautiful, broken patterns that seemed to mock the fracturing of her future. Three months until the wedding. Three months to figure out how to tell her fiancé that the woman he proposed to was not the woman he would marry.

OUTSTANDING   TECHNIQUE   REQUIRED OUTSTANDING CONTROL. Grace stared at her shaking hand suspended over the ignition button, betrayed by a body that had just become her enemy. Start the car. Drive to the studio. Teach the next lesson. Simple steps that now felt impossible. The lupus information lay buried in her bag on the passenger seat. Even without touching it, its presence was enough to make breathing harder. Her phone buzzed, sending a jolt through her shoulders. Probably another question from her wedding planner.

The clinic's parking lot stretched before her, heat waves dancing off the asphalt. She needed to leave. Her new student would arrive in forty minutes, but sunlight through the windshield caught every tremble in her fingers—each twitch an uninvited confession of her body's unwelcome truth.

No. She wouldn't give in to this. Years of dance discipline had taught her how to push through pain, how to maintain optimal form even when her muscles screamed. This was no different. She'd manage it, like she managed her thriving dance studio, like she managed planning her wedding, like she managed every detail in her courtship with Andrew until he proposed. Landing the Gulf Coast's most eligible bachelor hadn't been easy, but she'd done it. This was just one more challenge to overcome. Grace jabbed the ignition button. The engine's hum filled the car, drowning out the rapid thud of her pulse. One more deep breath. She could do this. She had to do this.

Traffic crawled along Highway 90. Grace's fingers tightened on the steering wheel as another joint-stabbing ache shot through her wrists. The stumbles during Emma's last lesson flashed through her mind—the confused looks from her longtime student, the whispers between her and her mom. Grace couldn't let that happen again. Not with this new girl. Not with her first private lesson.

The sun glared off the Gulf waters, and Grace squinted as her vision blurred at the stoplight. Three blinks to clear it. Four. The car behind her honked. Her foot slipped off the brake. She jerked forward before catching herself.

Thirty minutes until the lesson. The local dance community lived on gossip, and her studio's reputation for teaching flawless techniques had taken years to build. One shaky performance was already too many. If word got around that she couldn't demonstrate proper form...Her phone buzzed again. The wedding planner probably needed an immediate answer. But Grace's hands trembled too much to reach for it. Everything had to be impeccable—her nuptials, her dance business, her entire storybook life.

Andrew's family expected nothing less. As did the coast's social circles.

The lupus packet spilled out of her bag as she turned into the studio lot. The sound of paper sliding against paper might as well have been a gunshot. Her wedding was fast approaching. Too little time to figure this out. How could she ensure no one discovered just how badly her body was revolting.

Grace pulled into her reserved spot behind Grace Ballet Academy. Needles stung her knee as she applied the brake. Another warning to be considered. Another warning to be ignored. Had to be ignored.

Ten minutes until the lesson. She leaned her forehead against the steering to try and steady her breathing. The previous stumbles with Emma had been basic moves—a simple développé, an elementary port de bras. This afternoon wouldn't be quite as challenging. She could do it. She must do it.

Andrew's voice echoed in her head. "Anything that's worth doing is worth doing perfectly." He'd said that the night he proposed, explaining why he waited three years to ask.

No backup teachers today. Calling in a substitute would mean explanations. Questions. The start of everything unraveling. She couldn't risk it. Not with a first lesson. Not with her future hanging by a thread.

Grace grabbed her gear, leaving the lupus packet buried in her purse. Mind over matter. She'd learned that lesson at nine, dancing through her first sprained ankle. At eleven, performing with a fever of 102. At twelve, earning her pointe shoes through bloody toes and sore muscles.

Her hands shook as she unlocked the door. Inside, the empty studio waited. Pristine hardwood floors. Mirror-lined walls. Her kingdom of precision and control. She had eight minutes to become the professional teacher everyone expected. After that, she needed to transform back into the flawless bride-to-be. Hopefully, her body's betrayal wouldn't define her.

Five minutes. She forced her spine straighter, chin higher. The face in the mirror looked like hers—same graceful neck, same elegant posture. But something shifted behind her eyes. A crack in the foundation. The consummate dance instructor. The flawless fiancée. Roles she'd performed with perfection. Until now. Her hands shook as she reached for the ballet barre. The cool wood beneath her palm used to feel like home. Now it felt like a lifeline. A prop in her performance of normalcy.

Four minutes to transform back into the Grace Thompson everyone expected.

Three minutes to bury the betrayal of her own body.

Two minutes to—

The entry door chimed.

FOUR

Nathan staggered under Hannah's dead weight, half-carrying, half-dragging her down their home's dark hallway. Her skin burned through her thin cotton pajamas, head lolling against his shoulder. Those eyes that always sparkled at him stayed closed, no matter how much he begged. "Stay with me, sweetheart. Stay with me." The words scraped raw in his throat.

Lily's wails pierced through the bedroom door—hungry, scared, alone. Six months old and needing her mama. But Hannah's head bobbed against his shoulder, her ragged breathing too shallow, too fast.

The key fob. Where was the...there. The bowl by the door. One arm tightened around Hannah's waist as he grabbed it, metal biting into his palm.

Lord, please. Not like this. Not tonight.

He could do this. Get Hannah to the car. Grab Lily. Drive. The emergency room was only twelve minutes away. Eleven if he ran the yellow lights.

Nathan sprinted back through the dark house to Lily's room, his t-shirt already sticking to his back in the June heat.

Her cries grew louder with each step. The pink nightlight cast shadows across her crib as she stood gripping the rails, face streaked with tears.

"Daddy's here, Lily-bug." His hands shook as he scooped her up, grabbing her diaper bag from the rocker. She buried her face in his neck, hiccuping sobs against his skin. The air conditioning hummed, fighting the Mississippi humidity. No time for shoes. No time to change her out of the light cotton onesie.

The thick, muggy air clung to his skin as he tore down the front steps. Hannah sprawled across the reclined passenger seat of their GMC Acadia, motionless. His stomach twisted. He dropped his cheek to her lips—her breath came shallow—almost not there.

"I know, baby girl. I know." His hands shook as he fumbled with Lily's car seat straps, every second feeling like betrayal. Hannah's breathing grew more labored beside him. The dashboard clock read 10:47.

Too slow. Moving too slow.

The engine roared to life. Go.

Red light. Nathan touched Hannah's clammy neck to find a racing pulse. Her head rolled toward him.

"Stay with me, sweetheart. Five more minutes."

Lily's wails pitched higher from the back. She scrunched her face red and raised tiny fists in the rearview mirror.

Green light. Both hands back on the wheel.

The Bluetooth crackled. "Merit Hospital Emergency, how can I—"

"My wife's unconscious. Type 1 diabetic. Four minutes out." His voice wavered. "She's breathing but—"

A horn blared. Someone cutting him off.

"Son of a—"

"Sir, we'll have a team waiting. Is anyone else in the car?"

"My six-month-old daughter," Nathan said as calmly as he could. "Almost there, Lily-bug." The mirror reflected only desperate little fists now. "Mama's gonna be okay."

Please let that not be a lie, Lord.

The emergency entrance blazed under harsh overhead lights. The Acadia's tires screamed as Nathan swung beneath the covered drive. Medical staff rushed the passenger side before he could shift into park.

"Type 1 diabetic, unresponsive!" He tore at his seatbelt. "She was acting strange all day, then—"

"BP's dropping," a nurse called as orderlies slid Hannah onto a gurney. "Get a glucose reading."

"Sir, you need to move your vehicle." A security guard called out.

Nathan's jaw clenched. "My wife is dying." The words came out raw and loud.

Lily's screams cut through the chaos as the gurney disappeared inside. Go with Hannah. Get Lily. Park the car. Every option a betrayal. No right choice—only wrong ones.

"I'll be right there," he called to the nurse, the promise feeling like ash in his mouth. He reached for Hannah's hand —cold, so cold now. "Baby, I'm only minutes behind you."

The team wheeled her through sliding doors, rattling off numbers that meant nothing and everything. Nathan jumped back into the Acadia to search for a parking spot. "Hold on, Lily. Just hold on."

He swung Lily's car seat out, her diaper bag pulling against his shoulder. Her sobs had turned to whimpers, tiny fingers reaching for him. No time to comfort her. Not yet.

The entry doors whooshed open to cool air and

controlled chaos. A line formed at the check-in desk. No time for that. He spotted the team surrounding Hannah inside an opening with urgent movements.

"Sir." A nurse stepped into his path. "You must—"

"That's my wife in there. Hannah Carter. They just brought her in."

Her expression shifted. "Follow me." She glanced at Lily. "Do you have someone who can take care of your daughter?"

"No. I mean, not yet. I haven't..." He needed to call Rachel. He couldn't handle this alone.

"Okay, let's get you both settled in the family room first. Then we'll—"

"I need to be with her." His voice snapped. Lily whimpered louder, straining against her car seat straps. "I need to be with my wife."

"The emergency staff is with her now. As soon as she's stabilized." The nurse touched his arm. "Let's take care of your daughter while we wait. Shall we?"

Wait sounded like a gunshot. *Wait for what?*

The family room's walls closed in like a cage. Nathan paced the small space with Lily clutching to him, her tears soaking his t-shirt.

"Shhh, Mama's getting help." His voice broke. Every second now with Hannah was a second not seeing what they were doing to Hannah. Not knowing if she...

No. Don't think it.

The wall clock moved to 11:25. How long since they'd wheeled her away? Ten minutes? An hour? His phone buzzed. Mom. He should answer. Should tell her... tell her what? That he'd missed the signs all day? That Hannah had sworn she was fine, just tired, and he'd believed her? Lily squirmed in his arms. Any other night, he'd have changed her immediately. Now, even that simple act felt impossible when Hannah might be dying just rooms away. His hands wouldn't stop shaking.

The door opened. Nathan spun, his heart hungry for news about Hannah—but it was the nurse with a bottle.

"Formula from our nursery," the nurse said with a gentle tone. "When you're ready, I can show you where to change her."

Words died inside him, his entire awareness consumed by Hannah. "Any update on my wife?"

"Dr. Montgomery has arrived." She set the bottle down. "Do you need help with your daughter?"

Need help? He needed Hannah to open her eyes. Needed to turn back time to this morning when Hannah had skipped breakfast, claiming nausea. "No." He swallowed hard. "Thank you."

The door opened again. Dr. Montgomery stood there in her white coat and a grave expression. Nathan's legs went weak. He sank into the vinyl chair, Lily secure in his arms.

"Nathan." Dr. Montgomery pulled up a chair, leaning forward. The same position she'd taken three days ago when warning them about Hannah's creatinine levels. "We've got Hannah stabilized, but her blood sugar was 600 when she came in. She's in diabetic ketoacidosis. Her body's basically turning on itself."

Lily squirmed, reaching for her bottle. Nathan's arms froze.

"We're moving her to ICU. The next twenty-four hours are critical. She's still unconscious, and her kidneys..." Dr. Montgomery's pause stretched too long. "They're showing signs of failure."

The room started to spin. Through the roaring, Nathan heard himself ask, "Can I see her?"

"In about thirty minutes. We're setting up dialysis now." Dr. Montgomery glanced at Lily. "Is there someone who can come for the baby?"

Nathan felt for the phone in his pocket. Had he called Rachel? Had he called his mother? Mom's missed calls. His sister's texts. A whole support system waiting, if he could just make his hands work. If he could just breathe.

The family room door opened. This time his sister Rachel slipped in, still in her pajamas under a thrown-on cardigan. The sight of her—familiar, capable Rachel who'd helped with Lily since day one—broke something loose inside him.

"Nate." She crossed the room in three steps, already reaching for Lily. "Mom's parking the car. What do you need?"

Lily stirred against his arms, whimpering. He should hand her over. Should let Rachel take her home to bed.

"She's..." The word caught. He tried again. "Hannah's..." He pressed his lips to Lily's forehead, breathing in her baby powder scent. As if somehow this might be the last normal moment before everything changed. Her tiny fingers clutched his shirt as he passed her to Rachel. "Her diaper needs changing. And there's a bottle..." He gestured to the untouched formula.

"Nathan." Rachel shifted Lily to her hip with motherly ease. "We'll figure it out. Go see Hannah."

Appearing at the threshold with her eyebrows pinched together, his mother wrapped him in a fierce hug. "We're here for you." Her voice wavered. "Tell Hannah we're praying."

Mom and Rachel's presence anchored him as he walked the sterile hallway toward the ICU. Each step away from Lily carved something raw in his heart, but Hannah needed him. Hannah, who'd warned him about days like this during their engagement. Who'd made him memorize her insulin routine before she'd even said yes. Who might not make it through the night.

Lord, please. I'm not ready. Lily's not ready. We need more time.

The ICU doors whispered open. Machines surrounded Hannah, their beeping piercing his skull. This couldn't be Hannah. His Hannah. The woman who danced with Lily in her arms just yesterday.

"Ten minutes," the ICU nurse said softly. "Talk to her. She might hear you."

Nathan sank into the chair beside the bed, clutching his wife's hand—her wedding ring loose on her finger. When had she gotten so thin? How had he missed it?

"Hey, sweetheart." His voice broke. "Lily's with Rachel and Mom. They're taking good care of our girl, so you just..." He swallowed hard. "You just focus on getting better."

Her chest rose and fell. Each breath was an answer to his prayers.

In sickness and in health.

The monitors' steady rhythm shattered into a piercing wail. Hannah's body jerked, her hand going limp in his.

"Hannah?" *Not now. Please God, not now.*

The ICU doors slammed open. Medical staff swarmed the bed, shoulders blocking his view. Someone yanked him back. His spine hit the wall, legs threatening to buckle. Dr. Montgomery barked orders over the chaos.

"Starting compressions—"

"—pressure bottoming out—"

"Push one of epi—"

Each command hammered into his core. He'd promised

to protect her. Now all he could do was watch. Watch and pray while strangers fought for his wife's life.

Nathan's heart stopped. "Hannah?"

Medical staff rushed in, their voices urgent but controlled. Dr. Montgomery appeared at Hannah's side. Nathan found himself backed against the wall, watching them work. Watching them save her.

Minutes stretched like hours until the alarms quieted. The crisis passed.

"Blood pressure stabilized," Dr. Montgomery said finally, turning to Nathan. "She's fighting, Nathan. And the dialysis is helping." She squeezed his arm. "Try to get some rest. The next few days will be hard, but Hannah's strong."

"You scared me, sweetheart." He raised her fingers to his lips. "But we've got time. We've got all the time in the world." Nathan reclaimed his seat by Hannah's bed, taking her hand again. The monitors beeped steadily now. Regular. Safe. But that could change in a millisecond.

FIVE

Rumbur Valley, Pakistan—Two Weeks After the Mission Slaughter

Joseph winced as the wire brush handle dug into his palm. Raw blisters pulsed beneath his fingertips, stinging with sweat and grime. He shifted his grip and resumed scrubbing the crusted dung from the goat's feeding trough, the harsh scraping echoing off the courtyard walls. The setting sun painted copper and gold across the distant mountains. Long shadows spilled across the stone-paved yard.

Six more troughs to clean before sunset prayers. Six more days until they left for Islamabad.

The sharp clank of the gate slamming against the stone wall cleaved through the evening hush. Joseph's head snapped up. A boy—no older than ten—charged through the entrance, his tan kurta flaring around spindly legs. His sandals slapped the dirt, kicking up clouds that hung in the air like smoke.

"Malik." The boy's voice quivered with panic. "Malik."

Joseph's brush slipped from his hand, clattering against

the flagstones. His heartbeat surged, loud and hot against his eardrums. A familiar chill crept over him. From the barn came the rasp of metal on wood. Hassan stepped into view, a rifle glinting in the dying light.

"Inside, Joseph." His voice was measured, flat—too calm. The same tone Joseph had heard only once before. He tried to move, but his legs refused. His lungs drew tight. That voice. That exact tone. The memory slammed into him—Papa's hands shoving him to the hidden door beneath the mission house. Mama's cry cutting through the darkness. The metallic sting of blood in the air.

The boy's rapid Pashto filled the courtyard, words tumbling over each other like stones in a flash flood—every word tightening the knot in Joseph's stomach. The muezzin's call to prayer echoed across the valley, mixing with the bleats of nervous goats. The boy gripped Malik's sleeve. Joseph caught fragments of their conversation—militants, search, blasphemer. The brush lay forgotten in the dirt. TPL was getting closer.

Inside the house, Malik reviewed what he had learned. "The boy works for Karim at the tea shop. He overheard TPL questioning his uncle about a Eurasian youth who performs healings." His hands shook as he fastened the shutters. "They're calling it black magic, saying Joseph mocks Allah's will. They searched the boy's uncle's farm. They're moving through the valley, village by village."

Hassan checked his rifle's ammunition. "How long?"

"They'll reach Rumbur by morning." Malik grabbed his coat. "I must go to market now, before dark. We need supplies, and I'll learn what I can about their movements."

Joseph's stomach churned. Why would they be searching for him? Did they believe the stories? He shook his head, trying to clear his thoughts. Perhaps it was a mistake, some misunderstanding. Maybe they were after someone else. But the fear took root. Could his gift truly make him a target? The chaos around him blurred his thinking as he recalled the bloodshed at the mission. Had his family suffered because of him? His thoughts haunted him as he struggled to prioritize the danger at hand.

"We should leave now," Hassan said.

"Wait until I return." Malik headed for the door. "Two hours. No more."

In those two hours that stretched like six months, Joseph helped Hassan pack the mules while keeping watch. Every snapped twig, every distant voice had him looking for cover. The sun fell beneath mountains. The door slammed open. Joseph flinched, nearly dropping the water skin he was filling at the tap. Malik staggered into the doorway, sweat streaking down his temples despite the chill in the air.

Hassan stepped forward, voice taut. "What did you learn?"

"They're here," Malik whispered. He stumbled inside and collapsed onto a stool. "TPL. Everywhere."

Joseph's throat clenched. His heartbeat pounded. The water skin slipped and hit the floor with a dull thud.

Malik's palms shook with uncontrolled tremors as his wife pressed a tin cup into his hands. "Checkpoints on every road," he gulped spilling water down his chin. "Armed men. Trucks. They're stopping everyone."

Joseph flattened his back against the wall, his legs weaker than a moment before. The room seemed to shrink around him.

"They have your description," Malik continued, his eyes finding Joseph. "A Eurasian boy. Nine, maybe ten. They're offering ten thousand rupees for information." He lowered his voice. "Twenty thousand if someone confirms your demonic abilities." The cup in his hand clattered on the table. Joseph flinched. His skin prickled with cold sweat. He caught Hassan watching him, concern carved into the lines at the corners of his eyes.

"The roads are blocked?" Joseph managed through a dry mouth. "We're trapped?"

Hassan crossed the room in three strides. The metallic click of the weapon being loaded got everyone's attention. "Not trapped," he said, his jaw set in determination. "We go through the high passes."

"The passes?" Malik lurched forward, grabbing Hassan's arm. "There's still snow. The mules."

"Better the snow than TPL bullets." Hassan's expression softened as he clasped Malik's shoulder.

Joseph's throat tightened as Malik's wife jammed a bundle of flatbread into his hands. Her touch was gentle, reminiscent of his mother's, grounding him momentarily. He couldn't afford to think of what she might believe if she knew the extent of his gift. The thought of being seen as the devil the TPL labeled him sent chills through him. He forced himself to focus, scanning the shadows for any sign of trouble. Time was running short, and they needed to move quickly to avoid detection.

Malik's shoulders sagged as he hurried them to the back gate. He squared his shoulders. "We'll tell anyone who asks that you passed through last month heading for Peshawar."

They led the mules into the deepening dusk. Joseph glanced back once—Malik's family framed in warm lamplight, unmoving, already receding into memory. His thoughts churned over the escape route Hassan had outlined. How far to the ridge? Would the mules survive the climb? He tallied their meager supplies in his head, estimating how far they might stretch.

Hassan's hand clamped down on his shoulder. "We need to reach the ridge before moonrise," he said, his voice tight and firm.

They'd barely started up the trail when an engine growled in the distance, echoing across the valley floor. Joseph dropped to a crouch, yanking the mule's lead close to the mountainside. Twenty paces ahead, a scatter of boulders offered partial cover. Headlights streamed through the trees below, sweeping the road like hungry eyes.

He drove his back against the stone, lungs tight, heart pounding against bone. Ready to bolt.

"Keep moving," he whispered. "Stay in the shadows."

The TPL had come early. And Joseph had a sinking certainty—just like at the mission, he wouldn't leave Pakistan without more bloodshed.

SIX

Nathan hesitated at Mike Santos's doorstep, his wedding band feeling heavier on his finger as he reached for the doorbell. Inside, the gentle murmurs of men's voices blended with warm laughter, typical of this weekly men's group meeting. Nathan needed this time as his world shattered into pieces. His Hannah, his beautiful Hannah, had almost slipped away from him two weeks ago.

The doctors' words kept him up at night—"renal failure," "permanent damage," "cautious optimism." Clinical terms that couldn't capture the fear of watching his wife's face grow paler each day, of seeing her hands—once so capable with their newborn daughter—now trembling with weakness.

Taking a deep breath, Nathan pressed the doorbell. The garden air around him carried the scent of Mike's wife's roses, the ones Hannah had always admired. He breathed in the fragrant air as though each whisper might nurture his faith into something unshakable.

The weekly prayer group had been his anchor through Hannah's hospitalization. These brothers in Christ had stood in the gap when Nathan's own prayers had faltered, when his faith had wavered beneath the crushing weight of fear. Men like Mike Santos, Jim Wheeler, and Steve Martinez seemed to have a direct line to heaven. God listened to men like them, didn't He?

The door swung open, and Mike's usual welcoming smile faltered as his eyes scanned Nathan's face.

"Nathan, brother, come in. We're just about to start," Mike said softly, stepping aside.

From the familiar living room, Steve Martinez's voice carried like a lifeline. "We were just talking about you and Hannah. How are you both holding up?"

The homey space enveloped Nathan like a warm embrace—well-worn leather couches bearing the imprints of countless gatherings, a coffee table adorned with dog-eared Bibles and journals filled with prayers answered and prayers still waiting. Family photographs lined the walls, testaments to God's faithfulness through generations.

Seven men looked up, their eyes reflecting a compassion that threatened to undo Nathan's fragile composure. Jim Wheeler, silver-haired and steady as an oak, cleared his throat gently.

"Nathan. How's our Hannah doing today?"

"She's..." Nathan's voice caught like fabric on a thorn. "The doctors say she's stable, but..."

"But stable isn't enough when it's your wife," Mike finished for him, mercy flowing through his words.

Nathan sank onto the nearest couch edge, his fingers gripping his knees to steady himself. A strong hand rested on his shoulder. Mike's voice was close and comforting. "Let it out, brother. That's why the Lord brought us together."

The concern in their weathered faces—men who had walked their own valleys and emerged still praising—broke something loose within him, like a dam giving way after the spring thaw.

"I can't..." The words tumbled out like stones. "I can't imagine doing this alone. I can't bear the thought of raising Lily without her. Hannah's home now, but her numbers are still concerning, and I..." His voice fractured. "Every time she holds our baby, I watch her hands for tremors. Every time she stands, I'm poised to catch her. I can't sleep, worried she might stop breathing."

Jim Wheeler leaned forward, his Bible resting in his lap. "After Karen's first cancer scare, I followed her everywhere. I couldn't let her out of my sight. As if my vigilance could somehow keep death at bay."

"My Sarah had severe preeclampsia with our second," Steve added, his gentle eyes holding understanding. "For months after Tommy was born, I'd wake in the dark just to make sure she was still alive."

"I remember that season," Jim nodded. "The whole church was storming heaven's gates."

"Day and night," Steve agreed, his voice warm with memory. "Just as we're doing for your Hannah now, brother."

Nathan wiped away tears with the back of his hand, not caring that these men saw his vulnerability. The knot behind his ribcage loosened just a fraction. These weren't just men who prayed—they were men who understood. They'd walked through fire and still believed.

Mike settled beside him, shoulder to shoulder. "You know what Scripture carried me through Amy's MS diagnosis? Psalm 121. 'I lift my eyes to the hills—where does my help come from? My help comes from the Lord, the Maker of heaven and earth.'" Mike's voice steadied as he continued, "'He will not let your foot slip—he who watches over you will not slumber.'"

"But what if..." Nathan forced himself to voice the fear that had been circling like a vulture since Hannah's condition worsened. "What if He doesn't help in the way we're asking? What if He takes her anyway?"

A silence filled Mike's living room—not the uncomfortable kind that begs to be broken, but the heavy quiet of men who had wrestled with the same question in their own dark nights of the soul.

"Son." Jim's gravelly, gentle voice broke the stillness. "Sometimes He does take them home. Karen's been cancer-free for fifteen years now, but that doesn't mean..." He folded his weathered hands slowly. "The Lord gives us today. Just today. And He gives us each other to help carry the load."

"The hardest part," Nathan admitted, "is pretending everything's fine for Lily. Putting on a brave face when I'm scared out of my mind."

"You don't have to pretend here," Mike said quietly. "Not with us. This is holy ground."

"Remember Job?" Steve's Bible pages rustled like prayer flags in the wind. "He said, 'Though He slay me, yet will I trust in Him.'" Steve's voice softened to reverence. "That's not a guarantee everything will turn out as we hope. It's choosing to trust even when the path leads through the valley."

The truth of their words burned hotter than false comfort would have, but it was a cleansing fire. Nathan's hands trembled like aspen leaves. "But Lily needs her mother." Fresh tears spilled unchecked. "I need my wife."

Mike's hand remained steady on his shoulder. "Then we pray, brother. We pray with all our might. But

Nathan..." Mike waited until Nathan lifted his gaze. "We also pray for strength to trust Him, whatever His answer may be. You're not walking this road alone. Not ever."

Nathan's gaze fell to the carpet, to the worn spot where countless prayers had been offered in this room. His daughter's entire life stretched before him—first steps, first words, first day of school—milestones he'd always imagined sharing with Hannah by his side. Now each future moment felt like a coin toss. Would his beloved be there, or would it just be him, navigating the waters of parenthood without his compass?

"I don't know how to live with such uncertainty," he confessed. "How do you keep putting one foot in front of the other when any day could be..." The words died in his throat.

"One day at a time," Jim said with the quiet authority of someone who had walked with God through deep waters. "Sometimes one hour at a time. You hold onto what's true in this moment. Hannah's home. She's with your precious Lily. And you have a church family that will surround you both with love, no matter what comes."

Murmurs of agreement rippled through the room. Nathan's shoulders sagged, not in defeat but in the blessed relief of sharing a burden too heavy to carry alone. The terror still lingered, the future still uncertain, but something else had taken root alongside it—a fragile seedling of strength, watered by the tears and prayers of faithful men who had faced their own impossible fears.

The evening's prayers gradually faded into a reverent silence. Nathan reached for his keys and rose from the couch, his knees steadier now than when he had arrived. Hannah's words before he left echoed in his mind: "Give Lily her bedtime bottle if I'm asleep when you get home."

Such a simple request. Such a precious, ordinary moment. How many more ordinary moments did they have left? A lifetime? A year? A heartbeat? These brothers' wives had survived their health crises. But what if Hannah... What if tonight was one of their last together? What if he had spent more evenings holding her hand instead of working late? More time treasuring their quiet moments instead of worrying about mortgage payments? What if he had insisted she see a doctor sooner, had been more attentive to the early signs?

The guilt pressed against his chest like a stone. Someone pressed a tissue into his hand. Jim's Bible closed with a gentle thump. The leather couch creaked softly as Steve moved closer.

"Can I..." Nathan's voice broke like thin ice. "Can I ever forgive myself if she dies?"

Steve leaned forward, elbows on his knees, eyes soft with compassion. "Nathan, when Tommy was fighting for his life in the NICU, I asked myself that same question every single day. I blamed myself for every ragged breath he struggled to take."

"How did you ever find peace?" Nathan asked, desperate for a map through this wilderness.

"Truth is, I couldn't do it in my own strength. Not completely. But I learned to surrender it to God, piece by painful piece. To lay it at the foot of the cross again and again."

Nathan went still, the most fearsome question of all rising to his lips. "But what if Hannah dies? Could I ever forgive God?"

Mike's grip on his shoulder tightened slightly. "Nathan?"

But Nathan pulled away, stumbling to his feet. His eyes

fell on the family photos adorning the wall—Mike's smiling wife and children, their presence and permanence a testimony to God's faithfulness. The promises Nathan couldn't guarantee for his own little girl.

Jim's weathered voice burst through the silence like a beam of light through stained glass. "You're asking the wrong questions, son. It's not about whether you can forgive God. It's about whether you can trust Him even if He asks you to walk a road you never wanted to travel."

Before Nathan could respond, his phone vibrated against his leg. Hannah's name illuminated the screen, causing his heart to stutter. With trembling fingers, he read her message—

"Come home now. Something's wrong."

"YES, SIR. SETBACKS FROM THE SHORELINE." Nathan flipped through his work binder, searching again for the casino's site plan while the zoning administrator waited on the phone. A maintenance cart rattled past, forcing Nathan against the wall of the ICU corridor. Late afternoon sun slanted through the narrow windows, adding light over his neglected-for-days blueprints for the Sunset Bay Resort and Casino.

The structural analysis for the forty-story tower couldn't wait much longer—he'd already pushed back two client meetings. His thumb caught on a fresh paper cut as he flipped past another insurance denial. *How'd that get in here?*

He squinted at his own cramped handwriting. "Fifty-seven feet. Would you like me to email—"

His phone beeped. Richard Barrett, Senior Partner of

Meridian Engineering. Third time today. Nathan's stomach clenched—fourteen days of pushed meetings and delayed reports. Even Richard's legendary patience had limits.

"I'm sorry, could you repeat your email address?"

Dear Lord, help me focus. Hannah needs me to focus.

The zoning administrator went on about utilities and infrastructure, coastal access, and environmental impact. Nathan pinched the phone against his ear to capture every detail. Six weeks in and out of the hospital, and he still couldn't get the three specialists to agree on a treatment plan. His mother had Lily again—third time this week. Guilt gnawed at him—for not being at his daughter's side, and for not being at the office. His phone chirped—10% battery.

Just what I need...

Dr. Montgomery rounded the corner, her pace slowing when she spotted him. Nathan tensed at her expression—that careful neutral mask he'd grown to hate.

"The latest numbers aren't what we hoped for." She kept her voice professional. "The dialysis isn't keeping up with—"

"Then we need to try something else." Nathan gripped the binder until his fingers ached. "Different medications, different schedule, different—"

"Mr. Carter." She shifted the tablet in her arms. "Nathan," she said softly. "We've adjusted her treatment plan three times. The kidney damage from the diabetes is simply too extensive."

Extensive. Progressive. Irreversible. More words that meant giving up.

"What about the Mayo Clinic?" The words tumbled out. "Or Johns Hopkins? There must be experimental treatments, new protocols—"

Dr. Montgomery's shoulders dropped a fraction. "Even if we could arrange a transfer in her condition... her insurance wouldn't cover it."

"I don't care about the insurance." His voice echoed in the corridor, too loud. A nurse glanced their way. Nathan forced himself to speak softer. "She's thirty-two years old. We have a six-month-old daughter. You can't just give up."

Dr. Montgomery touched his arm—the first time she'd ever done that. Her eyes softened behind her wire-rimmed glasses. "Nathan. I know you're doing everything possible. But Hannah needs you to hear what I'm saying."

The binder slipped from his grip, scattering papers across the floor. He knelt to gather them. She crouched to help, but he waved her away.

"I'll be up to check on her again before my shift ends," she said, straightening. "Try to get some rest. You can't be there for Hannah if you run yourself into the ground."

He stayed on his knees, staring at the scattered documents until her footsteps faded. *Lord, I trusted You. I believed. Where are You in all of this?*

His phone vibrated again. Barrett. The casino blueprints peeked from beneath an insurance form.

Everything was slipping away, and he couldn't catch any of it.

Nathan gathered the last of the papers when his phone lit up again. Not Richard this time—Rachel.

"Lily's running a fever. Mom tried calling, but your voicemail's full. Should I take her to urgent care?"

He lost his balance before steadying himself against the wall. "I'll meet you there," he typed, then deleted it. Hannah's monitors had been erratic all afternoon. If he left now...

A memory sliced through him—Hannah in the nursery,

showing him where she kept the infant Tylenol, explaining about checking Lily's temperature under her arm instead of her mouth. "Just in case," she'd said. "You need to know these things."

Had she known he'd be in this situation then?

His phone chimed again. Rachel.

The nephrologist's voicemail still needed a response. Richard would be calling again any minute. The casino developers wanted updated plans by Friday. And now Lily...

Something cracked inside him. A sound escaped his throat—half laugh, half sob. He'd been so sure he could fix this—find the right doctor, the right treatment, the right prayer. But Hannah kept slipping away while he juggled papers and phone calls, pretending he had any control at all. He pushed himself to his feet, his decision crystallizing. He scrolled through his contacts and hit dial. "Richard? It's Nathan. I know we're knee-deep in the casino, but I must take a leave of absence. Starting now."

Nathan watched the sun sink behind the Gulf, bathing the hospital windows in its angry glow. "I'll understand if you reassign the Sunset Bay project." His voice steadied. "But my wife and daughter need me more than that casino needs another tower."

He'd go to Lily first. Then return to be with Hannah. Everything else would have to wait.

His phone died as he reached the elevator, plunging him into silence before Richard could respond.

SEVEN

Grace shoved the lupus pamphlets into her desk's bottom drawer, burying Dr. Lawson's treatment plan beneath old programs. Her phone buzzed against the metal desk, alerting her of a new text. Andrew's name lit up the screen.

"Remember. We're having dinner at my parents' tonight. Mom's making that salmon you love." More command than a question.

The walls of her tiny office at Grace Ballet Academy closed in around her. The Fayard dinner meant two hours of wedding talk. Two hours of Sandra's attention to detail. Two hours of Grace keeping her hands steady, her smile fixed, her secret buried.

Grace's fingers lingered over the phone. A stabbing ache pulsed through her fingers—the same ache that she struggled with during today's beginner class. She forced her trembling hands to type—

"Not feeling 100%. Rain check?"

No answer for what seemed like an eternity. Finally, three animated dots inside a speech bubble, then his answer. "Mom cooked salmon for you special."

Grace nearly laughed. Salmon was Andrew's favorite, not hers—she'd only mentioned liking it once, and Sandra had transformed that into "Grace's favorite" ever since. Another Fayard family myth she'd learned not to contradict.

Another three dots. "Should I be worried?"

Worried? Andrew Fayard didn't do worried. Worried meant something was wrong, and nothing could be wrong. Not three months before their wedding. Her office door rattled—someone turning the handle.

"Just a moment," Grace called out, sweeping the medical paperwork into her drawer and slammed it shut. The handle jiggled again.

The door crept open without warning. Ms. Chen appeared, Emma's performance folder clutched against her like a shield. "Grace, I know it's late, but Emma's been crying all afternoon about her solo—"

Grace's phone buzzed against the metal desk. Andrew again. She flipped his image face-down with a quick snap of her wrist.

"Please, come in." Grace forced her lips into the reassuring smile she'd perfected for anxious dance moms. Each movement deliberate, she rose from her chair—ignoring the hot knife of pain that sliced through her hip—and pulled out the visitor's chair. "Emma's making wonderful progress."

Ms. Chen perched on the edge of the seat, her back ramrod straight. She flipped open the folder, revealing Emma's evaluation sheet with Grace's neat red marks. "It's this fouetté sequence." Her finger jabbed at the notation. "She practiced until midnight. Her feet were bleeding." Grace's phone vibrated again, rattling against the desk. Once. Twice. Three times in rapid succession. Ms. Chen's eyes darted to the phone, then back to Grace.

"I can demonstrate—" The words escaped before Grace could catch them. She gripped the desk's edge, steadying herself as she rose. The familiar weight shift sent fire racing from her ankle to her knee. She bit the inside of her cheek until she tasted copper.

Just get through this with proper form and optimal control.

"Watch carefully." Grace positioned herself in the narrow space beside her desk. Her right knee threatened to buckle as she established her preparatory fourth position. Sweat beaded at her hairline.

She initiated the turn, focusing on the framed ballet poster on the wall. Each rotation sent lightning through her joints. One. Two. Three. Her vision blurred on the fourth turn, but she held her spotting point with fierce determination.

"See?" Grace's breath came short and sharp as she settled back into fourth position. She pointed to her eyes, then to the wall. "Emma's dropping her focus here." She demonstrated the incorrect head position. "When it needs to stay—" She snapped her head back to the spotting point with military precision. "—right there."

Her phone lit up. Sandra Fayard's name glowed.

"Would you excuse me? Just for a moment." Grace took her phone into the hallway, heat warming her cheeks. Three missed calls from Andrew. Five texts. *Enough already.*

"Dad has the venue contract." "Tonight's not optional." "Mom's been cooking all afternoon." "What's really going on with you?"

The last one landed hard. "Is there something you're not telling me?"

Sandra's voicemail chimed in her ear—"Grace, honey,

Andrew says you're not feeling well again. I made that salmon, and Richard needs those contracts signed before his morning meeting. We're all getting a little worried about you."

A crash from her office had Grace silence Sandra's message. Spinning too quickly, Grace's vision blurred. Through the doorway, Ms. Chen gathered scattered papers —papers that had spilled to the floor from her not-quite-closed drawer. Including a bright purple pamphlet with "Living with Lupus" emblazoned across the top.

Ms. Chen's fingers closed around the purple pamphlet. Grace lunged forward, but her knee buckled. She caught herself against the doorframe, pulse thundering in her ears.

"Grace?" Ms. Chen's eyes darted from the pamphlet to Grace's white-knuckled grip on the doorframe. "Are you—"

"Research." The lie tasted bitter. "For a friend."

Her phone vibrated once more. And once more, Andrew's face filled the screen—an actual call this time. Grace declined it with a shaky finger. Another text followed immediately—"Dad's lawyer needs those prenup revisions also. Non-negotiable."

Ms. Chen set the pamphlet on the desk, smoothing its crumpled corner. "My sister has lupus."

The word hung between them. Grace's carefully constructed walls split open. She couldn't look at Ms. Chen, couldn't bear to see pity replace respect. Couldn't bear to imagine herself like some invalid, forced to give up everything she'd built.

"She still gardens." Ms. Chen said. "Different ways now, but she adapted. Found new techniques."

"Adapted." Grace's laugh came out harsh. "You can't adapt classical ballet. You can't modify perfection. I built my business on of my reputation as a skilled dance instructor. On perfection." *And Andrew picked me for the same reasons.*

"Emma worries about disappointing you." Ms. Chen stood, gathering her purse. "She thinks you shine like sterling. But maybe..." She hesitated. "Maybe she needs to see that even the best dancers face challenges. That grace isn't about perfection."

Grace's phone chimed. "Car's running. Be there in 20. Mom called the caterer, venue manager, and wedding planner. Stop being difficult."

"I can't—" Grace's voice broke. "This studio is my life outside my fiancé. If I start 'adapting,' if people see weakness..." Her fingers brushed the pamphlet. "Your sister's garden doesn't have dozens of students. Or a fiancé whose family name requires a flawless wife."

"No," Ms. Chen said quietly. "But she has something better now. Peace with herself."

Grace's phone purred with another alert. Sandra's name.

"Please don't tell anyone," Grace whispered.

"I won't say anything." Ms. Chen paused at the door. "But you can't hide it forever. Especially not from the people who love you." She hesitated. "My sister's name is Helen. If you ever want to talk to someone who understands."

The door clicked shut behind her. Grace sank into her chair, staring at Andrew's waiting texts, at the venue contract that needed signing, at the prenup that now felt like a trap, at the recital programs promising pieces her body might never let her demonstrate again.

Andrew's last message—"Dad's lawyer needs those prenup revisions tonight." The prenup. Of course. If she didn't show up tonight, they'd wonder why. Questions would lead to suspicions. Suspicions would lead to investigations. And investigations could lead straight to her health. Better to control the narrative now than let it control her later.

"Meet you there," she typed. "Need to finish something at work."

She should stop at the pharmacy first. Dr. Lawson's warning—steroids might help, but they weren't miracle workers. But they might get her through one dinner with the Fayards. One more performance of the impeccable Grace Thompson, future Fayard bride. Her reflection in the desk mirror showed a woman already at her breaking point, and the Fayards hadn't started asking questions yet.

THE CRYSTAL CHANDELIER sparkled like diamonds over the linen-lined table that could easily seat sixteen, though tonight only six place settings adorned its celeste-white surface. Grace adjusted her lace-trimmed napkin across her lap, grateful that the dim light Mrs. Fayard preferred for her dinners helped hide the pallor she knew had settled into her face. Through the floor-to-ceiling windows of the Fayard dining room, the carefully cultivated grounds of Destiny Plantation stretched into the twilight—five acres of cultivated landscaping punctuated by illuminated fountains and a white gazebo that glowed like a fairy-tale backdrop.

"Everyone, let's bow our heads before we begin," Mr. Fayard announced, his voice holding the same authoritative tone he used in boardroom meetings. He extended his hands to his wife and daughter, signaling the family's ritual of connection.

Grace reached for Andrew's hand, then Charlotte's, completing the circle around the table. Her fingers throbbed at the contact, but she maintained her composure. The cool metal of Andrew's Rolex pressed against her inflamed wrist, a small reminder of the wealth and expectations that surrounded her. A reverent hush fell over the dining room as Mr. Fayard cleared his throat. The delicate scent of roses from the centerpiece mingled with the aroma of roasted salmon, creating an atmosphere of cultivated perfection that seemed to demand equally flawless participants.

"Heavenly Father," Mr. Fayard began, his deep voice resonating through the room, "we come before You with grateful hearts this evening. We thank You for this abundance You have provided, for the hands that prepared it, and for the blessing of family gathered at this table."

Grace kept her eyes closed. Andrews fingers tighten around hers and she sensed Charlotte shifting beside her. The Fayard family had perfected this ritual over generations, their prayers as carefully structured as their business dealings.

"We thank You for Your constant provision," Mr. Fayard continued, "for the health and prosperity You've bestowed upon this household."

The word "health" landed like a stone in Grace's stomach. She swallowed hard, wondering if they could feel the unnatural heat radiating from her fingers, if they suspected the secret diagnosis she carried.

"We appreciate the strength You've given us to fulfill Your divine purpose in this community and beyond. Guide us to use our resources and influence according to Your perfect will."

A subtle emphasis on "strength" wasn't lost on Grace. The Fayards valued fortitude above almost everything else

—physical, mental, spiritual. Weakness was not tolerated, merely managed and hidden when necessary.

"Bless those who struggle with affliction," Mr. Fayard added, "and guide them to Your healing light. Teach us to be Your hands and feet to those in need."

Grace's heart stuttered. She risked opening her eyes slightly, peering through her lashes at the family circle. Mrs. Fayard's face remained serene, eyes closed in practiced devotion. Andrew's grandmother, Eugenia, nodded slightly at each phrase, pearls gleaming at her throat. No one appeared to be watching her for a reaction.

"And Lord," Mr. Fayard's voice softened slightly, "we ask Your blessing upon Andrew and Grace as they prepare for their union. May their marriage bring honor to this family and glory to Your name."

Grace felt Andrew's thumb move gently across her knuckles—a tender gesture that made tears prick behind her closed eyelids. Would he still offer that comfort if he knew the truth? Would the Fayards still welcome her into their lineage of perfection if they discovered her body was betraying her?

"In Your holy name we pray," Mr. Fayard concluded.

"Amen," the family echoed in practiced unison.

Grace's "Amen" caught slightly in her throat as she raised her head. For a brief moment, her eyes met Mrs. Fayard's across the table—something unreadable flickered in the older woman's gaze, something that made Grace wonder if her future mother-in-law's perception extended beyond her carefully maintained facade.

"Now then," Mrs. Fayard smiled, reaching for the silver serving dish, "who would like some salmon? Grace, I had it prepared especially for you."

Grace summoned her brightest smile, ignoring the pain

radiating through her joints. "It looks wonderful, Mrs. Fayard. Thank you."

"Please, I've told you a dozen times to call me Catherine," Andrew's mother insisted with a smile that didn't quite reach her eyes. "We're practically family."

The word "family" landed less like a promise and more like a test she had yet to pass. Grace reached for her water glass with steady determination, praying her body would allow her to maintain the illusion of wellness through just one more dinner.

"The salmon looks divine, Mother," Andrew's sister Charlotte said as she reached for her water goblet. At twenty-eight, she still lived in the guest house on the property and managed the family's charitable foundation.

"Divine indeed," Andrew's grandmother Eugenia nodded from the head of the table opposite Mr. Fayard. At eighty-two, she still maintained her weekly salon appointments and wore her pearls proudly. "Although not as good as my Josephine used to make it."

Grace carefully accepted the heavy serving dish, focusing all her energy on keeping her hands from trembling as the family resumed their polished dinner conversation. The blessing was over, but Grace couldn't shake the feeling that something in the atmosphere had shifted—as if the room waited for her carefully concealed secret to be loudly revealed.

Charlotte dabbed her mouth with her napkin. "Did you hear about Cousin Eliza? She's back in treatment again."

Mrs. Fayard's lips tightened. "Perhaps not at dinner, Charlotte."

"What's wrong with Eliza?" Grace asked, grateful for any topic that diverted attention from her untouched food.

A weighted silence fell across the table before Andrew's grandmother spoke.

"Weakness of constitution. Third generation in that branch of the family." She sipped her water. "Her mother was the same way. Some vessels simply aren't strong enough for God's work."

Grace's insides cinched. She reached for her water glass, her hand trembling slightly.

"Speaking of God's work," Mrs. Fayard redirected, "Andrew, tell everyone about your promotion."

Andrew straightened beside Grace. "Gulf Coast Trust is considering me for vice president of commercial lending. They'll make a decision by Thanksgiving."

"Excellent timing for the wedding," Charlotte beamed. "The Fayard legacy continues its upward trajectory."

"And your children will have every advantage," Mrs. Fayard added, her gaze lingering on Grace. "Assuming you're still planning on three?"

Grace nodded, swallowing hard. "Of course." The sauce for the salmon needed passing. She reached for the dish, a sharp pain shooting through her wrist. The silver server wobbled in her grip.

"Careful there," Mr. Fayard cautioned.

"Yes, dear. You don't want to spill anything on that lovely outfit," Mrs. Fayard said with a lopsided grin.

"Sorry," Grace murmured, steadying the sauce boat with both hands.

"Are you feeling well, dear?" Mrs. Fayard's eyes narrowed. "You seem off tonight."

"I'm fine." The lie hit her mouth like spoiled wine. "Just tired from recital preparations."

"You should consider hiring more help at that little studio of yours," Andrew's grandmother suggested. "A

Fayard woman has charitable obligations that will take precedence."

"The Wingo Foundation Gala, for instance," Mrs. Fayard added. "As a bank executive's wife, you'll be expected to serve on at least three committees."

Grace nodded, shifting in her seat as fatigue overwhelmed her. The pain throughout her joints intensified, a dull throb transforming into sharp needles. She glanced at her watch—time for another dose, but her medication was in her purse by the front door.

"Sweetheart?" Andrew's voice seemed distant. "You're sweating."

All eyes turned to her. The chandelier was suddenly too bright, the conversation too loud.

"I just need some water," she said, reaching for her glass. Her hands refused to cooperate, sending the crystal tumbling. Water splashed across the imported tablecloth, soaking into the pristine white fabric.

"Oh!" Charlotte jumped up, napkin in hand.

"I'm so sorry," Grace stammered, attempting to blot the spill with her own napkin. Her hands shook visibly now, beyond her ability to disguise.

"What's wrong with you?" Andrew's grandmother asked, her voice sharp with concern or criticism—Grace couldn't tell which.

Andrew's hand covered hers, stilling her trembling fingers. "Honey, you're burning up."

Five pairs of eyes fixed on her, waiting. The faultless facade she'd maintained cracked, then shattered completely.

"I have lupus," she whispered.

"Lupus?" Andrew's hand tightened. "Since when?"

"I found out yesterday." Grace's weak voice was barely

audible in the cavernous dining room. "Dr. Lawson confirmed it after my blood work came back."

Charlotte's hand flew to her mouth. "Oh, Grace."

The silence stretched, punctuated only by the gentle ticking of the grandfather clock in the foyer. Grace's admission drifted through the family like a delicate crystal ornament, waiting to shatter.

Mrs. Fayard recovered first. "Well." She folded her napkin precisely. "That explains your appearance tonight."

"What exactly is lupus?" Mr. Fayard asked, his businessman's tone taking over. "Is it contagious?"

"No, Gerald," Mrs. Fayard answered before Grace could. "It's an autoimmune disease. My college roommate's sister had it." She turned to Grace, her expression softening slightly. "It's treatable these days, isn't it?"

Grace nodded, relief filtering through her at the measured response. "Yes. Dr. Lawson started me on medication. There are good days and bad days, so I've been told. But many people with lupus lead normal lives."

"Define normal," Andrew's grandmother said, her pearls gleaming as she leaned forward. "Can you have children?"

"Mother," Mr. Fayard warned.

"It's a legitimate question," she insisted. "The Fayard name must continue."

Grace hadn't even considered that aspect yet.

Andrew's hand found Grace's knee under the table. "We'll cross that bridge when we come to it."

"And your dancing business?" Charlotte asked softly. "Will you still be able to teach?"

Grace swallowed against a dry tongue. "On good days, yes. I might need to adjust some things, hire additional help."

Mrs. Fayard stood suddenly. "I'll make some tea. Grace, you look like you could use something soothing." She disappeared into the kitchen before Grace could respond.

Mr. Fayard let out a pointed sigh. "The Lord tests those He loves most deeply." He clasped his hands together and bowed his head. "We should pray for healing."

The family joined hands again. Mr. Fayard's voice rose with fervency, asking for divine intervention and complete restoration of Grace's health. Words like "deliverance" and "freedom from affliction" washed over her as she kept her eyes downcast, watching a drop of water from her spilled glass slowly spread across the white tablecloth.

"The power of prayer can move mountains," Charlotte said when her father finished. "Let's hope it does here as well."

"God rewards the faithful," Andrew's grandmother nodded firmly. "Though sometimes His answer is 'not yet.'"

Mrs. Fayard returned with a silver tea service, her composure fully restored.

Andrew remained quiet beside her, his thumb tracing circles on her knee under the table. She couldn't read his expression.

"We should go to the sitting room," Mrs. Fayard suggested. "Grace needs to be comfortable."

As the family rose, there was a whispered exchange between Mrs. Fayard and Gerald. When Grace straightened, Mrs. Fayard offered her a sympathetic smile. "Come, dear," she said, extending her arm. "Let's get you to where you can relax. We're all here for you." Catching the light, her diamond bracelet flashed like a warning.

Grace took her elbow, her revelation settling in like a heavy cloak. The family's prayers and warm smiles surrounded her, but beneath the surface ran a quiet current

—something that spoke of contingency plans and quiet calculations.

As they moved to the sitting room, Mrs. Fayard glanced at Andrew with a look that spoke volumes about this new situation. As if the family would be there for Grace to display their Christian charity.

The question was—for how long?

EIGHT

Grace's heels clicked against the polished hardwood floor of Thirty Two, a restaurant she'd never visited despite Andrew's frequent name-dropping of it as one of Biloxi's most exclusive dining spots. Of course, he'd choose somewhere public yet private enough to contain any emotional fallout. At one o'clock on a Tuesday afternoon, the restaurant sat nearly empty—a jarring change from their usual intimate dinners at Ruth's Chris in the Hard Rock Hotel and Casino.

Her hands showed her anxiety as she smoothed her silk dress, the additional medical information from Dr. Lawson burning a hole in her designer purse.

Andrew was already seated at a corner table, far from the floor-to-ceiling windows with their sweeping views of the Gulf. His steel-gray suit was immaculate, his shirt perfectly pressed, and a chilled bottle of her favorite wine sat open before him. Did he see this as a special occasion or order the Sancerre to soften a blow? He started pouring.

His expression was carefully controlled, his posture rigid. Grace recognized this setup—the private, formal setting, the way he sat erect, like a cobra ready to strike. It reminded her of how he'd once described handling difficult client meetings.

"I've been thinking about what you confessed at my parents' last week." He straightened his tie for the umpteenth time since she'd arrived. "We need to discuss our future."

Her fingers curled around the folder in her purse. *No.* She wouldn't let him write them off so easily, not without hearing her out first. She hadn't spent the night building spreadsheets and printing medical studies just to sit here and accept defeat.

"I have something to show you first." Her voice came out stronger than she'd expected. She reached for her purse, her hand brushing against the documents she'd prepared last night. The same determination that had driven her to build her dance studio from nothing surged through her veins.

"Grace..." Andrew's jaw tightened.

"Please." She pulled out the evidence, her hands steady now. "After seeing how your family reacted, I've done more research. Dr. Lawson has already outlined a treatment plan." She spread the papers between them, covering the crisp tablecloth with hope printed in black and white. "Look, with the right medication and monitoring, many women with lupus lead completely normal lives."

He shot a quick look at the documents, then adjusted his watch—the gleaming Rolex he hadn't stopped flashing since buying it to celebrate his first promotion. Even now, in the middle of discussing her illness, he was fussing with his status symbols. "I understand you're trying to be practical about this, but—"

"I *am* being practical." She leaned forward, fighting to

catch his gaze. "The success rates for pregnancy with lupus are higher than ever. We'd need to be careful, plan everything with my doctors, but it's possible."

Her heart hammered as she pulled out another paper. "This study shows that with proper medical care, sixty percent of lupus patients—"

"Stop." His command came out strong. He pushed the papers away, hurriedly taking a sip from his water. "This isn't about statistics."

Heat crept up her neck. "Then what is it about? Because I'm still me, Andrew. This diagnosis doesn't change who I am or what we can have together."

"Doesn't it?" His voice stayed level, controlled, but his face flushed red. He straightened his tie again—that nervous tic she once found endearing but now recognized as a sign that something threatened his precise order. "Our five-year plan, Grace. The beach house. Starting a family. Everything we talked about."

"Can still happen." She reached for his hand, but he pulled back. The gesture sent a chill through her. "We might need to adjust some timelines, maybe push the wedding back a few months to adjust our plans."

"A few months won't fix this." He finally met her eyes, and the carefully crafted sympathy there made her stomach turn. It was the same look he'd described practicing in the mirror for difficult clients. "Don't you see? This changes everything. The uncertainties, the medical bills, the risks. I can't build a future on maybes."

The truth hit her like a storm surge. This wasn't just about her illness. She studied the man she'd agreed to marry as the world around him blurred. Every straight line of his suit, every practiced gesture, every chosen word—it all screamed of his need for control. For certainty. "You're scared." The words slipped out before she could stop them.

Andrew's expression flickered, a chink in his polished armor. "I'm being realistic. My position at the bank, my reputation—everything I've worked for requires stability. I can't—" He paused, realigning his knife and fork to perfect parallels—the same way he organized his life. "We can't move forward with so many variables."

Grace gathered her papers with trembling fingers. She'd come armed with facts and figures, prepared to fight for their future. But how did you fight someone's fundamental nature? The realization settled inside her like lead— Andrew hadn't just lost faith in their relationship—he'd lost faith in her the moment she became a risk he couldn't manage. Her hands stilled over her arsenal of information that was now meaningless. You couldn't reason with a man who'd already calculated the cost of caring.

"Variables?" she said. "That's what I am now? A liability to your five-year plan?"

Andrew's shoulders stiffened. He reached for the untouched wine bottle and filled his glass. "You're twisting my words. I care about you, Grace. That's why this is so difficult."

"Difficult?" Her laugh came out hollow. "Tell me something, Andrew. Did you decide this the night I told you and your family about my lupus? Or did you wait until after I left?"

"I'll handle the cancellation fees for the venue," he said, his voice even. "The deposits, the vendors—you won't have to worry about any of it. I've already spoken to my attorney."

"Your attorney?" The room tilted. She gripped the table. "When?"

He wouldn't meet her eyes. "This morning." He slid his chair back an inch, adjusting his tie again. "And Grace...I'll need the ring back."

The clink of silverware and idle chatter from nearby tables seemed to stop. The lingering sweetness of her coffee turned flat on her tongue. She eyed his outstretched hand—the same hand that had slipped that ring on her finger six months ago at Ruth's.

"The ring?" Her voice sounded distant.

"It's been in my family for three generations." He pulled a small envelope from his breast pocket. "You understand."

Of course. While she'd been gathering information to reassure him after that disastrous dinner, he'd been planning his exit strategy. Minimizing his losses. Her lungs constricted, each breath shorter than the last.

Steadying her fingers, she twisted off the ring and held it at eye level. The diamond scattered afternoon light while Andrew's careful mask slipped into alarm. Then, with drama worthy of a Daphne du Maurier novel, she dropped it with great ceremony into his full wine glass.

"Grace." He reached across the table, not quite touching her hand. "You'll see this is better. Cleaner. For both of us."

She stood. Her chair screeched against the hardwood floor. Several heads turned their way. She forced herself to smile with lips so dry no amount of water could quench them. Let them see. Let them whisper about how Andrew Fayard's fiancée had made a scene at Thirty Two. She walked out, shoulders back, head high, determined to maintain her composure. But now she had another problem. If her health continued to deteriorate, how could she save her dance studio without the massive Fayard family safety net?

NINE

Nathan jerked awake, his internal alarm clock now set to Hannah's medical schedule since bringing her home from the hospital two months ago. The bedside clock's red numbers glared 2:17 AM. He was late for her blood sugar check.

He reached across to the supply table, where her insulin pump supplies, prescriptions, glucose meter, and test strips were organized with military precision. The 2:00 AM check had become their solemn ritual, but the long days of an engineer and the long evening of caring for Hannah and Lily finally caught up to him. He'd overslept by seventeen minutes. "Sweetheart?" His hand brushed her arm. Ice cold. The insulin pump attached to her abdomen beeped softly— he'd slept through three low blood sugar alarms. The display flashed an urgent warning—42 mg/dL and dropping.

She lay motionless, her skin a waxy gray against the white pillowcase. The same sickly pallor she'd had during her last crash, but worse. Much worse.

"Hannah!" His voice fractured like thin ice. He

fumbled for the bedside lamp and knocked over a prescription bottle. Pills scattered across the floor as light flooded the room. Her chest didn't rise. Her lips had taken on a bluish tint. Panic clawed up his throat as he touched trembling fingers to her neck. "Come on, baby. Wake up."

A faint flutter beneath his fingertips. Too slow. Way too slow.

The emergency glucagon kit. He yanked open the nightstand drawer and clutched the orange case. The needle gleamed as he pulled it out with shaking hands. They'd used her last backup three days ago when the pump site failed. He'd meant to fill the new prescription yesterday.

Nathan jammed the needle into her thigh through her pajama pants, just as the diabetes educator had drilled into him. One-one-thousand, two-one-thousand, three-one-thousand...He counted to five and withdrew it.

Nothing. No response. Her lips remained blue. The glucose gel was next—he squeezed it between her cheek and gum, knowing it was probably too late for that. Her body wasn't absorbing anything.

He grabbed his phone, muscle memory taking over as he punched in 911. They'd done this dance before—four times in two weeks. But something in his gut screamed this was different. The dispatcher's voice faded in and out as he rattled off their address. He focused on Hannah's breathing.

"911 service. What's your emergency?"

"My wife is unconscious. Diabetic shock. I've given glucagon and glucose gel, but she's not responding. Her pump alarm shows 42 and dropping." The information tumbled out, clipped and mechanical.

"Sir? Is your wife breathing?"

Was she? He couldn't tell. The dim light from the lamp

played tricks on his vision. He leaned closer, his cheek hovering above her parted lips. No warm puff of air met his skin.

"No," he said with conviction.

"Emergency services are three minutes out. Do you know CPR, sir?"

"Yes." He'd certified last month. "Just in case," the instructor had said. Just in case was now.

He disconnected her insulin pump with one practiced motion, setting it on the nightstand. Then he grabbed Lily's baby monitor from the charger and clipped it to his waistband. Their six-month-old daughter slept peacefully down the hall, oblivious to the nightmare unfolding.

"Tell them to come through the back door," he said as he positioned himself over Hannah. He started keeping it unlocked after the second emergency in as many weeks. "We're upstairs."

He interlocked his fingers across her sternum just like he'd been taught. One-two-three-four—Don't think about how fragile she feels. Five-six-seven-eight. *Nine-ten-eleven-twelve—God, please.*

Sirens wailed in the distance. Growing closer. The same route they'd taken four times before. He kept counting, kept pushing, kept breathing for her.

Heavy boots thundered up the stairs. "In here." His voice rasped. His arms burned from compressions. But he refused to stop.

The paramedics burst in—they'd been here before. Recognition flashed across their faces as they swarmed the bed. "Sir, we need you to step back."

Nathan stumbled away, his legs wooden. The paramedics worked with efficient speed—checking vitals, starting an IV, calling out numbers that meant Hannah was slipping away.

"Blood sugar critically low. No response to glucose."

"BP barely registering."

"Starting emergency protocol."

Through the fog of medical jargon, one phrase cut through: "She's coding."

The hallway seemed to stretch as Nathan followed the gurney. The paramedic who'd been here for Hannah's last three crashes touched his arm.

"We need to move fast."

Lily. Still asleep in her crib. He couldn't leave her alone. Couldn't go with Hannah. The choice tore at his insides.

Nathan fumbled for his phone, his vision blurring as he hit Rachel's number. Seven rings before his sister answered.

"Nathan?" Rachel's voice was thick with sleep. She knew what a middle-of-the-night call meant.

"Hannah's..." His throat closed around the words, a sob threatening to break free. The paramedics were already loading her into the ambulance. "She's not breathing, Rach. They're taking her to Merit again," he said frantically. "I need to go, but I can't leave Lily."

"I understand." The sounds of movement came through the phone—Rachel getting dressed. "I'm coming right now. Is she..." The unspoken question hung between them.

"It's bad. Worse than before." The admission felt like betrayal, but Rachel needed to know.

"Ten minutes, tops. I'll call Mom on the way. Nathan..." she said softly. "You've done everything you could."

The simple acknowledgment nearly broke him. "Just hurry."

"I will. I'll take care of Lily."

He logged off, his hand shaking so badly he almost

dropped the phone. Rachel had been their rock through every crisis with Hannah—the one person who never offered empty platitudes or false hope. The one who understood what they were facing.

The paramedic squeezed Nathan's shoulder. "We'll take good care of her. Wait for your family."

The ambulance doors slammed shut. Hannah disappeared behind them, wrapped in a cocoon of wires and tubes. Just like the other times. But worse.

Nathan stood in the driveway, watching red lights fade into the pre-dawn darkness. The baby monitor clipped to his waistband remained silent. How long before Lily woke, asking for a mother who might never return.

No. Don't think it. Just breathe. Wait for Rachel. One minute at a time.

Rachel arrived at the hospital twenty minutes after Nathan. Mom kept Lily at home. His daughter shouldn't have to spend another night in this place. She'd already logged too many hours here in her short life.

Dr. Montgomery's expression as she'd pulled Nathan aside told him everything. The same gentle tone she'd used two weeks ago when discussing Hannah's discharge. "We need to prepare for difficult decisions, Nathan."

Difficult decisions. Code for deciding when to let go.

Nathan sank into a chair, his body heavy with promises. He'd sworn to protect Hannah, to keep her safe. Now his wife lay behind those double doors, machines breathing for her while he sat here helpless. Useless.

The phone vibrated—Mom checking in. Lily was still sleeping, thankfully. His daughter's peaceful ignorance felt like a mercy and a curse. She wouldn't remember this moment. Wouldn't remember her mother at all.

His phone rang and he answered. "Nathan." Rachel's

voice. "Do you want me to call the prayer chain? Get Mike Santos here?"

How many times had those men prayed for Hannah's healing? How many times had he believed God would save her? How many times must God mock him with all these emergencies?

How much more could his faith take?

THE LINE on the heart monitor stretched longer between beeps. Nathan's fingers tightened around Hannah's cold hand, then forced them to relax. Three days at her bedside, watching her kidneys fail despite the dialysis, had taught him to treasure each moment. Be gentle, be strong. This could be the last time—no. Stay focused for Hannah's sake.

Dr. Montgomery's words from this morning echoed in his brain—"The combination of kidney failure and the infection is too much. Her body is shutting down." Despite the antibiotics, the infection had spread. Despite the dialysis, her toxin levels kept rising. Despite every prayer, every treatment, every hope, Hannah was slipping away.

His throat closed against the biblical passages he should be reciting, the words of comfort locked behind memories that dated back to middle school. Their first date. Their first kiss. The senior prom. Their wedding. The day they brought Lily home. Memories that were supposed to continue, not stop.

"Nathan." Hannah rasped beneath the oxygen mask. Her hands twitched in his grip, those same hands that caressed Lily's cheek not long ago.

Stay strong. She needs you strong. He leaned closer, wielding his voice like a shield against the terror building inside his belly. "I'm right here, sweetheart. Like I promised. Like I'll always be."

"Lily—" A harsh cough cut off her words. Her eyes rolled back momentarily, then focused again with frightening intensity.

The monitor's rhythm stumbled, and Nathan's heart lurched with it. A nurse appeared in the doorway, checking the readings, then disappeared again. Images of future moments crashed through his mind—Lily's graduation, her wedding, grandchildren—scenes that were supposed to include Hannah.

Not yet, God. Please, I'm not ready. We're not ready.

Hannah's fingers clawed at the oxygen mask. The movement so sudden, so desperate, his heart skipped. He caught her hand. "Shh, sweetheart, you need to rest."

She shook her head, raised her brow with an urgency he'd never seen before. Not even during her worst episodes. Her lips moved behind the fogged plastic, but the words came out garbled.

The beeping increased, each tone stabbing him viciously. He must keep her calm. "I'm here. Just breathe, okay? Nice and slow like Dr. Montgomery taught us."

But Hannah kept fighting, kept trying to speak. Kept looking at him with those eyes that could see straight through to his soul. Her hand pulled against his, weaker now, but determined. She had something to say. Something important enough to spend her precious remaining breath on.

God help me. The right choice and the safe choice warred inside him. Hannah's oxygen levels were already too low, but if these were their final moments....he couldn't let her go without hearing her last words.

Moving carefully, he lifted the mask for her to speak. "I'm listening, sweetheart."

Hannah's breath came in shallow gasps. "Promise me..." Her fingers dug into his palm. "That you won't blame God." She heaved, struggling for air. The monitor alarm sounded briefly before settling back into its irregular rhythm. Nathan almost replaced the mask, but her eyes pleaded with him.

"His plan...for you and Lily...trust it." Each word seemed to cost her, her face contorting with the effort.

An invisible band tightened around his ribs. How could he not blame God? They'd done everything right. Married in the church. Taught Sunday School together. Raised Lily in faith. And this was their reward? His gaze lingered on the dove pendant resting against his wife's wrist—the spirit symbol that caught his attention through every emergency room visit, every setback, every near tragedy.

"Nathan." Hannah's voice strengthened with unexpected urgency. "Promise me." Her body went rigid, her eyes unfocused for five terrifying seconds before returning to him.

He swallowed hard, forced the lie past his constricting throat. "I promise."

She drew a rattling breath. "Church...Lily...don't lose..." The words dissolved into coughing. He quickly replaced the mask, his heartbeat quickening as her oxygen levels dropped on the monitor.

"Don't talk anymore. Please, Hannah. Save your strength."

She shook her head stubbornly, pushing weakly at the mask again after several labored breaths. "She'll need...faith...when I'm—" She couldn't finish, her body wracked with another coughing fit.

Like a knife twisting deeper. *When I'm gone.* He nodded, unable to speak.

Hannah's eyes drifted closed, then snapped open with alarming suddenness. "One more..." Her voice had weakened to just a whisper. "After time...find..." The words faded as her energy flagged.

"Shh, don't worry about anything else. Just rest."

"No." Her fingers tightened. "Lily needs...mother. Someone..." Each word was a battle now, her breathing growing more labored between fragments. "Promise...won't be...alone."

"No," he burst out.

"Promise." The single word held all her remaining strength.

Tears spilled down his cheeks. How could she ask this of him? How could she think anyone could replace her? But her eyes pleaded, and he couldn't deny her. Not now. Not ever.

"I promise," he choked out. "But Hannah, please...just stay with me. Stay with us."

The monitor's warning tone changed pitch. Her eyes fluttered closed, then flew open again. She struggled to speak once more.

"Someone who...makes you happy. Who'll love...our Lily." Each word was a battle now, her face contorting with the effort.

Nathan couldn't imagine it—sharing his life with another woman, sharing Lily with a stranger. The very thought felt like betrayal. But Hannah's eyes pleaded, and he had never been able to deny her anything.

"I promise," he whispered, the words feeling like ash in his mouth. "I promise I'll find someone who makes me happy. Who'll love Lily." His voice broke. "But Hannah, please don't go. Not yet."

He positioned the mask back in place, his own breath coming faster. "Stay with me, sweetheart. Please. Lily needs you. I need you."

The monitor's shrill alarm pierced the room. Her eyes found his. A tear slid down her cheek as her lips moved beneath the mask. Nathan leaned closer, his ear nearly touching the plastic.

"Love...you...both..."

"We love you too. Hannah, please..." He wept. "Fight a little longer." He wasn't ready. How could he ever be ready? How do you tell your six-month-old daughter that she'd never see her mother again?

Hannah's fingers twitched in his grip. One small squeeze. Then her hand went slack.

A steady tone filled the room. No more beeps. No more peaks. Just one long, endless line. One long, endless tone, sounding the end.

TEN

Marcella Hills, Pakistan

Jagged stone bit into Joseph's back as he flattened himself against the mountain face. His leg muscles screamed from crouching, but he didn't dare move. Not with three TPL trucks crawling along the road thirty feet below, close enough he could hear gears clank as the drivers shifted.

Hassan's fingers waved to stay still. A scatter of loose shale broke free under Joseph's boot, clattering down the slope. The plink-plink-plink of falling rocks froze his lungs.

Militant voices carried up through the pre-dawn mist.

A child's scream shattered the air.

The sound yanked Joseph's gaze downward. Through gaps in the scrub brush, a woman's bright hijab flashed in a mud-walled courtyard. She rocked back and forth, clutching a bundle wrapped in a blanket to her breasts.

"Joseph," Hassan called over the rumble of engines. "Ten minutes to the city."

The lights of Islamabad painted the clouds ahead in an

amber promise. But heat bloomed in Joseph's palms. That familiar burn began to build.

The bundle in the woman's arms shifted. He caught a glimpse of a child's face—flushed skin, glassy eyes that reflected the dawn light. Something in the weak movements reminded Joseph of little Samira from the mission, how she'd looked before his father prayed for her. The warmth in his palms grew hotter.

The boy's ragged breathing reached Joseph's ears, clawing at his conscience. Hassan tugged Joseph's sleeve, pointing silently. Following his guide's gesture, Joseph spotted a narrow goat path ten yards ahead, winding up into deeper shadow. Their escape route.

"Ya Allah," the woman's Urdu drifted up to their hiding spot in a mother's desperation. "The fever takes him."

Brakes squealed. The lead truck stopped.

Joseph's thighs trembled from holding still. Below, car doors creaked open. Boot steps crunched on gravel. The mother's cries grew more desperate.

"Please, my son needs a doctor."

"Be quiet." A man's voice, hard with authority. "Have you seen any strangers pass through? A foreign boy?"

The burn in Joseph's hands pulsed stronger. He clenched his fingers into fists, but that only intensified the sensation. The child's whimpers grew weaker.

Hassan tugged Joseph's sleeve. Ten yards ahead, a narrow goat path wound into shadow. Their escape route. But the boy's ragged breathing clawed at Joseph's conscience. More vehicles approached, their headlights sweeping the mountainside. Joseph flattened deeper into the rock face, his heart thundering so hard he feared the militants would hear it. The beam of light passed just below their position.

"Search the houses," someone ordered. "They can't be far."

The woman's soft weeping merged with her son's fading breaths—the same sounds that had filled the mission the night cholera swept through the village. The night Joseph first discovered his gift, when little Samira struggled at death's edge.

Hassan's grip tightened—a warning, a plea.

But the familiar fire spread up Joseph's arms, and in his mind, his mother's voice commanded clear as the morning— *"Remember your gift. Your purpose."*

Flashlight beams cut through the darkness below. From his position, Joseph could see militants entering one house, then another. Shouts carried up the slope, followed by cries that made his stomach tighten. A child wailed somewhere in the village. Another joined in. Joseph's fingers dug into the rocky soil beneath him.

"The boy will die before they finish searching," he whispered to Hassan.

Hassan's eyes reflected starlight. "If you go down there, it will be us who dies."

The militants entered another house. Their commands grew fainter.

Joseph's hands burned hotter. He could almost feel the child's fever from here, like a beacon calling to the fire in his palms. The woman had stopped wailing, but her silent rocking hadn't ceased.

"We must reach the city before dawn," Hassan's grip stayed firm on Joseph's arm. "Your parents died to get you to safety."

The militants' voices faded around a corner. A dog barked in the distance. The narrow path down to the courtyard lay in shadow.

Joseph pulled free of Hassan.

"Five minutes," he whispered. "Watch for their return."

Hassan's face hardened, but he nodded once. "May the Lord Jesus protect us both."

Loose stones shifted beneath Joseph's feet as he crept down the rocky slope to within five meters of the woman and her child. The boy's breathing was so shallow it was difficult to hear.

Closing the distance, Joseph touched the woman's shoulder. She flinched. Her eyes widened at his Western features, but before she could cry out, he placed a finger to his lips. Understanding dawned in her tear-streaked face.

The boy's skin burned against Joseph's palm as he placed his hand on the child whose heart fluttered like a trapped bird.

A whistle cut through the darkness—Hassan's warning. Flashlight beams swept back toward them.

Joseph closed his eyes. The familiar fire surged through his arms, but exhaustion from two weeks on the run made his head spin. He swayed, catching himself on the courtyard wall.

Remember your gift. Your purpose.

The power flowed slower than usual, like honey instead of water. Joseph's own strength drained with it, but he felt the boy's fever breaking, his breathing deepening. The child's eyes fluttered open, clear and bright.

Another whistle, more urgent. The child giggled.

Joseph squeezed the mother's hand once, then staggered back to the mountain. His legs trembled with each step. Voices grew louder behind him—the militants returning.

Hassan's arm caught him before he fell. "You cannot heal the whole world, Joseph."

"No." Joseph leaned against his friend as they climbed. "But I can heal those God puts in my path."

Dawn's first light touched the eastern sky. Islamabad's glow seemed further away now, with TPL trucks between them and safety. But the boy's heartbeat had been strong when Joseph left him. For now, that was enough.

Joseph's vision blurred. Every step drained energy from his legs as they moved higher into the mountains, away from their planned route into the city.

Hassan studied the valley below. TPL vehicles still choked the main road, their headlights sweeping the darkness. "We must circle wide." He pointed east, away from the roads. "There is a dry riverbed that leads into the city's outskirts. But it will take hours."

The mountain path grew steeper. Joseph stumbled, his hand scraping against rock. The healing had drained him more than usual. Or maybe it was the two weeks of running, of sleeping in caves, of the hollow ache that opened whenever he thought of home. Of Mama and Papa.

A truck engine roared to life below. Voices shouted commands in Pashto.

"They're mobilizing the search." Hassan gripped Joseph's arm, steadying him. "Can you continue?"

Joseph nodded, though his legs shook with each step. The first rays of sun pierced the mountains, painting their shadows long against the rocks. Soon the light would expose them to the valley. But somewhere in that village, a child's heart beat strong and sure. A mother and her son who were whole and healthy. Even with the TPL militants swarming between them and safety, Joseph couldn't regret his choice.

Hassan pulled him behind a boulder as more vehicles thundered past on the road. They were running out of darkness. Running out of time.

"We must reach the riverbed before daybreak." Hassan's voice held an edge of fear Joseph had never heard. "If they catch us now..."

The sun climbed higher. Joseph forced his legs to move, one step at a time. Engines echoed off the mountain walls as the TPL began their hunt anew.

Joseph's boots lost traction on the steep embankment. Loose shale shifted under his feet, sending him sliding too fast. His knees hit rock. Pain shot up his thighs. He pitched forward, arms windmilling, until Hassan's fingers clamped around his wrist. "I've got you," Hassan whispered, steadying him as they skidded the last few feet into the dried riverbed.

Joseph's legs trembled and threatened to fold. Each breath burned in his lungs. The high banks offered some cover, but the sky blazed orange now. Soon the sun would climb above the mountains, giving away their position.

Hassan pulled Joseph behind a fallen tree. "Stay down. TPL patrols the bridge ahead."

Joseph's ribs seemed to shrink, leaving little room to breathe. Through gaps in the dead branches, he glimpsed the concrete bridge spanning the riverbed. Two militants stood guard, rifles ready. Beyond them lay the outer edges of Islamabad—so close, yet unreachable.

A convoy rumbled overhead. Both guards straightened, raising their hands in greeting.

Hassan's whisper carried urgency. "When the next motorcade passes, we run. There's a water tunnel beneath the bridge that will hide us."

Joseph nodded, not trusting his voice. His limbs felt like lead. But they had no choice. Dawn's light crept down the riverbank, exposing more of their position with every passing minute.

Engine noise grew louder. More vehicles approached.

Hassan squeezed Joseph's arm. "Ready yourself."

The guards above turned toward the oncoming trucks. Hassan tensed beside him, coiled to spring. The convoy thundered overhead. He pushed Joseph forward. His legs nearly gave way with the first step. Adrenaline surged. Each stride sent pain shooting up his spine, but the fear of capture prodded him. They half-ran, half-stumbled through ankle-deep silt, Joseph dragging in ragged, desperate gasps.

"Hurry," Hassan urged, supporting Joseph's weight as they staggered the twenty yards toward the tunnel entrance.

Shouts erupted above them. A rifle cracked. Bullets kicked up dirt near Joseph's feet. Ten yards.

Hassan shoved Joseph ahead of him to the dark mouth of the tunnel. More shots sounded off the concrete. Hassan grunted—a sharp, pained sound.

"Hassan."

"Keep moving."

They plunged into darkness. Freezing water soaked Joseph's socks. Hassan's labored breathing hissed in the confined space. They stumbled forward, feeling their way along slimy walls.

Voices carried from both ends of the tunnel now. Flashlight beams probed the blackness.

"Here." Hassan pulled Joseph into a narrow mainte-nance alcove, pressing them flat against the wet cement. Moisture ran down Joseph's neck. His heart thundered so loudly he feared it would give them away.

Boots splashed. A beam of light swept past their hiding spot. Joseph held his breath.

Hassan's grip on his arm weakened.

"You're hurt—" Joseph whispered.

"Quiet."

More footsteps approached from the other direction. They were trapped.

Blood trickled down Hassan's arm, hot on Joseph's shoulder in the freezing tunnel. The familiar burn of healing tingled in Joseph's palms. He reached for Hassan's shoulder.

"No." Hassan's grip tightened despite his wound. "Not enough time for that."

Flashlight beams crisscrossed at the tunnel's center. Voices bounced off the concrete walls. "Check every alcove."

Hassan's breathing grew ragged. Joseph's hands burned. The power surged through him like electricity, demanding release.

A beam of light swept toward their hiding place.

Hassan took them deeper into the shadows, but not before the glow caught the water pooling at their feet.

A shout went up. "There."

Gunfire shattered the silence. Hassan shoved Joseph lower, shielding him. There was splashing ahead—more militants closing in from the far end. He grabbed Hassan's arm. The power flowed, and Hassan couldn't stop it.

The wound sealed shut and his breathing steadied. "Foolish boy," he whispered, but his grip was firm now. "We run together."

They burst from the alcove as flashlight beams converged. Hassan led them through the crossfire, slipping between shadows. Bullets tore through the darkness, but their pursuers fired blind.

Light gleamed at the tunnel's opening—a rectangle of blinding gold. Joseph squinted, splashing through ankle-deep water. That light meant Islamabad. The American embassy and safety.

If they could only reach it.

———

GUNSHOTS. Screams cut short. Smoke.

The images flashed—his mother in the garden when the trucks arrived, his father shoving them to the hidden entrance, the tunnel door sealing out his parents' faces forever. Then the cracks of gunfire. Mama's scream, swallowed by silence.

They emerged onto the mountainside. Below, the mission blazed on the valley floor. Tears stung his eyes, mingling with the grit and smoke clinging to his skin.

His fingers found Mama's silver cross, warm against his chest as if it still held some fragment of her life. The compound where they had taught children and treated the sick was just a burning skeleton now.

The mountains watched—ancient, indifferent, silent witnesses to the tragedy in their shadow.

Then, cutting through his grief like sunlight through storm clouds, he heard it. Not with his ears, but somewhere deeper.

A voice, small and still—*"One day, you will return."*

Joseph blinked.

The ceiling fan above him spun in slow, lazy circles. Morning heat pressed against the grimy windows of the Islamabad hostel. From a nearby mosque, the call to prayer drifted through the clatter of traffic and the vendors' early cries.

He lay still for a moment, the echo of the voice lingering.

Everything else had happened—the tunnel, the fire, the screams. But the voice...that hadn't been there.

Not then.

His fingers found the cross at his chest—still warm.

One day, you will return.

He sat up slowly, the words turning over in his mind. Was it memory? A dream? Something else?

What did it mean?

Joseph flung his legs over the edge of the narrow bed, his feet touching the rough wooden floor of the dimly lit hostel. The musty air mixed with the odors of sweat and dust. Across the room, Hassan filled a plastic bucket with water from the communal bathroom. "You screamed in your sleep," he called over his shoulder, his voice echoing in the cramped space. "Bad dream?"

Joseph said nothing as he toed off the dirt-caked shoes he had worn for what felt like a lifetime. He ventured into the shower stall, bracing.

Hassan poured lukewarm over his shoulders. "I guess that's to be expected with all you've been through."

The grime washed away, but the hurt in his heart remained. His mind drifted back to his mother's laugh, the whiff of jasmine in the warm air. That life was gone. What lay ahead was a mystery.

After drying himself with the rough towel, he slipped into the fresh clothes Hassan had bought earlier. They were simple but clean, a welcome contrast to the tattered ones he'd left behind.

The cracked mirror reflected a stranger. Hollow cheeks. Dirt-smudged skin despite the shower. Eyes that looked older than ten. Joseph touched his face, wondering if Mama and Papa would recognize him now. Two weeks ago, he'd been just a mission kid helping in the garden. Now he was... what? A refugee? A fugitive? The only thing that was familiar was the cross hanging from his neck.

Hassan emerged from the bathroom and clapped him on the shoulder. "You look like a young man ready for an adventure."

Joseph forced a weak smile.

They stepped outside, and the heat struck him like a solid wall. The streets roared with life—vendors shouting over the din of traffic, children darting between carts, the scent of roasting meat thick in the air. It was overwhelming. The sharp contrast to the cold mountains made his stomach twist.

Hassan led him to a crowded bus stop. Joseph stood stiffly, every face around him unfamiliar—like he was a foreigner in his own country. The bus arrived in a cloud of dust, and they wedged themselves inside. The press of bodies, the lurch of the engine, the thick heat—it all closed in, squeezing his breath.

When they finally stepped off in front of the American embassy, Joseph's pulse hammered against his ribs. The building rose before them—all concrete, glass, and steel. Nothing like the mud-brick walls of home.

Armed guards stood at attention beside a massive gate. Joseph's throat went dry. Through those gates lay his future —whatever that meant now. His fingers found his mother's cross, clutching it like an anchor as the chaos of Islamabad swirled around him.

"Stay close," Hassan murmured as they approached the security checkpoint.

Bright lights replaced the dusty streets, their sterile glow making Joseph's head pound. A woman in Western clothes strode across the marble lobby, clutching files close to her.

"Joseph."

He hadn't had time to react before she pulled him into a fierce embrace.

Sarah. His khala. His mother's sister.

She stepped back, her dark eyes glossy. "I've been so worried. The assault on the mission was all over the news."

"We traveled two weeks from the Hindu Kush," Hassan said in rapid Urdu. "William and Lyla..."

"I know." Sarah's voice was tight. She flicked her eyes at the folders in her arms. "I have everything ready."

Joseph's stomach knotted. *Ready for what?*

Aunt Sarah knelt, meeting his gaze. "You're leaving in the morning." A brief hesitation. "To Biloxi, Mississippi."

The words meant nothing to him.

She pressed on. "Your father's brother, David—your uncle—he's a pastor there. You'll be safe with him."

Safe. The word felt foreign—like the city's heat, like the strange curve of English letters on the embassy walls. Everything he knew was slipping away—his parents, the mountains, the soil that was warm between his fingers the morning they were killed.

Hassan crouched beside Sarah, taking Joseph's hands. "Your gift isn't just for Pakistan, Beta. God has bigger plans."

Joseph swallowed hard, clenching his hands into fists. The warmth that had flowed through him—power he didn't understand. But where had it gone when his parents needed it?

Sarah's hand found his shoulder as she stood.

Was this God's plan? To send him halfway across the world?

His breath steadied.

No. God hadn't abandoned him. He was sending him.

A whisper of something stirred inside him—not peace, not yet. But something just as powerful.

Purpose.

He exhaled, lifted his chin, and followed Sarah through the towering embassy doors, hearing,*"One day, you will return,"* once again.

PART 2

ELEVEN

Six months later—Biloxi, Mississippi

Joseph froze at the door of the sixth-grade classroom, his new backpack suddenly heavy on his shoulders. Fifteen unfamiliar faces swiveled toward him like flowers tracking the sun. The room fell silent.

"Class, this is our new student, Joseph, "Mrs. Bennett announced, her voice too cheerful. "He's joining us all the way from Pakistan. Isn't that exciting?"

Joseph's fingers traced the edges of his mother's cross.

"You can take the empty seat by the window," Mrs. Bennett said, pointing to a desk in the third row.

He nodded, eyes downcast as he navigated between desks. He felt the stares like tiny pinpricks across his skin. His one goal today was simple—blend in. Be normal. Don't let anyone see what makes you different.

Six months since he'd left the mission compound, and still everything about America was foreign—especially this classroom with its strange white rectangle mounted on the wall where a chalkboard should be. When the teacher touched it, colorful words and numbers appeared like magic.

Uncle David had driven him to school that morning. "Just be yourself, buddy." But being himself was exactly what Joseph couldn't risk.

A boy with spiky blond hair and a shirt that probably cost more than a month's supplies at the mission leaned over as Joseph sat down. "Did you like live in a hut back in Pakistan?"

He set his backpack on the floor and sat. Today was going to be a long day for sure.

Mrs. Bennett scribbled numbers across the massive whiteboard. Fractions—three-fourths plus one-eighth, five-sixths minus one-third.

Back home, twenty children crowded around six shared desks, poring over five battered textbooks. Here, every student had their own desk. Their own books. Their own space.

The boy beside him unzipped a pencil case that glowed blue from the inside. Two rows ahead, a girl's sneakers lit up red with every step. Joseph tucked his plain, dusty shoes farther beneath his desk.

"Joseph, perhaps you'd like to try this one?"

His head jerked up. Mrs. Bennett was pointing to a new problem glowing on the board.

"Three-fifths divided by one-half," he read in a faint murmur.

Multiply the numerators, then the denominators. The answer came easily—it always did. Numbers made sense when nothing else did. But fifteen pairs of eyes were on him now. Watching. Weighing. The back of his neck tingled, the way it always did just before fear took hold.

"Six-fifths," he said, louder than he meant to."The answer is one and one-fifth."

Mrs. Bennett's smile softened. "Excellent. You may sit down."

The tingling faded.

Two hours later, the cafeteria doors opened to a wall of noise and smells—pizza, French fries, something sweet like cinnamon. Joseph clutched his brown paper bag. Hundreds of kids sat at long tables, laughing, shouting, trading food.

"Hey, Pakistan." It was the boy with spiky hair, waving from a table near the windows. "Over here." Joseph hesitated. His stomach clenched. With nowhere else to go, he walked over.

"I'm Zack," the boy said before pointing to his three companions. "This is Bryan, Madison, and Taylor."

Joseph hunched his shoulders and slid onto the bench edge, ready for a quick escape.

"What's in the bag?" Taylor asked. Her headband caught the light, throwing tiny rainbows across the table.

Joseph pulled out his sandwich. The peanut butter had soaked through the bread, making a dark stain on the plastic wrap.

"That's it?" Bryan's eyes widened. His tray overflowed with pizza, fries, an apple, chocolate milk, and a cup of blue jello.

Joseph stared at their trays. Back home, this much food would feed the entire mission staff for dinner.

"I'm good with this," he whispered.

"So what was it like?" Madison leaned forward, her eyes bright with curiosity. "Did you ride camels to school?"

"Were there, like, terrorists everywhere?" Bryan added through a mouthful of pizza.

"Did you have electricity?" Taylor asked.

How could Joseph explain the home he left behind? The garden where his mother taught him to grow vegetables. The evening generator that gave them three hours of light for homework. The families who walked miles to receive medicine. "We had a regular house," he said. "And a school. And friends. And electricity."

"But why were you even there?" Zack asked, biting into his pizza.

A crash echoed through the cafeteria. A small boy with glasses stood frozen, his lunch splattered across the floor. Chocolate milk pooled around his shoes.

Snickers rippled through the room.

The tingling returned, shooting down Joseph's spine like electricity.

Not dangerous. Just embarrassing.

The boy's face crumpled. Tears welled in his eyes. The laughter got really loud. The boy turned fast toward the door that went to the stairs. Joseph could see what was gonna happen next. The boy would run without looking and miss the first step and fall down the concrete stairs head first.

Joseph stood so quickly his knee banged against the table.

"Where are you going?" Zack called after him.

But Joseph was already moving.

The boy with glasses pushed through the stairwell door just as Joseph had predicted. He weaved between tables, dodging a teacher who reached out to stop him. "No running in the cafeteria."

The tingling intensified, spreading through Joseph's shoulders to his fingertips. The boy was inside the stairwell. Three more steps and he'd reach the first stair.

Joseph lunged, grabbing the boy's backpack just as his

foot missed the first step. For a suspended second, the boy teetered on the edge, arms pinwheeling. Joseph yanked him backward, and they both tumbled onto the concrete floor.

"Let me go." The boy struggled against him, tears streaming down his face.

"You were going to fall," Joseph panted. The tingling sensation receded, leaving his hands ordinary again. "The stairs—you would have gotten hurt."

The boy stopped struggling. "How did you know?"

Joseph released him and scrambled to his feet. "I just saw you running. It was obvious."

A teacher appeared just inside the door. "What's going on out here?"

"Nothing," Joseph said quickly. "He dropped his lunch, and I was helping him."

The teacher tilted his head, just slightly, the way someone might when they smell a lie. "Both of you back to the cafeteria. No running."

The boy wiped his face with his sleeve. "Thanks," he mumbled. "I'm Peyton."

"Joseph."

"You're the new kid. From Pakistan."

Joseph nodded, waiting for the inevitable questions about camels and terrorists.

Instead, Peyton asked, "How'd you get to me so fast?"

Joseph's hand went to his mother's cross. "Just lucky, I guess."

They walked back into the cafeteria together. The laughter had moved on to another target, but Joseph could feel Zack and the others watching him from their table.

"Want to sit with me?" Peyton asked. "I mean, if you're not already sitting with someone."

Joseph glanced at Zack and his companions. Bryan was

making exaggerated running motions with his fingers. Taylor nudged Madison with her elbow as both laughed.

"Yeah," Joseph said. "I'd like that."

THE FINAL BELL rang at 3:15. Joseph gathered his new textbooks—so many books, all for him alone—and followed the crowd to the front entrance. His shoulders finally relaxed as he pushed through the exit doors. He'd survived his first day in an American school.

In English class, the teacher asked him to read aloud. A girl in the front row giggled behind her hand at his accent. In history, they talked about countries he'd never even heard of. In science, when Ms. Garcia asked about different types of energy, he almost mentioned the Holy Spirit that gave him his gift.

Outside, a line of cars waited in the pickup lane. Joseph spotted Uncle David's blue Ford truck immediately. Unlike the shiny SUVs and minivans, the truck had a dent in the passenger door and faded paint on the hood. He climbed in to the smell of pine air freshener dangling from the rearview mirror.

Uncle David, a sturdy man with salt-and-pepper hair, greeted him with friendly ease. Deep-set emerald eyes, like Joseph's and his father's, sparkled with kindness. He wore a red flannel shirt and jeans that hinted he'd been doing yard work at the church where he pastored. "How was your first day?" he asked.

Joseph buckled his seatbelt. "Fine."

Uncle David studied him for a moment, then put the truck in park. "That bad, huh?"

"I didn't say it was bad."

"You didn't have to." Uncle David's green eyes crinkled at the corners, just like Papa's used to. "Tell you what—there's a place down the road that serves thirty-two flavors of ice cream. Might help with the first-day blues."

"What are the blues?" Joseph asked.

"It's when you feel down and out."

"I don't feel down and out," Joseph protested. "No blues." But his stomach growled at the suggestion of ice cream.

Uncle David chuckled and pulled away from the curb. "You know, your dad called me after my first week back from Pakistan. I was about your age—maybe a little older. I couldn't stop talking about everything I missed from the mission."

Joseph looked up. "You weren't born here?"

"Born in Lebanon. Your grandparents were missionaries there. Your dad and I grew up overseas until we were teenagers. "Uncle David turned onto a street lined with restaurants, each with glowing signs bigger than Joseph's entire classroom back home. "When we first moved to Biloxi," he said, "I couldn't sleep for days. The lights were too bright. The food portions were too big. Even the toothpaste," he chuckled, "had too many flavors. Your dad used to say Americans had a word for everything, and then five more words, just in case."

Joseph stared out the window at a billboard advertising the newest smartphone. It reminded him of what Papa told him about coming to America from overseas—how things were so big, so overwhelming. "At lunch, this kid had enough food on his tray to feed three people."

"America can be a bit much when you've lived somewhere simpler." Uncle David eased the car into a space beneath an awning with pink and turquoise stripes. A giant plastic sundae smiled down from the roof. "God called me to stay in America to start a church. But I don't forget my formative years. They were much like yours."

"And my father?"

"Your dad—he was more like your grandfather. Followed his calling to become a missionary himself. Left when he was twenty-two and never came back. Met your mother and made her country his home."

Joseph fingered his mother's cross. "Something happened today."

Uncle David turned off the engine. "What kind of something?"

"A boy was going to fall down the stairs. I knew it was going to happen before it did." Joseph took a lung-swelling breath.

Uncle David narrowed his eyes. "Did you say that you knew?"

"No. I just pulled him back. Mom told me never to tell people about my gift. They wouldn't understand."

Silence settled in for a long moment. "Your mother was a wise woman," his uncle finally said. "And she was right—most people won't understand. But don't use that as an excuse to hide who you are from anyone."

"What do you mean?"

With a hint of sadness in his eyes, Uncle David smiled. "Let's get that ice cream first. Then we'll talk about what makes you different—and why it's okay to be different, even if many people won't understand."

Traces of waffle cones and ice cream wafted through the open door. Inside, laughter floated out with the jingling bell, and the display case glowed with swirls of color—mint green, bubblegum blue, deep chocolate brown.

"What'll it be?" The teenage girl behind the counter said.

Joseph pointed at the plain white one. "That."

"Vanilla?" she said, her voice flat, like she'd said it a hundred times that day.

Uncle David ordered something with chunks of cookies and paid with a crisp bill. Joseph clutched his cup with both hands. At the mission, ice cream meant his father cranking the metal handle for an hour while Joseph and his mother took turns adding ice and salt. The treat was for celebration —Easter or Christmas or after a baby was born healthy in the community.

He dipped his spoon in and took a tiny bite. The sweetness exploded on his tongue, richer and creamier than anything he'd ever tasted. His eyes widened.

"Too much?" Uncle David asked.

Joseph shook his head, already digging into the mound for another mouthful. "Different," he said. "But a good different, I think."

For the first time that day, Joseph felt the tightness beneath his breastbone loosen. Maybe America would never be his home the way Pakistan had. Maybe he would be a weird kid from another country. But at least he, like Peyton, wasn't alone.

TWELVE

Why did it have to be so hard? Grace stared at the pale band on her finger, clutching the studio key in the predawn hours. Her stiff and uncooperative fingers refused to comply. She forced them to work, like she'd done every morning this week.

This is nothing compared to what's coming, she thought, steeling herself against the wave of uncertainty that threatened to overwhelm her. She had to find the strength to face whatever came next.

Inside, darkness cloaked the familiar scent of rosin. The hardwood floor creaked beneath her feet—5:02 AM, too early for even the most dedicated students. But she needed this time, needed the silence to think, to plan, to figure a way forward.

She flicked the light switch, illuminating her wall calendar in her precise handwriting—"Final Venue Payment—The Dance Loft." Her shoulders tensed. The same cursive filled several squares—dress fittings, cake tastings, meetings with the wedding coordinator—woven in with student evaluations and competition deadlines for the next three months. Red X's marred the wedding entries now, angry slashes across her carefully ordered life.

The midnight blue binder on her desk held four years of careful planning—her studio's growth projections, the expansion blueprint she'd developed during late evenings between classes. Everything she'd built herself, piece by piece, long before Andrew Fayard entered her life with his promises of forever and his family's expectations.

Dr. Lawson's information packet lurked beneath the planner—"Living with Lupus" in bold medical font. Grace slid it away, under competition entry forms. Three nights of obsessive research had only confirmed what Dr. Lawson had told her—chronic condition, systemic inflammation, potential disability. Words that had no place in a ballet studio. She'd memorized the treatment options, calculated the costs down to the penny, but refused to let those clinical terms define her future. She'd handle this diagnosis like every other obstacle in her life. With discipline. With control.

Her finger joints flared with sharp and persistent pain, but she forced her hand flat against the wedding vendor contracts. Contracts that would be paid in full by the Fayards—a minor expense to spare the embarrassment of a flawed wife and daughter-in-law. Her laptop screen glowed in the dim studio—$47,326. The expansion fund she'd built over six years of teaching. Years of budgeting, of skipping vacations, of late nights stretching every dollar while watching her girls stretch at the barre. Every recital ticket, every private lesson fee, every sacrifice had been for them. All of it—now a choice between her students' future or her own health, between their dreams and her survival.

"I'll take care of all the cancellation fees," Andrew had promised at lunch yesterday. But his tone had been cold, dismissive—like she was a business liability to manage. Not the tone he'd used when she'd mentioned the lupus diagnosis at his family dinner. Family pressure?

The treatment plan would devour her savings. Even with insurance, the medications Dr. Lawson prescribed would cost eight hundred monthly—the same as Emma's competition coaching. The new biological infusions could run thousands per dose—equivalent to a month of utilities for the expanded studio. Every dollar diverted to managing her illness was a dollar taken from her students' potential, from the empty storefront next door where her advanced classes could finally have enough space, from the spring floor that would protect her dancers' joints in ways she wished someone had protected hers.

It was as if broken glass ground through her knuckles as she pulled up the student roster—an unforgivable lack of control for a dancer. She steadied her fingers through the sheer will of a dancer.

Emma had a shot at the Youth America Grand Prix regionals in six weeks. Katie Marshall needed intensive coaching before her Joffrey audition. The spring recital loomed three months away, with thirty-two beginning students counting on her.

She reached for the floor plan. "Grace Ballet Academy Expansion" blazed across the cover in bold print. The architectural renderings showed her dream—two separate studios with professional spring floors, a dedicated conditioning room, proper changing areas. Everything her girls deserved.

Grace pushed to her feet, forcing herself to the wall of photos. Her fingers traced the gilt frame of Emma Chen at last year's competition—arms perfectly extended, chin lifted just as she had demonstrated countless times during private lessons. "Higher elbow, Emma. Imagine your arm growing from the center of your back," she'd instructed, physically adjusting the girl's position until it matched the classical ideal. Now that correction was immortalized in the photograph, Emma's form flawless enough for any conservatory brochure.

Next to it hung the moment Katie Marshall burst into tears clutching the Joffrey letter while Grace had maintained her composure, though her heart had soared more than any grand jeté. "Your hard work did this," she'd told Katie, "not talent. Talent is nothing without discipline."

Her gaze lingered on the junior company's trophy from Southeastern Regionals—five girls who'd arrived with sloppy technique and departed with gold medals. Countless hours of practice, individually tailored combinations, blisters on her own feet from demonstrating the same sequences repeatedly until her students could mirror them perfectly. Her legacy. Her life's work.

The studio's front window cast shadows across the photos, her reflection ghosted in the glass—straight spine, lifted chin, flawless posture. Always flawless posture. She moved into first position. Her body knew this, had known it since she was five years old. A simple demonstration for tomorrow's advanced class. Just a basic grand jeté, the kind she'd performed thousands of times.

Her muscles tensed for the preparatory plié. For a fleeting second, muscle memory tricked her—she was sixteen again, nailing the move across a competition stage, the rush of flight, the applause. Then the first shock of pain shot through her knees, insistent—the discomfort she'd taught dancers to push through during performances. Her arabesque wavered by two precise degrees, but she clenched her jaw and corrected her alignment. She had to prove she could still do this. Prove Andrew wrong. Prove

Dr. Lawson wrong. Prove that her body wasn't betraying the discipline she'd instilled in it since she was five years old.

The jump never happened. Her legs buckled, sending her crashing against the photo wall. Frames clattered to the floor around her as she slid down. The sound of shattering glass punctuated her fall.

Tears burned her eyes—an unprofessional display she never permitted during rehearsals—as she traced every detail of the scattered photos, at the shattered dreams they represented. She couldn't even manage a simple routine, a basic movement she'd executed flawlessly since childhood.

Her body had broken formation, had failed to execute the most fundamental combination. How could she teach what she could no longer demonstrate? How could she correct arabesques she couldn't hold, jetés she couldn't perform? How could she maintain the standard of excellence her students deserved when her own technique was crumbling?

But as she looked at Emma's captured arabesque among the shattered glass, a new determination took root. If she couldn't display, she'd find another way to teach. If she couldn't jump, she'd make her students soar higher than she ever had. She'd adapt. She'd overcome. She had to.

Her joints protested as she gathered the fallen frames, but she forced herself to move. She had five hours until her first class. Five hours until she would give instruction from a chair if she had to. She had a life to live and a studio to run. And she'd find a way to do it, even if it killed her.

THIRTEEN

"Nathan, let me take Lily," his mother whispered, her hand gently brushing his in the front row of the church sanctuary.

"No." Nathan jerked away, his voice hardly more than a breath, meant only for his mother. He hitched Lily higher on his hip, the diaper bag swinging hard against his leg. "I've got it."

She glanced down at the floor, then met his eyes again, her expression soft but uncertain. "Sweetheart...you don't have to carry everything by yourself."

Lily's tiny fingers grabbed at his collar, her dark eyes—Hannah's eyes—staring up at him. His arms tightened around her as Pastor Mike stepped behind the pulpit. "We gather today to celebrate the life of Hannah Marie Carter..."

Celebrate? Celebrate watching his twenty-six-year-old wife slip away before his eyes. Celebrate having to explain to Lily someday why her mother wasn't in any of her family photos .

"Her faith was unwavering," Pastor Mike continued, "even in her final moments."

Easy for Pastor Mike to say. He hadn't been there, holding her hand while the monitors flatlined. Hadn't heard her last words, that impossible third promise about finding someone new. Something beneath Nathan's breastbone twisted. *Faith.* He used to understand that word. Used to believe in it. He could still hear his own voice—six years ago, standing at that very altar, Hannah's hands in his. And now, in that hospital room, he'd begged. Bargained. Promised her anything if she would just stay. But she didn't stay. Instead she'd begged him to promise three things with her last breaths.

Lily arched her back, face reddening. The bottle nipple missing her mouth, formula dribbling down her chin. "That poor man" filtered from somewhere behind him. "The nursery workers would be happy to take Lily," his mother said not for the first time.

"Through Hannah's suffering, God's plan..."

Plan? Nathan's free hand curled into a fist. *Some plan.* Leave a six-month-old without her mother. Leave him trying to warm bottles one-handed while his daughter screamed. Leave him alone with Hannah's last words echoing in his head and her Bible burning a hole in the diaper bag and—

"Though we don't understand His ways..."

Lily's cry hit a new pitch. The bottle dropped again. This time, when his mother reached for the baby, Nathan couldn't stop her. His arms felt leaden, useless. Just like that night. When all his love, all his prayers, all his desperation hadn't been enough to keep Hannah from dying.

His mother swayed with Lily at the end of the pew, his daughter's cries softening to hiccups. The familiar motion— Hannah's motion. The same motion she'd perfected over six months of midnight and early-morning feedings.

"In her final days, Hannah showed us all what it means to trust in the Lord's wisdom..."

The hymnal creaked in Nathan's grip. *Trust?* Hannah had trusted. Prayed. Nathan had followed every doctor's order. Checked her glucose levels four times a night. Done everything right. And still—she died.

"Even knowing she would leave behind her loving husband and daughter..."

The hymnal's spine bent. Rachel's hand touched his arm, but he shrugged it off. His mother had moved to the back of the church with Lily, her sobs echoing through the quiet sanctuary.

"Hannah's last words were of faith..."

No. Her last words were about Nathan finding someone new. About not blaming God. About taking their daughter to church. Promises he couldn't keep. Shouldn't have to. The room tilted sideways. Hannah's portrait—that smile—those eyes, faded to forever gone.

"Let us join in singing Hannah's favorite hymn, 'Trusting God.'"

The organ swelled. The congregation rose. The hymnal fragments slipped from his fingers as his mother approached, Lily reaching toward Hannah's casket with a soft babbling sequence that sounded like mama. The sound shattered his soul. He stumbled to his feet, shouldering past Rachel, past his mother's startled gasp. Past sympathetic faces.

He needed his child. Needed to run. Needed to get out of this church.

He clutched his daughter's warm body, drawing her close as he fled down the center aisle. Away from Hannah's smile in the portrait, from the lies about God's plan, from everything except his daughter and the impossible promises crushing his heart.

The church doors slammed shut behind him. The hymn cut off by the roar of distant traffic. The sanctuary's cool darkness surrendered to the blinding September sun, turning the world white-hot and wavering. Nathan's shoes hit the concrete steps with a clap that echoed off the brick walls. His lungs seized as the humidity hit him like a vengeful sauna claiming its newest victim. Lily squirmed, her skin sticky against his neck, but he couldn't let her go.

Sweat instantly soaked through his black suit, his damp shirt clinging to his spine. The world was too bright, too loud, too real after the artificial quiet of the sanctuary. Behind him, "Trusting God" filtered out—the words about God never failing. Well, there was no trust here. Not anymore. Because God said no to his heartfelt prayer.

Just the concrete steps of the church, outside where he and Hannah were married six years ago. Where he'd carried Lily down these same steps after her dedication. Where he'd promised God he'd raise his daughter in faith, back when he'd believed promises meant something.

Lily's tiny hand patted his cheek, wet with what he refused to call tears. He had to keep going. Had to strap her into her car seat. Had to drive home to an empty house, half-empty insulin bottles, and half-finished plans.

The diaper bag was stolen;; inside.

Hannah's Bible tucked in the side pocket, the one she'd read every morning during her dialysis sessions with her her favorite verses underlined—"Love bears all things, believes all things, hopes all things, endures all things."

Nathan pushed the ignition, Lily secure in her seat. He wouldn't go back in. Not today, next Sunday., or ever again.

Let them talk about God's plan. Let them whisper about faith and grace and promises.

He had his own promise to keep. The only one that mattered now.

He'd protect Lily all alone. From everyone and everything.

FOURTEEN

Grace deleted the seventeenth take of her tendu demonstration caught in the confines of her dance studio. The camera's memory card showed enough space for fifty more attempts. The pain in her hip suggested maybe three. She checked her watch—forty-five minutes until Emma's lesson.

The new tripod squeaked as Grace adjusted its height to just below her knee, the optimal angle to capture footwork. Here she could show her students flawless technique, even if she could only provide it through recordings now.

"Take eighteen," she breathed, pressed record, and stepped into first position. The working leg extended, toe pointed. A familiar burn crawled down her side—not the healthy sensation of muscles in action, but the hot, jagged sensation of inflammation. Like someone had replaced her joint fluid with ground glass.

Her supporting leg trembled. Invisible to most, perhaps, but to a dancer, it might as well be an earthquake. She locked her quadriceps, gritted her teeth behind lips trained to smile through distress. Three more seconds. The trembling intensified. Sweat beaded at her hairline. Not from exertion—a simple tendu shouldn't make her perspire—but from the effort of fighting her own body.

Two.

Her silhouette dancing across the mirror showed excellent form from the knee down. Beautiful lines. But she caught the slight angle of her hip, compensating for the discomfort. Wrong. All wrong.

One.

Grace released the position and tapped the camera's playback button. The tiny screen revealed what she feared—every micro-tremor magnified, every hint of strain visible in high definition—the subtle rotation in her hip, the almost imperceptible shift of weight that screamed amateur, not teacher.

She jabbed the delete button with more force than necessary. The camera beeped in protest.

"Again," she whispered, though no one was there to hear. She hesitated to push record. Eighteen failures already documented and erased. How many more before her body surrendered completely? The red light blinked on. Take nineteen.

Again, the playback revealed every hint of strain. Delete. Start over.

Her phone buzzed. Ms. Chen texting—"Running 10 minutes early today. Emma can't wait."

Grace's spine straightened to performance tension. The basic positions weren't enough. She needed to record the fundamental barre work—pliés, relevés, rond de jambe.

Take twenty. Her toe traced the arc along the floor, muscle memory fighting against joints that grew stiffer by the minute. The burning spread from hip to knee. But she kept her face serene, the way she'd taught Emma. A dancer never shows pain.

The tendu was flawless. Technical perfection captured in digital permanence. One movement preserved before her body could steal it away.

Her phone shuddered with another message. Ms. Chen —"Parking now."

Grace retrieved her prescription bottle from beneath the expansion fund receipt—six thousand dollars meant for new barres and mirrors now invested in camera equipment and medications. She swallowed the pills dry. Time to face a different method of teaching without moving. At least she had one flawless recording. For now.

Smoothing her leotard, Grace guided Emma and Ms. Chen into the studio. Emma froze mid-pirouette when she spotted the tripod. "What's all this?" Emma's nose wrinkled at the setup.

"I'm creating a digital library of proper technique." Grace kept her voice steady, professional. "This way you can practice at home with precise examples of each movement."

"But you always show me. Correct me." Emma clutched her pink dance bag closer. "That's what makes me better."

Ms. Chen touched her daughter's shoulder. "Like your math videos, Emma. Remember how helpful those were?"

"Exactly," Grace said, her shoulders loosening a fraction. "And I'll still be right here, watching your form, making corrections—"

"Making sure you point those toes." Ms. Chen winked at Emma. "No slacking just because it's on video."

Emma's gaze drifted from the camera to the shaking in Grace's hands. Her brow furrowed, lips parting as if she was about to ask something—but she didn't. Instead, she clutched her tote bag tighter around the straps.

Grace forced her voice to steady. "Let's get started, shall we?" She pressed play on the tendu demonstration. Her recorded self executed the movement perfectly—toe extending, leg lifting, each angle precise. No hint of quivering or hesitation. "Watch how the working foot brushes through first position," she said, nodding at the screen.

Emma's form showed more confusion than concentration. The young dancer's typical eagerness had dulled to cautious observation.

This has to work. Grace's expansion fund might be gone, but she refused to let her teaching standards drop. Even if every correction now required rewinding and replaying.

"Okay, Emma. Your turn. Remember to keep your supporting leg straight."

Emma attempted the tendu, her movement hesitant.

"That's...close." Grace fought the instinct to demonstrate. "Let's watch it again. Pay attention to how the heel leads the point."

A simple touch to the ankle would fix this. Her student struggled with concepts that had always come naturally through mirroring.

From the corner of her eye, Grace caught a stir. Ms. Chen shifted in her chair, uncrossing and recrossing her ankles. The leather-bound notebook lay open on her lap—the same one she'd brought to every lesson since Emma started at age six. Page after page of meticulous notes in her architectural handwriting—"Emma's turnout improved," "Work on fifth position," "Arabesque showing excellent progress."

Ms. Chen's Mont Blanc hovered over the pristine page.

The tip didn't move. No scratch of ink against paper. No nodding as she recorded Grace's instructions for home practice. Six years of lessons. Six years of copious notes documenting every correction, every bit of improvement, every exercise before next week. Ms. Chen had once joked that she could publish "The Complete Guide to Emma's Ballet Education" from those notebooks. Now, nothing.

Grace's stomach tightened. That empty page spoke volumes—louder than any complaint, more damning than any criticism. Ms. Chen, who documented her daughter's achievements with photographs and journal entries, had nothing worth recording today. The pen finally moved, but only to tap silently against the notebook's edge. A rhythm of impatience or concern? In six years, Grace had never seen Ms. Chen's notebook remain blank.

Forcing her attention back to Emma, Grace rewound the video demonstration again. "Watch the alignment of the supporting leg here," she said, voice steady despite the hollow feeling spreading through her.

Ms. Chen closed the journal with a soft snap. First time ever.

"One more time." Grace ignored the stiffness penetrating her lower back. "Notice how—"

"I see it," Emma said with an edge Grace had never heard before. "But it's different when you show me. I can feel what you mean then."

Heat crept up Grace's neck. "The recording shows every detail perfectly." She gestured to the screen where her recorded self demonstrated again. "Try to match the exact angle of—"

"But Miss Grace, when you demonstrate, I know exactly what to do."

"Emma." Ms. Chen's quiet interruption carried maternal authority. "Let's do it your teacher's way."

Your teacher's way. The phrase twisted in Grace's stomach. This wasn't her way. Her way was hands-on corrections, immediate demonstrations, dancing alongside her students until each movement flowed naturally.

Emma returned to first position, determination replacing frustration. Her tendu extended, closer this time to the recorded version.

"Better." Grace allowed genuine pleasure to warm her voice. "Now for the rond de jambe combination."

As she cued up the next video, Grace caught her form cast across the mirror. Flawless posture, serene expression, completely still. Too still. A ballet teacher should flow like water, not stand rigid as a statue. But Emma was progressing, however slowly. Perhaps this could work. Grace's joints screamed otherwise.

"Again." Grace rewound the recording for the seventh time in twenty minutes. The studio clock's minute hand crawled forward with excruciating slowness. Her hip throbbed in time with her heartbeat. Emma's posture showed slumping shoulders before she forced them back. The girl's ponytail had begun to droop, wisps of hair sticking to her flushed cheeks.

"Remember to keep your supporting leg straight through the entire rond de jambe." Grace's finger drifted over to the pause button, fighting the urge to simply stand beside Emma and physically help her with the proper arc.

Emma nodded, determination tightening her jaw. She positioned herself and extended her working leg.

"Better," Grace said, though the movement still lacked Emma's usual flow. Like watching a butterfly with a damaged wing—all the right motions but none of the grace. "But your arms need to be more expressive."

She reached for the remote to rewind again, but her fingers seized. The device clattered to the floor.

"I've got it," Emma said, scooping it up before Grace could bend down.

"Thank you." Grace accepted the device, careful to grip it with her whole hand this time. "Let's try the combination from the beginning."

Emma's eyes flickered to the clock. They'd spent forty minutes on what typically took fifteen. The girl's breathing slowed with concealed frustration as she moved into first position.

This time, Emma's rond de jambe extended in a graceful arc. Her arms floated into second position with textbook precision. Every angle of her body matched the recorded demonstration. And yet. The movement was hollow. Technical perfection without a soul—like sheet music played without dynamics. Emma was dancing with her muscles, not her heart. But it was correct. It would have to be enough.

"Well done, Emma." Grace stopped the playback, maintaining a grin despite the deep ache across every flex point. "That's a wrap for today."

"You did beautifully," Ms. Chen added.

Emma packed her dance gear with uncharacteristic silence. No excited chatter about next week's choreography. No impromptu pirouettes by the door.

The studio door clicked shut behind Emma and Ms. Chen. Grace held her spine straight as a plumb line until their shadows disappeared from the frosted glass.

One. Two. Three. Count it out, like a final hold.

Her performer's mask cracked. Her shoulders slumped,

then she folded forward, as if someone had snipped the invisible strings holding her upright. The pain she'd been holding back surged in, sudden and overwhelming—like floodwaters breaching a levee. She took one step toward her office chair. Her hip locked mid-stride. "No, not now." The words escaped through gritted teeth as she leaned on the barre. The same barre where she'd demonstrated arabesques for years was reduced to a crutch.

She dragged her right leg forward, the joint grinding with each movement. Three more steps. Her body trembled, not with the familiar muscle fatigue after a challenging adagio, but with the aftermath of pretense—of forcing stillness when every instinct screamed for relief. She fell into the chair as her legs gave way. The vinyl cushion exhaled a soft hiss beneath her weight. Grace's hands shook violently now that no one was watching, the tremors she'd hidden from Emma breaking free like wild birds from a cage.

Sweat dampened between her shoulder blades. From standing still. From doing nothing but maintaining the illusion of the capable teacher, the flawless dancer.

Her reflection stared back from the wall of mirrors—her hair still in its neat ballet bun. Only her eyes betrayed her, bright with unshed tears and something worse—fear. She'd survived the lesson, but barely. And tomorrow there would be eight more students. Eight more performances of strength she no longer possessed. She poised her fingers over the keyboard. The advanced girls needed to perfect their grand jetés for next month's showcase. Even with precise video demonstrations, they'd need to...ah—

A spasm shot through Grace's hip, sharp enough to steal her breath. She gritted her teeth, forcing her spine to stay upright. The ache wasn't just in her hip anymore—it radiated down her thigh, into her knee, a slow, obstinate fire. Some things couldn't be taught through a screen.

She had to find a better way—before she lost everything she'd built.

Grace scrolled through her phone's contacts with trembling fingers, the studio lights reflecting off the screen as they dimmed on their automatic timer. The empty dance floor stretched before her like a silent accusation, its polished surface holding the ghosts of a thousand arabesques she might never demonstrate again. Outside, twilight gathered at the windows, highlighting the walls where photographs of her star students hung in formation. Her thumb hovered over her rheumatologist's name—the last thread of hope in a world unraveling one painful movement at a time.

GRACE SMOOTHED the manila folder across Dr. Winters' desk with the same precision she used when setting up to teach a class. Every motion deliberate. Control. Technique. Focus.

Across from her, Dr. Winters adjusted her wire-rimmed glasses, the silver strands in her hair catching the light like fine threads of mercury. Her eyes—gentle, but sharp—scanned the contents. Grace tracked every nod.

A leather-bound Bible rested on the desk's edge beside a stack of medical journals, its cracked spine and softened corners hinting at years of study. "CAR T-cell therapy is showing promise in advanced cases," she said, tapping a finger against the printouts. "It reprograms your immune system—to stop it from mistaking your healthy tissue as the enemy."

Grace stole a look at the highlighted statistics and circled remission rates. She'd compared the proposed treatment timeline around her teaching schedule. "How soon could we start?"

Dr. Winters leaned back, removing her glasses. "Before we discuss timing, we need to address some realities about this treatment."

Shifting in her chair, Grace sat ballet-straight. She'd anticipated this part. "I understand there are risks. The cytokine release syndrome, potential organ—"

"The financial realities, Grace." Dr. Winters folded her hands on the desk. "While your insurance will cover a portion, CAR T-cell therapy costs between three hundred seventy-five and four hundred seventy-five thousand dollars. Most patients face significant out-of-pocket expenses."

The number hit Grace like a missed landing. Her expansion fund totaled only $40,176 after her video equipment purchases. She'd memorized the balance just yesterday, checking it twice before bed.

Dr. Winters' expression softened. "There are payment plans available, though they rarely cover the full amount. And given the progression rate we're seeing…"

Grace studied the red numbers, each one dropping like her dancing ability—day by relentless day. "How long will it take before I experience the benefits?"

"To achieve an optimal outcome?" Dr. Winters leaned forward, her voice softening. "We should begin within the next eight weeks. I've seen remarkable recoveries when we start treatment early—some almost miraculous." She traced an invisible pattern on her notepad. "The simple answer is the sooner we start, the better."

"What about a modified treatment plan?" Grace pulled

out her studio calendar, already marked with competition dates and recital preparations. "Something that would let me keep teaching, even part-time?"

"As you well know, the traditional treatments aren't managing your inflammation levels." Dr. Winters tapped Grace's latest lab results. "And you're right, without aggressive intervention, you're facing increasing joint damage, fatigue, and potential organ involvement."

"I understand." Grace studied her teaching calendar closely, as if its careful columns of times and dates could shield her from the doctor's words. "What if we adjusted the dosing schedule?"

"Grace." Dr. Winters' voice gentled. "Before we discuss schedules, may I ask what support systems you have in place? Family? Church community?"

"I have my studio. My students." Grace straightened her papers, precise angles matching the desk edge. "I'm not particularly religious, if that's what you're asking."

"I see." Dr. Winters studied her for a moment. "Two years ago, I had a patient with nearly identical markers to yours. The inflammation levels, the progression rate—everything matched. Modern medicine had exhausted its options, but she experienced a complete recovery. She attributed it to her faith, her church community's prayers, and, to be frank, divine intervention."

"Are there any clinical trials accepting new participants?" Grace kept her voice gentle, acknowledging Dr. Winters' good intentions while steering them back to a concrete plan.

Dr. Winters returned to Grace's file. "There's a promising study at the University of South Carolina, but the waiting list..." She shook her head. "Given your progression rate, I wouldn't recommend delay." She pulled out a pad from her desk drawer. "I have some pull with that research committee. I can get you in immediately. But whether it's CAR T-cell therapy or a clinical trial, you'll need to suspend teaching. At least temporarily."

Temporarily somehow sounded more permanent than was probably intended. Her fingers clutched her studio calendar, where next month's competition dates filled every weekend in red ink.

"I know this is overwhelming." Dr. Winters slid a business card across the desk—her personal number handwritten on the back. "Take a couple of days to consider your options. But remember what we discussed about your test results. Without intervention..." She tapped the numbers in red. "Your body won't sustain your current teaching schedule much longer."

Grace slipped the card into her folder, aligning it perfectly with her research papers. Her expansion fund wouldn't cover even a quarter of the treatment costs. And closing the studio, even temporarily...

As if Dr. Winters could read her mind, she laced her fingers and leaned forward. "And don't discount a faith support system. I find myself depending more and more on spiritual intervention the longer I practice medicine."

"Thank you for your time, Dr. Winters." Grace stood, gathering her materials. "I'll review the clinical trial information."

"One more thing." Dr. Winters reached for a different business card, this one cream-colored with gold lettering. "The patient I mentioned—she's part of a prayer ministry at Victory Chapel. They meet on Thursday evenings."

Grace accepted the card out of politeness, tucking it behind Dr. Winters' contact information. "I'll keep it in mind."

Standing in Dr. Winters' doorway, Grace's hip twinged —a sharp reminder of everything slipping away.

Eight weeks. She had eight weeks to find almost half a million dollars or watch her body betray her completely. The expansion fund suddenly felt like spare change, and her dreams of a second studio as fragile as a dancer's final bow.

The elevator doors opened to the parking garage. Grace's sensible black flats clicked against the concrete, echoing like a metronome counting down time she didn't have. Behind Dr. Winters' business card, the gold lettering of Victory Chapel caught the fluorescent light. Grace exhaled sharply, turning it over in her fingers. The doctor's voice echoed in her mind—*"some almost miraculous."*

No. She set her jaw, slipping the card beside the medical referral, as if burying it under something tangible, something real. The glove compartment snapped shut, sealing it away next to her studio keys—the keys she'd have to surrender if she chose her body over her dreams.

FIFTEEN

Four Months After Hannah's Death

The stringent scent of marker ink flooded Nathan's nostrils as he smoothed the thin tape across the whiteboard, checking the line's angle with a critical eye. Not quite right. He peeled it back and tried again, satisfaction settling in when the line ran perfectly parallel to the whiteboard's edge.

From her playpen, Lily rattled a plastic ring, her ten-month-old giggles filling his home office. Toys scattered the confined space—evidence of his daughter's busy morning— while his desk maintained its typical order.

"What do you think, sweetheart?" He stepped back, surveying the grid he'd created. "Looking good, right?"

Lily squealed and bounced, tiny hands clapping together.

"I'll take that as approval." He lifted the corner of his mouth—his first smile since Hannah's funeral. This would work. It had to work. The schedule would help him be a single parent and a successful engineer.

Nathan uncapped a black marker and wrote "Daily

Schedule" at the top of the whiteboard reminding him of Hannah labeling Lily's bottles. He pushed the memory away, focusing instead on time blocks. 6 AM—Wake up, bottle feeding. 6:30 AM—Daddy's shower while Lily plays in her bouncer...

Lily swayed in her pink onesie as she watched him, dark eyes tracking his every movement. He swallowed hard and kept writing.

7:15 AM—Drop-off at Little Sprouts Daycare. 7:45 AM—Arrive at Meridian Engineering. The schedule filled out under his precise block writing, each time slot another piece of control over the chaos his life had become.

"See, Lily? Everything's going to run like clockwork." He turned to find her dozing off, one hand clutching her favorite giraffe—the stuffed animal Hannah had picked out during her final hospital stay.

Nathan gripped the marker tighter and forced his attention back to the whiteboard. Tomorrow would be his first day back at work since...since everything. He had to get back on track—for Lily's sake.

Grabbing a red marker, Nathan entered an emergency list for him to have in stock at all times—one large pack of diapers, wipes, diaper rash cream, and baby powder. Extra clothes, blankets, and pacifiers for comfort. He wrote the pediatrician's emergency number—bringing him back to Hannah's last night at home. Lily's soft snores filled the quiet office. He checked the office clock—2:30 PM. Right on schedule for her afternoon nap. The first successful data point for his new system.

A text lit up his phone—Mom. "Do you need me to watch Lily tomorrow?"

Nathan's jaw tightened. He could handle this. He had to. He'd drafted proposals for million-dollar projects and

managed entire construction teams. One baby. One schedule. That shouldn't be beyond his capabilities. His thumbs
circled the keyboard. A simple "Yes" would be easier. But
easier wasn't the same as right. If he couldn't manage this on
his own, what did that say about him? About the promises
he made to Hannah?

"Got it covered. Thanks." He hit send before he could
second-guess himself.

The whiteboard gleamed with possibility, each time slot
a promise of order restored in a life that had spiraled out of
control. Nathan programmed alarms into his watch—
feeding times, medicine checks, daycare drop-off. If he
perfected this schedule, perhaps he could prove to himself
and to others that he could master being a single dad.

Lily stirred in her playpen, dark curls stuck to her forehead. Hannah's curls. Nathan blinked hard and focused on
setting one more alarm, channeling the grief into precision.

The whiteboard filled quickly—blue for the regular
schedule, red for emergencies, green for work commitments,
yellow for tasks not a priority. Stepping back, Nathan
surveyed his creation. This was what he could control when
everything else had been ripped away. The colors created
clear boundaries between his responsibilities. No overlap,
no confusion, just organization.

"This is how we survive, Lily," he whispered, his engineer's mind seeking refuge in systems and schedules.
Hannah had been the spontaneous one. He needed this
structure now more than ever.

His phone chirped—3:30 PM. Time to feed Lily. Right
on cue, she stirred, fussing softly.

He scooped her up, breathing in the soft scent of baby
powder. "See? The system works." For a split second, he
almost called out to Hannah to warm the formula—before

the silence reminded him. He could handle this part. The warmer was already set. Four minutes exactly for the right temperature. He'd make this work. He'd make Hannah proud. Tomorrow he would prove it.

Lily nestled into his arms, her tiny hand curling around his neck—the same way she used to cling to Hannah. Nathan swallowed hard and stared at his whiteboard masterpiece. Straight lines. Vivid colors. Structure. Control. No space for grief when every minute had a purpose. The warmer beeped. Time to begin.

Lily latched on eagerly, her dark eyes locked on his. Nathan settled into Hannah's old rocking chair and checked his watch. Ten minutes for feeding, then burping, then playtime.

His phone buzzed. Rachel—"Need anything for tomorrow?"

Nathan exhaled sharply and rubbed his temple. *Not you too.*

Across the room, Lily stirred, her tiny face scrunching. Not now. Not when everything was finally falling into place.

He tapped the message, started to type—then deleted it. The constant offers of help weren't kindness. They were thinly disguised accusations of everyone waiting for him to fail. Like they didn't believe he could do this on his own.

He shoved the phone into his pocket and turned back to Lily. He didn't need help with his daughter.

Lily finished her bottle right on schedule. Lifting her to his shoulder, Nathan patted her back with a rhythm he'd perfected over the past two weeks. Tomorrow he'd prove he could balance everything.

"Just you and me, Lily-bear." He kissed Lily's forehead as she let out a tiny burp. "We've got this figured out."

But as he laid her back in the playpen, his smartphone stirred in his trousers with a new notification. Nathan hesitated, staring at the whiteboard filled with meticulous plans. Expectations from all sides, heavy and unrelenting. Failure wasn't an option—not now. With a deep breath, he reached for his phone, ready to silence any doubts. Tomorrow, he had a schedule to follow—a life to manage.

"Let's do this," he murmured to himself, his resolve hardening as he prepared to face whatever lay ahead.

AS NATHAN FINISHED DRESSING Lily in the early hours of his new routine, the pungent smell hit first, followed by yellow-brown sludge that oozed up her back and soaked through the carefully selected daycare outfit.

"No, no, no..." The wipes container rattled empty. The backup package sat on the changing table, three steps too far away. His gaze darted to his phone. 6:59 AM. Each passing second shredded his buffer time.

At 7:19, brake lights flared across two lanes of traffic. Nathan's fingers cramped around the steering wheel. A silver minivan swerved into his lane, stealing another two car lengths. His morning was not off to a good start.

Lily babbled in her car seat, her nonsense sounds filling Nathan's ears. He adjusted the overhead mirror to catch a glimpse of her. Hannah would have handled this delay differently. She'd make up silly songs during traffic jams, turning mundane moments into memories. The thought stung his eyes as he inched forward in the gridlock.

At 7:33, Miss Patricia's floral perfume hit him like an accusation as he rushed through Little Sprouts' entrance balancing Lily on his hip. The daycare director's smile tightened at the corners. "There's our Lily-girl." She glanced pointedly at the Mickey Mouse clock on the wall. "You almost missed the morning snack."

Eighteen minutes late. His stomach knotted as he lowered his little girl into Miss Patricia's waiting arms. The other children were already seated at tiny tables, plastic cups and cheerful plates arranged in front of them.

"Sorry," he mumbled. "Traffic was horrible."

"Just sign her in, Mr. Carter." Miss Patricia's voice held the patience of someone who'd heard every excuse.

Nathan fumbled with the pen ripping through the paper as he scrawled his signature, leaving a rumpled tear across the pristine sign-in sheet. Another failure to add to the morning's tally.

"Da-da." Lily reached for him from Miss Patricia's arms as she carried her to the snack tables.

"I'll be back at five, sweetheart," he called to her through a tight throat. "Be good for Miss Patricia."

The Anderson Street shortcut might save four minutes if he hit the lights right. Maybe he could salvage something from this disaster of a morning.

At 8:13 AM, the familiar creak of his office chair should have been comforting. Nathan slumped into it, his breath still coming too fast. His monitor hummed to life, Outlook calendar immediately assaulting him with a missed meeting notifications and urgent emails.

Twenty-eight minutes behind schedule.

Studying the workload, he was unsure where to begin triaging the damage. His iPhone vibrated against the desk surface. Little Sprouts' calling.

What now?

"Mr. Carter?" Miss Patricia's voice carried a distinctive

tone—one that managed to be both sympathetic and judgmental at once. "The diaper bag?"

The realization hit like him like Conner MacGregor inside the octagon. Nathan closed his eyes. The perfectly pack pinked bag lay next to Lily's car seat.

"I'll bring it right over," he said, barely holding back a sigh.

His morning lost. His schedule in ruins. Day one was already in complete shambles.

SIXTEEN

Three Years After Hannah's Death

"Bedtime soon," Nathan called out from his home office as he studied the proposal he'd been working on since after dinner. He glanced at his watch—7:46 PM. Fourteen minutes until getting Lily to bed. This nightly routine took him and his daughter three years to perfect.

From down the hall, the cheerful voice of *Curious George* and Lily's giggles drifted into his office. At four-years-old, she still laughed at the same monkey antics that had first caught her attention when she could barely sit up on her own.

The numbers on his screen blurred as he fought against his exhaustion. He'd started his workday at 5:00 AM, pausing to drop Lily at daycare before going to his office, picking her up, throwing together dinner, and bathing her. Lunch had been an afterthought, lost somewhere between meetings and phone calls at Meridian Engineering. He couldn't afford another late night—not if he wanted to wake up on time and drop off Lily at preschool by 7:30.

He needed a promotion to Project Manager. Better pay.

More control over his schedule. The same control he'd been seeking since stepping down to part-time when Hannah died, leaving him alone with a six-month-old. A chance to prove his self demotion hadn't derailed his career permanently. Rumor had it the position might open up by year's end, and Nathan intended to be ready.

Lily's giggles had stopped, though *Curious George* played on. Her sudden silence reminded him of those first terrible months, checking her crib every time she grew quiet. "Lily?" he called out, scrutinizing his figures. "Everything okay, sweetie?"

A rustling sound answered from somewhere in the house.

"Just a minute." He forced his attention back to the proposal. One more section to review. He'd factored in every contingency, outlined clear solutions. This had to be right.

His cell phone buzzed. A text from Rachel—"How are you two holding up tonight?"

"All good. Lily's watching *Curious George*. I'm working." He typed quickly, trying to head off one of her check-in calls. For three years since Hannah's death, his mother and sister seemed to think he'd fall apart without their constant monitoring.

Another noise. Closer. Like cardboard scraping against cardboard.

"Lily?" He pushed back from his desk, straining to identify the sound's location. "What are you getting into?"

The monkey's voice from her television chirped on about helping his friend, but Lily's usual commentary didn't follow.

Nathan checked his watch again. "Eight minutes before bed. Go brush your teeth."

Lily didn't answer. No "five more minutes" or "after this part." Nothing. Just the TV and that scraping sound again. He craned his neck toward the doorway. The noise seemed to be coming from... his bedroom?

"Lily?" He stood and strolled to the hallway. Her empty room on the right, television still playing. "Come on, sweetie. Bedtime."

More rustling. Definitely his room.

He rounded the corner, curious as to what he would find. Hannah's old closet door was open, light spilling onto the carpet. A box lay overturned on the floor, its contents scattered.

And there, in the middle sat Lily, cross-legged among scattered boxes, holding a leather-bound Bible he hadn't seen in three years. Hannah's Bible. The one she'd read every morning since she was a teenager, the one she'd intended to share with Lily when she was old enough to understand. The one Nathan had hidden away along with her breast pump, the unfinished baby book, and all other reminders of the future they'd planned together.

On the carpet lay a pair of faded pink satin ballet slippers, the ribbons frayed at the edges from years of use, preserved by her mother and passed down when Hannah and Nathan had married. Another piece of her he'd tucked away, unable to face.

His breath hitched at the sight of the Bible in Lily's hands and the slippers beside her. Three years of carefully avoiding this moment, of deflecting questions about the woman in the photos at his mother's house, of changing the subject when Lily pointed at his wedding ring.

He remained frozen at the opening, pulse thundering. Hannah had read from that Bible every morning, her notes filling the margins. She'd marked passages about faith, about marriage, about being a mother. Words meant for her daughter to learn someday.

But not now. Not at four years old. Not when Nathan still couldn't make it through a day without missing her. Not when he'd built his entire life around keeping Hannah's memory locked safely away where it couldn't hurt either of them.

He should grab the Bible and slippers. Return them to the box. Distract Lily with a bedtime story. Maintain the careful walls he'd constructed between then and now. She carefully opened the Bible, her small hands treating the worn leather with unexpected reverence, turning pages as if the book held something precious. She glanced down beside her. "Pretty shoes," she whispered.

His nightly schedule began to crumble. Their routine couldn't protect Lily from this moment. It couldn't protect him. He eased into the closet, his decision made. He couldn't hide Hannah forever.

Where do I start?

"Daddy?" Lily looked up from the Bible, her face glowing in the overhead light, one hand still on the open bible. "Who wrote all these letters? And whose shoes are these?"

Nathan's throat closed. He lowered himself to the carpet beside her. "Those are from your mama." His voice stumbled on what he'd been avoiding for so long, through first steps, first words, first days of preschool. "And those were her ballet slippers when she was a little girl."

My mama?" Lily's finger moved along Hannah's flowing script in the margins. "Where did she go?"

The question he'd dreaded since the funeral. The one he couldn't dodge anymore. His carefully constructed world of schedules and routines offered no defense against a four-year-old's curiosity. "Your mama..." Nathan pulled Lily into his lap, her warmth anchoring him to the moment. "Your mama went to heaven when you were just a tiny baby."

Tilting her head, she studied his face. "Why?"

Nathan's throat constricted. All the times his mother had turned away, dabbing her eyes while holding Lily. All the photos she'd framed of Hannah with a newborn. His little girl had noticed. Had been watching. Had been wondering.

And he'd been too wrapped up in his schedules, his routines, his desperate need for control to see it.

His wife's handwriting flowing across the pages like a road map he'd refused to follow. The small ballet slipper still clutched in Lily's hand—a tangible piece of the mother she'd never known. He'd failed them both. Failed his wife by hiding her memory. Failed his only child by thinking he could protect her from the truth.

His daughter's question hung between them, waiting. No spreadsheet could solve this. No routine could make it easier. Nathan drew a ragged breath and held Lily closer. For the first time since those early days of desperate grief, he let the walls crumble.

The digital clock on his nightstand blinked 8:17. Bedtime had come and gone, and his schedule had shattered. But Lily's fingers still traced her mother's handwriting, and for once, Nathan didn't check his watch.

"Did Mama dance?" Lily whispered, holding up the slipper.

"She did when she was little," his voice softening with the memory. "Your grandma has pictures."

Lily slipped her toes halfway into the satin shoe, which was far too big for her. "I want to dance too."

Nathan looked down at Hannah's Bible, at the ballet

slipper engulfing his daughter's small foot, at the daughter they'd created, at the life he'd tried so hard to organize into sections of time. "Yeah, Lily-girl. Maybe you can."

"Can you tell me about Mama?" Lily whispered, leaning back against him.

He gently took the Bible from her lap. "I can, Lily-girl. I can."

SEVENTEEN

Four Years After Lupus Diagnosis

Grace soared across the studio in a grand jeté, her body moving with a precision she hadn't felt in four years. Impossible until six weeks ago. The mirrored wall flashed past, catching the line of her legs, the crisp turnout, the lift through her torso. Precision. Control. The kind of technique that had once made Grace Ballet Academy a name worth promoting. No pain. No tremors. Just movement, clean and free. Classical form, hers again.

"Brava." Melissa's voice startled Grace as she landed. Her accountant stood at the entrance, laptop tucked under one arm, grinning. "I'd say you're officially back."

Grace smoothed her leotard, fighting a smile. "Those CAR T-cell treatments were expensive, but after thirty-four months of remission..." She grabbed her water bottle from the barre. "Besides, moving out of my apartment to live upstairs and save rent has its perks. I can practice whenever I want."

"Speaking of saving money..." Melissa set her notebook

computer on the reception desk. "Ready to review these numbers?"

A knot cinched tight in Grace's belly. Despite selling almost everything and moving into the tiny efficiency upstairs, the medical debt loomed large. But for the first time since her diagnosis, she had hope. Dr. Winters' latest report showed stable markers, and her student roster was growing.

"Let's see how bad it is," she said, pulling up a chair.

Melissa opened her computer. "First, the good news. Last month you earned your best profit margin since reopening—$2,347. Cash flow is up, expenses remained steady."

"That's because of Ms. Chen." Grace smiled, remembering how her student's mother had championed her return. "She's sent me three new girls this month alone."

"About that." Melissa pulled up a spreadsheet. "You're at eighteen students now. If we can get to twenty-five by fall registration, we can bump your monthly revenue to $8,500." She paused. "But the medical debt..."

"Just say it."

"$387,432." Melissa's voice softened. "Even with the GoFundMe covering part of the treatment."

Grace twisted her water bottle cap. The amount still shocked her, even though she'd memorized every digit. "At least the collection agencies stopped calling."

"Because we have a payment plan in place." Melissa switched screens. "Look, if you maintain current enrollment and add those seven students, we can increase the monthly payments from $2,000 to $3,500. You'll be debt-free in—"

"Eight years and four months," Grace finished. "I did the math."

"And Dr. Winters is confident about your remission?"

Grace nodded. "My markers have been stable for almost three years. Although she warned I'm not out of the woods, she's moved me to six-month checkups."

Melissa closed her laptop. "Then we stick to the plan. Keep building enrollment, continue your light schedule, and—" She gestured at the ceiling. "—living above the studio cuts nearly two thousand a month from expenses."

The sound of a car door drew Grace to the window. Emma Chen climbed out of her mother's SUV, ballet bag slung over her shoulder. In seven years, her student had transformed from a timid beginner into an artist on the precipice of professional dance.

"My five o'clock is early." Grace gathered her water bottle and towel. "Same time next month?"

"About that..." Melissa reached into her briefcase. "You might want to see this first."

She handed Grace the phone without a word.

On the screen, Grace spun in tight fouettés, her form sharp as if the years hadn't passed at all. The studio lights flared with each turn, catching in the mirror, in her eyes. Below the video, Emma's caption read—My teacher is back. Followed by hashtags Grace had never imagined under her name again—#CoastalBallet, #Inspiration.

She blinked. Three thousand hearts. And counting.

Something stuttered inside her—like awe, or fear. Or both.

Grace followed the numbers climbing under Emma's post. "When did she film this?"

"Haven't a clue," Melissa tapped the screen. "Look at the comments."

Is this THE GraceBallet Academy? My daughter would love to train there.

Amazing control. Are you accepting new students?

I remember taking classes here. So glad they're back.

Her insides burst with butterfly tremors—the same sensation she'd experienced when she'd first opened. Before Andrew, before the diagnosis, before her life changed. She handed the phone back to Melissa, blinking hard.

"This could change everything," Melissa said. "If even half these inquiries turn into students."

"Let's not get ahead of ourselves." But Grace couldn't help smiling. "One step at a time."

"Speaking of steps..." Melissa gathered her things. "Don't forget to sign the loan modification papers. I need them by Monday."

Reaching for the pen, a slight tremor in her right wrist made Grace pause. She flexed her hand, dismissing the familiar ache. She signed her name with deliberate care, refusing to acknowledge the stiffness where bone met bone.

Just stress. Nothing more.

EACH STAIR SEEMED STEEPER than the last, her hips protesting with a dissonance that no dancer could ignore. Grace gripped the railing, mentally marking the difference between yesterday's fluid ascent and today's stilted movement—a subtle change that only years of body awareness could detect.

She gritted her teeth, attributing the discomfort to the vigorous petit allegro demonstration from her intermediate class. Yet, the twinge in her joints hinted at something more sinister, an echo from a past she strove to outrun.

The small room welcomed her with familiar sights—posters of prima ballerinas on the walls, her childhood music box on the dresser, and the gentle afternoon light filtering through gauzy curtains. She'd transformed the former storage space into a home of sorts, though cozy was a generous description for a room just large enough for a twin bed and kitchenette.

Grace set her dance bag down and rolled her shoulders, planning a quiet evening before tomorrow's full schedule. The ache threading through each limb and ligament whispered warnings she wasn't ready to hear. Not now, when things were finally looking up. Simple dinner tonight—just soup and maybe some toast. Pulling a pot from the cabinet, she winced as her fingers protested the grip—the same fingers that should be capable of the delicate port de bras she'd demonstrated just hours ago.

The regular movements of cooking usually soothed her, but tonight each motion was heavier than the last. Her knuckles ached as she twisted the can opener. The tomato soup's aroma filled the small space, but Grace couldn't focus on its warmth. Instead, her attention fixed on the way her wrists and ankles started to swell, and her knuckles grew tight and angry. Hands that should articulate precision now betrayed the artistry she'd fought to reclaim. She recognized these signs with intimate knowledge of her body—had seen them before, four years ago when her life had crumbled around her. The hands that had just executed flawlessly for Emma's class now looked like a stranger's.

"No," she whispered, stirring the soup. "Not now. Not when I'm finally getting ahead."

The spoon clattered against the pot's edge as a sharp pain shot through her wrist. Grace stumbled back from the stove, her heart thumping. The swelling was undeniable now, her fingers puffy and stiff—just like that first morning in her old apartment, when everything had changed.

Grace staggered to her bathroom mirror, leaning into the sink. The face that stared back confirmed her fears—the telltale butterfly rash across her cheeks, faint but unmistakable. Her skin held that sickly pallor she remembered too well.

The room spun slightly as memories crashed over her—Dr. Winters explaining treatment options, Andrew walking away at thirty-two, the day she'd moved her few remaining possessions up these same stairs. She'd rebuilt everything from scratch—her life, her studio, her independence. The thought of starting over again...

Her phone sat on the dresser. Dr. Winters. More tests. More treatments she couldn't afford. More battles just to make it through each day.

The soup burned on the stove, forgotten, as Grace sank onto her bed. She punched in the number, her swollen knuckles making even this simple task difficult. As it rang, she stared at her ballet posters—all those taut bodies frozen in eternal grace. The irony wasn't lost on her. She'd fought so hard for this life—rebuilt it from the ground up. Calling meant acknowledging what she already knew. She exhaled shakily as the line connected.

"Doctor's office," a cheerful voice answered. "How may I help you?"

"This is Grace Thompson." She closed her eyes. "I...I need to schedule an appointment."

EIGHTEEN

Four Years After Leaving Pakistan

The murmurs of high school freshmen huddling over their shared microscopes filled the biology lab. Fourteen-year-old Joseph squinted at the stained onion root tip cells, adjusting the fine focus until the purple chromosomes came into sharp relief. "Got it," he said, sliding the microscope to his lab partner. "I think that's prophase—see how they're condensing?"

Peyton barely glanced through the eyepiece. "Yeah, cool." He jotted something in his lab book without enthusiasm, then sighed. "Sorry, man. I'm kind of distracted today."

Joseph sketched the cell in his own notebook, carefully labeling the parts Ms. Peterson expected them to identify. Three years at Coastal Christian Academy had taught him the importance of meeting expectations, of blending in. "Everything okay?"

"Not really." Peyton's voice dropped. "My Uncle Rob was in this construction accident last week. A metal support beam collapsed and basically crushed his leg."

Joseph's pencil paused. "That's terrible. Is he going to be all right?"

"Surgery's tomorrow, but..." Peyton swallowed hard. "The doctors aren't making any promises. He might never walk normally again."

The familiar tingling sensation began in Joseph's palms, subtle at first, then spreading to his fingertips. He set his pencil down to hide his hands on the lab table.

"Mom's been crying for days," Peyton continued, adjusting their slide. "He was supposed to walk my sister down the aisle at her wedding next month because my dad's deployed overseas."

The tingling intensified. Joseph hoped the sensation would stop. This was a South Mississippi biology class—not a dusty tunnel in Pakistan. He was a normal American teenager, a wide receiver on the JV football team. Not a healer. Not an oddball. "That's rough," he said, reaching for his pencil again. "Hey, I think I found metaphase on the right side of the slide. Want to take a look?" The tingling continued. Joseph flexed his fingers.

Peyton sketched a telophase cell with distracted strokes. "The doctors said they'll have to put in all these metal pins. And even then, he might need a walker."

Joseph tried to concentrate on the purple-stained cells beneath the microscope lens. The burning sensation felt like he was back in Pakistan with Hassan when he healed the boy dying from cholera—when the power had flowed through him—when healing occurred with a touch. "My sister's freaking out." Peyton was oblivious to Joseph's discomfort. "She's talking about postponing the wedding, but Uncle Rob keeps saying she shouldn't. He's always been like that—putting everyone else first."

Ms. Peterson circled near them. "How are we doing, gentlemen? Finding all the phases?"

"Yes, ma'am," Joseph answered quickly, grateful for the interruption. "We've identified four so far."

"Excellent. You have ten more minutes to complete your drawings."

As she moved to the next table, Peyton leaned closer. "The worst part is his kids. He's got three, and he's a single dad. Construction is how he supports his family."

Joseph's throat tightened. Three children suddenly without their father's protection. A family shattered in an instant. The words carried him back to when militants stormed his parents' mission. "What about their mother?"

"She died in a car accident two years ago," Peyton said. "That's why this is hitting everyone so hard. My cousins already lost their mom, and now their dad might never work again."

Joseph knew too well what those children were feeling —the terror of possibly losing a parent, the ground shifting under their feet when everything familiar crumbles away. "That's really tough," he managed, forcing himself to turn the page in his notebook. "We should probably finish these drawings before—"

"Look," Peyton said, pulling his phone beneath the lab table. "This is him. The picture's from yesterday when I visited him."

Joseph half-heartedly peeked at the screen. A middle-aged man lay in a hospital bed, his right leg suspended in a complex frame of metal rods and pins. Despite the obvious pain in his eyes, he smiled for the camera, one arm around a young girl who couldn't have been more than seven. The heat in Joseph's fingers flared so intensely he had to clench his fists. He could almost see the damaged bone and tissue beneath the bandages, could almost feel how the healing would flow if he just placed his hands on that shattered leg.

"Which hospital?" The question slipped out before Joseph could stop it.

"Merit. He's having surgery there tomorrow morning." Peyton tucked his phone away as Ms. Peterson looked in their direction. "My mom's taking me to visit him tonight after dinner."

Merit Hospital. The same place Uncle David constantly visited his congregants nearly every week. The same place he'd been subtly suggesting Joseph come with him for months now.

"Time's up, everyone," Ms. Peterson announced. "Please clean your slides and return all materials to the front table."

As Joseph carefully placed his notebook in his backpack, grateful for the distraction from the persistent tingling in his hands, Peyton asked him, "You'll be at football practice this afternoon?"

Relieved by the change of subject, Joseph nodded. "Yeah. Coach said he might let me run with the varsity today."

"Sweet. You've got the best hands on the team." Peyton grinned, unaware of the irony of his words. "See you there."

Joseph gathered his books, but as he turned to leave, Peyton caught his arm.

"Hey, I almost forgot. My mom asked me to invite you for dinner tonight. We're having gumbo, then we'll visit Uncle Rob." Peyton's expression was hopeful. "You could come with us to the hospital after if you want."

The burning in Joseph's hands surged again, as if

responding to the invitation. He shoved them deep into his pockets.

"I can't," he said, the words catching in his throat as the tingling in his hands intensified. Part of him desperately wanted to go—to help—but the larger part feared what might happen if he did. "My uncle needs help with...some stuff at home." The lie tasted like vinegar, bitter because he could probably be used to heal Peyton's uncle and chose not to be labeled a freak if word got out.

The school bell rang, signaling the assembly that had been announced that morning. Joseph followed the stream of students to the gym, his hands still tingling uncomfortably in his pockets. As they filed into the bleachers, the principal introduced a guest speaker—a veteran talking about service and sacrifice. The gymnasium lights dimmed for a video presentation, and suddenly Joseph wasn't in Mississippi anymore.

The flickering screen transformed into flashes of memory—gunfire outside the mission walls, his mother's terrified face as she pushed him toward the hidden tunnel, Hassan pulling him through darkness as explosions shook the earth above them.

"—and that's why we honor those who've given everything," the veteran was saying as Joseph snapped back to the present, his breath coming in short gasps.

Peyton, sitting beside him, nudged his arm. "You okay? You look like you've seen a ghost."

Joseph nodded stiffly, wiping cold sweat from his forehead. "I'm fine," he whispered, though the memories still pressed at the edges of his thoughts. The assembly continued, but he hardly heard a word, lost between his current American world and the violent Pakistani past he tried so hard to forget.

Three hours later he sat alone in the empty locker room, football practice long over. He'd made three spectacular catches, earning approving nods from Coach Matthews and midair shoulder bumps from teammates. Joseph's body had moved on instinct as the football spiraled to him. For those few seconds in the air, the tingling in his hands transformed into something useful—something ordinary. His fingers closed around the ball for a great catch, and the cheers from his teammates momentarily drowned out the voice that whispered he was meant for something greater.

Coach Matthews gave him a thumbs-up, and in that moment, Joseph felt like just another teenager with a talent for football, not a boy carrying the load of a divine gift he was afraid to use. Now, in the silence, he couldn't keep his eyes off his hands. They looked normal—no visible glow, no mark of his supernatural gift. Yet the tingling continued, a reminder of what he could do and what he chose not to. His phone buzzed with a text from Uncle David—"After I pick you up, we need to go to Merit Hospital and pray for Peyton's uncle."

He typed back—"Go without me. I can catch a ride with a friend." He reached for the silver cross hanging beneath his shirt, the one his mother had given him before she was murdered. His fingers traced the familiar contours as he closed his eyes. "Lord," he whispered in the empty locker room. "You gave me this gift to help people, but I just want to be normal." He fondled the cross between his fingers, remembering how his mother's gentle voice encouraged him to trust God's plan.

Remember your gift. Your purpose.

The locker room remained silent, but for a moment, Joseph felt less alone. He tucked the cross back beneath his shirt, the impression of its shape lingering on his palm alongside the persistent tingling. A locker slammed somewhere down the hall, making him jump. He grabbed his football gear. Time to go home, to the quiet house where Aunt Rebecca would ask about his day and give him that look—the one that said she understood Joseph's struggle but wouldn't push.

As he shouldered his backpack, his phone vibrated once more. A text from Peyton—"At hospital now. Uncle Rob not doing great. Surgery moved up to tonight. Keep him in your prayers, man." Attached was a photo—Peyton's uncle, looking pale and drawn, surrounded by worried family members. The little girl from the earlier photo was crying on her father's shoulder.

The healing heat in Joseph's hands flared so intensely he nearly dropped the phone. He shoved them deep into his pockets and clenched his teeth. This wasn't his problem. This wasn't his responsibility. "I'm just a kid," he whispered to the empty room. "A typical American boy." He typed back quickly—"Praying for him. See you tomorrow." Then switched off his phone before he could change his mind.

The locker room door swung open. Coach Matthews stood just inside the door, surprise evident on his face. "Joseph? Thought everyone had cleared out." He stepped inside, eyeing the boy's troubled expression. "Everything okay, son?"

Joseph swallowed hard. "Yes, sir. Just...thinking about the game Friday."

Coach Matthews nodded. "You looked sharp out there today. Keep it up and you'll be starting."

Starting. Playing football. Being normal.

"Thanks, Coach," Joseph said, banishing the image of Peyton's uncle on the hospital bed. "I should get home."

As he moved past Coach Matthews, the man's hand

found his shoulder. "You know, Joseph, you've got a great gift. Focus on what you're good at, and things will get easier as you grow older."

Joseph froze.

"The way you snagged those passes today," Coach added with a smile. "You've got a gift for being a great receiver. Don't waste it."

Joseph nodded, relief flooding through him. "I won't, Coach."

He strolled out into the fading afternoon light. Each step away from the locker room felt heavier than the last, as if invisible chains were pulling him back toward his phone, toward Merit Hospital, toward the choice he refused to make.

The sensation in his palms intensified to white-hot. They appeared normal—deceptively so—but the power surging beneath his skin sent tremors through his fingers. His mother's cross poked his spirit like a persistent cattle prod. He stumbled to a stop at the parking lot's perimeter, doubling over as queasiness hit his stomach. Images flashed through his mind—Peyton's uncle, his terrified children, the shattered leg that could be fixed with a single touch.

Stop. He pressed his palms to his temples. *Please stop.* But the visions only intensified—the frightened kids morphing into memories of himself at ten, when his parents died, burdened with the same helplessness that Peyton's cousins were dealing with now. Joseph straightened, gasping for breath as sweat beaded on his forehead. He would be a normal American teenager—a receiver, not a healer. But the divine power burning in his hands spread up his arms and into his shoulders. Was he delaying the inevitable? How long could he ignore what his mother had called purpose?

Around him, the ordinary world of football and studies continued unaware, while within him, an extraordinary power was demanding recognition. The line between the boy he pretended to be and the servant he was created to become was impossible to cross without sacrificing one for the other.

NINETEEN

One Year Later

A notification illuminated fifteen-year-old Joseph's phone in the half-light of his bedroom. Tommy Martinez Spinal Cord Recovery Fund. The image on his Instagram was depressing. Tommy horizontal in a hospital bed, neck immobilized, arms resting uselessly atop sterile white sheets. Machines behind him. A calendar on the wall marked three months since the crash, each day X-ed out in patient anticipation of progress that hadn't come.

Joseph flexed his fingers, feeling the familiar warmth bloom beneath his skin. His maroon and gold jersey hung in the window, catching light—not just fabric and numbers, but proof that he belonged here. That he was just another kid in high school. No miracles required. No voice in his head telling him what to do. Just play football.

The playbook creaked as he pulled it into his lap—X's and O's, River Valley's defensive patterns. Something real he could touch, understand, control. The pillow vibrated with another alert, and heat climbed his arms. Two days until playoffs. Two days until he could prove himself like any other player.

Another buzz. His hands trembled with something that wasn't just nerves.

Downstairs, Aunt Rebecca's voice rose and fell, talking about mission board meetings, the rhythm as familiar as church songs. Uncle David's deeper tones rumbled in response competing with the sound of bacon sizzling. Joseph opened the image again.

"Joseph." Uncle David's voice came from below. "Breakfast."

He closed the laptop hard, like he was trapping something dangerous inside. Two days until playoffs. That was what mattered. Not healing. Not purpose. Not this thing that felt both weird and familiar.

"You'll be late for school."

He grabbed his bag and went downstairs to the kitchen, surrounded by the smells of coffee, fresh toast, and bacon. Uncle David stood at the counter, a Bible open beside his plate like he was making a point. "Your donation went through," he said, sipping from a mug with crosses on it. "Twenty dollars."

Joseph tensed. Midnight. Anonymous. It had felt like doing something good then. "Better than nothing," he said, the words sounding flat.

The Bible was open to Acts. Of course it was.

"What did your mother always say?"

Joseph's jaw tightened. The pressure in his arms pulsed like a second heartbeat. "I've got a team meeting before school." He stood to leave.

Uncle David's voice followed him. "Don't forget who you are. Or why you're here."

Joseph stepped outside. Morning sunlight made everything look sharp and bright. Travis's truck sat by the curb, exhaust puffing in the cool air. Mrs. Peterson worked on her flowers, each bloom fighting against the coming fall. Normal life just kept going.

Buzz. $42 from Anonymous Donor. $151,938 to go.

The pressure didn't go away. He climbed into the passenger seat anyway.

"Yo," Travis said, not noticing Joseph's mood. "Did you see the film on River Valley's defense?"

"Yeah. We'll be fine." The words felt empty.

Another buzz. Another reminder of what he was trying to ignore.

Travis talked about the opposing defensive line for the entire drive to school, excited while Joseph stayed quiet. Focused on routes. On coverages. On anything but Tommy.

The school appeared—red brick, same as always. Posters covered the walls with different messages.

GO WARRIORS. CRUSH RIVER VALLEY. HELP TOMMY WALK AGAIN.

Someone had put musical notes around Tommy's photograph—him at his drum set before the accident, before everything changed.

"You coming?" Travis called, already halfway to the entrance.

The poster moved in the morning breeze. The pressure in Joseph's arms built like water behind a dam.

"Yeah," he said. "Coming."

In the locker room, Coach Matthews paced in front of the whiteboard, his marker squeaking out plays and possibilities.

"Matt, wait for Joseph to clear the coverage—then hit him between the hashes."

More arrows. More squeaks. More pretending these drawings would matter when Friday's lights came on.

Joseph tried to focus, but his phone kept buzzing, pulling at his attention. Tension built in his chest—pressure looking for a way out.

"One more thing." Coach capped the marker with a click. "Mandatory fundraiser assembly first period. For Tommy Martinez."

Joseph's fingers curled.

Coach's voice dropped to a whisper. "Let's take a knee and pray for Tommy."

Bodies folded around him. Joseph stayed upright—the only one still standing among all the bent heads. He stared at his hands, these normal-looking things that held something not normal at all.

"Lord, we lift up our classmate..."

After the others left, Joseph lingered by his locker. He turned his palms up. The warmth from that evening outside Islamabad stirred again.

Not now. Not here. Not again.

"Hey." Matt's voice cut through the quiet. "Assembly time."

Joseph slammed his locker shut and followed.

The assembly hall buzzed with teenage energy. Joseph found a spot in the back row beside Matt, Peyton, and Travis, grateful to disappear in the crowd.

"$23,042 raised so far," the principal announced. Tommy's face filled the screen. The neck brace. The arms that wouldn't move. That same beep marking time in a life that had stopped. Joseph's ears filled with the sound of his own pulse. The burning got stronger, a private shame. He knew without looking—another donation alert, another push he was fighting.

"...medical bills, therapy equipment, a hospital bed for the house..."

Tommy's mother's voice broke into pieces. Joseph stared forward, his breathing quick and shallow.

Matt leaned closer, worried. "Dude... your hands are shaking."

Joseph hid them under his legs, like hiding evidence.

Tommy's father came to the microphone, grief written in new lines on his face. "We're still praying for a miracle."

Joseph stood up fast, a sudden movement in the stillness. Matt caught his sleeve. "Where are you going?"

But Joseph was already moving. Away from the image. Away from the screen. From Tommy. From the fire building inside him that threatened to burn down his carefully built normal life. He had routes to run. A game to win. A life to pretend was his.

Miracles could wait.

Behind him, Tommy's father's voice broke over the speakers. "The doctors say he'll never walk again."

Joseph clenched his fists against the feeling. But the heat pulsed stronger. Angrier. More insistent.

A gift or a curse, but his to carry either way.

TWENTY

Five years after Hannah's death

"Read it again, sweetie?" Nathan said, his attention split between the road ahead and the rearview mirror. Lily's small finger traced the text in her Children's Bible, her dark curls forming a halo around her head in the morning light. His pride swelled as he listened to his daughter read on her first day of kindergarten, a milestone he'd both dreaded and anticipated for months.

"And Jesus said, 'Let the little children come to me,'" Lily read carefully. She paused, her finger tracing the page. "Daddy, this is a hard word?"

Nathan checked the mirror. "Which word, sweetie?"

"This one. For-for." She bobbed her head with each syllable.

"Forbid," he answered from memory. He checked the dashboard—7:42 AM. The conference call was at 8:30, and they still had to navigate her new school's drop-off line.

"'Do not for-bid them,'" Lily continued with a hint of pride in her tone. "'For the kingdom of heaven belongs to such as these.'"

Nathan's phone buzzed on the console—probably Richard about the morning meeting. The device fell silent, then immediately lit up again. Through the windshield, brake lights flared red across three lanes of traffic.

"Son of a—," Nathan caught himself. He'd promised to stop using those words in front of Lily. He took a composing breath, remembering his mother's advice about modeling calm behavior. The sound of pages turning from the back seat mixed with the soft tick of the turn signal. "Daddy, will Jesus tell Mommy it's my first day of school?"

His throat tightened. These questions kept coming ever since Lily had found Hannah's Bible and ballet shoes. The gridlock inched forward. Nathan drummed his fingers on the steering wheel, calculating minutes until the conference call. Missing it would tank his chances at project manager. He needed that promotion, especially with Lily's tuition and the rising cost of after school childcare.

"'The good shepherd loves his sheep,'" she read on, oblivious to his tension. "'He leaves the ninety-nine to find the one that is lost.'"

Another buzz from his phone. No texting with Lily in the car. That was one of his rules, written in black Sharpie on the schedule grid hanging in his office. The rules that kept them safe. The rules that kept them moving forward.

The school's brick entrance finally came into view. Cars snaked through the school parking lot. Mothers and fathers strolled with kindergarteners to their first day. Nathan hadn't planned for this. His timetable allowed for a quick drop-off, ten minutes max.

"Look, Daddy. Mia's here." Lily crammed her face to the window, watching her Sunday School friend walk in with both parents, backpack bobbing from her shoulders.

The phone jolted a fresh reminder. 8:15 AM.

"Can we take pictures like Mia's family?" she asked, "with a sign that says 'First Day?'"

Nathan swallowed hard. Hannah would be better organized for photos to place on the refrigerator memorializing Lily's first day at school.

"Just a quick picture, sweetheart," Nathan said, pulling into a parking space. "We need to get you to class."

His phone lit up again. Richard Barrett's direct line. Nathan silenced it as he helped Lily out of her booster seat. She clutched her Bible to her with one hand, gripping his fingers with the other. The tightness of her small hands made his schedule-focused mind falter. These were the moments his meticulous planning couldn't account for—the weight of her trust in him.

"Miss Tammy said to wait by the blue door."

Nathan steered them to the kindergarten entrance, where a cluster of parents huddled with cameras ready. A mom in yoga pants arranged letter boards and props for her daughter's photo shoot.

Lily tugged his hand. "Can we do that?"

"Honey, I've got to—" Nathan stopped. Lily's lower lip trembled as she watched Mia posing with her parents. He glanced at his watch. 8:22 AM. The conference call would start in eight minutes. He had a presentation on an upcoming project to present. His whole career trajectory could pivot on this morning. Of all mornings. But his daughter's hand in his turned his heart.

She looked up at him, Hannah's eyes staring from Hannah's face. "Please, Daddy? Just one picture?"

Nathan pulled out his phone, work notifications stacking up on his messages. He opened the camera app. "Okay, baby. Stand by the wall and show me your brave kindergarten smile." She held up her Bible, beaming. The morning sun caught her silver heart necklace—Hannah's childhood jewelry.

8:24 AM.

"One more," Lily pleaded.

Through the school's glass doors, Nathan watched Miss Tammy greeting students. A text from Rachel—"Don't forget to take pictures."

8:26 AM.

Lily swapped her Bible for her unicorn backpack, still smiling. Other parents brushed past them, some offering knowing looks that made Nathan's heart drop.

"Time for class," Nathan said, reaching for Lily's hand. Her palm clammy against his as they approached the line. Each step toward the blue door seemed to make her movements more hesitant. Nathan checked his watch again, feeling the seconds tick away.

8:28 AM.

He guided Lily forward, watching her shoulders tense as they merged with the stream of excited kindergarteners. Other parents were already turning to leave, some wiping away tears, others checking the time like him. As they neared the threshold, Lily's pace slowed. Her grip tightened on his hand, and he noticed her breathing quicken. Before he could address the warning signs, she froze completely at the doorway. She spun, wrapping her arms around his legs, eyes wide with sudden fear.

"What if I'm not smart enough for kindergarten?" she whispered, her voice trembling.

Nathan knelt down, his phone buzzing against his knee. "Hey, look at me." He tucked a curl behind her ear. "You're going to do great. You're the smartest five-year-old I know."

Lily clutched his neck as if he planned to leave her forever. Pulling her close, he breathed in the strawberry scent of her shampoo. In that moment, his schedule did not matter.

Another buzz—the alarm warning the conference was starting. He reached and silenced it without looking. The promotion, the project, Richard's expectations—all of it faded with his daughter in his arms.

Some meetings couldn't wait—but this time with his daughter couldn't either.

TWENTY-ONE

Five Years After His Parents' Death

Sophomore wide receiver Joseph Freeman cut hard left, his cleats tearing into the wet grass. The River Valley safety took the bait, overcommitting to the inside. One quick step to the right, and Joseph was free, sprinting down the side-line. The roar from the home stands swelled with each stride.

Fifty yards to go. Forty. Footsteps pounded closer behind him. He tucked the ball tighter, pushing harder. Section C, row twelve—Uncle David would be on his feet, Aunt Rebecca clutching his arm and screaming like she did at every game. The Channel 13 cameraman scrambled but couldn't keep pace with Joseph as he flew past the thirty-five.

The defender dove, clipping Joseph's ankle at the twenty-yard line. He stumbled, fought to keep his balance, but his momentum slowed. Two more River Valley players swarmed in, driving him out of bounds at the fifteen.

The ref's whistle cut through the noise as Joseph pushed himself up from the sideline. Coach Matthews was already signaling the next play. First and ten. Eight minutes left. Score tied at fourteen.

Joseph rushed back to the huddle, his jersey caked with mud from the soft turf. The floodlights caught the mist rising off the field, creating halos in the November night. Matt's voice was steady despite the stakes. "Split right, twenty-seven power. Joseph, seal the edge. On two."

They broke into formation. Joseph lined up in the slot, stealing a glance at the defensive end. Seventeen years since Coastal Christian had made the playoffs. His gaze drifted to the boom camera hovering overhead, then whipped back to Matt in shotgun formation.

"Down." Matt barked. "Set."

The River Valley defensive end shifted, cheating to Joseph's side.

"Hut. H—"

The snap was early and high. Matt stretched, barely getting his fingers on the ball. Joseph turned to block when a blur of blue and white shot through the gap. A sickening crack echoed across the field like a bat splitting wood, followed by a strangled "woof" that somehow cut through the wall of crowd noise.

Joseph spun toward the sound. Ten yards away, a River Valley player stood, then clutched at his chest as if struck by a bullet. His legs wobbled for two desperate steps before buckling completely. His face hit the turf like a sack of sand dropped on concrete. His teammate, number 24, approached with casual concern that evaporated at the sight of the motionless body. "Let's go, Marcus, next play," he said, tapping the fallen Marcus's shoulder pad. Marcus remained frozen, limbs splayed at unnatural angles. Panic flashed across number 24's face as he frantically waved toward their sideline. "He's out cold!" he shrieked with a tremor that electrified every nerve in Joseph's body.

Three River Valley trainers charged onto the field, medical kits thudding against their hips. One dropped to his knees beside Marcus, voice low and urgent as he spoke into the helmet, two fingers pressing against the player's neck. "Scissors," he snapped, eyes sharp with panic. In one swift motion, he sliced through Marcus's jersey, barking commands over his shoulder—sharp, staccato orders that struggled to pierce the thunder pounding in Joseph's ears. Cutting the shoulder pad strings, he leaned down, ear to Marcus's heart. "Nothing. Starting compressions."

Each thump on Marcus's frame echoed across the suddenly silent stadium, matching Joseph's own racing heartbeat. The trainer's counting compressions were like desperate prayers—"One-two-three-four..." Around him, both teams sank to one knee, the soft rustle of uniforms and whispered prayers creating a terrible contrast to the violent struggle for life playing out on the field. The sharp smell of wet grass and sweat mingled with fear. Joseph's mouth went dry as he watched the trainer's face redden with effort, veins standing out on his forehead as he fought to restart Marcus's heart.

With trembling fingers, Joseph found the chain on his neck and pulled up his mother's silver cross, as if it had been waiting for this moment. Ten yards separated him and Marcus—ten yards and a wall of players, coaches, and trainers.

But that wasn't what kept him frozen. It was four years of hiding his gift—his failure to make God's power known. Would God still use him after four years of hiding? After failing to visit Peyton's uncle in the hospital? Or ignoring

Tommy Martinez? Had Joseph buried his gift so deep God wouldn't bother to revive it?

But this was different than Peyton's uncle or Tommy Martinez. Marcus was dying right in front of him.

Joseph's palms burned, that familiar sensation he'd felt with the young boy in Pakistan—like holding his hands too close to a flame. The power moved through him, trickling at first, then rushing down his arms into his fingertips. His hands glowed faintly in the stadium lights—or was that his imagination?

His mother's last words flooded his mind, clearer than they had in years.

The trainer started another round of compressions. Time slowed. The choice crystallized—remain invisible or become who he was meant to be. The mist, the crowd, the lights—all faded as Joseph's vision tunneled inward. Then he was no longer on a football field. He was back in Pakistan. Back at his parents' mission. Back in the tunnel where their screams rang. He'd stood frozen while they died. He couldn't move then. Couldn't move now.

A camera crew edged onto the field, recording everything.

I can help. Should help.

But what if he failed? What if he succeeded? The cameras. The crowd. His teammates. All those eyes. All those questions.

Whump, whump, whump. A helicopter's rotors reverberated from above, "AirCare" emblazoned on its belly as it hung suspended in the sky.

The trainer's arms pumped faster, his movements growing desperate. "Come on, kid. Stay with us." The words slurred together as Joseph's present and past collided.

Marcus's family would be in the stands right now. Or

worse—at home, watching their son die on television. Helpless. Just like Joseph when TPL militants had stormed his
family's mission. Not again. Not when he could do
something.

Joseph took one step forward, then another. The movement broke some invisible barrier inside him. A soft hum
vibrated beneath his skin, like static before a lightning
strike. He marched forward. Couldn't stop. Couldn't return
to hiding his purpose. Couldn't deny who he was and why
God had spared him that day in Pakistan.

Remember your gift. His mother's words prodded him
forward. *Your purpose.*

God's energy burned inside him, searing hot. His teammates parted to make a path.

"Clear the field so the helicopter can land," cried a
frantic policeman. Bits of blown turf and paper debris
whipped past Joseph as he got nearer.

The trainer's arms faltered, then dropped. "Lost him
again." His voice spilled out lost emotion. "Where's that
AED?"

Five yards to Marcus. The TV camera's red light pulsed
like an accusation—a silent witness that would broadcast
whatever happened next to the entire world. Joseph's throat
constricted around a sob he refused to release. By morning,
his quiet life would vanish. No more blending in. No more
silence. His friendships, his safety—gone. Exposed, he
wouldn't just be a high school athlete anymore. He'd be the
freak. A story. And stories got dissected.

Remember your gift.

Power pulsed in his fingertips, a living current
demanding release.

A policeman, his badge catching the stadium lights,
blocked his path. "Son. Let the trainers do their work."

Five feet to cover.

Your purpose.

"I can help him," Joseph whispered.

The officer held up his hand.

"Please." His voice broke like a fragile thread snapping. "I have to."

A second policeman joined the first. "Back up, kid."

Remember your gift. Your purpose.

"Here's the AED," cried the school nurse as she rushed the field. "Give me room."

Both policemen turned. Joseph dropped his shoulder, edging his way closer. Two quick steps, then his knees hit turf beside Marcus, whose lips had gone blue.

Hands grabbed Joseph's shoulders, pulling him back. The energy spiked—sharp, blinding, like sunlight reflected off glass.

He lunged and demanded. "In the name of Jesus Christ —live,"

Light exploded through his fingers.

Marcus gasped.

For a heartbeat, no one moved. The trainers froze, eyes wide. The officers froze, mouths open. Joseph shook as the power flickered away. God had done it. Marcus was alive.

Then—

A murmur rippled through the stands. Someone whispered, "Did you see that?" Then another. Then a roar.

Marcus blinked, color flooding back into his face. He breathed in a steady rhythm.

Phones rose like fireflies in the bleachers. The TV camera came within inches of Joseph's face. Questions pelted him from every direction.

"How did you—"

"What just—"

"Who are—"

Marcus sat up, touching his chest where Joseph's hand had landed. Their eyes met. Joseph saw his own fear—the fear of being different, of being seen.

Remember your purpose.

The helicopter's blades faded in the distance. Joseph pushed to his feet. Faces closed in. Too many faces. Too much attention.

Bodies pushed closer. He stumbled backward. His secret was out, now he must get off the field. Away from the cameras. Away from the curious looks.

Coach Matthews appeared appeared out of nowhere. "Let's go, son." His grip steady on Joseph's elbow, yanking him toward the locker room.

Marcus stood. "What happened?"

The questions would come now. All those years of keeping quiet—gone in a second.

Where was Uncle David? Aunt Rebecca?

Joseph glanced toward their section. Empty. He yanked free from Coach Matthew's grip and ran—past the end zone, through the gate. His cleats clattered in the concrete tunnel, echoing like a countdown. Everyone had seen. Everyone knew.

He burst through the double doors, lungs burning, heart hammering in his ears. The locker room buzzed with ESPN highlights—some college player diving for a touchdown. *Will what happened with Marcus end up on that screen?* Please, God. Don't let it.

He dropped onto the bench, elbows on his knees, struggling to breathe.

The door creaked open. Coach Matthews stepped inside. "Joseph—"

"I had to leave," he said, snatching his bag. "I couldn't—"

"Son." Coach's voice softened. "That boy's alive because of you."

Joseph froze. Not from shame. Not from fear. But because he knew—it wasn't about him. It was about Jesus. And because of what Jesus did—and would continue to do—Joseph's life was about to become very complicated.

No more hiding. No more running. Just doing what he was chosen to do.

TWENTY-TWO

Six Years After Hannah's Death

Nathan's phone vibrated on the conference room table at Meridian Engineering. He glanced down to see Ms. Peterson's name. Lily's first-grade teacher again—probably another update about his daughter's advanced aptitude in math or reading. He flipped the device face-down, forcing his attention back to the structural modifications projected behind him. The Tier One Imports representative narrowed his eyes, obviously unhappy with the interruption.

"As you can see, the foundation reinforcement for the Stone County site will require—"

The buzzing continued, rattling against his presentation notes.

Richard Barrett, his managing partner, leaned forward in his chair.

Twenty minutes. He needed twenty uninterrupted minutes to prove he could handle this assignment. It had been six years since Hannah's death, six years of being a single parent, of putting off career advancement to care for his only child. He'd put his career on hold. Every attempt at advancement had been derailed—school calls, fevers, recitals. But this was his first real shot, and he had to make it count. Lily's future depended on it.

The phone buzzed a third time.

Nathan squared his shoulders, gesturing to the cost analysis spreadsheet with practiced precision. He'd rehearsed this presentation during the quiet hours after Lily's bedtime, tracking every variable, anticipating every question.

Another vibration. The screen flashed like a warning light. A tight coil of dread wound in his gut as the buzzing continued.

Focus. He needed to focus. Nathan switched slides, his usually steady hand grazing the HDMI cord. The Power-Point presentation flickered black, his carefully crafted slideshow vanishing before his eyes. Of all the times for technology to fail him. "Just a moment." He jiggled the connection between the laptop and the television monitor. Nothing.

His phone buzzed twice in rapid succession. Richard coughed into his fist.

Nathan forced his hands still, remembering the nights he'd spent perfecting these calculations while Lily slept. He would not lose this opportunity. "I have backup prints," he said as calmly as he could.

The phone lit up again. This time, the school principal's name appeared. Richard's voice cut through the room. "Take the call."

Joseph dug through his briefcase for the printed plans. "I can handle this." The same words he'd repeated to church members, to his mother, to everyone who'd offered help since Hannah had died.

The developer stood. "Mr. Carter, clearly you're not prepared—"

The phone rang this time, loud and shrill. He must have unmuted it the last time he touched it. Lily's school picture flashed on the screen—her mother's eyes staring back at him, accusing.

The Tier One representative checked his watch.

Nathan's thumb lingered over the ignore button. One more dismissal. One more time choosing work over—what? Over the one person who mattered most? Hannah would never have ignored that call. The ringing stopped. Relief followed. Then crushing guilt. What kind of fathers ignore calls from they child's school?

His phone lit up with a text from the same number—*911 EMERGENCY. CALL NOW*.

His professional facade cracked. Six years of pretending he could do it all, handle it all, be everything Lily needed—all of it collapsed under those four words. Richard saw it. His expression softened, but his voice remained firm. "Nathan. Look at your phone. For God's sake, go."

He didn't argue this time. The deal was lost. His shot at project manager, gone. But none of that mattered anymore. Punching the school's number, Nathan rushed out of the conference room. Three voicemails. He floated his fingers over the play button, but he couldn't press it. Not yet. Not until he was moving.

The brass elevator doors opened with a cheerful ding that didn't cheer him. Two junior engineers stepped out, their greetings dying on their lips as Nathan pushed past. "Level P1," he commanded the elevator's electronic display. His voice was calm. Too calm. His heart pounded as the doors closed in front of him. He felt disheveled, unraveled—the same rising panic he'd had his last night with Hannah.

Lily had her mother's eyes. What if she had inherited something else?

His phone rattled again for attention. And again it was Lily's school. This time, he answered.

"Mr. Carter," a woman said with a high pitch of relief. "Finally—"

"I'm on my way." He jabbed the call button repeatedly, willing it to descend faster. "What's wrong with my daughter?"

"She fell during first period. Hit her head on the corner of a desk."

The elevator settled with a gentle bounce. "Is she conscious?" Nathan broke into a run across the parking garage, his dress shoes scratching against the concrete.

"Yes, but she's very upset and disoriented. We've got ice on it, but there's quite a bit of blood. Protocol requires that we contact you."

"I'll be there in ten minutes." Throwing his briefcase onto the passenger seat, he slid behind the wheel as he terminated the call. His mind raced. Blood. Head injury. The gear shift grew slick beneath his palms as he jammed the car into reverse. Too fast—the yellow column appeared in his peripheral vision and he yanked the wheel, tires squealing as he aimed for the exit.

The morning commute had never felt so slow. Nathan wove between cars, his pulse hammering in his throat. He should be in the conference room right now. Should be proving himself. Should be securing his future, his ability to provide for Lily.

Instead—

A horn blared. Yanking the vehicle back into his lane, he cursed under his breath. *Focus. Drive. The rest can wait.*

Back Bay Elementary came into view, its red brick

facade a beacon through the morning haze. He swung into the first empty spot, tires catching the curb. Too rushed to straighten it.

He burst through the security door to the chaos of children's voices, straight to the principal's office. The principal emerged from an open doorway, her usual warm smile tight with concern. "She's right here, Mr. Carter. In the nurse's station."

Lily sat on the examination table, her pink dress spotted crimson, an ice pack across her forehead. Her face was blotchy from crying, but her eyes lit up when she saw him. "Daddy." She reached for him with her free hand. "I didn't mean to climb so high."

Nathan's legs nearly buckled as he crossed to her. The sight of blood in her hair—like when Hannah had fallen with low blood sugar. A sense of inadequacy rushed through him. Six years of being both mother and father, and he still wasn't prepared for moments like this. Her mother would have known exactly what to say to comfort her.

"The bleeding's slowed," the nurse said gently, lifting the ice pack. "But she'll need a stitch or two. She was trying to reach the butterfly puppet on top of her class's bookshelf."

Nathan examined the gash above Lily's left eyebrow. His hands were steadier now that he could actually do something.

"Does it hurt bad, sweetheart?"

"Only when I scrunch my face." Lily demonstrated, then winced. "My teacher said I was very brave."

"She was," the nurse agreed. "But Mr. Carter, our policy requires documentation for head injuries. I've already started the incident report."

"I understand." Nathan's mind shifted to logistics.

Emergency room or urgent care? His mother could meet them. He just had to call and admit he needed help.

"Lily, where are your shoes?"

"In my cubby. Can I bring Sparkles to the doctor?" Her voice wavered, that same tiny tremor he'd heard in his own voice at Hannah's funeral. The beginning of delayed shock. "She's worried about me too."

Nathan nodded without hesitation. "Of course. Go get her." He watched as Lily carefully lifted her beloved purple unicorn from the backpack, cradling the worn plush toy against her chest.

Sparkles had been her constant companion since she was three—through thunderstorms, first days of school, and now this. "And my ballerinas?" she asked.

"And your ballerinas." Nathan answered through a relieved smile. "I'll bring her to her pediatrician," Nathan told the nurse as he grabbed Lily's unicorn backpack. Sparkles' purple tail dragged slightly as Lily carried her. "I'll have her send you her treatment notes for your report."

The nurse's expression softened. "Would you like me to call ahead?"

He hesitated. Then, finally—"Yes. Thank you."

Lily slipped her small hand into his, Sparkles tucked securely under her other arm. He squeezed back, grounding himself in that single moment. He could handle this.

But he had to admit, he struggled handling this alone.

TWENTY-THREE

Six Years After Lupus Diagnosis

Two years had passed since Grace's lupus remission ended. Two years of managing relentless flare-ups, of cycling through medications that worked less and less, had brought her back here—to the rheumatology waiting room at Merit Clinic. The same stiff vinyl chairs, the same calming scent. She had sat here at twenty-four when she first heard the diagnosis, and again at twenty-eight when the symptoms crept back. Now, at thirty, she was here again, bracing for whatever came next.

The warm, sweet smell of vanilla lingered, wrapping around her like a ghost of the past. It pulled her back six years—Dr. Winters' solemn gaze, the soft *plink* of her engagement ring vanishing into Andrew's wine glass, the *For Lease* sign she'd nearly hung behind her studio window.

Two elderly women beside her exchanged photos of rosebushes and grandchildren, their voices light with ordinary concerns. On the wall-mounted television, Channel 13 News played footage of a high school football game. The camera zoomed in on a cluster of players and coaches huddled around a fallen player on the field. A red banner scrolled across the bottom—*"MIRACLE AT COASTAL CHRISTIAN STADIUM?"* The reporter's voice cut through the waiting room chatter. *"According to multiple eyewitness accounts, sixteen-year-old Joseph Freeman broke through players, police, and emergency responders surrounding Marcus Williams, who had been rendered unconscious and had no pulse following a severe collision. Within moments of Freeman's contact with the victim, Williams regained consciousness and appeared to make a complete recovery. Emergency medical personnel couldn't explain the incident, citing it medically inexplicable."*

The footage switched to a shaky cell phone video showing a dark-haired teenager with emerald green eyes touching a motionless player in a white jersey. The fallen boy suddenly jerked upright as stadium lights flashed and the crowd erupted.

"Publicity stunt," one of the elderly women muttered.

"My grandson plays for Coastal Christian," the other woman countered. "Says the boy really was dead. Blue lips and everything."

Grace scanned across the low partition that separated the rheumatology waiting area from the pediatric section, to a man standing near the reception desk, his attention fixed on the same news segment. Tall, with khaki pants that held straight creases and a blue button-down rolled precisely to mid-forearm, he balanced a leather messenger bag against his hip while pressing a phone to his ear. A little girl, maybe six or seven, sat in a nearby chair next to a stuffed unicorn, making two tiny ballerina figurines pirouette on her armrest. She wore crisp shorts and a navy polo, a butterfly bandage stretched across a thin red line over her eyebrow.

The girl's straight brown hair was tidily braided, tied off with simple blue bands that matched her polo. No pink bows, no frilly dress—just practical, well-coordinated clothes that showed a masculine eye for detail.

"Hold on, Richard." The father cupped his phone, eyes remaining on the television a moment before turning to his daughter. "Lily, careful with those."

Too late. A figurine slipped from the girl's hand and spun across the floor, sliding under the partition to Grace's feet in rheumatology. The girl slid from her chair, but her father touched her shoulder. "I'll get it. Just give me a minute to wrap this up," he said. "Sorry again. Lily bumped her head and needs a stitch or two. I'm afraid I'll have to take another personal day."

As he ended the conversation, his eyes flicked back to the television, where the reporter was interviewing specta-tors from the game. His expression held something Grace recognized—a curiousity mixed with skepticism. The look of someone who wanted to believe in miracles but had seen too much reality. She reached for the fallen figurine, wincing as her joints protested the movement. The small plastic dancer wore a pink tutu, its arms raised in fifth position.

"She's doing ballet." The girl—Lily—bounced around the partition, her navy polo still perfectly tucked into her khaki shorts. "See?" She demonstrated with her other figu-rine, twirling it in circles. "I want to learn to ballet."

Her father followed the girl into rheumatology, slipping his phone in his pant pocket. "Sorry about that." His smile appeared to come easily. "Lily, let's not bother the lady."

"Do you dance?" Lily asked Grace, hope bright in her small face.

The question stole Grace's breath, as if the girl was

prophetic. "I do...Well, I want to continue..." she managed, nodding to the clinic's entrance.

Lily positioned her figurines side by side on the armrest between their chairs. "Like this?" She turned her feet out in a wobbly first position.

Grace's hands lifted instinctively to demonstrate, then froze. The familiar ache pulsed through her fingers. "I used to teach ballet." The words caught like thorns on the way out.

Lily's eyes widened. "Where?"

"At Grace Ballet Academy."

"The blue building by the beach?" Lily's eyes lit up. "With the big windows?"

Her father settled into the chair across from Grace. "I'm Nathan." He spoke with the measured tone of someone accustomed to explaining things. "We drive past there on the way to her school."

"Grace Thompson," she offered her hand. "Your daughter is precious. How long has she been interested in dancing?"

"Since last year when she found her mother's ballet slippers."

"Does her mother still dance?"

Nathan's eyes dropped. "She passed away six years ago."

Grace's heart shuttered. "Oh, I'm so sorry."

The news segment caught both their attention as the reporter summarized, "Doctors remain unable to explain Marcus Williams' recovery. The teenager who allegedly performed the healing has declined all interviews..."

"Strange story," Nathan said, nodding at the screen. "Wonder what really happened."

"I was wondering that too," Grace replied. "Seems too incredible to be true, but..."

"But sometimes you want to believe," he said, his expression shifting as he checked the television—the same look she recognized in her own mirror on days when hope felt necessary and foolish.

"Lily Carter?" A nurse called from the pediatric door.

"That's us." Nathan stood. "Come on, sweetheart."

Lily clutched her figurines. "Can we drive by the ballet studio after? Please?"

Grace shook her head slowly. "It's...it's closed for the rest of the day."

"Oh." Lily's shoulders dropped.

Grace pulled a business card but hesitated. *What are you doing? After this visit with Dr. Winters, do you really think you'll be able to take on another student?* "If you're interested in lessons, I may be able to help."

He took the card, brushing her fingers with his. A warmth fluttered in her belly.

"Thank you," he said. "We may do that."

"Miss Thompson?" The rheumatology nurse appeared in the other doorway. "Dr. Winters is ready."

Grace stood slowly, precise, measured. The effort of standing without grimacing stole her breath.

"Bye." Lily waved her figurine in a final pirouette. "Thanks for helping my ballerina."

Nathan guided Lily with a gentle hand on her shoulder. Such a normal gesture. Such an everyday moment between father and daughter. Grace turned toward her own consultation about a future she couldn't control. Behind her, Lily's voice drifted through the partition. "Daddy, can we call about ballet tomorrow?"

Grace forced herself to keep walking. To not look back at the little girl who still believed in pirouettes and endless possibilities. But as she followed the nurse down the hall-way, her mind split in two directions—half dreading Dr. Winters' news, half fascinated by a teenage boy who could possibly heal with a touch.

TWENTY-FOUR

Grace had spent six years climbing back—restoring her health, restructuring her business, reclaiming her dreams. Years poured into her studio, proving she could still dance—despite the diagnosis, despite the finances. And now, everything she'd fought for hung in the balance, shadowed by whatever news this visit would bring.

Inside Dr. Winters' office, the blinds let in thin lines of light, casting a warmth Grace refused to feel. Not in this room—the same room where she'd sat six years ago, discussing the same disease with the same doctor, learning how her life would be upended.

Not this time. She had eighteen girls counting on her. Emma's regional competition in six weeks. Peggy's scholarship audition. The Christmas recital deposits already collected. She'd find a way to adapt her teaching, to push through whatever Dr. Winters was about to reveal.

"Just tell me what I need to do," Grace said from the leather chair, her spine dancer-straight despite the ache in her lower back. "I have students who need me. Recitals coming up." She could manage the joint pain. Could modify her instruction.

"Your bloodwork shows antibodies are back, and your kidney function is declining." Dr. Winters spread the lab results across her desk, each page a death sentence for the renewed confidence in Grace's future.

"There must be some mistake." Grace leaned forward to argue with facts she knew she couldn't change. "I've been following the maintenance protocol exactly. Taking every supplement. Getting enough rest." Her voice caught. "I haven't missed a single dose."

Dr. Winters folded her hands beneath her chin. "Sometimes, despite doing everything right, lupus can—"

"I modified my work schedule," Grace said with emphasis. "Cut back my demonstration time. Started using more verbal cues." The pressure in her connective tissue screamed for attention, but she continued. "I even installed mirrors on the back wall so I don't have to turn as much while teaching."

"Grace." Dr. Winters' gentle tone broke through her desperate litany. "The test results are clear. Your body is attacking itself again, and this time..." she tapped the topmost page. "This time, the progression is more aggressive."

Grace's fingers curled around her compact, the metal cool against her discomfort. All those careful adaptations. All those little victories. All those moments she'd thought she was winning. "We need to start an assertive intervention immediately," Dr. Winters continued. "There's a protocol combining Benlysta with targeted immunosuppression. But it requires three days a week of treatment, and Grace..." she leaned forward. "You cannot continue teaching. The physical strain is accelerating the damage."

"I've already tried everything," Grace whispered. "The CAR T-cells were my miracle. They were supposed to be my cure."

"Medical science is advancing every day." Dr. Winters pulled another set of papers from her desk drawer. "But right now, you should focus on stabilizing your condition before we lose more organ function."

Grace studied the new stack of lab results, each figure a nail in her studio's coffin. She sighed as she concentrated on the numbers. CRP levels elevated. Complement proteins low. Creatinine climbing. She'd learned this language already. Back when she believed she could dance her way back to normal.

"How long?" The question barely made it past her lips.

"Two weeks. Maximum. Then we need to begin aggressive treatment."

Grace's mind raced through her calendar. Emma's competition piece wasn't finished. Peggy hadn't mastered her fouettés for her scholarship audition. The Christmas recital costumes weren't even ordered yet. "There has to be another option," she said, palms flat against her thighs to stifle their trembling. "What if I cut back to just private lessons? Or only work with the advanced students?"

Dr. Winters shook her head. "I know what the studio means to you. But you can't teach ballet if you can't move."

The truth of those words hit harder than any diagnosis. Grace lifted her right arm, attempting a simple port de bras. Pain shot through her shoulder to her fingertips, leaving her arm suspended awkwardly in mid-air. Three years of rebuilding her life, and her body was betraying her again.

"I understand the physical demands of teaching." With a sympathetic nod, Dr. Winters leaned forward. "But this isn't just about joint discomfort anymore. Your kidney function is at risk."

"My students." Grace choked through the lump in her throat. "Some of them have been with me since I opened the studio. They trusted me when no one else would." She thought of Emma, who'd stayed even when Grace could only demonstrate through verbal instruction during her first bout with lupus. Of Emma's mother—she'd shown up early to help Grace arrange the studio for easier movement patterns. A tear trickled down Grace's chin.

Dr. Winters pushed a tissue box across her desk. "What about taking on a position with a competing dance company in an advisory capacity?"

"No." Grace swiped at her cheeks. "That's not me. I'm different. The way I teach is different. We focus on proper technique, on building confidence. On..." Her voice cracked. "On helping each student develop their art." The irony of her words hit her. The very thing that had defined her life—as a dancer, as a teacher, as a person—was slipping away again.

"You've been so focused on your students for so long," Dr. Winters said, pulling a brochure from her desk drawer, "on being strong for them. But it helps to have a place where you don't have to be strong. I know this is overwhelming," Dr. Winters produced another folder from her desk. "Let me outline the treatment protocol." She spread out a new set of papers, each one filled with schedules, medication lists, and testing requirements.

Grace forced herself to look at the documents, but the words blurred together. Three days a week of therapy. Weekly blood draws. Monthly kidney function tests. The schedule alone would destroy her business.

"The Benlysta infusions take approximately four

hours," Dr. Winters continued. "Most patients find they need the rest of the day to recover."

Four hours. Grace's mind raced through calculations. That meant closing the studio three afternoons a week. Canceling twelve private lessons. Losing nearly half her income. The medical debt from her first round of treatments still haunted her credit report, and now...

"What about the CAR T-cell therapy?" she asked, grasping at anything that might let her keep her business. "It worked before."

"Your antibody levels are too high for that to be effective now." Dr. Winters' voice softened. "And I doubt your insurance would approve coverage for a second round."

Of course they wouldn't. Grace remembered the numbers—$375,000 for the treatment that had given her these three precious years of remission. Years she'd spent teaching, rebuilding, believing she could outwork this disease. She tried to shift in her chair, but her hip locked. The same hip that had to work perfectly for tomorrow's advanced pointe class.

"The longer we wait," Dr. Winters said with an incline of her head, "the more damage your immune system will do to your organs. Especially your kidneys."

Grace touched her compact again, feeling its smooth surface beneath her trembling fingers. Inside was the reflection she'd been trying to hide from all morning—not just the butterfly rash, but the swelling across her knuckles and knees, the shadows under her eyes, the tightness around her mouth that betrayed her pain.

Dr. Winters pointed to a graph. "Your kidney function declining—fast." Dr. Winters traced a line with her pen, licating a downward trend. "At this rate—"

"Stop." Grace held up her hand. She didn't need to see

the projection. Didn't need another reminder of how quickly everything could slip away. Just like last time when she reviewed bankruptcy paperwork from a hospital bed. She'd promised herself never again.

"There's one other thing we should discuss," Dr. Winters said. She reached into her desk drawer and withdrew a glossy brochure. "I lead a small group at my church with men and women struggling with chronic illnesses like yours. Many find it helpful, especially during treatment transitions."

Grace's fingers protested as she took the pamphlet, the shiny paper slipping through her swollen fingers. A fissure formed in the wall of isolation she'd built around her life— not hope exactly, but perhaps a recognition that she couldn't fight this battle alone. "Did you hear about what happened at that high school football game?" Grace asked, surprising herself with the question. "People in your waiting room couldn't stop talking about it."

Dr. Winters' eyes brightened. "At Coastal Christian? Quite extraordinary, don't you think?"

"They're reporting that a local boy healed another player?" Grace's skepticism colored her words. "That sounds... impossible."

"I thought so too, until I saw the video." Dr. Winters reached for her tablet. "Would you like to see it?"

"I did. On television."

Dr. Winters shook her head. "Not this one. A young girl in my group sent me this last night. She's a cheerleader and shot this on her phone on the field." She turned the screen toward Grace. The monitor showed frantic trainers performing CPR on a downed player, his cut jersey and shoulder pads on the ground beside him.

Grace leaned forward, her heartbeat quickening as the

recorded drama played on. The camera zoomed in. The medical team frantically worked over the fallen player's body, their movements increasingly desperate. Then a Coastal Christian player—lanky and dark-haired—pushed through the circle of medical staff. Something in the boy's expression—intense concentration mixed with terror—made her fingers tighten into fists.

The phone camera shook as he knelt and placed his hand on the player. "Four minutes with no response..." Dr. Winters's eyes widened. "Now wait for it."

The unconscious boy suddenly jerked. His eyes flew open. He bolted up into a sitting position.

Grace flinched back in her chair, her mouth opening and closing. "Could that be edited?" But it was clear it wasn't from the bewildered joy on the revived player's face, from the look of relief on the boy who'd touched him.

"They brought the injured boy here." Dr. Winters softened her posture. "I've spoken with the ER doctor who examined him afterward. No damage to his heart. No sign of the concussion his trainers initially suspected. Completely healed as if nothing happened."

Grace marveled at the frozen image. "You're saying it was some kind of...miracle?"

"Yes. I believe it was." Dr. Winters's voice carried a surprising certainty. "In thirty years of practicing medicine, I've witnessed things I simply cannot explain."

"But you're a physician. You believe in faith healing?"

"I believe in medical science." Dr. Winters folded her hands on the desk. "But I also have come to realize that God sometimes works beyond those boundaries."

Grace frowned. "So you're suggesting I can, what—pray my lupus away?"

"I'm suggesting that faith can be a powerful component

of healing." Dr. Winters's eyes held Grace's. "Not instead of medical treatment, but alongside it."

"My mother died of ovarian cancer," Grace said flatly. "I don't recall God stepping in then."

"I don't pretend to understand why some experience miraculous healing and others don't." Dr. Winters' voice softened. "But I've seen enough in my practice to know that trusting God changes things—sometimes physically, always spiritually."

Grace looked away, uncomfortable with the direction of the conversation. "I've never been much for religion."

"This isn't about religion." Dr. Winters' voice was smooth as still water. "It's about recognizing that there are forces at work beyond what we can see or measure."

The video still played silently on the tablet. The boy—Joseph—looked terrified by what he'd done, even as the crowd erupted around him.

"If God heals people," Grace whispered, "why are your waiting rooms so full?"

Dr. Winters didn't answer immediately. When she did, her voice carried no judgment. "That's the mystery of faith, isn't it? I don't have all the answers. But I've learned to remain open to possibilities surpassing my understanding."

She reached into her desk drawer and pulled out a small pamphlet. "This is my church. We have a healing service the first Sunday of every month." She held it out. "No pressure. Just an invitation."

Grace hesitated. Her instinct was to refuse. She wasn't the kind of person who went to church or relied on God for anything. God hadn't protected her relationship with Andrew or saved her business. What could He possibly do for her now?

But her fingers curled around the brochure before she

could stop herself. Not an acceptance—just...taking it. A piece of paper. Nothing more. "I'll take your brochure," she said, sliding the pamphlet into her bag. "But no promises."

As she stood to leave, her thoughts wavered. She was not the poised ballet teacher she'd fought so hard to become again, but a patient—just another person needing help instead of giving it. And maybe, just maybe, someone who needed to consider the possibility of her own miracle.

TWENTY-FIVE

Should I call her?

Nathan held the business card between his fingers. Grace Thompson had stirred something in his heart he hadn't felt since Hannah was alive. What was Grace's story? Why did she seem so sad? Stupid question. She was at a clinic at the same hospital where his wife had died.

What if he called her? For Lily's sake, of course. He could ask for advice about getting Lily involved with dancing. But would calling her remind Grace of what she'd lost? It was clear that whatever brought her to a rheumatologist was preventing her from teaching ballet. The grandfather clock in the foyer chimed, counting down to Lily's bedtime.

"Can we look at the baby pictures again?" Lily's voice carried that eager tone she'd used at the clinic when talking to the ex-dance instructor. "Please, Daddy?"

Since Lily had found Hannah's box of stored items, she'd been craving more information about her mother.

"Sure, princess." He opened the album, and the first photo punched him in the gut—Hannah in the delivery room, exhausted but radiant, cradling her newborn daughter. The smile he'd fallen in love with in college, the one that could light up a room.

Lily's small finger jabbed at the picture. "Mommy was so pretty."

"Yes, she was." Saying the word was like swallowing sand. Page after page chronicled their life—Hannah with Lily at one month, two months, and so on. Their only Christmas together. Each memory a reminder of everything he and his daughter had lost. Everything he couldn't change.

"That dance teacher today was pretty too." Lily's words dropped like a stone in still water.

Nathan's heart sank. What Hannah had planted six years ago resurfaced—*"Find someone new. Lily needs a mother."* A knot of emotion formed in his throat, making it difficult to swallow. Was it too soon to think about that?

"She knew all about ballet," Lily said. "Did you see how she made my dancers move?"

He hadn't noticed the figurines moving. He'd noticed the woman's tired but kind eyes—like Hannah's had been near the end. The familiar look of fighting to stay strong.

"Can she teach me to dance? Please?" She twisted around to face him, hands clasped under her chin. "She gave us her card."

He'd been acutely aware of that fact all evening. "Honey, I don't think so," Nathan said. "I don't think she's teaching anymore. She was visiting a doctor who treats very sick people."

"But she said she had that whole ballet school." Lily bounced on the cushion, jostling the album. "And she showed me the right way to point my toes and everything."

A flash of Grace demonstrating the move, even at the clinic, her face lighting up for a moment before a shadow crossed it again. He closed the scrapbook. "Sometimes people have to stop doing things they love, princess. Even when they don't want to."

"Like when Mommy had to go to heaven when she wanted to stay with us?" Lily's voice went small.

Nathan's heart seized. The room spun for a second as past and present collided. He hugged her tighter, needing her warmth to anchor him to now. "Yes, sweetheart," he managed, though the words felt like glass in his throat. "Something like that."

"Daddy?" she tugged his sleeve. "Could we just ask her? Maybe she could teach me at our house instead?"

Would it be so wrong to call her? Nathan grabbed his phone. Grace Ballet Academy. Even the script looked elegant, like Grace herself. Professional. Polished. Until you looked closer and saw the cracks.

"Can we call her now?" Lily nuzzled against his arm, trying to see the card.

"It's too late tonight, sweetheart." His thumb traced the embossed letters. "Besides, we don't know if she's..." *Available. Willing. Well enough.* "—teaching private lessons."

"But you'll ask her?" she asked with a raised brow.

The photo album slid onto the coffee table as she climbed into his lap, wrapping thin arms around his neck. She smelled of baby powder and lavender from the same bedtime routine Hannah had started when Lily was an infant.

"Please, Daddy?" Her voice carried the soft lift of hope.

Find someone new. Hannah—clear as the chiming clock. *Lily needs a mother.*

"I'll think about it." The words didn't sound like a betrayal.

"TEN MINUTES LATE," Nathan said to himself. He checked his watch again, fighting the urge to pace Merit Health's pediatric wing. Simple stitch removal shouldn't wreck his entire schedule, but the thought of postponing another client call made his stomach clench. He'd spent three years perfecting their routine—he couldn't afford any disruptions now.

"Daddy, look." Lily held up the ballet figurine she hadn't put down since their chance encounter with the dance teacher. "She's doing an arabesque."

"Very nice, sweetheart." He fired off a quick email to reschedule to 10:30. Plenty of time.

"Lily Carter?" A nurse appeared with a clipboard. "Follow me, please."

He gathered their things, following Lily, who skipped ahead down the familiar hallway to exam room three. The nurse opened the door. His steps faltered. Dr. Stevens wasn't alone. Dr. Montgomery, Hannah's endocrinologist, stood beside him, reviewing a thick medical file. The last time Nathan had seen her was the night his wife had died.

"Hello, Lily." Dr. Stevens crouched down with a bright smile that crinkled the corners of his eyes, his voice deliberately cheerful. Then he straightened, his mouth tight, his eyes darkened with professional concern. That look— Nathan recognized it from every doctor who'd ever delivered bad news about Hannah. His collar constricted around his throat as if someone had yanked it tight.

"Let's check those stitches first, shall we?" Dr. Stevens said.

Lily hopped onto the table, paper crinkling beneath her. "Will it hurt when you take them out?"

"Not a bit." Dr. Stevens examined her forehead. "You've healed up nicely."

Nathan forced himself to look at Dr. Montgomery, who had treated Hannah's diabetes for eight years. The doctor's presence in pediatrics could only mean one thing.

"Nathan." Dr. Montgomery's voice triggered a cascade of hospital memories he had spent three years trying to forget. "The blood work from Lily's ER visit showed some concerning glucose levels. Dr. Stevens consulted me, and given her mother's history, I ordered additional tests."

Nathan gripped the back of a chair as the room swayed around him. On the exam table, Lily made her ballet figurine pirouette across her knee, humming to herself.

"What are the numbers?" The question came out hollow, mechanical. He already knew. Dear God, he already knew. The lingering antiseptic smell became overpowering. Nathan forced his quivering hands into his pockets, trying to hide them from his innocent daughter.

"Glucose is 186," Dr. Montgomery said, her tone gentler than it had been during Hannah's final days. "The A1C came back at 6.8 percent. We also found elevated autoantibodies, which confirms she has Type 1 diabetes."

A sharp, sour taste flooded Nathan's mouth. The overhead lights seemed to pulse. She was just a toddler when Hannah's monitors flatlined. And now...

"Look, Daddy." Lily's voice cut through the memories. "My ballerina can do a split." She demonstrated with a figurine, completely unaware that her world had just changed forever.

"Lily, sweetheart." Dr. Stevens pulled a rolling stool next to the exam table. "We're going to teach you about something called diabetes. It means your body needs a little help from some special medicine."

She tilted her head, still playing with her tiny ballerinas. "Like vitamins?"

Nathan's insides compressed as if caught in a slowly closing fist. He started counting ceiling tiles, desperate for something to focus on besides his failing to protect his daughter.

Dr. Montgomery stepped closer. "Nathan, I know this is overwhelming..." she glanced at Lily before adding, "I wish I weren't speaking about diabetes with you again. But we caught it early, and treatment options have advanced significantly over the years. But we'll need to start insulin therapy immediately," Dr. Montgomery said. "I'll also schedule an appointment with our diabetes educator. You know, for her routine."

"I remember the routine." Nathan's voice cracked. He'd watched Hannah do it for years—pricking her finger every few hours, counting carbs, adjusting insulin doses.

Nathan reached for his phone, desperately needing to make lists, to create a plan, to establish some kind of control over this recurring nightmare. Hannah's last coherent words sliced through him—"Promise me you'll keep taking Lily to church. That she grows up with faith." Had she somehow known then that Lily would face the same battle?

His fingers brushed against paper tucked in his pocket— the business card from Grace Ballet Academy. Grace's tired smile flashed through his thoughts, how his daughter had lit up around her in a way he hadn't seen in months. It had been unsettling, watching someone else reach his daughter so effortlessly when he struggled daily to be enough for her.

Dr. Montgomery was still talking. "...need to monitor her carefully for the first several weeks. The glucagon kit..." She paused, studying his face. "And I'd like for you and Lily to join a support group."

"I've got it under control." The response came automatically, but even as he said it, he knew it was a lie. The same lie he'd been telling himself for six years.

"Here's our initial care plan." She handed him a thick folder. "Emergency numbers, dietary guidelines, monitoring schedules."

The words blurred together. He tried to focus, but all he could see was Hannah's medical alert bracelet catching the harsh hospital lights that final night. Would Lily wear one just like it? "Did you see that news report?" He blurted out, interrupting her. "The football player. The one who collapsed during that high school game last week."

Dr. Montgomery paused, her expression shifting to something between concern and mild annoyance. "Marcus Williams? The boy who supposedly recovered instantly?"

"Yes. The video is viral on YouTube." Nathan leaned forward, lowering his voice so Lily wouldn't hear. "The news reported a student—Joseph something—healed him right there on the field."

Dr. Montgomery's professional demeanor hardened. "Nathan, I understand you're looking for hope. But whimsical stories and viral videos won't help your daughter." She tapped the folder. "This will. Proven medical science, careful monitoring, and consistent treatment."

"But what if it was a miracle?"

"In over twenty years of practicing medicine, I've seen patients abandon sound medicine for miracle cures. It never ends well." Her tone softened slightly. "Especially with diabetes. I don't have room for magical thinking when managing my patients' healthcare."

Nathan's momentary spark extinguished under her clinical certainty. He nodded, shoulders slumping as he accepted this reality again.

"This," Dr. Montgomery held up what looked like a small white disc, "is called a Dexcom ONE. It's much better than the old finger-prick methods. The sensor goes on her arm or tummy, and it tells you her sugar numbers right on your phone."

"Like a fitness tracker?" Lily's eyes widened. "Can I pick what color?"

The innocent question shattered what remained of Nathan's composure. Six years of careful control crumbled as he observed his daughter with the same disease that took her mother, asking about a device that would rule her life. Would track her survival. Would warn when—

"Nathan?" Dr. Montgomery's voice seemed to come from far away. "Do you need a moment?"

He shook his head, fighting to rebuild his walls. Lily needed him steady, strong, to be enough this time.

"Daddy? Can my ballerina wear a tracker too?"

Dr. Montgomery smiled. "We'll make an appointment to see Lily on Friday to check how she's doing with the sensor."

Friday. Nathan's mind raced. The day was jam-packed. The quarterly review meeting that afternoon. Lily's after-school program. The groceries. The laundry. His schedule was unraveling faster than he could catch the threads.

"I'll have the nurse bring in the Dexcom applicator and some information packets." Dr. Montgomery touched his arm, the same gentle gesture she'd used the night she'd told him Hannah wouldn't make it. "And please consider the support group I mentioned earlier. Parents, children, young adults—all learning to navigate chronic conditions together." She handed him a pamphlet.

Nathan took in the brochure, its cover showing a circle

of chairs filled with smiling faces of all ages. A photo of a mother and daughter made his breath catch painfully.

"I know it's not your style," Dr. Montgomery added, her tone shifting from suggestion to medical authority. "But managing Type 1 diabetes requires help and encouragement—a big part of Lily's recommended treatment plan. Just like the Dexcom One, just like the insulin regimen."

A support group would be another hit to his routine.

"Take a few minutes," Dr. Montgomery said softly. "This is a lot to process."

He tucked the brochure into his pocket, letting it rest beside Grace's business card—two rectangles of paper carrying more weight than they should. One was a diagnosis. The other...maybe a possibility. Maybe hope.

His hand hovered over his phone for a moment. Then, with a breath he hadn't realized he was holding, he opened his calendar and canceled every appointment. The remainder of the day belonged to Lily, which may include a visit to a ballet studio.

PART 3

TWENTY-SIX

"I can't lose her too, Rachel," Nathan said, gazing at the setting sun through his kitchen window. Medical pamphlets and insurance forms covered his usually spotless counter. "It's Hannah all over again."

"Where's Lily now?" Rachel's voice came through the speaker.

"Asleep. Finally." He rubbed his eyes, exhausted from the day's crisis. "They loaded us down with so much information—insulin schedules, glucose monitoring, dietary restrictions. It's overwhelming."

"Just like with Hannah."

"Exactly. Like. Hannah," he said in a desperate cadence. "I keep thinking about how it ended with her, and now Lily..." He shuffled through the papers, trying to organize them into some semblance of control. "I have to do better this time. I can't fall apart."

"What did Dr. Montgomery recommend?"

"Three appointments next week. Blood work, endocrinologist consult, diabetes education classes. They installed a blood sugar monitor and an insulin pump on her abdomen."

Nathan pinched the bridge of his nose. "I don't know how I'll manage. Barrett's already frustrated with my downtime."

"Nathan—"

"And Lily's school. They're not equipped for this." He stood to pace the kitchen. "I could work remotely, maybe. Schedule ZOOM calls between doctor visits and treatments."

"You can't do this alone," Rachel cut in. "You tried that after Hannah died, remember."

"What choice do I have?" He stopped at the window. Stars were appearing in the darkening sky. "Mom's up in years. And you have three kids of your own. Plus, I'm all Lily has."

"That's not true. I can help more than you think. And so can Mom. You must build a support system. For Lily's sake, if not your own."

"At the clinic today, she got excited about ballet." Nathan remembered how she'd found Hannah's old slippers years ago. "We met this dance instructor. She gave me her card when Lily asked her about dancing as if she's trying to connect somehow with Hannah."

"That sounds about right. Finding magic in the middle of chaos." Rachel paused. "Maybe it's not just coincidence. She'll need normal things too, activities that aren't about being sick."

"Dance lessons?" He shook his head. "With everything else going on?"

"Why not? Hannah would have wanted that for her."

Nathan's breath shallowed at the allusion to Hannah. He pictured his young daughter holding those worn ballet slippers, asking questions about her mother. "I have to keep her safe. That's what matters now."

"You must let her have her childhood. One that

includes more than glucose monitors and insulin pumps and doctor visits."

Nathan studied the business card—Grace Ballet Academy. "Maybe you're right. This dance instructor..." he squinted to read the fine print, "Grace Thompson. She seemed to understand. The way she looked at Lily reminded me of how Hannah used to look at her in her crib."

"Grace Thompson? I know that name..." Rachel's voice rose in excitement. "Now I remember. One of my neighbors had her daughter enrolled at Grace Ballet Academy. She gave Grace high praise."

"That's her. She made Lily smile. Made me smile." Nathan set the card on the table. "But with everything else —the medical appointments, the monitoring, and work."

"Nathan, listen to me. You can't protect her from life while trying to save it." Rachel paused. "Hannah knew that balance. Maybe it's time you learned it too."

He contemplated the card, remembering how Lily's eyes had lit up at the topic of dancing. "I don't know. But the timing..."

"Is never perfect," Rachel finished. "But she needs this —something that she can focus on besides her illness."

Nathan ran his thumb over the embossed letters of Grace Ballet Academy. The same studio he'd driven past countless times. "You're right," he said finally. "Hannah would've wanted this for Lily." He said goodbye to his sister and sat in the growing darkness, the card between his fingers. He picked up his phone, hesitated, then tapped the screen.

GRACE THRUST the key with a trembling hand, missing her studio's entry door lock. She leaned against its frame, took in a lengthy draw of air, and tried again.

Click.

Inside, twelve versions of herself stared back from the wall of mirrors. A thin film of dust floated in the light, settling on the hardwood floors she'd polished every Sunday. Her footsteps echoed. No music. No voices. No shuffle of ballet slippers. Only one cardboard box waited in the center of the room, its flaps spread wide like an insult. Memorable photos adorned her office—ten years of teaching, ten years of memories, ten years of her life. Grace couldn't tear her eyes away from the first one. Opening Night. Ribbon cutting. Chamber of Commerce photo op. Back when she'd thought owning her dream meant her life was falling into place—perfectly.

The next one—Emma Chen's first recital. Such a timid little thing back then, hiding behind her mother's legs. Now she danced with Jackson Ballet's summer intensive, all limbs and lightness, as if she was born on pointe. The acceptance video still sat in Grace's phone, Emma bouncing, ponytail flying. "Miss Grace. I got in."

The next frame—Regional Dance Competition, 2020. The advanced class, lined up in formation. She clutched the frame for a closer look. A sharp pain shot through her wrist. The photo slipped, glass cracking against the hardwood, shards tinkling across the floor. Grace rocked back on her heels. She reached to pick up her latest mishap. A piece of the broken glass nicked her palm—a thin line of red welling up, blooming, slow and inevitable—like her life slipping through her fingers.

What next?

Ten minutes later she sat at her breakfast nook in her

upstairs apartment, the kettle's whistle piercing the silence. Steam billowed over Dr. Winters' treatment protocol spread on the counter. Three days per week. Eight hours per session. Non-negotiable.

The teapot kept shrieking. Grace didn't move.

Sunset colored the walls in amber and rose. The same walls she'd painted herself three years ago, celebrating remission with a fresh start. Now medical papers littered her usually immaculate Formica surface—lab results, insurance forms, hospital schedules. A calendar printout of her teaching schedule lay buried beneath them, student names neatly blocked into color-coded time slots. She reached for the kettle. The simple motion sent pain through her wrists. The teapot slipped. Scalding water splashed across the treatment protocol, blurring the words she'd been avoiding since leaving Dr. Winters' office. *Aggressive disease progression. Kidney function declining. Intervention required.*

Grace grabbed a dish towel, dabbing at the wet paper with precise, methodical movements. She could fix this. She must reorganize her schedule. Adjust her teaching methods. Adapt. Like she had before. She just needed a plan. Her phone chimed with another student message about the upcoming recital. She'd deal with that later. Right now, she must focus on logistics. On solutions. On anything except the growing certainty that this time, determination alone wouldn't be sufficient.

She opened her laptop, forcing herself to face the spreadsheet she'd been avoiding. The studio's finances glowed back in stark black and red. Eighteen students. After expenses, barely enough monthly revenue to cover utilities and insurance. Her fingers trembled over the keyboard, adjusting figures that refused to balance. The stack of medical bills beside her computer told the real story—her debt from the first round of treatments. Her liquidated savings, maxed-out credit cards. The new protocol would add another $200,000. Insurance would pay for some. But she couldn't afford the premiums.

A payment reminder from Merit Health Center flashed across her screen. $2,000 due next week. She clicked delete, but like her symptoms, it didn't go away. She pulled up her bank statement. The expansion fund she'd built penny by penny over six years. Not even enough for the next procedure. "We must begin immediately," Dr. Winters had said before Grace left the clinic.

She'd spent everything she had on doctors and treatments and drugs, only for lupus to declare victory. There had to be somewhere to find relief. She curled her fingers around the lukewarm mug. The tea tasted tepid and oddly thick. *I need a miracle?*

Her phone buzzed—another text from another student about next month's recital. The recital she'd planned for months. The one she couldn't cancel without refunding tuition payments she'd already used on keeping her studio open. She pulled up the clinical trial website Dr. Winters had mentioned. Requirements scrolled past—no strenuous activity. The instructions blurred as she calculated costs—rent, insurance premiums, medical debt. Even if she sold everything, liquidated the expansion fund...

A sudden spasm gripped her hands. The mug slipped, tea splashing across her laptop keyboard. She grabbed for paper towels, but her joints locked. Dark liquid seeped between the keys, shorting out the screen. The spreadsheet flickered and died, taking with it any illusion of control.

No. No. No.

Grace stumbled to her feet, knocking over the chair. She had to get downstairs, had to check the studio's desktop computer. All her financial records, student applications, music recordings—everything that kept her business running lived on that hard drive. She couldn't lose those files. Couldn't lose one more thing.

The stairs had never seemed so steep. Her knees buckled halfway down, forcing her to clutch the railing. In the mirror wall below, her reflections wavered—every one showing a woman she didn't recognize. A woman who'd exhausted it all chasing a dream slipping further away. When had she started looking so...old?

Her phone rang, displaying an unknown number. Probably another bill collector.

She let it go to voicemail, focusing on each step down to the first floor. The desktop computer hummed to life, its soft whir echoing in the empty space. The spreadsheet opened, numbers marching across the screen in rows. Six years of careful planning reduced to cold math. Even if she doubled class sizes, raised tuition, cut every possible expense—the figures still spelled defeat. She couldn't outwork this, couldn't scheme her way free. Not this time.

The phone rang again. Same number. She reached for it, then stopped. What was the point? No payment plan could fix this. No doctor could promise a cure. She'd spent everything—money, strength, pride—trying to hold onto a life that was fleeting.

The sun had set. Darkness enveloped her studio—her dream, her life, her future.

The phone rang a third time.

Why not? What more could life take from her now?

TWENTY-SEVEN

Nathan was three digits into calling Grace Thompson for the third time when he received an incoming call—Richard Barrett, his firm's managing partner. Nathan's stomach tightened. He glanced at his watch—6:59 PM. Nothing good came from the boss wanting to talk after hours. He switched over.

"Richard," he answered, trying to sound alert despite the exhausting day.

"Nathan, glad I caught you. How's Lily?"

Nathan hesitated. Did he want to share Lily's health issues with work so soon? "She went to bed early. It's been a long day."

"Sorry for the late hour. I have a partners' meeting first thing tomorrow and need to touch base tonight."

Nathan reached for his coffee mug and found it empty. The kitchen table around him was covered with the evening's debris—homework sheets, insurance paperwork, diabetes information brochures. "No problem," he lied, his eyes still on Grace Thompson's business card, the conversation with his sister still in his head.

"Good news," Richard continued. "Westshore Distribution finally got green lit. I'm assembling the team now. I'm trying to decide if I want you as project manager."

Nathan's breath caught. His heart thumped. The promotion he'd been angling for since he graduated. The salary bump that would cover medical expenses without draining his emergency fund every month.

"That's...wow." He straightened in his chair, suddenly wide awake. "I appreciate your consideration."

There was a pause of three beats before Richard continued. "I need to be upfront—this is going to require a serious commitment. Weekly client meetings, site visits, coordinating with contractors. Not exactly nine-to-five."

From the hallway came the soft pad of footsteps. "Daddy?" Lily appeared in the doorway, clutching her stuffed rabbit. "My tummy feels funny."

Nathan covered the phone with his hand. "Just a minute, sweetie. I'll be right there." He tried to keep his voice steady, though his heart rate doubled.

She frowned, hugging her rabbit tighter. "It hurts where they put that thing."

The Dexcom ONE they'd attached at the hospital that morning was causing discomfort. He nodded. "Go sit on the couch. I'll check it in just a second."

"Everything alright?" Richard asked as Lily shuffled to the living room.

"Fine." Nathan watched her small frame disappear around the corner. "Just a...household issue."

"That's actually what I wanted to discuss." Richard took on that careful tone executives used before delivering difficult news. "The Westshore venture is critical for the firm. We need someone who can give it their full attention."

Nathan's grip tightened on the phone. "I understand the commitment required."

"Do you? Because I remember you turning down the Bayside lead last year."

Nathan shifted his gaze to the kitchen table covered with the diabetes care instructions from Dr. Montgomery. "That was different," Nathan said. "Lily was younger then."

"And now she's in school," Richard continued. "But I've noticed you've taken several personal days recently. The partners are concerned about your availability."

Nathan reached for the receiver that was supposed to be kept within six feet of her new monitor. The screen showed 110 mg/dL. *She's fine.*

"The circumstances were unexpected," Nathan said carefully. "But I've adjusted my schedule. The project would have my full commitment."

Richard sighed. "I want to believe that, Nathan. You're the best designer we have. But this position requires early morning meetings, evening client dinners, weekend site visits—"

"I can make it work." Nathan was more forceful than he intended. He lowered his voice as Lily appeared at the door again, face pinched. "I've already lined up additional child-care options." A lie, but he'd figure it out. He had to.

"There's also travel involved," Richard added. "Atlanta, Charleston, possibly New York. Sometimes on short notice."

Nathan's mind raced. His mother could help occasion-ally, but her arthritis limited her ability to manage Lily's medical needs. Rachel had her own kids. The after-school program ended at 5:30. The new endocrinologist wanted weekly appointments for the first month.

Lily approached the table, hand against her abdomen

where the monitor was attached. "Daddy, when can we call the ballet lady?"

Heat crawled up Nathan's neck. He covered the phone again. "Not now, Lily-bear," he whispered "Go wait in your room for five minutes."

Her face fell, but she padded back down the hall.

"Look, Richard," Nathan said, turning away from Lily's retreating figure. "I want this position. I need this position." He took a centering intake of air. "And I can handle whatever it requires."

"I'm glad to hear your commitment." Richard's tone warmed slightly. "This project could put you on track for partnership in a few years."

Partnership. The salary increase alone would cover Lily's medical expenses, but partnership meant security— the kind of financial safety net that could protect Lily no matter what complications her diabetes might bring in the future.

"I won't let you down," he said, his voice steadier than he felt.

"Good. The kickoff meeting is Wednesday at 7:30 AM. I'll need you to present the preliminary designs to the investors."

Wednesday. Nathan glanced at his calendar on the refrigerator, where he'd penciled in "Lily—Endocrinologist —8:15" in red marker.

"I'll be there," he said, already calculating. If he dropped her at his mother's by 7:00, she could take Lily to her appointment. He'd have to prep all the paperwork and write detailed instructions for the glucose monitoring.

"Perfect. And Nathan..." Richard paused. "Congratulations. I'm counting on you."

After they hung up, Nathan sat motionless at the

kitchen table, staring at the space where Grace Thompson's business card had been. He'd set it aside when he took Richard's call. Now it lay face up beside the pile of medical brochures, the elegant script of "Grace Ballet Academy" catching the light.

He picked it up, turning it over in his fingers. Dance lessons. A normal childhood activity. Something that had nothing to do with blood sugar levels or insulin doses or carb counting. Nathan reached for his phone, then stopped. The reality of this opportunity settled over him like sunlight after years in the shade. But the commitment would be challenging—early meetings, client dinners, weekend site visits, travel.

Where would ballet fit into that schedule? Where would anything?

He opened the kitchen drawer and placed Grace's card inside, closing it with a soft click. Later. He'd contact her later, when he had a better handle on this new routine.

Nathan stood, squaring his shoulders as he headed to Lily's room. First, he needed to check her monitor. Then he had to call his mother about Wednesday's doctor appointment. After that, he'd update his grid on the whiteboard, recalculating every minute of their lives to accommodate his new responsibilities.

One step at a time. That's how he'd survived after Hannah died. That's how he'd manage now.

As he entered Lily's room a small voice said he needed more help. Nathan pushed it away. He could do this.

But across the house, in the drawer where he'd placed her card, Grace Thompson's name still whispered like a possibility.

THE PHONE BUZZED AGAIN, skittering across Grace's desk and bumping against a pile of overdue medical bills. The sound grated—sharp, insistent, impossible to ignore. She flinched. Shoulders tensed. Another collector? The hospital again? Her thumb hovered over the decline button. Let it ring. Let it go to voicemail. Let it be someone else's problem. But the screen kept pulsing, patient and unrelenting.

But running wouldn't solve anything. She exhaled slowly and accepted the call.

"This is Grace Thompson." She kept her voice professional, bracing for the inevitable demand for payment.

"Grace, it's Dr. Winters."

Grace's fingers curled around the phone. Her rheumatologist calling at 7 PM couldn't be good news. She straightened in her chair, wincing as pain shot through her lower back. "This is a surprise." Her gaze drifted through her office doorway. Darkness had overtaken her studio. Only the dim light from the desk lamp cast a long rectangle across the polished floor. The empty barre stood guard against the mirrored wall, a reminder of everything she fought to preserve.

"I apologize for calling after hours," Dr. Winters' tone climbed with each syllable, "but this couldn't wait until morning. Do you have a moment?"

"Of course." Grace shifted the phone to her other ear, trying to ignore the throbbing in her swollen fingers as she checked the expense spreadsheet on her computer monitor.

"I've received some information that might be significant for your case," Dr. Winters continued. "There's a new clinical trial at Mayo Clinic that I believe you should consider. It's specifically for lupus patients with kidney involvement who haven't achieved lasting remission with previous treatments."

Closing her eyes, Grace tried to absorb what was said. Another treatment? Another round of hope followed by disappointment? More medical expense? She'd been down this road before.

"What kind of trial?" she asked, reaching for the pen beside her keyboard, automatically preparing to take notes despite her aching joints.

"It's called Selective Immunoproteasome Inhibition," Dr. Winters explained. "It works differently than the CAR T-cell therapy you underwent. This targets the cellular structures involved in the immune response rather than modifying your T-cells."

Grace scribbled the term on her notepad, her handwriting jagged from the stiffness in her fingers. "And the results?"

"Promising. Especially for patients with kidney involvement." Dr. Winters' voice took on an urgent edge. "In the first group, sixty-seven percent showed a significant reduction in disease activity. For those with lupus nephritis specifically, seventy-three percent demonstrated improved kidney function."

Grace's pen stilled. Those numbers were better than anything she'd heard before. She pushed aside past-due notices to make room to take notes. "What's the catch?"

"Several, actually." Dr. Winters paused. "The trial is being conducted exclusively at Mayo Clinic in Rochester, Minnesota. If selected, you'd need to relocate there for eight weeks of intensive treatment."

"Eight weeks?" Grace's gaze darted to her class schedule detailed on her whiteboard. Eighteen students. Recital preparations beginning next month.

"The protocol requires three weekly on-site treatments plus continuous monitoring. There's no way to do this remotely or commute."

Grace thrust her palm against her lower back, feeling the familiar ache that had grown steadily worse over the past month. "When would this start?"

"That's the other catch. They must have a decision by nine tomorrow morning. If you say yes, initial screening is in Minnesota starting five days from today."

"*Five days?*" Grace stood abruptly, regretting it as pain flared through her joints. She limped to the window overlooking the darkened parking lot. "That's impossible. I have a business to run."

"I understand, but..." Dr. Winters' tone softened. "If we don't address your kidney function soon, you're looking at possible dialysis within twelve months."

Dialysis. Grace rested her forehead against the cool glass.

"The trial covers all medical expenses," Dr. Winters continued, "but you'd need to handle travel and living costs."

And close my studio.

Grace turned back to her desk, her eyes landing on the studio's financial records. Even with eighteen students, she was just breaking even. Closing for eight weeks would mean losing them all.

"There must be alternatives," Grace said, more to herself than to Dr. Winters. *Maybe hire an instructor to cover the classes.* But she couldn't afford to pay an instructor.

"I should mention," Dr. Winters added, "your specific case history makes you an ideal candidate. Your previous response to CAR T-cell therapy, followed by recurrence with kidney involvement, fits exactly the profile they're seeking. There are only twelve spots remaining, and they're reviewing candidates tomorrow."

Grace sank back into her chair. "So I either close my studio and go to Minnesota, or I stay here and watch my kidneys fail."

"I wish there were better options." The regret in Dr. Winters's tone was genuine. "But this trial represents your best chance at meaningful improvement, possibly even a permanent remission."

Grace studied a framed photo on her desk—herself at twenty-two, mid-leap across a Broadway stage, body perfectly aligned, face radiant with joy. A body that worked. A body that obeyed. "I'll have to think about it," Grace said, her voice almost inaudible.

"Of course. But I'll need your answer by eight tomorrow to submit your information before their deadline."

After ending the call, Grace sat motionless, listening to the distant sound of traffic on Beach Boulevard. Eight weeks in Minnesota. Her studio closed. Her students scattered to other teachers. Her finances in tatters. She clicked the YouTube window on her computer, where she'd saved the clip Dr. Winters had shown her weeks ago—one high school football player's touch, another's impossible recovery. She'd replayed it countless times, wavering between skepticism and desperate hope.

"Faith healing," she whispered, shaking her head as she closed the video. If her options had come down to miracles versus medicine, she wasn't ready to put her trust in some-thing so fantastic. At least the Mayo Clinic trial offered tangible results and measurable outcomes.

She pulled her keyboard closer, wincing at the effort, and began researching the Mayo Clinic trial. Each new detail confirmed Dr. Winters' assessment—this was cutting-edge medicine with positive early outcomes, especially for patients like her.

She studied the class schedule. Emma Chen had finally mastered her arabesque after months of work. Jayden was two weeks away from attempting his first solo.

Her phone buzzed with a text from Dr. Winters—"Sending consent forms now. Please review if you're considering."

Grace opened her email to find twenty pages of medical documentation. As she scrolled through dense paragraphs of potential side effects and treatment protocols, a sharp pain knifed through her lower back, as if her failing kidneys were making their vote known. She pushed herself to her feet, ignoring the protest within her skeletal framework. She crossed to the studio floor, her reflection ghostly in the wall of mirrors. Without turning on the overhead lights, she moved to the barre, placing her hand on the smooth wood.

She attempted a simple plié, the most basic movement taught to every beginning ballet student. Her knees revolted. Her form in the mirror showed a woman barely resembling the dancer in the framed photograph. This wasn't about dancing anymore. It wasn't even about teaching. It was about survival.

She returned to her desk and picked up her phone. Her fingers trembled as she dialed. "Dr. Winters? It's Grace." She took a steadying breath. "I'll do it. I'll go to Minnesota."

"I think that's the right decision," Dr. Winters said with obvious relief. "I'll submit your information immediately. We must move quickly with the paperwork."

"I understand." Grace's gaze settled on the photograph of herself in full dance regalia and form. "What happens next?"

"I'll send you the complete packet tonight. If selected, the Mayo Clinic coordinator will contact you tomorrow. You'll need to be in Rochester by Monday."

Monday. Five days to shut down her life here.

After finishing the call, Grace opened a new document on her computer and began typing—"Dear Students and Parents." She glared at the blinking cursor, unsure how to explain that she was closing the studio indefinitely. Her computer alerted her of an incoming email—the promised paperwork from Dr. Winters. As she printed the documents, she noticed a missed notification on her phone. An unfamiliar local number.

Grace frowned. *Who could that be?*—a potential student —another commitment she couldn't keep now. She set the phone down without returning the call. Whatever it was would have to wait. Right now, she needed to focus on what mattered—fighting for her life, even if it meant leaving everything else behind. Returning to her letter, her fingers moved more confidently across the keyboard. "Due to an unexpected medical issue, Grace Ballet Academy will be temporarily closing effective immediately." She paused, then added, "I believe this absence will ultimately allow me to return as a stronger teacher for all of you."

She hit save and leaned back in her chair, feeling a strange mix of terror and relief. Did she have a clear path forward to a normal life? Would that path lead to restoring everything she'd built? She turned back to her computer to send the goodbye letter to her students and their parents, while outside her window, darkness settled completely over the Gulf Coast.

TWENTY-EIGHT

New Orleans, Louisiana

The light fixtures hummed overhead as third-year seminary student Joseph Freeman shifted in his wooden chair, his notebook open on the desk before him. Twelve other seminary students settled into their seats for Wednesday's systematic theology class at River of Life Seminary. The familiar scent of old books and coffee filled the high-ceilinged classroom, a converted chapel that still bore stained glass windows and arched beams.

At twenty years old, Joseph was midway through his junior year. Four years had passed since that pivotal high school football game when he'd publicly used his gift to heal an opposing player on the field—an event that had confirmed his calling to ministry and led him here to New Orleans.

"Today," Dr. Marshall announced, closing the classroom door with a soft click, "we're diving into one of the more...spirited areas of theological debate." His eyes crinkled behind wire-rimmed glasses. "Spiritual gifts."

Joseph's heart quickened. He straightened in his seat as

he opened the AudioNote app on his iPhone to record and outline the lecture. After nearly two years at seminary, he'd learned which topics would generate passionate debate, and this ranked near the top. More importantly, it was personal. His childhood memories of Pakistan pressed against his consciousness—the smell of dust in Islamabad, the warmth flowing through his hands, the crying mother of a dying infant, the look in her eyes when she realized her son had been healed.

Dr. Marshall began writing on the whiteboard—"Cessationism" on one side, "Continuationism" on the other.

"As future ministers and church leaders," Dr. Marshall said, turning to face the class, "you will inevitably encounter these differing perspectives within your congregations. Understanding both views thoroughly is essential, regardless of where you personally land."

Joseph nodded. He hadn't come just for academic answers but to understand why God had given him this gift —how to carry it, how to use it.

Dr. Marshall adjusted his glasses. "Let's begin by defining our terms. Who can articulate the cessationist position for us?"

Several hands shot up around the room. Joseph kept his down.

"Cessationism," began Trevor, a lanky student in a pressed button-down, "is the theological position that certain spiritual gifts—specifically the miraculous ones like prophecy, tongues, and healing—were temporary provisions for the apostolic age." He sat up straighter. "First Corinthians 13:8-10 tells us that 'when the perfect comes, the partial will pass away.' Many scholars interpret 'the perfect' as referring to the completed canon of Scripture."

Dr. Marshall nodded. "And what biblical support do cessationists offer beyond that passage?"

"Hebrews 2:3-4," Trevor continued. "It says God bore witness to salvation 'by signs and wonders and various miracles.' The past tense suggests these signs confirmed the apostles' message but weren't meant to continue indefinitely."

Joseph's pen tapped silently against his notebook. He'd heard these arguments before, but they'd never aligned with his experience. The warmth that flowed through his hands when he prayed for Marcus, the opposing safety in his high school state playoff game, hadn't felt temporary or obsolete.

"Thank you, Trevor," Dr. Marshall said. "Now, who can present the continuationist perspective?"

Bethany's hand shot up from the front row. Her flowy skirt brushed the floor, and her notebook was already open and color-coded. She leaned forward, enthusiasm sparking in her voice. "Continuationists believe all spiritual gifts remain active today," she said. "Jesus commissioned his followers to heal the sick and cast out demons—commands that weren't time-limited. Paul encouraged believers to 'eagerly desire spiritual gifts,' especially prophecy. Why would God inspire that instruction if these gifts would soon disappear?"

"What about the argument regarding the completed canon?" Dr. Marshall prompted.

"The 'perfect' in Corinthians more likely refers to Christ's return or our glorified state," Bethany replied. "Besides, spiritual gifts aren't adding to Scripture—they're confirming it, just as they did in the apostolic age."

The discussion intensified as more students joined in.

"But why don't we see the same scale of miracles today?" asked Micah from the back row.

"Who says we don't?" Bethany challenged. "In my church—"

"Anecdotes aren't evidence," Trevor interrupted. "The charismatic movement is full of exaggerated claims and emotional manipulation."

Dr. Marshall raised his hands. "Let's maintain respect for different traditions."

Joseph felt the familiar tension building in his chest. He hesitated. Speaking up meant inviting scrutiny—academic, theological, personal. If he framed his words wrong, would they dismiss him? Debate him? Demand explanations he wasn't ready to give? His fingers curled around his pen as he finally raised his hand.

"Joseph," Dr. Marshall acknowledged with a nod.

"I believe Scripture supports the continuationist view," Joseph said carefully, "but I also think we sometimes focus too much on debating whether gifts exist rather than on how they should be properly used." He paused, measuring his words. "Paul spends more time addressing the proper use of gifts than arguing for their existence. Maybe our focus should be on discernment and responsible stewardship of whatever gifts God provides."

A momentary silence fell over the classroom.

"An excellent point," Dr. Marshall said, his eyes twinkling with interest. "Theological positions matter, but practical application matters more. Whether you believe all gifts continue or some have ceased, we can agree that God still works through His people in various ways."

As the discussion continued, Joseph retreated into his thoughts. He'd spoken from conviction but had carefully avoided mentioning his own experiences. The last thing he wanted was to become a theological exhibit—either celebrated or scrutinized based on others' preconceptions.

When class ended, students gathered their books amid continued debate. Joseph lingered, watching Dr. Marshall erase the whiteboard. The questions he really wanted to ask remained unspoken—

How do I know when to use this gift? What if I get it wrong? What if people see it as a parlor trick instead of God's work?

Dr. Marshall turned, catching Joseph in his thoughts.

"Something on your mind, Joseph?" he asked, setting down the eraser.

Joseph hesitated, glancing toward the door where the last students were filtering out.

"I was wondering..." he began, then stopped, unsure how to proceed. He'd never discussed his gift with any of his professors before.

Dr. Marshall leaned against his desk, giving Joseph his full attention. "Take your time."

"How do you know?" Joseph finally asked. "If God has given you a gift—a specific gift—how do you know when or how to use it properly?"

"That's quite a theological shift from our classroom debate," Dr. Marshall observed with gentle humor. "Are we speaking hypothetically, or is there something more personal behind your question?"

Joseph's fingers tightened around the strap of his messenger bag. The classroom was empty now, just the two of them beneath the colored light filtering through stained glass. Outside, the New Orleans afternoon hummed with distant traffic and birdsong.

"It's personal," Joseph admitted. "Since I was young, back in Pakistan, I've experienced...something when I pray for people who are sick." He forced himself to meet Dr. Marshall's gaze. How would he react? With cautious curiosity, like a scientist studying a specimen? Or with the quiet reverence Joseph longed for—an acknowledgment that this wasn't theory to him, but a burden he didn't fully understand?

Dr. Marshall's expression remained neutral, neither skeptical nor overly eager. "Your uncle told me about your family's mission work, though he said you rarely speak of it."

Joseph's eyes widened slightly. He hadn't expected this connection.

"Go on," Dr. Marshall encouraged gently.

"There's a warmth in my hands," Joseph continued, the words coming easier now. "And—people get better." He shook his head. "I don't tell many people. Scared that they'd think I'm making it up. Or want me to be some kind of miracle worker."

"And what do you think it is?" Dr. Marshall asked.

"I believe it's a gift from God," Joseph said firmly. "But I don't understand why He gave it to me or when I should use it. What if I hold back when I shouldn't? What if I step forward when I shouldn't? Sometimes I worry I'm not using it enough, that I'm letting fear make me passive. Other times I worry I might misuse it, turn it into something performative instead of sacred."

Dr. Marshall nodded slowly. "The apostle Paul faced similar questions in the early church. That's why he emphasized gifts being for the common good, not personal glory." He studied Joseph thoughtfully. "Have you had any theological mentoring specific to this gift?"

"No, sir. In my father's church in Pakistan, we accepted such things without much analysis. Here in America, it seems everyone has a theory, but few have experience."

Dr. Marshall smiled. "Theory without experience is hollow, but experience without a theological framework can be directionless." He walked to his bookshelf and ran his fingers along several volumes. "I'd like to suggest we meet regularly to discuss this. There's rich biblical teaching on healing that goes beyond the cessationist-continuationist debate."

Hope rose in Joseph's chest. "You'd be willing to do that?"

"Of course. That's why I'm here." Dr. Marshall pulled a book from the shelf and handed it to Joseph.

Joseph read the title aloud, running his fingers over the cover. "'Showing the Spirit: A Theological Exposition of 1 Corinthians 12-14' by D.A. Carson."

"It's an excellent exegetical work on the key biblical passages related to spiritual gifts," Dr. Marshall explained. "Carson is a respected New Testament scholar who provides a thorough analysis of these chapters and addresses some common misunderstandings in charismatic and Pentecostal interpretations. I think you'll find it illuminating."

"There's something else," Joseph said, his voice quieter now. "Something I haven't shared with anyone at seminary."

Dr. Marshall settled against his desk, giving Joseph his full attention. "Your uncle told me about what happened to your parents' mission in Pakistan," Dr. Marshall said gently. "The attack, your escape with Hassan. I know it was traumatic, especially for a ten-year-old boy."

Joseph's fingers absently touched the outline of his mother's silver cross beneath his shirt. "What Uncle David doesn't know is that I've been having this recurring dream since coming to America." His gaze drifted to the stained-glass window where colored light spilled across the floor. "I see the ruins of the mission—the blackened walls, my mother's garden overgrown with weeds. But then I hear this small, still voice telling me I must return someday. That I must rebuild what was destroyed."

"And you believe this is divine guidance?" Dr. Marshall asked thoughtfully.

"I do." Joseph met his professor's eyes with unexpected conviction. "It's not just about honoring my parents' memory. When the militants destroyed our mission, they silenced the only Christian witness for miles. If no one returns, if no one rebuilds, the Gospel loses its foothold in that region."

Dr. Marshall walked to the window, sunlight illuminating his thoughtful expression. "So your uncle knows about the dreams?"

"He does, but he doesn't understand them the way I do," Joseph said, a note of frustration creeping into his voice. "He thinks I'm holding onto the past, that I should focus on ministry here in America. But this isn't about the past—it's about the future God has planned."

"Many would say such a mission is impossible—even dangerous," Dr. Marshall observed.

"That's what Hassan told me the night we escaped," Joseph said with a faint smile. "I was only ten, but I knew even then that with God, nothing is impossible."

"So your theological studies here—"

"Are preparation," Joseph finished. "I need to understand my gift. How to use it wisely. How to bring healing not just to bodies, but to a place wounded by violence and hatred."

Dr. Marshall turned back to Joseph. "Your journey reminds me of Christ's parable of the talents." He gestured toward the book in Joseph's hand. "The master entrusts his servants with resources according to their ability. Those who faithfully steward what they're given—even in small

matters—are eventually entrusted with greater responsibilities."

Joseph hadn't considered it that way before. "So the
hospice ministry..."

"Is not separate from your calling to rebuild the
mission," Dr. Marshall said, his voice warming with
certainty. "It's preparation. Faithful stewardship in smaller
settings prepares us for larger ones. The Lord's pattern
throughout Scripture is clear—those who prove faithful
with little are entrusted with much." He placed a hand on
Joseph's shoulder. "This hospice ministry I mentioned—
serving the forgotten, bringing comfort to the suffering—
consider it not just practical training, but spiritual preparation for the greater restoration work God has placed on your
heart."

Something settled in Joseph's spirit—a confirmation that
resonated with that small, still voice from his dreams. For
the first time, he could see how each piece of his journey
connected, forming a path that led back to Pakistan. Back
home.

TWENTY-NINE

Eleven Years After Lupus Diagnosis

Grace's fingers struggled with the computer keyboard as an elderly man leaning on his cane waited for directions. After a month on the job as a receptionist at Merit Health Center, she still hadn't mastered the labyrinth of various physicians and departments.

"I need to reschedule my cardiology follow-up," the man said, tapping his cane against the floor.

Grace forced a smile, self-conscious of her telltale butterfly rash that had reappeared last week. Four years ago, she'd closed Grace Ballet Academy to pursue an experimental treatment in Minneapolis. Eight weeks of hope, six months of relief, but ending in failure. Now she never imagined she'd be here—learning insurance verification codes instead of teaching fundamental dance positions and techniques.

At least she still owned the building, her apartment above the empty studio providing one small constant in her unraveled life. But when her lupus returned after the Mayo Clinic failed, Dr. Winters arranged this position at

Merit Health Center, complete with the employee health benefits Grace desperately needed. The position suited her well enough, and she found her years of running a business came in handy. Scheduling, talking with people, handling the occasional problem—all these past experiences made the job feel comfortable, almost familiar. She settled into the role with little difficulty, quietly pleased that her previous work life had prepared her so thoroughly for this new chapter. New chapter, yes, but not her dream.

"Of course, sir. Let me pull up Dr. Melancon's calendar." Grace's fingers stroked the keyboard, the dates swimming on the computer. The specialty code hovered just out of reach, buried in the fog of her mind. She'd learned it in training—used it this morning, even—but now it felt distant, like trying to grasp something through thick molasses.

A young mother hand in hand with a toddler appeared behind the man.

A familiar voice cut through her rising anxiety. "Good morning, Grace." Dr. Winters passed by quickly with a patient chart in hand. "Don't forget we have small group tonight."

She nodded. Dizziness followed. Her cheeks warmed as Dr. Winters strolled to her office. The irony wasn't lost on Grace—she used to teach coping with the rigors of ballet at her studio. Now she learned and prayed with others how to deal with her chronic disease.

"I see Dr. Melancon has an opening next Thursday at 2:15," she said, though the numbers on the calendar kept blurring. She blinked hard, trying to force her lupus-fogged brain to focus. "Or there's...wait." She squinted at the schedule again. Had she already offered that time slot to someone else earlier that morning?

The young mother lifted her toddler to her hip and sighed.

"Take your time, dear," the elderly man said. His kindness only made Grace's cheeks burn hotter. She'd once run a successful ballet studio, coordinating dozens of students' complex schedules. Now she struggled with simple appointment software.

A well-dressed woman burst to the counter, cutting in front of the others. "I need to see Dr. Harrison right now. It's about my test results."

"I'm sorry, but Dr. Harrison is booked all morning," Grace said, her fingers trembling slightly on the keyboard. "I can help you schedule—"

"You don't understand. I left three messages yesterday." The woman leaned over the desk. "I'm not leaving until I see him."

Grace's mind went blank. What was the protocol for demanding patients? The procedures she'd learned in training scattered like startled birds. "Ma'am," Grace started again, forcing her voice to remain steady. "Let me check the schedule one more time." She focused on the elderly man first, carefully typing in his information. One task at a time. Just like when she'd taught nine-year-old girls their first plié. "There we go, sir. Thursday, 2:15 with Dr. Melancon. Would you like an appointment card?"

The elderly man smiled, and for a moment, a spark of her old confidence surfaced. She might not be teaching ballet anymore, but she could learn this. She had to. "Now," she turned to the young mother, speaking quickly before the well-dressed woman could interrupt again. "How can I help you?"

"I need to schedule an appointment with Dr. Stevens," the mother said, shifting her toddler higher on her hip.

"Of course." Grace pulled up the pediatric calendar. "Dr. Stevens has an opening next Tuesday at 10:15 or Wednesday at 2:30."

"Tuesday works," the mother said. The toddler squirmed as Grace entered their information and printed an appointment card. Now she focused on the well-dressed woman. "Mrs...?"

"Peterson. And I've been more than patient."

Grace pulled up Dr. Harrison's message queue. "I see your messages here. Let me contact Dr. Harrison's nurse about your test results." Her fingers moved steadily now. "If you'll have a seat, I'll make sure someone calls you within the hour."

The woman's shoulders relaxed slightly. "Within the hour?"

"Yes, ma'am. I'll mark it urgent."

After Mrs. Peterson settled into a waiting room chair, Grace allowed herself a steadying breath. The morning rush had passed. A name on Dr. Stevens' schedule caught her eye. Her fingers froze on the keyboard—Lily Carter, 9:30 tomorrow morning.

Was it the same Lily? The little girl who'd clutched a pair of ballet figurines in Dr. Winters' waiting room four years ago? The one whose father—Nathan—had watched with quiet pride as she twirled them on the chair beside him? Grace swallowed. That had been the day her body betrayed her—again. She'd given the father her business card just before the diagnosis that sent her to Minneapolis.

She studied the name, half-expecting it to disappear. If it was the Lily she'd met with her father, they'd have to pass her desk tomorrow morning. Would she recognize Grace after all this time? Would her father? She exhaled, forcing her hands to move again. One thing at a time. Her work phone lit up, startling her from her thoughts.

"Merit Health Center, this is Grace speaking."

"Hello," came the familiar male voice that jolted her system. "I need to confirm an appointment for Lily Carter."

FIVE YEARS *After Lily's Diabetes Diagnosis*

Nathan sat before a grid of glowing rectangles—twelve faces boxed into neat little frames, each window its own world of blurred backgrounds and digital nods. He unmuted the mic above his own ZOOM frame. "The final phase of Gulf Shores Distribution should complete ahead of schedule."

Just then, the door to his home office creaked open. Lily burst in, all energy and movement, her brown ponytail bouncing behind her like punctuation. She wore her sixth-grade PE uniform, socks mismatched, cheeks still flushed from the ride home.

"Dad. Dad. Look what I learned today in dance class."

Nathan clicked mute again—his team's expressions softening into smiles with a few chuckles.

"First position." Lily planted her heels together with exaggerated care, toes turned out in a shaky V. "Miss Kelly says I have natural turn-out."

Behind the closed door of Nathan's office, the conversation rolled on—final inspections, budget closeouts, ribbon-cutting schedules. Four years of work wrapping up. And here, in a flash of movement and breathless pride, was the life that mattered more than any of it.

"Second position." Lily slid her feet apart, arms curved at her sides like she was hugging a beach ball.

The Dexcom ONE alarm on his smartphone beeped. Nathan's eyes darted from his daughter's impromptu dance demonstration to the concerning pattern on the software's display. Lily's glucose had been swinging between 180 and 75 since yesterday morning. She'd need a snack soon, but her eager grin made him pause. He should wrap up this call, but the Gulf Shores timeline couldn't afford more delays.

"Third position." Lily crossed one leg in front of the other, her PE shorts and T-shirt a far cry from the dance leotards she'd been begging for. "The front heel goes right here on the back foot."

Keeping one eye on the Dexcom display, Nathan nodded. The downward trend made his stomach clench.

"Fourth position is like third, but..." she slid a wobbly foot forward. "You move your foot out more."

His assistant's voice came through the earbuds. "We need your input on the landscaping specs, Nathan."

"Fifth position is the hardest." Lily's tongue poked out in concentration as she attempted to cross her feet. "Miss Kelly says most dancers my age can't do it right."The Dexcom arrow displayed a changed glucose level. Nathan checked the timestamp—thirty-six hours of moderate readings outside of pre-set high and low thresholds. He should document this pattern for Dr. Stevens tomorrow and possibly give Dr. Montgomery a call. The pediatric endocrinologist had been helpful with day-to-day management, but these readings were eerily similar to patterns he'd seen before. Dr. Montgomery had treated both Hannah and Lily, understanding the family history in a way other doctors couldn't.

Lily teetered, catching herself against the wall. "Did you see that, Dad? I almost had it."

The competing demands weighed on him—his daughter's proud face, the waiting project team, and the glucose monitor that never stopped requiring his attention.

Nathan unmuted his call. "Guys, I need two minutes. Lily's blood sugar is dropping." He switched off his camera and pushed back from his desk. "Lily-bug, amazing dance moves. But we must check your numbers."

"I know." Lily's shoulders slumped. "The beeping already told you."

"Hey." He turned his daughter to face him. "Those positions were spot on, especially that fifth one. Maybe we can talk about real ballet classes after we see Dr. Stevens tomorrow."

Lily's face brightened. "Really?"

"Really. Now scoot upstairs and get your homework started. I'll bring you a snack in fifteen minutes."

Lily scooped up her backpack. As she twirled toward the door, a bright blue flyer slipped from her PE clothes onto the hardwood floor. The Merit Health logo caught Nathan's eye—something about community programs.

He'd grab it later. Right now, he had too much going on.

Nathan unmuted and switched his camera back on. "Let's talk about those landscaping specs." But his eyes kept drifting to the Dexcom display, where Lily's glucose numbers told a story he wasn't sure he was ready to face.

That evening, he transferred her glucose data to his laptop resting on the kitchen table while chicken breasts baked in the oven. The thirty-six-hour graph showed a moderate swing between 40 and 60, with no obvious trigger. Not an emergency, but—

Nathan's stomach clenched. That pattern—too familiar. Too close to one that preceded him rushing Lily to the hospital a year ago.

He reached for his phone on the counter to open the

Dexcom app—the routine as ingrained as breathing now. Log the numbers. Stay on top of the data. Stay in control.

But his thumb hesitated, then slid right. The YouTube logo glowed beneath his fingertip, a silent temptation. The kitchen light reflected off the screen as his finger trembled slightly before tapping. Just one more viewing, he told himself. One more analysis of what happened on that miraculous evening.

One tap on favorites, and a frozen moment from three years ago—a thumbnail of a boy with outstretched hands titled "Miracle at High School Stadium." His pulse ticked faster. He knew the clip by heart. He had watched it in the darkest hours after Lily's diagnosis, when fear had him scouring the internet for something—anything—that could undo reality.

The video loaded. A rush of noise, shaky footage, bodies crowding the frame. The confusion of an emergency unfolding. Coaches shouting, medics scrambling. Then—Joseph Freeman. A wiry kid forcing his way through the chaos, dodging security. The camera zoomed, unfocused and jerky. Joseph placing his hand on the fallen player. A second's pause. Then movement.

The oven timer shrieked. Nathan flinched, thumb jerking against the screen. His cheeks burned as he set the phone down and reached for his laptop again. He should be reviewing Lily's glucose patterns, not wasting time on unverified videos.

What am I doing? This isn't data. This isn't evidence.

He opened the spreadsheet where he tracked her glucose numbers, fingers moving mechanically through the familiar process of inputting the latest readings. Evidence and data—these were his anchors in uncertainty, his reliable constants. Not wishful thinking. During Hannah's final weeks, she put more faith in miracle cures and prayer circles than medical protocols. It was he who kept her treatment schedule on track, an experience that had hardened his resolve. With his daughter, he would not falter. The rigorous discipline of numbers and medication would be his framework of care.

"Watch this, Dad. A pirouette." Lily demonstrated in the kitchen doorway, her white ankle socks turning on the hardwood.

"That's great, sweetheart." Nathan tabbed through glucose readings, noting times and potential correlations.

"Miss Kelly says if I practice every day, I can be in the talent show," she added, her eyes bright with excitement.

Nathan looked up from his laptop. "A talent show? When is that?"

"Two weeks. We get to wear costumes and everything." She slid her feet apart. "Chaînés."

Her feet slipped. She caught herself on the doorframe, giggling.

"Careful there, ballerina. Maybe we should get you proper dance shoes."

"Can I get pink ones with ribbons?"

The oven timer beeped. He hit print and set his laptop aside. "We'll see. First, dinner. Then homework."

"Then more practice?" Lily pleaded, following him to the kitchen.

"Then bath. Then bed." He pulled out the baking sheet. "Big day tomorrow."

"Because of my doctor's appointment?" She reached for a paper napkin.

Three years of managing Type 1 diabetes had taught him to trust his instincts. And at that moment, every parental instinct told him something wasn't right with his little dancer's numbers.

"Dad? Is something wrong?"

Nathan forced a smile. "Nothing we can't handle."

As he turned back to the oven, he added another item to his mental checklist—call Dr. Montgomery's office first thing in the morning. These patterns warranted a specialist's opinion.

THIRTY

Grace winced as her fingers locked while she pointed. She flexed, willing the stiffness away as she explained the best path to Dr. Lowenstein's office for the young woman with the telltale glow. "Take the west elevator to the third floor, then follow the pink line." Grace motioned toward the bank of elevators across the massive lobby. "Women's Health is at the end of the hallway. They'll assist you in checking in for your appointment."

As the woman thanked her and walked away, Grace couldn't help but notice the protective way she rested her hand low on her still-flat abdomen. First trimester, if Grace had to guess. Once, she'd imagined herself making that same walk, that same unconscious gesture of connection with a growing life. But at thirty-six, with lupus medications that carried stern warnings about pregnancy, that particular dream had faded into the realm of impossibility.

Grace rubbed her knuckles beneath the desk. Two more visitors waited in line, each face bearing a blend of anxiety and impatience unique to medical centers. Behind them, the automatic doors slid open, revealing a familiar pair—a tall man with worried eyes and a young girl who danced her way into the clinic.

Nathan and Lily Carter. The girl, six years older now, moved as if she'd been taking rudimentary dance lessons.

"I can help who's next," she called, hoping her voice sounded steadier than her hands felt.

A woman with a sleeping infant stepped forward, but Grace found her attention divided. From the corner of her eye, the young girl rose to relevé while waiting, her weight distribution a tad uneven. Even from this distance, it was obvious the girl's stance wasn't quite balanced—a common beginner mistake that stirred memories of Grace's teaching days.

By the time she'd directed the new mother to pediatrics and helped an anxious college student find the lab for blood work, the Carters had reached the front of her line. Up close, she could see the changes the years had brought. Lily's childish features maturing, though she still had the same bright eyes that had looked up at Grace when she'd retrieved the fallen ballerina figurine years ago.

"Good morning," she said, her professional smile firmly in place. "How can I help you today?" Nathan stepped forward, his expression a mixture of recognition and uncertainty. "We need to see Dr. Montgomery in endocrinology," he paused as if uncertain, "I think we've met before. Years back?"

"You remember," she said, surprised he recalled their brief encounter. "Your daughter dropped her tiny dancer." She turned to her computer, grateful for the excuse to look away from Lily's impromptu movements. Each time Lily attempted what looked like a dance position, Grace felt that old teaching instinct stir—the same feeling she'd had in her past life when she'd watched new students make similar mistakes in her studio.

"Does Dr. Montgomery have an opening in her schedule today?" Nathan said, lowering his voice. "Lily's glucose numbers have been all over the place this week."

Glucose numbers. Diabetes. Grace's heart sank as she nodded, understanding the urgency in his tone. She'd heard it countless times at this desk—the careful way parents tried to convey medical concerns without alarming their children.

"Let me check her schedule." Her fingers moved across the keyboard, each keystroke sending tiny jolts of pain up her wrists. The scheduling system crawled today, overwhelmed by the morning rush. "It looks like Dr. Montgomery is booked solid for the next three weeks."

Nathan's face fell. He glanced at Lily, who had wandered a few steps away to study the massive directory board, still unconsciously practicing her ballet positions.

"Three weeks is too long," he said, running a hand through his hair. "Her insulin needs keep changing, and she has a dance recital coming up. I'm worried about her managing both."

The casual remark about a recital caught Grace's attention. "She's dancing?"

"Started lessons this year at school. It's been good for her, but with her diabetes..." He trailed off, watching the poor girl attempt a wobbly pirouette near the water fountain.

The computer system froze mid-search. Grace forced a smile and tapped Ctrl-Alt-Delete, acutely aware of the line forming behind Nathan. "I'm sorry about this," she said, gesturing to her screen. "Technology, right?"

While waiting for the system to come back online, Dr.

Winters walked briskly through the lobby with multiples files tucked under one arm. The rheumatologist caught her eye and tapped her watch meaningfully. Grace had completely forgotten about her afternoon appointment—the one where they'd discuss her latest lab results.

The computer finally responded, and she resumed her search. "Let me check for cancellations. Sometimes spots open up."

She scrolled through the calendar, conscious of her trembling fingers and Nathan's worried gaze. The lobby grew busier, voices echoing off the high ceilings as more patients arrived. A security guard directed an elderly man in a wheelchair toward Grace's desk, but she held up one finger, asking him to wait.

"I need to be thorough here," she explained to Nathan, scrolling through Dr. Montgomery's packed calendar. "Endocrinology appointments are hard to come by."

Lily returned to her father's side, rising again to attempt relevé. "Dad, can we get something to eat after? I'm starving."

"We must check your numbers first," he replied, the familiar caution in his voice that Grace recognized from her own medical routine.

Her search continued, day after day of fully booked slots. The security guard cleared his throat impatiently, and two more people joined the line. Grace's neck tensed as she felt the pressure mounting, her symptoms intensifying with her stress.

Then she saw it—a small gap in today's schedule. "There's a cancellation at 11:30 this morning," she said, her pulse quickening as the time registered. "Dr. Montgomery had a patient reschedule."

Nathan's expression brightened. "Today? That would be great."

She tapped the keyboard to enter Lily's information. 11:30 AM—the exact time of her appointment with Dr. Winters. The appointment she'd been dreading, where they would discuss her worsening symptoms and likely adjust her medication again.

"Miss?" The security guard's voice was more insistent now, the elderly man in the wheelchair looking increasingly uncomfortable.

"One moment, please," she said, her professional tone strained. Grace turned back to Nathan. "All set."

"Great," he said, the tension in his eyes softening. "Thank you."

She smiled at Lily—still attempting wobbly dance moves with the uninhibited joy she once felt. Was dancing with diabetes as challenging as with lupus? She printed the appointment confirmation. "They have your insurance information on file, so you're good to go."

"Thank you again." He took the card and waved it. "This is a big help."

"You're welcome." She nodded, already reaching for the phone to call Dr. Winters' office. "Bye, Lily."

Lily stopped her dancing and looked directly at Grace. "I remember you," she said suddenly. "You fixed my ballerina a long time ago. You said she just needed to find her balance again."

Grace's hands stilled on the receiver. "You remember that?"

"Yeah. I started taking real ballet classes now." Lily demonstrated a passé that made Grace's teacher instincts flare. Her weight was completely off-center, her supporting leg locked instead of engaged.

"That's wonderful," Grace managed, resisting the urge to correct Lily's form. "Ballet teaches discipline that helps with everything else."

"Even diabetes?" Lily asked.

"Especially with managing health conditions," Grace replied, surprised by the thickness in her voice. "It trains you to listen to your body."

Nathan studied her with interest. "Are you still teaching ballet?" The line behind him had grown to six people now, and the security guard shuffled his feet purposefully.

"Afraid not."

"We should let you get back to work," he said after a quick look over his shoulder. "Thank you again for fitting us in."

Grace watched them walk away, Lily attempting another wobbly rise to her toes while waiting for the elevator. Even from this distance, the girl's natural enthusiasm for movement was obvious—something no amount of proper technique could replace, reminding Grace of her own students, before her body had betrayed her passion.

When they disappeared into the elevator, she turned to the growing line of patients.

"I can help who's next," she called, gesturing to the elderly man in the wheelchair.

The security guard nodded gratefully and wheeled him forward. She tried to push thoughts of Lily Carter and Nathan and chronic illnesses to the rear of her mind, focusing instead on the directory screen in front of her. Some days, helping others find their way through the medical maze felt like the only dance she had left.

STUDYING the glucose trend lines on Dr. Montgomery's computer screen, Nathan mentally calculated the standard deviations before the doctor even mentioned them. Three years of managing Lily's diabetes had turned medical terminology into a second language—one he'd first learned during Hannah's illness and never wanted to become fluent in again.

"Her A1C is holding at 7.2," Dr. Montgomery said, clicking through the charts. "Not ideal, but not concerning given her age and activity level."

"The overnight basal rates need adjusting," Nathan pointed out, gesturing to the monitor. "She's dropping too low between two and four AM, then rebounding too high before breakfast."

Dr. Montgomery nodded. "Good catch. We'll modify her pump settings." She glanced at Lily, who sat in the corner chair flipping through a dance magazine she'd brought along. "How are you feeling about those nighttime lows, young lady?"

"Dad always catches them," she answered without looking up. "He's like the alarm on my monitor."

The casual confidence in her voice made Nathan's chest tighten. The 2:00 AM checks had become so routine that she barely acknowledged them anymore—as if all fathers naturally woke in the middle of the night to check their child's blood sugar levels.

"Speaking of activities," Nathan said, steering the conversation to his main concern, "Lily has been dancing at school and she wants to start ballet lessons. With her glucose variability, is that something we should consider, or would it complicate her management too much?"

His phone vibrated—the fifth time in ten minutes.

Ignoring it, he focused on Dr. Montgomery's response. The Gulf Shores project would have to wait.

Dr. Montgomery leaned back in her chair and rubbed her chin. "Dance is actually excellent exercise for diabetic children. The consistent activity helps with insulin sensitivity, and the scheduled nature makes her blood sugar levels more predictable."

Lily's head snapped up from her magazine. "So we can do it?"

"I don't see why not," Dr. Montgomery said with a smile. "We'll need to monitor how it affects your levels initially, but many of my patients are physically active."

Nathan's phone quaked with successive vibrations indicating multiple incoming messages. He slipped it from his pocket just enough to glimpse the screen—

"URGENT: Drainage test failed on east parcel. Final inspection tomorrow. Call immediately." "County inspector arriving 9 AM. Landscaping not compliant with revised codes." "Nathan—are you getting these texts? Entire timeline at risk."

He suppressed a sigh as Dr. Montgomery continued discussing dance-specific management strategies. This was the part of single parenting he found most impossible—the constant tug-of-war between Lily's needs and work demands that couldn't wait.

"You'll want to check her levels before class, have fast-acting carbohydrates available, and monitor for at least two hours after to establish her pattern," Dr. Montgomery explained, printing out a sheet of instructions. "I'd recommend reducing her bolus by about twenty percent before her lessons."

Nathan nodded, committing the instructions to memory

while his phone continued its silent protest. "And if they drop during her lesson?"

"Fifteen grams of carbs and recheck after fifteen minutes," the doctor replied. "Easy to remember."

The appointment concluded with medication adjustments and a follow-up scheduled for six weeks. As they strolled into the hallway, Nathan's phone buzzed again—Richard Barrett's name flashing. After three ignored calls, he couldn't put it off any longer.

"Lily, stay close," he instructed while answering the call. "Richard, I'm at Lily's doctor's appointment. What's the situation?"

As the managing partner launched into drainage issues and county inspectors, Nathan guided Lily to the exit, one hand on her shoulder while his mind split between the conversation and navigating the busy corridor.

"The retention pond design was approved last month," he argued, lowering his voice. "They can't change the requirements now."

Lily moved forward as Nathan slowed his pace, focusing on the phone conversation. The corridor was crowded with medical staff and patients, but he could still see Lily's pink backpack a few steps ahead.

"No, I specifically addressed that in the revised plans," he insisted, frustration mounting. "Page fourteen of the submission clearly shows—"

He looked up just in time to see Lily suddenly stop and place her hand against the wall for support. Her shoulders slumped, and even from behind, he could sense something was wrong. "Richard, I need to go." Nathan rushed forward. "Lily?" He reached her in three quick strides, turning her gently to face him. Her skin was pale, with a slight sheen of sweat across her forehead. "What's happening, sweetheart?"

"I feel funny," she mumbled, her eyes unfocused. "Kind of dizzy."

Nathan pulled out his phone, opening the monitoring app connected to Lily's sensor. The number flashed red— 68 mg/dL with a downward arrow. "You're dropping," he said, already reaching for her backpack where they kept her emergency supplies. He unzipped the front pocket and grabbed the container of glucose chews. His hands weren't quite steady as he twisted the cap. One slipped from his fingers, bouncing across the polished floor.

"Here, take these." He shook three orange-flavored tablets into her palm. "Chew them all, okay?"

She nodded weakly, bringing them to her mouth. Nathan guided her to a nearby bench, then moved to retrieve the fallen tablet. He looked up to find Grace Thompson standing a few feet away, her eyebrows drawn together, crow's feet crinkling as she studied them. "Is everything okay?"

"Lily's blood sugar is low," he explained, straightening. "She'll be fine in a few minutes once these tablets kick in."

Grace approached. She smiled at Lily. "Us dancers must stick together. Mind if I sit with you?"

Lily glanced at Nathan. Nathan nodded, surprised by the relief he felt at her presence. "Please."

She settled beside Lily. "Those orange ones look pretty sour, are they?" she asked with a sympathetic smile.

Lily made a face as she finished chewing. "They taste like medicine trying to be candy."

"I know. I take medicine too," Grace confided, earning a small giggle from the young girl.

Nathan checked the app again—72 mg/dL, with the

arrow now horizontal. "Starting to come up," he said, more to himself than to them.

"Dad was talking about boring water pipes when it happened," Lily explained to Grace, color already returning to her cheeks.

"Drainage systems," Nathan corrected automatically, then winced at how that sounded. "Work emergency. I got distracted."

Grace's expression held no judgment. "It happens. Sickness has its own schedule, regardless of ours."

Her voice eased something tight in Nathan's chest. The shared knowledge felt unexpectedly comforting.

After another five minutes, Lily's reading had climbed to 98 mg/dL. She stretched her legs and declared, "I'm hungry."

"That's a good sign," Nathan said, repacking her supplies. "We should get some real food into you."

Lily's eyes brightened as she looked between him and Grace. "Do you want to have lunch with us? Dad usually lets me have a milkshake if my numbers are too low."

Nathan opened his mouth, surprised by her boldness, but Grace spoke first.

"That's very sweet of you to ask," she said, glancing at Nathan with a quiet questioning in her eyes.

He found himself nodding before he'd fully considered it. "We'd enjoy the company, if you're free."

Nathan's phone buzzed again—Richard, no doubt, wondering why he'd hung up abruptly. He reached for it, finger over the screen, then deliberately hit the power button to silence it.

"Let me just grab my purse," Grace said, rising from the bench.

He extended his hand to help Lily adjust her backpack,

her energy already bouncing back like nothing had happened. "Patio 44 okay with you?" he whispered to his daughter as Grace hurried back to her desk.

Lily looked up at him with a grin. "Is this a special occasion?"

He tightened the strap over her shoulder. "Maybe."

But as they walked to catch up with Grace, his thoughts circled back to his daughter's question—and for the first time in a long while, he hoped it would be.

THIRTY-ONE

Grace followed the hostess behind Nathan and Lily, past the central bar with its hanging blue lights, into the dining room overlooking a sundeck.

"Window seat, please," Nathan requested, his hand protectively on Lily's shoulder.

The restaurant hummed with lunchtime conversation. Professionals in crisp polos and pantsuits mingled with tourists in breezy sundresses and linen shirts. The aroma of garlic and seared fish made Grace's stomach rumble, reminding her that she hadn't eaten breakfast that morning.

Lily pressed her face against the pane, pointing at colorful canopies flying over the gulf. "Look, Daddy. Para-sailing."

Nathan pulled out Grace's chair before she could reach for it.

"Thank you," she murmured, surprised by the courtesy. How long had it been since someone had done something so gentlemanly without the pitying glance that usually accompanied help? As she settled into the cushioned chair, she watched Nathan quickly check his phone, his eyes scanning what must be Lily's blood glucose app.

"Have you been here before?" he asked, seeming satisfied with whatever numbers he'd seen.

"Actually, yes." Grace smoothed her skirt, grateful she'd worn something comfortable yet professional to work that morning. "I used to come here to celebrate after my students' recitals."

Lily's eyes widened. "You had parties here?"

"Small ones." Grace smiled at the memories of happier times. Before the diagnosis, before everything changed. "Just me and the student who performed a solo, sometimes their parents."

"That sounds nice," Nathan said, his voice carrying a note of genuine interest that caught her off guard. She was used to the kind of politeness that barely concealed discomfort. Their server appeared with water glasses. "Welcome to Pier 44. May I take your drink order?"

Nathan leaned over to Lily, studying her menu with focused attention. "Let's see what we've got here, sweetie. The grilled chicken has fifteen carbs, and the mac and cheese has forty-two. Which sounds better to you?"

Grace found herself watching them. The easy way the father navigated his daughter's needs without making it seem like a burden touched something inside her. For the first time since leaving the clinic, she realized her shoulders had relaxed—no fidgeting, no need to keep stiffness at bay—just observing Nathan's and Lily's routine with quiet interest.

The server returned with their drinks—sweet tea for Nathan, a strawberry lemonade for Lily, and sparkling water with lemon for Grace. When she reached for her glass, A tremor ran through her fingers—a subtle yet stubborn reminder of her condition. Before she could withdraw her hand in embarrassment, Nathan casually slid the drink closer to her, his movement so natural it could have been coincidental. He didn't comment. Didn't offer a pitying glance. Just silent understanding that caught her off guard. Most people either ignored her lupus or overcompensated with sympathy. This man did neither.

"Miss Grace, do you know all the ballet positions?" Lily asked, sipping her lemonade through a twisty straw.

"I do." Grace smiled, grateful for the child's straightforward curiosity. No walking on eggshells, no careful avoidance of topics that might remind her of what she'd lost. "There are five basic positions for the feet and arms."

"Can you show me the third one? I keep forgetting."

"Lily," Nathan interjected gently, "maybe now isn't the best time for a demonstration."

"It's fine," Grace assured him. She positioned her arms, pleased when the movement felt more fluid than it had in weeks. The medication adjustments must be working. "Like this. And your feet would be one in front of the other, heels touching."

"Did you know Daddy can't dance at all?" Lily announced with an eleven-year-old's brutal honesty. "Not even a little bit."

Nathan's self-deprecating smile revealed a cute dimple in his right cheek. "Guilty as charged. Two left feet and neither one knows what the other is doing."

Grace laughed without effort for the first time in ages, without thinking about it first. "Dancing isn't about perfection. It's about joy in movement."

"That's what I keep telling him," Lily exclaimed, as if delighted to have an ally.

Their food arrived—fish tacos for Nathan, grilled chicken tenders for Lily, and a grilled shrimp salad for Grace. She noticed how Nathan discreetly checked Lily's plate, making mental calculations before returning to his own meal. The gesture was so similar to her own daily tallies—how many steps she could take, how much energy each task would cost, which medications to take when.

"So, you were a dance instructor for how long?" Nathan asked, squeezing lime over his meal.

"Three years." Grace speared a cucumber slice with her fork. "I opened Grace Ballet Academy after a short stint on Broadway."

Nathan's eyebrows rose. "Broadway? That's impressive."

"Perhaps. But teaching has always been my dream." Grace paused, surprised by her willingness to share. With most people, she kept conversation superficial, tired of the awkward silences that followed disclosures about her condition. "I was on track to really make a difference for young girls, until..." She stopped herself, not wanting to dampen the mood with talk of her diagnosis.

"Until life had other plans?" His tone was more understanding than prying.

Grace met his eyes, finding no pity, just recognition. Recognition of someone who'd also had to adjust to life's unexpected detours. "Exactly."

"Miss Grace, did you ever teach beginners?" Lily asked, dipping a chicken tender into a small pool of ketchup.

"I did. Some of my favorite students were beginners."

"Really." Nathan said, seeing genuinely interested. "What made them your favorites?"

Grace considered the question, appreciating that he'd asked something meaningful rather than the usual "How are you feeling today?" She smiled at Lily. "Their enthusiasm. Their willingness to try without fear of looking silly. And the way they dance with their whole hearts, not just their bodies."

A comfortable silence fell as they ate. Grace found herself watching Nathan interact with his daughter—the way he checked her glucose monitor while she chatted about school, how he asked about the number of carbs on her plate. He didn't hesitate, didn't second-guess himself. Every motion was effortless, like second nature.

The lines around his eyes spoke of worry she recognized all too well. Not just the exhaustion of a bad night's sleep, but something deeper—the kind of weight that didn't lift, only settled in more comfortably over time.

A server pushed through the patio door, letting in a gust of wind that sent napkins fluttering across their table. Grace reached automatically to catch one—her fingers collided with Nathan's as he grabbed for the same napkin. An unexpected warmth spread up her arm, a sensation that had nothing to do with joint pain. She withdrew quickly, as flustered by the pleasant feeling as by the contrast to the discomfort she'd grown accustomed to.

"Sorry," he said with flushed cheeks. His phone buzzed from his pocket. He pulled it out and peeked, furrowing his brow slightly. He returned it without comment, focusing on their conversation rather than whatever message had come through.

"You mentioned adapting techniques for students," Nathan said. "What does that look like?"

Grace set back her shoulders, her joints momentarily forgotten. It had been so long since anyone had asked about her teaching, not her treatment. She felt a spark of the old passion rekindling—the same passion that had carried her through twelve-hour days before her lupus diagnosis. "Everyone deserves to dance in their own way. I've had girls as young as three who mastered the most basic positions."

"Like building a high-rise," Nathan said, lifting his chin slightly. "You pour the foundation, then add steel, brick, and mortar—layer by layer, floor by floor." He exhaled sharply. "Then one day, you're standing on a rooftop."

Grace nodded. "I guess it's the same with ballet. You start with the basics—footwork, posture, rhythm—then build from there. But at some point, it becomes more than just technique. It becomes as natural as walking."

"I wish you were still teaching," Nathan said, his voice carrying a note of something she couldn't quite identify. "For Lily."

Their eyes met across the table, and for a moment, she felt seen—not as a patient, not as a former dancer, but as herself. "Me too. But like diabetes, lupus requires lifestyle changes."

"Lupus?" Nathan's body locked for a heartbeat, ribs rigid, lungs frozen mid-breath. Then, just as fast, the air left him in a slow exhale. "Oh, I'm so sorry."

"No worries," she brushed off his comment with a wave. "I've been living with it for eleven years. So long it's like part of my family."

"Eleven years. That's how long it's been since my wife—"

"Can I have dessert, Daddy?" Lily said as she pushed her plate away, oblivious to their conversation.

Nathan glanced at his watch, his expression shifting. "We should probably head back. I have a few work emergencies."

Grace felt a pang of disappointment. Their lunch was

ending too soon. Had bringing up lupus changed something? It usually did.

"But they have key lime pie," Lily protested, pointing to the dish being delivered to a nearby table.

"Maybe next time," Nathan fixed his gaze on Grace. "How do you feel about a next time?"

The question caught her by surprise. "I'd like that," she replied, the words slipping out before she could analyze them.

Nathan's smile widened. "Good."

The server brought their check, which Nathan immediately took. When Grace reached for her purse, he shook his head. "Please, let me. It's the least I can do after you helped us earlier."

"You don't owe me for that," Grace said softly.

"I know." His eyes held hers. "That's what makes it worth doing."

As they gathered their things, Lily tugged on Grace's sleeve. "Miss Grace, do you think I could be a professional ballerina even with my diabetes?"

Grace knelt to Lily's level, ignoring the protest in her joints. "Some of the best dancers I've known have had challenges to overcome. What matters most is your heart, not your pancreas."

Lily giggled at "pancreas," but her eyes remained serious. "So I could do it?"

"With the right teacher and maintaining your glucose levels? Absolutely."

"See, Daddy?" Lily beamed. "Miss Grace says I can."

Nathan's expression softened as he looked from his daughter to Grace. "Well, if Miss Grace says you can, I suppose we should listen."

Outside the restaurant, the coastal sun glinted harshly,

forcing Grace to shield her eyes. She squinted against the bright glare, wishing she'd brought her sunglasses. Her sensitivity to light was just one more unwelcome gift from her condition.

"Where are you parked?" Nathan asked.

"A block this way," Grace replied, pointing east.

"We're in the other direction. I guess this is where we part ways..." Nathan paused as he pulled out his phone. "Would it be okay if I got your number?"

When was the last time someone asked for her contact information for non-medical reasons? The gradual loss of friends after her diagnosis still stung at times. "Of course," she said, her heart swelling as she recited her number. She watched him enter each digit carefully, his focus reminiscent of how he'd monitored Lily's needs during lunch.

"I'll text you so you'll have mine," he said, tapping the screen.

Her phone buzzed in her purse.

"Thank you for lunch," Grace said. "It was..." She searched for the right word to express what the past hour had meant without sounding overly sentimental, "normal. In the best possible way."

Nathan nodded, understanding in his eyes. "Sometimes normal is the most extraordinary thing we can hope for."

As Grace walked to her car, she realized her condition hadn't dominated her thoughts or conversation. For an hour, she had simply been Grace—not a patient, not a medical record, not a collection of symptoms.

For the first time since her diagnosis, she felt a flutter of something she thought was lost forever—possibility.

She turned back once to see Nathan helping Lily into their SUV, his hand protectively on her head as she climbed in. The sight made Grace's heart twist in a way unrelated to her lupus and entirely connected to the man who balanced so much on his shoulders yet still pulled out her chair.

Later, when she checked her phone, she found a simple message: "Thanks for making today better. —Nathan."

And maybe tomorrow would be a little brighter because of it.

THIRTY-TWO

Six Months Later

"Are you going to keep me guessing all night?" Grace asked.

The Saturday evening traffic on Highway 90 moved steadily as the Biloxi sunset painted the sky in layers of amber and rose. Through the passenger window, the gulf stretched like burnished copper, whitecaps glinting where they caught the fading light.

Nathan gave her a side-eye glance from behind the wheel. "Patience," he said, his voice carrying a playful lilt she'd grown to recognize over the past few months. "We're almost there."

Grace settled back against the leather seat of his SUV, her fingers absently tracing the edge of her phone that she'd recently silenced all notifications. Tonight belonged to them alone.

"Fine," she conceded, watching as he signaled for a turn. "But you should know I've cataloged every restaurant between your house and downtown in my head."

"Is that so?" Nathan raised an eyebrow as they passed

the Hard Rock Hotel, its neon guitar silhouette already glowing against the darkening sky. "And what's your conclusion, Ms. Thompson?"

A flicker of recognition stirred within her as Nathan passed the Beau Rivage. When they turned onto Caillavet Street, the sight of the MGM Park Stadium brought an almost forgotten memory rushing back. The towering structure of the IP Casino grew larger in the windshield, its windows reflecting the sunset in a mosaic of orange and gold. Her throat tightened as the horrible memory materialized.

"Are we...?" she murmured under her breath.

Nathan's expression remained carefully neutral as he guided the SUV into the casino's garage. "Are we what?"

The parking levels muffled the outside world as they ascended, each turn bringing them closer to a destination Grace had sworn never to revisit. Twelve years ago, she had walked out of Thirty-Two restaurant humiliated after abandoning an engagement ring in a wine glass. With each floor they climbed, the ghost of past shame crashed against, despite Nathan's warm presence, her excitement of a romantic evening.

As they stepped through the casino's entrance, a symphony of slot machines and animated conversations bombarded Grace's eardrums. The air carried that distinct blend of perfume, tobacco, and the excitement that casinos cultivated. Twelve years hadn't changed that.

"I've driven past this place a hundred times on my way to one of my projects," Nathan said, his hand finding the small of her back as they navigated through the crowded gaming floor. "But I've never actually been inside."

Grace nodded, grateful for his voice anchoring her to

the present. Each step across the patterned carpet felt heavier than the last.

"Have you been here before?" he asked, glancing at her as they weaved between clusters of gamblers. They passed a roulette table where a crowd erupted in cheers.

"Once," she replied, raising her voice above the revelers. "Seems like a lifetime ago."

They approached the bank of elevators, and Grace's steps faltered slightly. Nathan pressed the call button, then turned to her with a smile. "A client recommended this place," he admitted. "Supposedly the chef does something amazing with sea bass."

The elevator arrived with a soft chime, its polished interior empty. Nathan gestured for her to enter first, then followed, turning to the control panel. He pressed the 32 button.

Grace stiffened slightly, her breath caught somewhere behind her ribs as the elevator began its climb. Each floor was a countdown. The walls seemed to press inward, the air growing thinner.

"Grace?" Nathan's voice tugged her back. He studied her face, concern etched in the tight set of his jaw. "You've gone pale. Are you okay?"

Clutching the handrail behind her, she forced herself to breathe. A voice inside urged her to tell him. Tell him now before her past influences her present. Get everything out in the open before this relationship goes any further.

But Nathan had planned this evening carefully. The tenderness in his eyes as he waited for her response bore no resemblance to her ex-fiancé. This was Nathan—who checked Lily's glucose levels while helping her with homework, who remembered how Grace took her coffee, who listened when she spoke about her love of dance.

"I'm fine," she managed, releasing her grip on the rail. "Just...a little vertigo from the elevator. It'll pass."

Nathan stepped closer, his hand finding hers. "We can go somewhere else if you're not feeling well."

The genuine concern in his voice steadied her. This wasn't twelve years ago. She wasn't the same person who had walked into Thirty-Two restaurant that afternoon, hopeful and desperate to be accepted despite her illness. "No," she said, squeezing his hand. "I'm curious about this sea bass you mentioned earlier."

The elevator slowed as it approached the 32nd floor. Grace took another deep breath, steeling herself against the memories that waited in the dining room.

The doors parted, revealing the restaurant's elegant entrance. Polished hardwood stretched beneath crystal chandeliers. Floor-to-ceiling windows framed the glittering coastline below. The hostess stand was exactly where Grace remembered, with the same discreet logo etched in gold.

Her feet refused to move.

"Grace?" Nathan's voice sounded distant, his hand steady at her forearm, grounding her to the present as the past threatened to drag her under.

A young hostess approached. Her sleek chignon and tailored black dress embodied refined elegance. Her lips curved into a welcoming smile that reached her ebony eyes as she greeted them with professional confidence. "Good evening. Do you have a reservation?"

"Yes, Carter for two," Nathan replied, his eyes still on Grace.

The young woman consulted her screen. "Of course, Mr. Carter. We have your table ready. Please follow me."

Nathan's thumb traced a small circle against Grace's arm and extended his elbow. "May I?" he asked.

She nodded, unable to form words as they followed the hostess through the dining room. Each step felt like moving against a high tide. The tables were arranged differently now. Small mercies.

"Is this suitable?" the hostess asked, gesturing to the pristine white tablecloth and the panoramic view of Biloxi, Back Bay, and the coastline.

"It's perfect," Nathan said, pulling out Grace's chair.

Grace lowered herself into the seat, her fingers trembling slightly as the hostess spread a napkin across her lap. The table setting hadn't changed—the same as the day Andrew ended everything. The same silverware set in perfect symmetry. The same crystal glasses catching the light like nothing ever went wrong here. Everything the same except for the man who sat across the table. He kept proving to be different from Andrew in every possible way.

Nathan's eyes widened as he took in the coastline. "Wow. They weren't exaggerating about the view."

"No," Grace managed. "It's quite breathtaking."

A server in a crisp white button-down, black bow tie, black dress pants, black waistcoat, and glossy black patent shoes appeared with water and menus, explaining the evening's special. Grace heard none of it. Her eyes kept drifting to the area where Andrew had explained how her lupus would be too much of a setback for his life's plans.

When the server departed, Nathan reached across the table and gently touched her hand. "You haven't been okay since we got in the elevator. What's going on?"

The concern in his eyes disarmed her. She took a breath she hadn't realized she'd been holding. "The last time I was here," she said quietly, "was twelve years ago. With Andrew."

Nathan's expression shifted from concern to confusion. "The man you were to marry?"

"Yes." She stared out where the sea met the sky, a blaze of molten gold and bruised lavender. "This is where he ended our engagement after he'd learned I have lupus."

Understanding dawned in Nathan's eyes. Then dismay. "Grace, I had no idea. Why didn't you say something in the elevator? We could have gone anywhere else."

"You seemed so excited about this place." She managed a small smile. "And I didn't want to ruin your surprise."

Nathan shook his head, his hand tightening around hers. "I would never want to bring you somewhere that holds painful memories. We can leave right now."

The immediate offer—so different from Andrew's insistence on controlling every situation—made her pause. She looked at Nathan, really looked at him. Where Andrew had always dominated conversations, Nathan waited patiently for her to continue. Where Andrew had criticized her choices, Nathan's eyes held only support. His presence somehow made her feel both protected and strong.

"Actually," she said, surprising herself, "I think I'd like to stay."

"Are you sure?"

She nodded, more certain with each passing second. "This place has held enough power over me. I've spent four years avoiding it, letting that afternoon define it. Maybe it's time to create a new memory here."

Nathan's smile spread slowly across his face. "I'd be honored to help with that."

While he studied the menu, still lacing his fingers with hers, something unlatched inside Grace. Andrew walking away no longer felt like a tragedy. It was—unexpectedly, undeniably—a blessing.

"So," she said, opening her own menu with her free hand, "are you joining me in ordering the sea bass?"

THIRTY-THREE

What if this is too much? We should've texted first about coming with takeout and a movie...

Nathan stood outside Grace's dance studio, the glow of her upstairs apartment window spilling onto the sidewalk. A takeout bag from Shaggy's dangled from his left hand while he held Lily's with the right. When Grace had called to cancel their weekly Friday dinner because of a lupus flare, the disappointment in her voice had been unmistakable. He knew those episodes well enough by now—the fatigue, the rash, the joint pain that made simple movements a struggle.

"Are you sure Miss Grace won't mind us surprising her?" he asked Lily, not for the first time since they'd left the restaurant.

"Dad," Lily rolled her eyes with all the exasperation a ten-year-old could muster. "You said she sounded so sad about missing dinner. And you said yourself she probably hasn't eaten anything good all day."

Nathan shifted the takeout bags from Shaggy's beachfront restaurant, warmth seeping through the brown bags against his thigh. He'd ordered all of Grace's favorites—blackened redfish, sweet potato fries, and Caesar salads. But what if she really just wanted to be alone? What if he was overstepping?

"I'm going to warn her," he said, reaching for his phone.

But Lily bounded up the steps to the side entrance that led to Grace's apartment.

"Lily, wait," he called, but it was too late to stop her.

The chime echoed faintly through the door, and Nathan's stomach tightened. There was no turning back now. He hurried up the steps to join his daughter, hoping Grace wouldn't mind their impromptu dinner delivery.

The door opened, and there stood Grace, wrapped in a soft gray cardigan over yoga pants. Her hair was pulled back in a messy bun, and despite the faint redness across her cheeks, her eyes widened with genuine surprise.

"Nathan? Lily? What are you doing here?"

"We brought dinner!" Lily announced, bouncing on her toes. "Dad said you weren't feeling good, so we brought a movie too!"

Grace's expression shifted from surprise to something softer. "I...uh...you didn't have to do that."

"We wanted to," he said, lifting the bags slightly. "But if it's a bad time..."

"No, no," Grace stepped back, opening the door wider. "Come in. I'm just...not exactly dressed for company."

"You look wonderful," Nathan said, then felt heat rise to his face. "I mean—comfortable. Which is good when you're not feeling well."

Grace's small apartment was exactly what he'd imagined—compact but thoughtfully arranged, with a few dance photos over a cabinet with a turntable and a bookshelf holding an assortment of books and vinyl albums. The scent of lavender hung in the air, mingling with something medicinal.

"I was just about to heat up some soup," Grace said, gesturing toward the kitchenette where a can of Campbell's sat unopened on the counter.

"Well, now you don't have to," Lily declared, already heading for the small dining table by the window. "Dad got your favorite—blackened redfish."

"With extra butter and lemon, just how you like it," Nathan added, setting the bags down.

Grace tucked a loose strand of hair behind her ear. "You remembered that?"

"Of course." He began unpacking the containers while Lily chattered about her day at school, the words flying out as she arranged napkins and plastic utensils. "—and then my friend said her mom might let her take dance lessons too. I told her you used to be the best teacher ever—even though I never got to take lessons from you."

The tension drained from Nathan's shoulders. There was no strain in Grace's expression, though she moved carefully—favoring her right side—as she settled at the table.

As they ate, Nathan caught sight of a framed photograph on the bookshelf—Grace frozen in a mid air, her white costume brilliant against the stage darkness, her body stretched in a flawless horizontal line high above the floor.

"Juilliard's spring showcase, my junior year," Grace said after following his gaze. t me."

"You look amazing," Nathan said before continuing. "You are amazing."

Grace's eyes met his, something vulnerable flickering there. "Some days it's hard to remember what that felt like."

"I get that," he said, surprising himself. "Work called yesterday. They're giving the partnership to Brad Jacobs."

"The promotion you were up for?" Grace asked, setting her fork down.

Nathan glanced at Lily, who happily dipped a sweet potato fry in ketchup. "Yeah. Richard said I wasn't showing enough 'commitment to the firm's growth objectives.'"

"That's ridiculous," Grace said. "After all the extra hours you've put in."

"Extra hours that weren't enough, apparently." He shrugged. "Richard needs someone who can travel more, work weekends."

"But you have Lily to think about."

"Exactly." Nathan took a sip of his water. "It stings, but I knew what I was choosing."

"Still allowed to be disappointed," Grace said, her voice gentle.

"What are you guys talking about?" Lily asked, looking up from her plate.

"Grown-up work stuff," Nathan said. "Nothing important."

"Dad didn't get the big promotion," Grace explained, more directly. "Because his boss wanted him to work all the time."

Lily frowned. "That's not fair."

"It's okay, kiddo," Nathan said. "Some things matter more than work."

"Like what?" Lily asked.

Nathan met Grace's eyes across the table. "Like being there for the people who count on you."

Something unspoken passed between them—a recognition that went beyond words.

"Can I use your bathroom?" Lily asked after eating the last bite of her redfish.

Grace pointed toward a door just outside the kitchen area. "Right in there, sweetie."

As soon as Lily disappeared, Nathan leaned forward, lowering his voice. "Thanks for not making a big deal about the promotion in front of her. She already worries too much about being a 'burden.'"

"She said that?" Grace's brow bunched in the middle.

"Not in those words." Nathan pushed his plate aside. "But after Hannah died, everything changed. One day I had a plan—career, family, the usual dreams. The next, I was raising my daughter alone, trying to figure out daycare and pigtails."

Grace's shoulders fell. "And then her diagnosis."

"Yeah." Nathan glanced at the bathroom door. "The diabetes added a whole new layer. Blood sugar checks, insulin calculations, emergency kits everywhere." He rubbed the back of his neck. "Some days I wonder if I'm failing both her and my job."

"I think you're doing better than you give yourself credit for," Grace said, reaching across to touch his hand briefly. "Lily's amazing. Happy, smart, confident."

"She is, isn't she?" He drew a deep breath. "But there are days when I'm so focused on her numbers and carb counts that I forget to just be her dad, you know?"

Grace nodded, the lines on her forehead smoothing away. "Balance is hard when health is involved. I had to close my business because I couldn't find it."

The mention of her dance school opened a door Nathan had been careful not to push through. "Was that when you got diagnosed?"

"Shortly after." Grace traced the rim of her water glass. "I had this whole life planned out too. The studio was grow-ing, I was engaged to Andrew, who asked for his engagement ring back after I told him about my diagnosis. Apparently, he didn't want to test that 'in sickness and in health' clause in the marriage contract."

Nathan tightened his jaw. "What a jackass."

Grace's laugh was genuine. "That's one word for him. He said he 'couldn't risk tying his future to someone with such uncertain health prospects.'" She mimicked a pompous tone. "His family had 'expectations' about the kind of wife he should have."

"Their loss," Nathan said, voice low but with conviction. "Big time."

"Maybe." Grace looked down at her hands. "But it was mine too. The stress triggered a massive flare. I couldn't teach, couldn't demonstrate. Students started dropping out. Medical bills piled up. Eventually, I had to close."

"I'm sorry," Nathan said, wishing the words weren't so inadequate.

"It's funny, though" Grace continued, her voice steadier now. "I spent so long being angry at my body for betraying me. But in some ways, the lupus saved me from marrying someone who would have eventually made me miserable."

The bathroom door opened, and Lily emerged. "Miss Grace, your soap smells like cookies."

"Vanilla and almond," Grace said, her expression changing seamlessly back to warmth. "My favorite."

The shift in Grace's demeanor was like stepping from shadow into sunlight—effortless, radiant, and a little awe-inspiring. How did she do that? One moment her eyes had held a look that revealed a past torment—the next, all warmth and presence for Lily. Unlike his own ghosts that he fought to keep at bay, Grace seemed to carry hers with a quiet acknowledgment that never diminished her capacity for joy.

"Dad, let's watch the movie," Lily said, climbing back into her chair.

"If Miss Grace is feeling up to it," Nathan said, studying Grace's face for signs of fatigue.

She smiled. A genuine smile, not fake or forced to be polite. "Well, let's see what you brought."

"Enchanted!" Grace exclaimed, holding up the DVD Lily had pulled from her backpack. "I love this one."

"Me too!" Grace beamed.

"Dad says the songs are too corny and there's not enough action."

"Men have no heart when it comes to movies," Grace said with a wink at Nathan.

They settled into Grace's small living area—Lily sprawled on her stomach on the floor with a pillow under her chin, while Nathan and Grace took the loveseat. The only other seating option was a rocking chair that looked like an antique, its cushion embroidered with ballet slippers.

As the movie began, Nathan found himself more aware of Grace beside him than the story unfolding on screen. The loveseat wasn't large, and their shoulders occasionally brushed when either of them shifted position. He relished how she tucked her feet beneath her and smiled at the scenes, the quiet laugh that escaped her when something particularly amusing happened.

Patrick Dempsey's character appeared on screen—the cynical divorce lawyer who didn't believe in fairy tales.

Nathan shifted slightly, the parallel not lost on him as he remembered Grace's earlier words about her ex.

Suddenly, the princess was singing about true love in Central Park, drawing crowds of strangers into her impromptu musical number.

Nathan thought about Hannah—how they'd fought

sometimes, loved fiercely, built a life that wasn't perfect but was genuinely theirs. He couldn't imagine reducing her to a line item in a career strategy.

Without thinking, he placed his hand palm-up on the cushion between them. An invitation, not a demand.

After a moment, Grace's fingers slid into his. The touch was light, tentative at first, then settling with quiet certainty.

"Had you called first, I would have asked you not to come," Grace whispered, leaning close enough that her warm breath brushed his ear. "But now that you're both here, I couldn't have asked for a better evening."

Something expanded in Nathan's chest—not just attraction, though that was certainly there, but a deeper recognition. Grace understood what mattered to him. She saw his choices not as career failures but as priorities correctly ordered.

On the floor, Lily giggled at the movie, completely unaware of what unfolded behind her. Nathan squeezed Grace's hand gently, feeling the delicate bones beneath her skin, the quiet weakness in her fingers.

For the first time since Hannah died, he didn't feel like he was failing at balancing his roles as father and provider. Instead, sitting here with Grace's hand in his, watching his daughter laugh at a silly movie after the three of them shared a meal, there was a sense that he was exactly where he was supposed to be and who he was supposed to be with.

And for the first time in a long time, he looked forward to tomorrow.

THIRTY-FOUR

One Year Later

Grace inserted her key into the studio's front door, the lock catching as if the building itself resisted her return. The hollow echo in the vacant space was a ghost of her past life as a dance instructor. Afternoon sunlight slanted through the windows, cutting across the hardwood floor where dozens of little feet used to practice pliés and relevés. Empty barres lined the walls, a thin layer of dust now covering the polished wood where eager hands once balanced young dancers. It had been six years since she'd closed Grace Ballet Academy, and still, her chest tightened at the loss. But she needed to keep today a good day. Her discomfort was minimal, and she was excited about the evening she had planned. Dinner at Nathan's. A movie with him and Lily afterward. No stress. No flare-ups. That was the plan. The key lime pie from Pelican Bakery that Lily loved was in her car, purchased during her break at the clinic. She wasn't staying here long. Just in and out to change her clothes and grab the mail.

She emptied the slot, flipping through the usual stack—

flyers, bills—until her fingers hit something thicker. Stiffer. The manila envelope with her bank's logo made her pause. Bills she expected, but an official correspondence rarely brought good news. The world around her went still. The studio's temperature seemed to drop ten degrees. Her breath caught, and for a second, she couldn't move. The letter grew heavier in her hand. Open it now or later? The lupus had been in relative remission these past few weeks— a blessing she'd attributed to the stability Nathan and Lily had brought to her life. Stress was her worst trigger, and right now, this envelope threatened to unleash a flood of it.

With a slow measured breath, she slid her finger under the envelope's seal. Better to know now than worry about it all evening. Her eyes immediately caught the bold red "NOTICE OF SEIZURE" on the cover page. "Oh no," she whispered, scanning through the legal jargon for the critical details. "Due to a judgment for unpaid debts, First Gulf Bank will proceed with seizing the property at 1422 Harbor Drive unless payment of $15,000 is received within 30 days of this notice..."

Leaning against the open front door, her knees suddenly weakened. Fifteen thousand dollars. In thirty days. The amount might as well have been fifteen million. Her clinic job barely covered her medical copays, groceries, and utilities. A sharp pain radiated through her wrists and up her forearms—her body's immediate response to stress. She took a deep breath, trying to implement the techniques Dr. Winters had taught her. Four counts in. Hold for seven. Eight counts out.

The studio had been her dream—her identity—before lupus had stolen her ability to dance. Teaching had been her life's mission, ballet her life's passion. When the symptoms had grown too severe to demonstrate proper technique, she'd closed the academy, but she'd never been able to bring herself to sell the property. Instead, she hoped against reality to someday reopen.

Her phone chimed with a text. Nathan—"Chicken Piccata is simmering and Lily's setting the table. Can't wait to see you." The message included a photo of Lily, grinning proudly beside a table set with the good dishes, a hand-colored place card propped against each plate.

Friday night dinners had become their ritual over the past few months—a bright spot in her week that she looked forward to with growing anticipation. The easy comfort of being with Nathan and Lily was the only happiness she'd known since her diagnosis. But now, seeing Lily's excited face, Grace felt the weight of what she might lose. Not just the studio, but the stability that had brought such peace to her life. How could she walk into their warm home carrying this burden? How could she smile and laugh and pretend everything was fine when her world was crumbling?

Grace glanced at her watch. If she didn't leave now she'd be late. She moved to the studio office. Dust coated everything, evidence of her failure. A framed photo still hung crookedly on the wall—Grace with Emma Chen after her first solo performance, both beaming with pride. Emma's transformation from terrified student to confident performer brought a smile to Grace's face, even now.

She dialed Melissa, her former business manager.

"Grace. Hey there," Melissa answered cheerfully. "Been a minute."

"The bank is seizing my studio," Grace said, her voice cracking. "I need fifteen thousand dollars in thirty days or I lose everything."

"Oh no," Melissa paused for several beats. "But I hate to say I saw this coming..."

"I know, I know. You've been telling me to sell for six years."

"Because it makes financial sense," Melissa said. "And have you seen what's happening in that neighborhood? Property values have skyrocketed. That developer built those luxury condos across the street, and now every building in a three-block radius has tripled in value."

Grace frowned. "So, what do I do?"

"You sell now. You could not only cover what you owe the bank but probably clear enough to pay off most of your medical debt too."

Grace's gaze drifted to the window, where she could see the gleaming glass towers of the new development. She'd been so focused on what she'd lost that she hadn't noticed the neighborhood transforming around her.

"There's a real estate brochure in my mail," she said, pulling out the glossy trifold. "Century 21."

"Call them. Tomorrow," Melissa said firmly. "But Grace? You need to be prepared to let the studio go."

Let the studio go. The words stayed with her after she hung up. Selling meant admitting the studio would never reopen. That the dream was truly over.

Her phone buzzed with another message from Nathan. "Everything okay? You're usually here by now."

Grace stared at the screen, her thumb hovering over the keyboard. Nathan and Lily were waiting for her. They'd prepared dinner, set the table with care, made Friday night special like they always did. She thought of Lily's hand-colored place cards, of Nathan's patient smile, of the way they'd both made space for her in their lives despite her limitations.

She couldn't bring this burden to their table—not yet. But she was tired of carrying things alone.

She glanced at the letter again, its red headline stark against the white page.

NOTICE OF SEIZURE.

She closed her eyes, drew a steady breath. Four counts in. Hold for seven. Eight counts out.

She would go to dinner. She would smile, eat key lime pie, ask Lily about her art project, listen to Nathan talk about next week's recipe . She would hold onto that joy.

And afterward, she would tell him. Not because she wanted to. Because she had to.

She picked up the envelope and tucked it into her bag, then wiped the dust from the framed photo of Emma and herself. Her past would always matter—but she was still writing her future.

As she locked the studio behind her, the late sun caught the glass of the condos across the street. For the first time, she really saw them.

Then she turned toward her car.

NATHAN ADJUSTED the vase of fresh tulips—Grace's favorite—making sure the small velvet box remained hidden behind the blooms. He stepped back, surveying the dining room table with a critical eye. The good china gleamed under the soft chandelier light, which he'd dimmed just enough to make the candles' warm glow the focal point. Lily's handmade place cards and carefully folded napkins added a touch of homey charm.

"Is it time yet?" Lily bounced into the room, her special occasion dress—a pale pink number with tiny silver stars—swishing around her knees. At twelve years old, she carried herself with the solemn importance of someone entrusted with a great secret.

"Almost, sweetheart." He checked his watch. "She should be here any minute."

"Can I see the ring again?" Lily whispered, though they were alone in the house.

Glancing toward the front window in search of Grace's headlight, he carefully extracted the box from behind the flowers. He opened it to reveal the princess-cut diamond set in white gold, simple and elegant—just like Grace.

"Do you think she'll like it?" he asked, a flutter of nervousness in his stomach that surprised him. After one year together, he knew this woman better than anyone save Lily and Hannah, yet this moment felt monumental.

"She's gonna cry happy tears," Lily declared with the certainty only children possess. "Like she does during those movies she loves watching."

Nathan chuckled, tucking the box back into its hiding place. "Let's hope so. Now, what does Dad need to remember tonight?"

Lily straightened, taking her role as proposal co-conspirator seriously. "Don't put the ring in food or drinks. That's dangerous and gross."

"And?"

"Wait until after the main course but before dessert."

"And..."

She tapped her chin thoughtfully, "Oh. I'm supposed to say I'm tired and go to my room when you give me the signal."

"Exactly." He held up his hand for a high-five, which Lily enthusiastically returned. "How's your number looking?"

Lily automatically reached for the Dexcom reader in

her dress pocket, a habit as natural to her now as breathing. "One-twenty-seven. Green arrow."

"Good job managing today." Nathan squeezed her shoulder, pride swelling in his chest. The daily vigilance of diabetes management was now their normal, but he never took for granted how well Lily had adapted.

The timer on his phone chimed softly. "Time to check the chicken."

As he moved to the kitchen, Lily trailing behind, he felt a strange sense of everything coming full circle. After Hannah had died he couldn't have imagined finding love again. Now, he couldn't imagine life without Grace—her steady presence during Lily's hospital stays, her laughter filling their home, the way she'd seamlessly become part of their family routines. Tonight would make it official.

After dinner, he would ask Grace to be his wife, to make their Friday night dinners a permanent arrangement. Lily was thrilled about the prospect of Grace becoming her step-mom. It was what he wanted. The timing was right. Nothing could possibly go wrong.

His phone buzzed with a text. Grace—"Running a few minutes late. Bringing key lime pie. Sorry."

Nathan smiled, typing back a quick response. A slight delay wouldn't derail his plans. He had waited six months to ask this question—he could wait a few minutes more.

"Dad, she's twenty minutes late now," Lily announced, peering through the front window curtains for the fifth time.

"She's coming," he assured her, adjusting the temperature on the oven to keep the chicken warm. "She texted that she's running a little late."

"There she is," Lily said with no constrained excitement.

Nathan's heart skipped a beat as he heard Grace's car door slam outside. He smoothed his shirt and checked his reflection in the hallway mirror. "Remember, act normal. It's just a regular Friday dinner until I give the signal."

"I know, Dad," Lily rolled her eyes with the exasperation only she could muster. "I can keep a secret."

The doorbell rang, and Lily rushed to answer it while Nathan lit the candles with hands that weren't quite steady. After a year of dating, Grace still made him feel like a teenager sometimes.

"Miss Grace." Lily's excited voice echoed from the entryway. "You look so pretty."

"Thank you, sweetie. So do you. Why are you so dressed up?"

Nathan rounded the corner to see his prospective fiancée kneeling to admire his daughter's outfit, a store-bought key lime pie balanced in one hand. Her hair was slightly windblown, and there was something in her eyes—a tightness around the edges—that immediately caught his attention.

"Hey," he said softly, leaning in to kiss her cheek. "Everything okay?"

"Fine," Grace said quickly, standing. "Sorry I'm late. I got delayed at the studio."

Nathan noted how she avoided direct eye contact. "No worries. Dinner's ready whenever you are."

As Grace moved past him to the dining room, he caught the floral scent of her perfume—the same one she'd worn on their first date.

"Wow, Nathan," Grace paused at the entrance, taking in the candles, flowers, and elaborate place settings. "This is...fancy for a Friday. What's the occasion?"

"Can't a guy make a nice dinner for his two favorite people?" he deflected, setting the pie on the sideboard.

Grace smiled, but her gaze lingered too long like she'd heard something that didn't quite add up. "Of course. It's beautiful."

Lily bounced in her chair. "Dad made calamari appetizers."

"Yum," Grace said, settling into her usual seat. She shakily placed her napkin in her lap, her fingers twisting, creasing the fabric while her gaze seemed fixed on something far beyond the dining room.

He plated the appetizers, eyeing Grace and the tension in her shoulders he recognized from the early days of their relationship. She jumped slightly when he touched her shoulder, then overcompensated with a too-bright smile. Something was definitely off.

"Wine?" he offered, holding up the bottle of Sancerre she preferred.

"Please," she nodded. "But just a small glass."

Conversation flowed haltingly through the first course. Grace asked Lily about school and responded appropriately to Nathan's questions about her day, but her mind seemed elsewhere. She kept glancing at her phone, though it hadn't buzzed, and twice she caught herself mid-sentence, as if losing her train of thought.

Nathan had just finished serving the chicken piccata, his mother's specialty, when he noticed she'd barely touched the calamari.

"You're not hungry?" He slid into his seat across from her. "Or is something wrong?"

"I'm okay," Grace said quickly, spearing a piece and taking a dutiful bite.

He exchanged a glance with Lily, who shrugged before

digging into her own meal. Something was definitely off. Grace had arrived fifteen minutes late, flustered and apologetic, clutching the key lime pie like a shield. She'd kissed him briefly, complimented the table setting, but seemed distracted throughout their usual pre-dinner ritual.

"Tell me about your day," he said, passing the vegetables.

Grace's hand trembled slightly as she accepted it. "Nothing much to tell. Just the usual Friday chaos at the hospital." She looked away, then added, too quickly, "Tell me about yours, Lily."

Lily launched into a story about her science project, filling the silence. Nathan watched Grace nod and smile at appropriate moments, but her mind was clearly elsewhere. When she reached for her water glass and nearly knocked it over, he decided enough was enough.

"Lil," he said during a pause in her story, "why don't you go wash your hands again before the main course?"

Lily looked between them, wise beyond her years. "Okay, Dad." She slid from her chair and disappeared down the hallway.

Reaching across the table, he gently took Grace's hand. "What's going on, Grace?"

"Nothing, I'm just tired." She attempted a smile that failed to land.

"Hey," he squeezed her fingers, "I know you better than that. Something's bothering you."

Her eyes suddenly welled with tears. She blinked rapidly, looking away. Alarm bells rang in Nathan's head. In two years, he'd rarely seen her cry.

"Grace?"

"I'm sorry," she whispered, pulling her hand away to wipe at her eyes. "I didn't want to ruin our evening."

"You could never ruin anything," he said gently. "Talk to me."

She took a shaky breath. "I found a seizure notice today. For my studio."

"Your studio?" he asked. "Oh, Grace, I'm so sorry."

Tears flooded her eyes. "In the mail. I almost missed it. Oh, Nathan, I can't believe this is happening."

He squeezed her hand. In a lot of ways, that studio was her connection to her life's passion. Instead of selling, which would have been financially optimal, she'd kept the building as her home. "How long have you been dealing with this?"

"I've been ignoring the late notices on my medical bills for weeks now," she said, her voice cracking. "I know it was wrong, but I'd been feeling so good lately, I didn't want the stress to disrupt my health."

Nathan moved his chair closer and extended his arm around her shoulder. "What's the timeline?"

"Thirty days according to the notice," Grace said, wiping her eyes with her napkin. "I haven't called the collector yet."

"That's something we can fight together," he said, his mind already working through solutions. "You won't lose your studio. We'll get this straightened out."

"I can't ask you to do that." Grace's shoulders slumped. "It's a problem I've been dealing with since before we started seeing one another."

"So. You know how I feel about you. And I know that building means everything to you. It's not just your home, but you have tons of memories there. It's part of who you are. Part of why I love you."

Reaching out from her chair, she wrapped her arms around Nathan's neck. "I don't deserve you."

"Hey," Nathan squeezed her hand. "First thing

Monday morning, we'll go to my bank. We'll take out a loan with me on the paperwork. You're not losing your studio."

Grace looked up at him, vulnerability and gratitude mingling in her expression. "We?"

"Of course, we." Nathan smiled softly. "Your problems are my problems. That's how this works."

"How what works?"

Nathan momentarily glanced at the flower arrangement hiding the ring. Should he ask her now? Right now? Grace wiped her eyes, then looked around. "Where's Lily? She's been gone a while."

The moment hung between them, heavy with unspoken words. Nathan felt the weight of the ring box behind the tulips, the carefully planned proposal now seeming impossible with Grace's world crumbling around her. How could he ask her to marry him when she was facing the loss of everything that mattered to her? The timing felt wrong, selfish even.

He cleared his throat, pushing down the disappointment. "I should check on her."

Nathan pictured his daughter listening in the hallway, waiting for his big question. But as the silence stretched, a different kind of concern began to creep in. "Lily?" he called out.

No response.

"Lily?" He said it louder this time, his voice echoing through the house.

Still nothing.

Grace's expression shifted from confusion to worry. "Lily?"

Nathan jumped to his feet, the dining room chair scraping against the hardwood floor. His footsteps echoed in the hallway as he moved toward the back of the house. "Lily?"

"Bathroom, maybe?" Grace said close behind him, her heels clicking rapidly on the tile.

He rapped hard on the bathroom door, the sound sharp in the sudden quiet. "Sweetheart? Are you in there?"

No answer.

He twisted the handle, and the door swung open. Lily lay slumped against the bathtub, her small body crumpled on the cool tile floor, the pink dress with silver stars now wrinkled and twisted around her legs.

"Lily." Nathan dropped to his knees, the hard floor biting into his kneecaps as his hands shook, reaching for her. Her skin was warm and clammy, slick with perspiration. Her chest rose and fell in shallow, irregular breaths.

Grace crouched beside them, her knees hitting the tile with a soft thud as she snatched up the Dexcom reader that had fallen from Lily's pocket. "Blood sugar's 180," she said, but her voice carried uncertainty.

Nathan gently tapped Lily's cheek, feeling the heat radiating from her flushed skin. "Lily? Can you hear me, baby girl?"

Grace placed two fingers across Lily's wrist. "Her pulse is rapid." She laid her palm on Lily's forehead, frowning at the intense heat. "And she's burning up."

"That would mess with her readings." Nathan asked, panic clawing in his gut as he scooped Lily into his arms. Her body felt unnaturally light, and her head lolled against his shoulder.

Grace was already moving toward the kitchen, her footsteps quick and purposeful. "I'll get the backup meter."

Nathan carried Lily to the couch, feeling the fever's heat seeping through his shirt. Her breathing was too shallow, too fast. His mind spiraled through every worst-case scenario as he settled her limp form against the cushions.

The finger-stick test confirmed it—Lily's blood sugar wasn't 180. It was 340 and climbing.

"Sensor's failing," Grace said, already prepping an insulin dose with steady hands. The tremor that had plagued her all evening was gone, replaced by the fierce precision Nathan had seen during Lily's worst episodes. "Her breathing's too shallow."

"We're not managing this at home." Nathan stood, gathering Lily's fevered body close to his chest again. Her weight felt both precious and terrifying. "Let's get her to the ER."

Grace was already grabbing her car keys from the counter, the metal jangling in her grip. "I'll drive—you monitor her."

The warmth from Lily's fever spread across Nathan's chest as he held her tight. "I need her emergency bag."

"Got it." Grace hoisted the backpack over her shoulder and yanked the door open, cool night air rushing in.

They rushed to the car, leaving behind the elaborate dinner, the candlelight producing dancing shadows on their half-eaten dinner, and the engagement ring tucked inside the centerpiece's tallest tulip.

Nathan slid into the backseat, cradling Lily's small form in his lap. Her dress was damp with sweat, and her breathing had become more labored. Fear churned through him, but so did something else—gratitude. Gratitude for the woman who, even while her life was unraveling, had shifted seamlessly from needing support to providing it.

The car engine roared to life, and Grace's hands gripped the steering wheel tightly. In the rearview mirror,

Nathan caught her watching him, her jaw set with determination.

The proposal could wait. What mattered most was that they were facing this crisis together, supporting each other when it counted.

She navigated toward the hospital with calm precision, the familiar route allowing her to focus on speed rather than direction. Lily's small chest rose and fell in an irregular pattern against Nathan's arm, sending fresh spikes of fear through him.

"She's getting worse," he said, his voice tight as he checked the backup glucose meter again. The digital numbers glowed ominously in the dark car. "And her sugar's still rising."

A flash of Grace's expression in the mirror drew Nathan's attention—her eyes widened, her jaw clenched as she processed the information. The car accelerated, weaving smoothly through traffic with practiced urgency.

"We're eight minutes out. Talk to her, Nathan."

As he whispered encouragement to his unconscious daughter, Lily stirred weakly in his arms. Her eyes fluttered open momentarily, unfocused and glazed, before rolling back. That distant look—the same expression he'd seen on Hannah's face in her final weeks—sent a chill through him despite the fever radiating from Lily's body.

The glucose meter beeped again, its sound sharp in the confines of the car. Grace pressed harder on the accelerator, the engine's hum growing more urgent as they whooshed past stopped traffic and ran a red light.

The hospital was still nowhere in sight.

Nathan clutched Lily closer, feeling her ribs expand and contract too rapidly beneath his palms. "Stay with me,

Lil," he pleaded softly, his voice barely audible over the rush of wind and engine noise. "Stay with me."

THIRTY-FIVE

"Jesus, please," Nathan prayed for the first time since Hannah's death, his gaze fixed on the emergency room's double doors. "Please don't take her too."

It had been two hours since he and Grace rushed his daughter here, her small body limp and cold, her glucose levels dangerously high. The overhead lights flooded the waiting room with the same sickly hue he remembered from eleven years ago. He glanced at his phone. Three missed calls from his mother. Four from Rachel. All straight to voicemail. His frantic text to his sister sparking the calls— "With Lily at the ER. It's serious."

"Here." Grace's soft voice broke through as she slipped next to him, offering a paper cup of water. "You need to drink something."

He took it but didn't sip, his throat too tight. "Thanks for driving us," he said, the words feeling inadequate as flashes of the drive replayed in his mind—Grace's steady hands on the wheel while he cradled Lily in the backseat, her calm voice as she called ahead to the hospital despite the chaos swirling around them.

"Any word?" she asked, glancing toward the nurses' station.

"Nothing," he said with venom. "Just like with Hannah. They take her away, and then...nothing."

Grace's hand found his arm, grounding him in the moment. "Let me check again. Kelly's on shift—she'll have updates."

Nathan watched as Grace approached the counter. Unlike his earlier frantic questioning, she moved with purpose, her posture composed and assured. The nurse recognized her immediately. Grace spoke in low tones—too quiet for him to hear—but he caught the nod of acknowledgment from Kelly, the promise of information sealed with a phone call.

Nathan's legs ached from pacing, but he couldn't sit—not while Lily was behind those doors, unprotected.

Grace returned, her expression steady. "They're running more tests. Dr. Montgomery is overseeing everything."

"Hannah's doctor." The words slipped out, hollow and heavy. "She told me there was nothing more they could do before Hannah died."

Grace's calm demeanor gleamed. She took his hand, her cool fingers wrapping around his clammy palm. "This is different, Nathan. Lily is different."

"Is it?" He pulled his hand away, frustration bubbling. "The symptoms started the same way. I should have noticed sooner."

"You got her here," Grace countered firmly. "You did everything right."

The double doors swung open, and a nurse stepped out, clipboard in hand. "Mr. Carter?"

Nathan's heart raced. Grace moved closer.

"Dr. Montgomery would like to speak with you about Lily's condition," the nurse said. "If you'll follow me."

Grace's hand brushed his elbow. "Do you want me to come with you?"

Nathan hesitated, then nodded. "Please." He couldn't face this alone—not again.

The nurse led them down the corridor. Grace's fingers entwined with his, providing an anchor in the storm of his fears. They entered a small consultation room.

"Dr. Montgomery will be right with you," the nurse said, shutting the door behind them.

Nathan felt frozen. He couldn't sit. He wouldn't move.

Grace simply stood by his side, a solid presence amidst the chaos, offering him strength without words.

"I can't lose her too," he whispered, the weight of his despair crashing over him.

"I know." Grace's voice was quiet yet firm—two simple words that somehow held deep understanding.

The door swung open, and Dr. Montgomery entered, her demeanor grave enough to twist Nathan's stomach. The same expression she'd worn the night Hannah died.

"Nathan," Dr. Montgomery said with compassion. She extended her hand, nodding at Grace with a warm smile of recognition. "Grace."

"How is Lily?" Grace asked, her voice steady as she shook the doctor's hand.

"Please, sit." Dr. Montgomery gestured to the chairs.

Nathan hesitated, unable to move until Grace nudged him gently into a seat next to her.

"We've stabilized her blood sugar," Dr. Montgomery began, "but I'm concerned about some other numbers."

Desperate for support, Nathan squeezed Grace's hand tighter.

"What other numbers?" he said barely above a murmur.

Dr. Montgomery raised her clipboard. "Lily's creatinine levels are elevated, and we're seeing proteins in her urine. Both are indicators of—"

"Kidney function," he finished for her, his heart sinking as memories of Hannah's battle flooded back. The room spun, and he leaned into Grace, seeking her strength.

She leaned back, grounding him with her presence. "What's your immediate plan?" Grace asked, her voice clear and resolute.

"We're admitting her to PICU," Dr. Montgomery said. "I've called in Dr. Park, our pediatric nephrologist. He'll be here within the hour."

As the rest of the information blurred, drowned out by the roaring in his ears, Grace's hand moved soothingly across his back, tracing circles of comfort.

Nathan felt his throat tighten as he choked out, "Is this...is this what Hannah went through?"

Dr. Montgomery's expression softened. "We don't know yet. There are similarities, but Lily is responding well to treatment."

"Can I see her?" he asked, the pleading in his voice unmistakable.

Dr. Montgomery nodded. "They're moving her now."

Nathan barely registered the rest of the conversation. All that mattered was seeing Lily.

"I know the way," Grace said softly, rising and offering him her hand.

Together, they followed the nurse down the hallway. Nathan moved because Grace moved, finding solace in her unwavering support.

When the elevator doors opened onto the PICU floor, he froze.

The air hit him first—sharp and sterile. Then came the sounds—monitors beeping, soft-spoken voices—the same lull of despair he'd known before.

Grace's hand tightened on his arm. "Let's go see Lily," she whispered. "I'm right here."

COFFEE SPILLED over the rim of the flimsy paper cup as Grace steadied herself against the hospital vending machine. She counted her breaths as Dr. Winters had taught her, then turned to return to Nathan, who sat solemnly at the corner table.

Eight hours since Lily had collapsed. Four hours since the doctors had stabilized her glucose levels. One hour since Nathan had left Lily's bedside in Pediatrics ICU for the first time in the pre-dawn hours.

Balancing the two cups carefully, Grace wove between scattered tables in the fluorescent-lit cafeteria. The competing aromas of microwaved pasta, burnt coffee, and an abandoned orange peel created a strange sensory backdrop to the night's crisis. A janitor pushed a mop across the far end of the room, the wheels of his bucket squeaking against the tile.

Nathan sat hunched at a corner table, staring at his phone. His shoulders formed a tight line under his button-down—the same shirt he'd worn to dinner, though now the sleeves were rolled unevenly, the collar askew. The romantic dinner setup flashed through her mind—candles, flowers, Lily's excited smile as co-host. All abandoned in an instant when they'd found her unconscious.

"Here." Grace set the coffee in front of him. "It's terrible, but it's hot."

Nathan looked up, red-rimmed eyes dull with exhaustion. "Thanks." He wrapped his hands around the cup but didn't drink. "Rachel's staying with Lily so I could... breathe for a minute."

Sliding into the chair across from him, Grace's knees bumped his under the small table. She didn't pull away. The last time she'd shared a meal with Andrew was the day he broke off their engagement. The stark contrast between then and now wasn't lost on her. "She's going to be okay." Grace covered his hand with hers. His skin felt cold despite the warm cup beneath his fingers.

Nathan turned his hand over, inviting hers. A simple gesture she'd grown to cherish. The cafeteria's harsh lighting softened around the edges as something shifted between them.

"The doctors think so," he said. "But her blood sugar—it dropped so fast. One minute we're dealing with your problem, the next..." His voice faltered, betraying exhaustion.

Grace squeezed his hand. *Her problem.* It seemed so small now, compared to what he was going through with Lily's illness. What Grace felt, too. The tremor in her own hand steadied with his strong grip.

For months, they'd existed in a carefully maintained triangle—Nathan, Grace, and Lily. Movie nights with Lily's commentary. Dinners with her chatter filling any awkward silences. Conversations about ballet connecting her with a young student. Now, in this sterile cafeteria with its buzzing lights and squeaking tile floors, it was just the two of them. No buffer. No distraction. No escaping to less serious matters.

And despite everything—despite the fear and exhaustion etched into Nathan's face, despite the hospital smells and the terrible coffee—within this solitude with him, Grace felt something unlock inside her chest.

Nathan sighed, running his free hand through his already disheveled hair. "Although her numbers are stabilizing, the doctor wants to monitor her kidney function. Something about the fever combined with the high blood sugar..." He trailed off, the technical details clearly overwhelming him.

Grace nodded. "I've been reading about diabetic ketoacidosis. The best way to manage it is with hydration and electrolyte balance. When Lily is released, I'll share the information I found at the clinic."

He looked up, gratitude momentarily replacing the exhaustion in his eyes. "You always know exactly what to research, don't you?"

Heat crept up her neck. "I can't help myself. When something matters to me, I dive in completely."

"Most people just say 'that must be hard' and change the subject." A ghost of a smile touched his lips. "After all this time, you're still learning new things about her condition and that means everything to me."

The simple gratitude in his voice made something twist in Grace's chest. With Andrew, everything had been about appearances—the perfect wedding, the perfect wife, the perfect life. Every conversation had centered on how things would look, what people would think, whether they were maintaining the right image. The last time she was with him, they were at an expensive restaurant ordering an expensive lunch.

But with Nathan, their relationship was substance. He didn't care if Lily's glucose monitor went off at the wrong time. He worried if her blood sugar levels were stable, not how her condition might inconvenience their social calendar. When Grace had canceled Friday night dinner recently because of a lupus flare, he'd shown up at her upstairs apartment with Lily and Shaggy's sea bass and classic movies instead of complaints about changed reservations.

His love for his daughter wasn't performative—it was bone-deep, cellular, as essential to him as breathing. And his concern for Grace felt the same way—not a show for others, but something real that existed whether anyone was watching or not.

Nathan glanced at his phone, checking for messages from Rachel. Grace squeezed his hand.

They let the quiet settle for a moment, the fluorescent buzz overhead filling the space between them.

Nathan studied her face. "You're different than when we first met at the clinic."

"Am I?"

"Yes. That day, you were...I don't know. Holding everything together so tightly. Like if you loosened your grip for a second, you'd fall apart."

Grace chuckled. "Maybe that's how it felt."

"And now?"

She closed her eyes briefly, remembering the fear that had gripped her when Lily collapsed, the desperate drive to the hospital, the way she'd found herself in the waiting room, head bowed, whispering words she hadn't never spoken. *Please, God. Not Lily.*

She hadn't prayed for herself when her own diagnosis came, hadn't asked for help when Andrew left, hadn't sought comfort when her body betrayed her and her dreams crumbled. But for Lily—for this child who wasn't hers but somehow had claimed a piece of her heart—she'd prayed without hesitation. "Now I know some things are worth more than control," she said finally.

Nathan nodded slowly, understanding in his eyes.

"Remember that video we saw that day in the waiting room?" Grace said. "The high school football player who collapsed, and that boy who healed him on the field?"

Nathan's brow furrowed. "Right. That story from the Coastal Christian's game. Why?"

She traced the rim of her cup. "I used to think those stories were ridiculous. People desperate to believe in something."

"And now?"

"Now I'm not so sure."

Nathan didn't dismiss her as he dismissed God at Hannah's funeral. He just watched her—as if her words had settled into the part of him that still needed to believe in something. "I wonder where that healer is now."

THIRTY-SIX

Joseph had found his stride. In his final year at River of Life Theological Seminary, he no longer questioned where he belonged. His gift had been tested in the sterile corridors of University Hospital, but now, beyond the halls of academia and the walls of medicine, he led freshmen and sophomore seminarians into the early morning streets of New Orleans.

The smell of freshly baked bread hung in the air as he stacked donated loaves into boxes, their crusts still whispering of the ovens they'd just left behind. Nearby, his team debated pneumatology—the study of the Holy Spirit's works—prophetic dreams, signs, wonders, miracles. Joseph let their voices drift past him. Among this city's forgotten souls, the gifts of the Holy Spirit should not be a spectacle. Rather, they should be woven from the quiet, steady work of God's hands.

He thought of his parents and their ministry in Pakistan. He understood them better now. True ministry didn't always announce itself with miracles—it unfolded in simple moments, one life at a time. His gift would come when it was needed. For now, he had a purpose—preparing food for the hungry.

Twenty minutes later, Joseph pulled the seminary van beneath the shadow of the Crescent City Connection. He scanned the makeshift community before killing the ignition—noting who was missing, who had new bandages, who might need extra attention today. The concrete overpass sheltered dozens of homeless men, women, and children, many of whom now greeted the seminarians by name after months of these visits. Familiar faces brightened as Joseph and his team stepped out, several calling and waving. Connections with the vulnerable mattered more to him than any academic achievement he could earn at school. He waved back warmly as he and the others began unloading boxes into the morning shadows cast by the massive bridge.

Sarah grabbed his arm. "Joseph, look." She lifted her chin toward an elderly man propped against a support column. His wheezing carried over the rumble of traffic overhead. The man's shoulders heaved, his chest barely moving as he desperately gasped for air.

"This guy needs a hospital," Michael said, setting down a box of bread.

The man fought to breathe with the muddy Mississippi rolling behind him. Joseph's gut clenched.

Old instincts resurfaced—Should he help this man? The lessons from seminary and his years of discernment had taught Joseph patience. Wait for the prompting. For God's timing.

Go to him.

A gentle nudge from the Spirit—the same voice that had guided him since childhood in Pakistan. He set his box down and walked to the man, responding not with the eagerness of a miracle worker but with the obedience of a servant.

The closer he got, the louder the wheezing. Sweat poured from the man's weathered face.

"Sir?" Joseph knelt beside him. "May I pray with you?"

The man's eyes opened. He managed a slight nod between gasps.

Joseph laid his hands on the man's shoulders. "Father," he whispered, "in Jesus' name..."

Power flowed through Joseph. But the man's breathing grew more ragged, more desperate. He clutched Joseph's arm. Panic filled his eyes.

Trust me, the Spirit said.

The wheezing turned to a rattling cough that drew concerned looks from the other homeless. Sarah took a step forward, but Michael held her back.

Then, like a wave pulling back from shore before rushing in, everything went still. The man took in one clear breath. Then another. "What did you do?" he asked as his eyes widened. "I can breathe." He stood, sucking air into his lungs again and again. "I can breathe."

A woman who'd been watching shuffled to Joseph, dragging her right leg. "Please," she said. "My leg. The infection..."

Yes. Her too.

Joseph helped the woman sit on a plastic milk crate. A crater had formed in her left calf, its edges an angry red against her pale skin. Through her worn sock, the wound was weeping.

"How long?" he asked.

"Three months." She looked away. "The hospital sent me home with antibiotics, but..." She gestured to her makeshift bed under the bridge.

Joseph knelt in the gravel beside her. He placed one hand on her ankle, the other just below her knee. "Father..." This time the healing came like spring rain. Color returned to the dead tissue. The gash closed with the skin knitting together. The woman gasped; tears streamed down her face.

Soot-faced men and women clustered around him. Some reached out in desperation. Others called out their ailments. A burning in Joseph's spirit intensified.

Yes. This is why I brought you here.

For the next hour, he moved among them, the Spirit guiding each interaction.

"My back," whispered an elderly woman, her spine curved from decades of labor. "Can't stand straight since I was seventeen."

As he touched her shoulders, he felt the power flow differently than before—not like a sudden wave but like a gentle stream, realigning vertebrae and easing muscles that had forgotten how to relax. Her soft gasp as she stood upright reminded him of his mother's face when he'd healed others in Pakistan.

A man with clouded eyes approached next, guided by a friend. Joseph touched his temples and watched as recognition and wonder spread across his face at the gift of sight restored.

Person after person came forward. Arthritis-twisted fingers straightened. Infected wounds closed. Decades-old injuries mended. Each healing uniquely flowed through Joseph's hands, yet all bore witness to God's tender mercy for these forgotten souls beneath the bridge.

When the last had been healed and the final box emptied, Joseph stood quietly, humbled by what God had done through him. Not just today, but throughout his journey from that frightened refugee boy to the man he'd become.

Even under this noisy overpass, among the forsaken, God's power had moved—awesome, undeniable, full of love.

As they packed up, Joseph flexed his fingers. Residual warmth tingled in his hands, but something else lingered—a pull he couldn't identify. He turned to the Mississippi, watching its muddy current churn south, racing toward the gulf.

The thought dissolved as images overtook his mind— white sand. A pier stretching into shady brown waters.

Biloxi.

The vision was so vivid it stopped him mid-step. His heart quickened as fragments of home emerged—Uncle David's weathered porch, the salty breeze, his first uncertain days in America. He hadn't consciously thought of the place in months, yet now the connection felt undeniable, as if today's ministry had been preparing him for something there.

"You okay?" Sarah asked.

Joseph nodded slowly. "Yeah... I think God's showing me something."

The whisper came again, gentle but certain.

Your preparation is complete. Return to where I first sent you.

"Biloxi," he murmured.

Michael shut the van's rear door. "What about it?"

"It's where I'm supposed to go next. After graduation."

He couldn't explain why, but purpose stirred within him. He had first arrived to that community as a frightened boy, fleeing persecution. Now, God was calling him back— not as a refugee, but as a servant.

And Joseph couldn't wait to see what lay ahead.

THIRTY-SEVEN

"How bad is it?" Grace asked, her voice hoarse with sleep and worry. She stretched across two plastic waiting room chairs, swollen joints aching in protest.

"Around three a.m., the alarms started," Rachel lowered herself into a chair across from her, eyes hollowed by exhaustion. "Lily's fever skyrocketed. One minute Nathan was dozing, the next the room was swarming with nurses. They were shouting numbers—104, 104.5—and then packing her in ice."

Grace could picture it—Lily's small body buried under blue packs, Nathan pushed back against the wall, helpless as strangers fought to cool his daughter's body. The thought of her own fever-drenched nightmares made her shudder.

Morning sunlight streamed through the wide windows, marking twelve hours since they'd rushed Lily through the emergency room doors. "And her glucose?" Grace asked, watching Nathan pace in front of the nurses' station. He hadn't slept, hadn't eaten—just moved in tight, anxious circles, leaning his forehead to the glass whenever they let him near her room.

Rachel shook her head. "Still unstable. Dr. Montgomery says her body isn't responding to the insulin the way it should."

Grace swallowed back a wave of nausea that had nothing to do with Lily—and everything to do with her own symptoms. Symptoms she'd hidden from him. Symptoms she couldn't burden anyone with. Not now. Somehow, she had to hold it together—for both of them. Forcing herself upright, she ignored the stiffness in her knees. Nathan needed her steady. Lily needed them strong. Grace's own crisis would have to wait. She pushed herself to standing, ignoring the stiffness in her knees to be the steady presence Nathan required right now.

"I brought snacks," Rachel said, pulling assorted options from her oversized purse. "Candy, chips, and those protein bars Nathan likes."

"Thanks." Grace reached for a Reeses Cup, but her visibly trembling fingers betrayed her. She quickly withdrew her hand. "Actually, I think I'll pass."

Rachel's eyes narrowed slightly. "You okay? You look flushed."

"Just didn't sleep well on these chairs," Grace said, touching her cheek self-consciously, feeling the telltale heat that signaled her rash was returning. The stress of the night had awakened symptoms that had been dormant for weeks. "I'm going to check on Nathan." She made her way across the waiting room. A wave of dizziness crashed over her, and she steadied herself against the wall, breathing deeply. *Not now. Please, not now. Must be strong for Nathan, for Lily.* For twelve years, her body had betrayed her. Today of all days, she needed it to cooperate. Her unsteadiness receded, leaving nausea in its wake. She swallowed hard and pushed forward.

"Any updates?" she asked, placing a gentle hand on his back.

He shook his head, eyes fixed on the window to Lily's room. "They're changing her IV again. Something about her veins collapsing."

"I need to use the restroom," she told Nathan. "I'll be right back."

In the harsh bathroom lighting, Grace rolled up her sleeve and froze at the fresh bruises spreading up her forearm. She hadn't bumped into anything. Just yesterday, she'd been fine, and now... She tugged her sleeve down and splashed cold water on her face, avoiding her reflection. When she returned, a hospital administrator approached Nathan with a clipboard.

"Mr. Carter? We need some additional insurance information for Lily's extended stay."

Nathan looked lost, staring at the forms.

"I'll handle this," Grace said, taking the paperwork. She squinted at the small print, the letters swimming before her eyes. "Do you have a pen I could borrow?"

As she struggled through the paperwork, Dr. Montgomery appeared at the entrance of the Pediatric ICU.

"Nathan? Let me update you on Lily's condition."

Nathan followed the doctor down the hall, and the space beside Grace turned cold and empty, as if she'd been excluded. She discreetly reached into her purse, retrieving her hydroxychloroquine and prednisone. She dry-swallowed the pills, grimacing at the bitter taste, then settled back into her chair to wait.

From across the room, she overheard two nurses discussing a young diabetic patient. Their hushed tones and concerned expressions told her they were talking about Lily.

"...still not responding to treatment the way we'd hoped," one said.

"More aggressive options are being discussed," replied the other.

She closed her eyes, the weight of worry pressing against her ribs, each heartbeat syncing with the throb in her fingers.

Nearly noon. Fifteen hours inside these walls, and her body was paying for every minute. Her phone screen blurred before clearing again; her hands were so swollen she could barely bend them, and the floor tilted under her feet if she moved too fast.

The scrape of dragging footsteps broke through the hum of the ward. Nathan sank into the chair beside her, his shoulders slumped, his face hollowed by exhaustion. His gaze found hers.

"Your face..." His voice shook, not with a father's worry, but something deeper, more personal.

Instinctively, she touched her cheek. The butterfly rash. No hiding it now.

"It's nothing," she said quickly. "What did Dr. Montgomery say about Lily?"

"They're trying a different protocol." Nathan scrubbed a hand over his forehead, his words slow, heavy. "She thinks..." His voice faded as he looked at her again—*really* looked—and something shifted in his expression. "You don't look right." He reached for her hand but froze when he saw the swelling. His jaw tightened. "You're sick too, aren't you?"

"I'm fine," she insisted with a lie.

Nathan's gaze flicked between her and Lily's door, torn in two directions. His hand brushed her forehead—and

PART 4

jerked back as if she'd burned him. His face twisted, fresh panic lacing his features.

"I can't... I can't handle you being sick too."

Shame crawled up her spine. She looked away. "It just started last night. Stress."

"You need to go home. Or maybe you should check yourself in here."

"No, no. I'll go..." she said. "But I hate leaving you here to deal with this alone."

"Grace." His voice was gentle, but unyielding. "Lily's stable for now. Rachel's here. You're no good to anyone if you collapse."

She opened her mouth to argue, to say she'd overhead a conversation to the contrary, but the room spun again. Her fingers clawed for the arm of the chair.

"I'll have Rachel drive you." Nathan said, steadying her into the seat. "Promise me you'll call Dr. Winters."

Reluctantly, she nodded, swallowing the lump in her throat. Rachel slipped an arm around her for support, but Grace hesitated, casting one last look at the man she loved. "Nathan..."

He caught her hand gently. "I'll call you the second anything changes with Lily." His voice dropped lower, rough with emotion. "But right now, I need to know you're taking care of yourself too. Please."

Only then, with her hand slipping from his, did she let Rachel guide her away—and every step felt like a betrayal.At the doorway, she turned back one last time to see Nathan watching her go, his face a complex mix of worry for her and fear for his daughter. In that moment, Grace realized that despite everything they'd been through, he still cared deeply about what happened to her.

And that was almost as terrifying as her symptoms.

THE GREYHOUND BUS rolled into Mississippi beneath a cloudless sky two months after Joseph's graduation. He leaned against the window, succumbing to the pull of sleep prompted by the steady hum of the rubber rolling on asphalt. Joseph drifted into a restless dream. He stood once again in the ruins of his parents' mission in Northwest Pakistan—blackened walls reaching toward an empty sky, his mother's garden choked with weeds. But this time, the vision expanded. He saw Pakistani Christians scattered across distant cities—Karachi, London, even some here in America—their faces turned toward their lost homeland with longing and fear. The voice, clear as mountain air, whispered through the devastation—One day, you will return.

He woke as the bus turned onto Highway 90, the familiar landscape unfolded—unchanged, unshaken coast-line—but as they passed through Long Beach, then Gulf-port, then Biloxi, he'd anticipated his return to the place he'd called home for twelve years.

The bus sighed to a stop. He stood and stretched, the familiar warmth in his palms—not painful, just present—reminding him of why he was here. God had sent him back to Biloxi for service and preparation for something far greater. He slung his backpack over one shoulder, rolled his Samsonite suitcase behind him across the tarmac. Was this how the prophets of old had felt when drawn to a purpose before they could see the path ahead?

Near the terminal entrance, Uncle David stood waiting, hands tucked into his jeans pockets, a gentle smile spreading across his weathered face.

"Joseph." His arms opened wide. "So good to see you."

He slipped into the embrace, the scent of bay rum stirring a flood of memories.

"It's good to be here," Joseph said, clapping his uncle's back.

"Where's Aunt Rebecca?"

"Home cooking you crab cakes and shrimp stew." His uncle held him at arm's length, eyes shining with quiet pride. "Hadn't seen you since you graduated. Have you made plans?"

Joseph smiled. "Not really. But God seems to want me here for the immediate future. He's preparing me for something."

They crossed the street to the same blue Ford pickup Uncle David had had since Joseph came to America—its dented fender and faded paint as welcoming as a front porch light.

"Preparing you?" Uncle David asked as they tossed Joseph's bags into the truck bed.

"Yes, but that's a long conversation." Joseph said. "Before I graduated—at the homeless ministry—it felt like I was living the Book of Acts. I've never seen anything like it."

"Well if my spiritual radar is tracking, I think the Lord has brought you back for something special." Uncle David said, easing onto Highway 90. "I believe He's led you here at exactly the right time."

Joseph glanced at him. "How so?"

A small smile tugged at the corners of Uncle David's mouth. "God is bringing revival to the Gulf Coast, getting people's attention through the miracle of healing.

Joseph's hands warmed with the familiar fire.

Uncle David chuckled. "Seems like only yesterday you came to the coast—a scared ten-year-old kid, fresh from Pakistan." He paused, his expression growing more serious.

"Our healing service has grown tremendously over the past few months, but I can't shake the feeling that God has more in store."

"I can't argue with that. We saw dozens of miracles in New Orleans this past year."

Uncle David nodded, then glanced sideways at Joseph. "Speaking of Pakistan—I've been getting some calls lately. Pastor Yousaf in Houston, the Gaza family in Detroit. They're concerned about the area you had to flee after your parents' deaths."

Joseph's grip tightened on the door handle. "Go on."

"They want to rebuild. To reclaim what was lost." Uncle David's voice carried a weight of understanding. "The mission your father started—its people have been scattered for twelve years. But they haven't forgotten your mother and father's work. Some are starting to wonder if maybe it's time to rebuild."

The dream rushed back—faces turned toward Pakistan with longing and fear. "What did you tell them?"

"That it would take someone with both the calling and the courage to lead them." Uncle David pulled into their driveway. "Someone who understands the cost but believes in the promise."

Joseph stared at the modest home where he'd spent his teenage years. The house looked smaller than he remembered, the oak tree in the front yard taller, but the feeling of safety remained the same. Safety—something those Pakistani families would never have in their homeland without someone willing to go first.

"I keep having this dream," Joseph said quietly. "I see the ruins, but I also see what the mission could provide again. Churches. Schools. Hope."

Uncle David turned off the engine. "And the danger?"

"Still there. Maybe worse now." Joseph met his uncle's eyes. "But if we wait much longer, there won't be anyone left who remembers why it mattered."

"I'd like you to minister with me tomorrow night—if you're willing," Uncle David said. "Victory Chapel has families that need a miracle. Could be a spiritual step back to Pakistan."

Joseph flexed his fingers. Sparks danced beneath his skin. "Sounds like you've been talking to Dr. Marshall."

"We go way back. Your room's just like you left it," his uncle said as they carried Joseph's bags inside. "Except I finally fixed that squeaky floorboard by the window."

Joseph chuckled. "The one that always gave me away when I tried sneaking in late?"

"That's the one."

He set his duffel on the twin bed and scanned the room. Posters of football players still adorned the walls. His high school graduation photo hung beside a map of Pakistan—a map he'd stared at countless nights, tracing the route back to his parents' mission with his finger. He crossed to the dresser where a picture showed him with his father and mother smiling in the mission garden.

He lifted it, feeling the weight of memory and legacy in his palm.

"I often visit this room to gaze at that photo," Uncle David said from the doorway.

Joseph touched the cross beneath his shirt. "I've been thinking about them a lot lately. About what they started, what they believed was worth dying for."

"They'd be proud of you," Uncle David said with a nod. "Very proud. And they'd understand what you're being called to do."

He sat on the bed, gazing at the framed image. "Tell me about tomorrow night. What should I expect?"

Uncle David leaned against the doorframe. "Should be standing room only."

"Doesn't matter how many show up," Joseph said. "God knows who needs to be there."

"That's what I told the elders." Uncle David smiled. "Service starts at six—worship, a short message, then we pray for whoever comes forward."

Joseph nodded. "Sounds great."

That evening, Joseph sat by his bedroom window, watching the sunset spill orange and violet across the horizon. The air conditioner hummed in the background, waves murmuring in the distance. He held his family photo, his eyes drifting to the map of Pakistan on the wall.

"I'm here, Lord," he whispered. "Show me what You want me to do. Here and...there."

He waited in the stillness, unsure if God would speak.

Then—

A dimly lit sanctuary filled with people. Faces obscured, but their desperation cut through the haze. Blindness. Sickness. Disease. The ache of faith stretched thin. Joseph was at the altar, hands raised, light pouring from his palms like liquid fire. People surged forward—drawn, reaching, grasping. A woman fell to her knees, catching the back of his blazer, her sobs breaking in relief as power flowed into her. Joseph's breath caught—not from fear, but from awe.

The vision changed. A hospital room. The beep of machines. A frail child beneath sterile sheets. Her breath shallow. A man stood beside her, shoulders bowed under an invisible weight. Grief clung in the air like humidity. Joseph reached for them—

Then the scene shifted again. Mountains. Dust. The

skeletal remains of his parents' mission rising from rubble like resurrection itself. But he wasn't alone. Men, women, and children walked beside him whose faces he couldn't quite see. They carried tools, Bibles, hope. Children laughed as they played among the construction. His Father's voice, carried on the wind—*Well done, my faithful son. Well done.*

He gasped, heart pounding, the last echoes of the visions burning behind his eyelids. Someone needed him—now. But farther ahead waited a greater purpose. Pakistan. The mission. Families who needed Christ. He stared out at the darkening sky, where distant stars blinked to life. He touched his mother's cross, hearing her whisper—*"Stay faithful to Our Lord, my love. Remember your gift. Your purpose..."*

The cross pressed warm against his palm, and a current stirred beneath his skin—steady, insistent, alive. Outside the window, the Gulf Coast night deepened to indigo, the moon's pulse threading in and out of the clouds like a heartbeat. In the distance, hospital lights glowed against the darkness—a constellation of suffering and hope.

Joseph stood between vision and action. Tomorrow's service was only the threshold. Somewhere ahead waited Desperate Souls, a woman clutching at his jacket, a frail child. And farther still—the ruins that could become foundations, the scattered who could become a congregation, the mission that could rise again.

The night thrummed with urgency, charged with miracles waiting for him to arrive.

THIRTY-EIGHT

Grace leaned into Rachel's steady support as they navigated the narrow staircase to her apartment above the studio. Each step became its own small mountain to climb, her body a map of territories claimed by pain.

"You should have had someone examine you at the hospital while you were there," Rachel said, her voice soft with concern as she pushed the door open. "You're pushing yourself too far again."

"Always the worrier," Grace said, attempting lightness. but her voice betrayed her. The lupus flare had ambushed her with familiar cruelty—joints aflame, exhaustion seeping into every cell, the distinctive rash spreading across her face like unwelcome watercolor. She recognized this pattern— crisis followed by collapse, her body's perpetual betrayal.

Rachel guided her to the couch, where Grace sank into the cushions, surrendering to gravity and fatigue. The effort of appearing stronger than she felt suddenly seemed absurd, a habit she couldn't quite abandon. "Nathan and Lily need you more than I need looking after."

Rachel arranged a glass of water beside Grace's medication with methodical care. "My mother's with him, and the doctors are continuing tests on Lily. I'm staying until I know you're settled."

The mention of Lily resonated through Grace like a bell struck at midnight. The child's fading presence amid the machinery haunted her—monitors tracing a fragile rhythm, Nathan's face a map of fear too painful to bear. His daughter's vibrancy, usually expressed through pirouettes and giggles, had been reduced to stillness against institutional sheets. And that hospital scent—antiseptic masking deeper notes of vulnerability. Grace knew it intimately from her own stays, but experiencing it alongside Lily's bed transformed it into something unbearable. Children were meant for sunshine and growth, not the harsh perils of intensive care.

"Promise me you'll actually rest," Rachel said, adjusting pillows with genuine affection.

"I promise." Grace meant it this time. The realization came with startling clarity—her stubborn self-sufficiency was just another form of control, as futile as trying to command the tide. "Just keep me updated. Please."

After Rachel left, silence settled around Grace like dust. Her body craved sleep while her mind spun elaborate futures where everyone she loved disappeared behind hospital doors. Across town, a child's life balanced on medical expertise and chance, while the man she'd cautiously begun to love faced the potential repetition of his deepest loss. And here she remained, rendered a spectator by her own rebellious body when participation mattered most.

She reached for her medication, her joints protesting each degree of movement. Her wrist seized, elbow grinding against invisible resistance. Pain shot through her arm, sharp enough to steal her breath. The glass wobbled in her grip, spilling cold water across her blouse, another small indignity in a day overfull with them.

Shifting position ignited her hip joint. She froze, waiting for the white-hot sensation to recede. Ten seconds stretched to twenty. The pain settled into throbbing, leaving her breathing in shallow sips of air. Such ordinary move-ments—just trying to find comfort. She regarded the distance to the kitchen with weary calculation. The space between intention and action had never seemed so vast.

She swallowed her pills dry, accepting their bitter taste as a form of penance for unknown transgressions. Changing her saturated blouse became a study in persistence, each button a puzzle her swollen fingers struggled to solve. When she finally pulled on a soft t-shirt, the simple accom-plishment felt like a small victory with a cost.

In the bathroom mirror, her reflection offered unwel-come truths. The butterfly rash spread its wings across her cheeks and nose, vivid against her pallor. She remembered Nathan's expression when he'd noticed it at the hospital— his concern for her layered atop his terror for Lily. His capacity for caring, even while drowning in fear, had pierced something long-calcified within her.

"Not now," she whispered to her reflection, to her immune system, to the universe. "Please, not now."

She checked her phone repeatedly, the screen remaining stubbornly empty of news. She drafted messages to Nathan and deleted them just as quickly. What comfort could she offer that wouldn't sound like a platitude? What words could possibly matter against the backdrop of moni-toring equipment and medical terminology?

Grace forced herself to eat a slice of toast, tasting noth-ing. Experience had taught her the false economy of skipping meals. As she chewed without pleasure, her thoughts remained with Lily's small form and Nathan's haunted eyes.

She scrolled through recent photos—Friday dinner, Lily proudly displaying artwork, Nathan laughing as Grace attempted to teach them ballet positions. The three of them at the park, ice cream commemorating an ordinary joy. Nathan's gaze, warm and unguarded, when he thought she wasn't watching.

They were becoming something she'd never quite believed possible for herself—a family, with all its messy complications and quiet certainties. Now two merciless diseases threatened this tentative happiness. She allowed herself a moment of pure, selfish grief for what might be lost before it had fully formed.

Her phone chimed with a WhatsApp notification from her support group. Someone posted about remarkable improvement after attending a healing service at Victory Chapel. Comments accumulated beneath, sharing similar testimonies.

Victory Chapel. Dr. Winters had mentioned it after Grace's diagnosis.

"*Some patients find comfort there,*" she'd said with careful neutrality. "*Sometimes medical science reaches its limits.*"

Grace had dismissed it then, the armor of skepticism firmly in place. Faith healing had seemed like desperation dressed as hope, a false promise she couldn't afford to entertain.

But now, with Lily's prognosis uncertain and her own body in revolt, Grace found herself navigating to Victory Chapel's website. Her finger hesitated over the screen before tapping the events page.

"Sunday Night Healing Service," the banner proclaimed. "With special guest Joseph Freeman, recently returned to Biloxi."

The young man in the photo appeared barely past twenty, green eyes radiating an earnestness that seemed both naive and compelling. Something about him tugged at her memory. She enlarged the image, studying his features with growing recognition.

This was the boy from that viral video years ago—the high school football player who had prayed over an injured opponent who subsequently rose, apparently healed. The video had circulated during Grace's darkest weeks of diagnosis, when she was still learning the language of chronic illness.

She'd categorized it then as coincidence or hysteria, safely filed away with other improbable hopes. But now, that certainty wavered.

Grace's analytical mind wrestled with her yearning heart. What did empirical evidence matter when a child's breath grew shallow? What was rational skepticism worth against the weight of Nathan's fear?

She flexed her swollen fingers, then studied Joseph's face again. The distance between her former certainties and present desperation yawned wide. Medicine was fighting for Lily, but medicine had fought for Nathan's wife, Hannah, too, ultimately surrendering to inevitability.

Grace couldn't bear to follow that thought to its conclusion. She picked up her phone, considering a text to Nathan. Doubt intervened immediately. His faith had shattered with Hannah's passing. Would suggesting a healing service seem cruel? Would it reopen scarred over wounds?

But the alternative—standing passive while Lily suffered

—seemed suddenly unbearable. The possibility of hope, however fragile, called to something long dormant within her. Perhaps this was what faith meant—not certainty, but the courage to reach beyond what seemed possible.

NATHAN SHOOK as he brushed a strand of Lily's dark hair from her forehead. His elbow bumped the cup on the bedside table, sending it toppling. Water splashed across the Pediatric ICU's floor, spreading beneath the bed where his daughter lay motionless.

He cursed as he lunged for the napkins beside the untouched tray, the sandwich still wrapped in plastic, the apple juice unopened.

The cartoon dolphins on the wall opposite his daughter smiled down at him with their permanent stares. Twenty-four hours earlier, she'd been helping prepare dinner, arranging flowers for his proposal to Grace. Now, tubes snaked from her arms, and the ventilator's hiss punctuated dead silence.

He mopped at the puddle with a napkin, his knees pressing into the hard floor. The same position he'd been in twelve years ago, beside Hannah, praying. Prayers that went unanswered. He hadn't uttered a single one since. The sodden napkins disintegrated in his grip.

The door swished open behind him. Rachel's hand squeezed his shoulder. "Any change?"

Nathan shook his head, not trusting his voice. He tossed the wet napkins into the trash and pulled himself up into a chair.

"Mom's on her way. She's bringing you a change of

clothes." With cheeks lined with tear tracks, Rachel settled into the chair on the opposite side.

With his gaze back to the monitors, he nodded. The numbers hadn't improved since Dr. Montgomery's last visit. Lily's kidney function was declining rapidly, her blood sugar impossible to stabilize.

Just like Hannah.

"Grace is home resting," Rachel said.

"She was pushing herself too hard." He rubbed his eyes. "Trying to hide how bad she felt." Seeing Grace's trembling hands and the rash over her cheeks had twisted something inside him. She'd been deteriorating right in front of him, and he'd been too consumed with Lily to notice until she nearly collapsed. "She wanted to stay," he added.

"She loves Lily." Rachel reached across the bed to take his hand. "And you."

His throat tightened. The engagement ring he'd planned to give Grace was still hidden among the flowers his daughter had arranged. Now everything was unraveling —Lily fighting for her life, Grace battling her own health crisis. The future he'd finally allowed himself to imagine was dying.

Dr. Montgomery entered, clipboard in hand, her face giving nothing away. "We've got the latest lab results," she said, her voice clinical. "I'm afraid they're not showing improvement. Her creatinine levels are continuing to rise." She referred to her papers. "Her kidneys are struggling to filter waste from her bloodstream."

Nathan lowered his head. "What does that mean for her recovery?"

Dr. Montgomery's professional mask slipped for a second. "I'm going to shoot you straight. Lily's condition is deteriorating despite our interventions. The combination of diabetic ketoacidosis and this infection has been devastating to her system."

"But she was fine yesterday," he said, his voice hollow. "We were making dinner, planning..." he paused, unable to continue.

"Type 1 diabetes can be unpredictable, especially in children. The fever triggered a cascade effect."

Rachel stood and moved beside him. "What are our options?"

"We're adjusting her insulin protocol and antibiotics. If her kidney function continues to decline, we may need to consider dialysis."

Dialysis. The news knocked the breath from Nathan's chest. Hannah died soon after going on dialysis.

"Dr. Patel, our pediatric nephrologist will be here in the morning," she added.

"*Morning?*" Nathan's voice rose. "What if she doesn't have until morning?"

"Nathan," Rachel warned of his tone.

Dr. Montgomery's expression softened. "We're doing everything medically possible. Lily is receiving the best care available."

Everything medically possible. Words that never comforted him.

Rachel squeezed his arm. "Should we pray? I know it's been a while, but—"

Dr. Montgomery let out a subtle scoff that cut through Rachel's suggestion. The doctor checked her watch. "I need to check on another patient. The nurse will be in shortly to adjust Lily's medication."

Nathan concentrated on his daughter's pale face. The last time he'd been inside a church was for Hannah's funeral, and he left angry with God.

"Nathan?" Rachel's voice was gentle. "I know you haven't been to church since Hannah died, but—"

"Because church didn't save Hannah." His bitterness slipped out before he could stop it.

"I know." Rachel's eyes filled with tears. "But what else can we do right now? The doctors are doing everything they can."

Nathan looked down at Lily's small hand, the IV taped securely to her skin. He'd promised Hannah he would take Lily to church, would keep her connected to faith even if he couldn't find his way back. He'd kept that promise, driving her to Sunday School every week, waiting in the parking lot rather than entering the sanctuary. "I don't know how to pray anymore," he admitted, his voice breaking.

"Then I'll start." Bowing her head, she took his hand. "Lord, we come before you tonight with heavy hearts. Our Lily is sick, and we're scared. You are the God who can heal all our diseases and forgives all our sins. We ask that you touch Lily and make her whole."

Nathan stared at his sister, the prayer not penetrating. He'd heard similar prayers twelve years ago. People had gathered at his men's group, hospital waiting rooms, formed prayer chains. None of it had mattered in the end.

"We cry out to you tonight, Lord, just as you did for Jairus' daughter when he asked," Rachel continued, her voice gaining strength. "You restored her to health, and we pray that you would do the same for Lily. By your loving compassion, people live and find new life."

He glanced at the monitors above Lily's bed. The numbers remained unchanged—dangerously elevated creatinine, unstable blood glucose. He'd clung to science, not faith, to determine whether his daughter would live or die. But science was losing.

"Lord, we're in distress and we need you to save us," Rachel prayed. "Bring your healing hand to Lily. Rescue her from this sickness. And please give the doctors wisdom. Guide their hands and their decisions."

Nathan's phone vibrated. He pulled it out, expecting a message from his mother about her arrival time. It was Grace. "There's a healing service at Victory Chapel tomorrow at 6 PM. I know you don't go for that sort of thing, but I'm considering it."

A healing service?

"...and I pray for my brother, Lord," Rachel's voice broke through his thoughts. "Give him strength during this time and restore his faith."

The monitor above Lily's bed beeped. Her oxygen levels had dropped two points. Not a dramatic change, but any decline sent fear coursing through him.

Beep. Beep. Beep.

The same sound that had filled Hannah's room signaling her death. Nathan had stood helplessly by then, watching the medical team's futile efforts to revive her.

He looked back at his phone, at Grace's message. He should dismiss such a suggestion outright. But, with Lily's life hanging in the balance...

"Maybe," he typed with shaky fingers.

Rachel finished her prayer with a soft "amen" and glanced at Nathan's phone.

"Grace," he explained, his voice rough. "She learned about a healing service at a church tomorrow evening."

Rachel's expression brightened.

"Probably staged," Nathan muttered, but without conviction.

"Could be," she conceded. "But what do you have to lose?"

Lily lay motionless, so small and fragile. The daughter he'd raised alone. The child who'd given him purpose. His phone vibrated with Grace's response—"I can meet you there if you want."

"I'll go," he said, as much to himself as to his sister. "Not because I believe in miracles, mind you."

"Because you love your daughter," Rachel finished for him. "And you'll try anything."

He nodded, his throat too tight for words. He reached for Lily's hand, careful not to disturb the IV.

"Hold on, sweetheart," he whispered. "Just hold on."

THIRTY-NINE

The smell of coffee drifted through the kitchen like an old Sunday hymn. Joseph wrapped his hands around the mug, the warmth tingling in his palms—as if the Spirit were already whispering. Less than twenty-four hours in Biloxi, and his past and present converged. He'd arrived as a reluctant refugee boy. Now, twelve years later, he was a servant—shaped by his parents' sacrifice, the ache of being different, Dr. Marshall's quiet guidance, and God's whisper beneath that New Orleans bridge.

Uncle David set a plate of scrambled eggs and toast in front of him, the china pattern unchanged in twelve years. "You're up early." The lines around his uncle's eyes had deepened since Joseph left for seminary. "Nervous about tonight?"

"A little." Joseph picked up his fork. "First time ministering at a healing service. Actually, first time ministering in a church at all."

His uncle sat across the table, the leather of his Bible creaking as he flipped it open. The book was worn, its margins filled with notes from years of preaching and teach-

ing. The silver in his uncle's hair glistened, a reminder of
how time had passed while Joseph was away, finding
himself. "That's why I was up before dawn," he said.
"Praying for you and the service."

Joseph took a bite of eggs, tasting not just the food but
the memory of countless mornings at this table. Of learning
to belong in a place that wasn't Pakistan, with people who
weren't his parents but had chosen to love him anyway.

"I had a professor who said spiritual gifts aren't about
us," he offered, remembering Dr. Marshall's kind eyes
behind wire-rimmed glasses. "They're meant to build up
the church, not ourselves."

The corners of his uncle's mouth lifted slightly. "'Eph-
esians 4. Christ gave apostles, prophets, evangelists, shep-
herds, and teachers—'"

"—'to equip the saints for the work of ministry, for
building up the body of Christ,'" Joseph completed the
verse, the words flowing from memory rather than conscious
thought.

They fell into silence then, the space between them
filled with unspoken history—of the day Joseph's gift had
first manifested, of the years he'd tried to bury it beneath
trying to fit in, of his eventual surrender to a calling he
hadn't chosen.

His uncle studied him with careful attention, as if
trying to acquaint himself with a stranger. "You've
changed," he said finally, his voice softer than before.
"Grown. I don't see the boy who questioned why God
anointed him."

Joseph's fingers found the silver cross hanging between
his collarbones. His mother had worn it until the day she
died—a simple token of a faith that had sustained her
through civil war, through exile, through the raising of a son

who God had chosen. Now it sustained him, a tether to her memory when so much else had faded. "I think I understand now," he admitted, watching dust motes dance in the sunbeam between them. "When I first came to America, I didn't want to stand out. I just wanted to be normal."

"And now?" His uncle leaned forward slightly, his breakfast forgotten.

"Now I know it was never about being different or like everyone else." Joseph laid his fork down with a soft clink of metal on ceramic. "First Peter says to be good stewards of God's grace, using whatever gifts we've been given to serve one another." The words sounded right, felt right, yet could he bear the weight of others' expectations, their desperate hope—and the disappointment when the miracle didn't come..

Uncle David braced his elbows against the table, a gesture so familiar it made Joseph's heart ache with sudden nostalgia. "Victory Chapel hasn't forgotten that football game when you were in high school. Neither has the town. You'll have a crowd tonight—some coming for miracles, some coming for a spectacle."

Joseph's stomach tightened as unbidden images flashed through his mind—cell phones raised to record his every movement, reporters transforming God's work into sensational headlines, old classmates wondering why he had returned to the place he'd once fled. What if one moment of weakness, one failure, undid everything God was trying to accomplish?

"That's what concerns me," he said voicing the fear that had followed him all the way from New Orleans.

His uncle's expression didn't waver. "Your job isn't to sift through their motives. That's God's work. Yours is to be faithful with what you've been given."

Joseph nodded slowly, acknowledging the truth in the words. His mind flickered to the nameless faces in New Orleans—homeless men and women who had nothing, who had received healing through his obedient hands. No cameras. No crowds. Just quiet wonders in a forgotten corner of the city.

"I've been reading First Corinthians 13 this morning," Uncle David said, turning a page in his Bible, the paper so thin it was nearly translucent. "Paul says that without love, spiritual gifts mean nothing."

"'If I have the gift of prophecy,'" Joseph recited from memory, "'and can fathom all mysteries and all knowledge, and if I have a faith that can move mountains, but do not have love, I am nothing.'"

"Exactly." His uncle closed the Bible with reverence, his weathered hands resting on its cover. "The gift of healing you have—it's powerful. But it's the love behind it that matters to God."

Later, in the quiet of his childhood bedroom—where New Orleans Saints posters still clung to the walls—Joseph knelt beside the bed, pressing his hands together as he had been taught to do as a child. The air seemed to thicken around him, charged with something he had never been able to fully explain. A presence just beyond his understanding. "Lord," he whispered, "help me tonight. Help me to use this gift as You intend. Not for attention, but for the love you wish to pour out to those you have chosen."

A familiar warmth stirred in his palms, an excitement he had once struggled against but now embraced as part of himself. The first time he'd felt it, as a child, he'd been terrified—certain he was ill or, worse, marked as different in a country where he already stood out. Now, he recognized it as something precious, if incomprehensible.

He recalled Dr. Marshall's gentle authority—his steady voice constantly quoting Paul during Joseph's final two years of seminary—*"Fan into flame the gift of God, which is in you through the laying on of my hands, for God gave us a spirit not of fear but of power and love and self-control. Power without love is dangerous."* he would explain. *"Love without self-control is reckless. But the balance of those three —power, love, and self-control—is what makes God's gifts so effective."*

The red numbers on the bedside clock glowed—10:17 AM. The service wasn't until six that evening, but the critical nature of the evening settled over him. He reached for his journal, flipping to a clean page—not preparations but memories—him and his mother in the garden, his father's baritone singing filling the mission grounds, tossing the football with Uncle David.

Whatever awaited tonight at Victory Chapel shouldn't alarm him. He was ready. Not because of his own strength, but because he understood what his mother had tried to teach him all those years ago.

Outside his window, Biloxi would be stirring to life. And by nightfall, some would arrive at Victory Temple seeking miracles. Others would come for proof that miracles didn't exist. Joseph closed his journal, accepting that he couldn't control how others received what he had to offer. He could only offer it with as much grace as he possessed. His gift was never about him. It was about *God's* purpose.

"For such a time as this," he murmured in the quiet room.

"NEED HELP, MA'AM?" the Uber driver asked Grace as if noticing her struggle.

"I'm fine, thank you," she replied, the automatic response of someone who'd spent twelve years hiding her illness. She eased herself from the car, steadying against the door as her knees threatened to buckle.

The Victory Chapel parking lot was already filled to capacity, with cars circling for spaces and families streaming toward the entrance. A banner stretched over the church entrance: "HEALING SERVICE TONIGHT - ALL ARE WELCOME."

She stood for a moment, catching her breath. Well, here she was, after years of medical care and experimental treatments, standing outside a church like a desperate pilgrim. But wasn't that exactly what she was? *Desperate.*

Despite her discomfort, an unexpected feeling washed over her—anticipation, perhaps even hope. There was no logical sense to it, yet she couldn't deny it. Something drew her, step by painful step, to the entry doors.

"Grace? Grace Thompson?"

She turned to see Dr. Winters, her rheumatologist, looking at her with surprise. "You're here," her eyes taking in Grace's obvious symptoms. "You've finally made it."

Grace managed a small smile. "I suppose I may have run out of other options."

"You're not the only one," her physician replied, nodding toward the slow procession of wheelchairs and canes shuffling through the entrance—faces hidden behind dark glasses, oxygen tanks rolling over concrete pavers. "Let's get inside before all the good seats are taken."

As they approached the double doors, Grace checked her phone for messages. Nothing. She caught her face in the glass entrance—the butterfly rash, the pallor beneath her skin, the shadows under her eyes. Breathing in to steady herself, she pulled open the heavy door and entered.

The aura was unlike any church she'd ever experienced. Vaulted ceilings stretched overhead, but there was no hushed reverence. A worship band played upbeat music pulsing with energy. Hundreds of voices sang in unison, creating an excitement that lifted her spirit.

Dr. Winters guided Grace to the middle section, but every pew was filled. People were along the walls and in the back, many with visible ailments—dark glasses, oxygen masks, bandages—the same desperate hope Grace saw in her mirror each morning.

"There's Joseph," Dr. Winters whispered, pointing at the stage. The young man stood slightly apart from the worship team, eyes closed, hands raised. Even from this distance, something about him commanded attention. Not the polished charisma of a televangelist, but something authentic, something the viral video hadn't captured—reluctance.

A spasm shot through Grace's lower back, making her wince. Her medication was wearing off, and standing was becoming increasingly difficult. She leaned against a pillar, willing her legs to support her.

"Excuse me," a deep voice said beside her. "You look like you could use this more than I can."

She turned to see a distinguished older man with silver hair and emerald green eyes. He gestured to his seat at the end of the sixth row.

"Oh, I couldn't possibly—"

"I insist," he said firmly. "You're here for a reason. I'm here every week."

His gentle authority made her accept without argument. As she sank into the cushioned pew, the man smiled and moved to the front of the sanctuary. The music swelled to a crescendo, then faded. The congregation sat down as the silver-haired man stepped up to the pulpit. A murmur of recognition rippled through the crowd. "For those visiting us today," he began, his voice resonant and warm, "I'm Pastor David Freeman. Welcome to Victory Chapel."

Grace straightened slightly. *Freeman.* This must be Joseph's uncle, the one who'd raised him after his parents' death.

The pastor opened his Bible. "This evening, I want to share something from James 5:14-15. 'Is anyone among you sick? Let them call the elders of the church to pray over them and anoint them with oil in the name of the Lord. And the prayer offered in faith will make the sick person well; the Lord will raise them up. If they have sinned, they will be forgiven.'"

He looked up. His gaze swept across the congregation, but it was as if he spoke directly to her.

"What excites me about this passage is God's responsiveness to the prayers of His people. God is not distant or uncaring but actively involved in the well-being of His followers."

Something ignited inside Grace—not the pain of inflammation, but something warmer, unfamiliar. Beautiful.

"James presents a holistic view of healing," Pastor David continued, his voice growing more passionate. "Not just physical, but spiritual and relational aspects of a person's life. Complete restoration is what God offers— wholeness that brings hope and joy to those who are unwell."

A tear slipped from Grace's lower left lash. She hadn't cried since her diagnosis twelve years ago and had prided herself on her stoicism. But something about these words penetrated the armor she'd built around her.

"The prayer offered in faith," Pastor David emphasized, leaning forward. "And if they have sinned, they will be forgiven. Complete healing. Complete restoration. Body, mind, and soul."

Something exquisite welled up inside her, starting somewhere in her core and radiating up to her head. A mysterious sensation washed over her, leaving her breathless. As the pastor concluded his message, he gestured toward Joseph. "Now, my nephew will begin praying for those in need."

The young man stepped forward with quiet confidence. The first person to approach him was an elderly woman in a wheelchair. Joseph bent down to her level, speaking softly before placing his hands on her shoulders. The sanctuary grew silent except for Joseph's fervent prayer.

Then it happened.

The woman's expression transformed—pain giving way to astonishment. She gripped the arms of her wheelchair and slowly, shakily, rose to her feet. A collective gasp rippled through the congregation.

"I can stand," the woman whispered, then louder, "I can stand!"

Grace's heart thumped like a percussion instrument. This was real. She had just witnessed actual healing.

A second person went forward—a middle-aged man with a visible tremor. Again, Joseph prayed, and within moments, the man's hands grew steady.

Lily. She needs to be here.

Grace reached for her phone, barely noticing the discomfort. Her swollen fingers made typing difficult, each letter requiring deliberate pressure. She blinked away tears to focus. "Nathan, bring Lily to Victory Chapel now. I just watched Joseph Freeman heal two people. This is real—trust me."

She opened a new message to Rachel. "I'm at Victory Chapel healing service. Very sick people are getting healed. NO EXCEPTIONS. Nathan needs to bring Lily NOW. Can you make this happen?" As she pressed send, more people were moving to the front and lining the altar, forming a line that stretched down the center aisle.

For the first time in twelve years, Grace allowed herself to hope for something beyond the management of symptoms, beyond merely slowing the progression of her disease. She glanced at her phone. No response yet from Nathan or Rachel. Time seemed to stretch as Joseph placed his hands on the shoulders of an elderly man. Whatever happened next, one thing was certain—something fundamental had shifted inside Grace's soul, something no medical test could measure or explain.

And if Nathan brought Lily—what then?

Grace fixed her eyes on the young healer, waiting for the courage to move. As if sensing her gaze, Joseph looked up from the man who was just healed from his affliction, scanning the congregation until his eyes met hers. For a brief moment, something passed between them—recognition, perhaps, or understanding. He gave her a slight nod before rubbing the eyes of a blind woman.

FORTY

The monitor unleashed a shriek that pierced Nathan's heart. Red numbers flashed, but he didn't need to read them to know Lily was slipping away. His baby girl—his whole world—lay so still in that enormous bed.

When had she gotten so small?

Her face looked hollow, dark smudges beneath her closed eyes. Nathan leaned closer, desperate to catch the rise and fall beneath the covers, terrified that each breath might be her last.

"We're losing her peripheral lines. Starting a central line now." The nurse's words blurred together, medical jargon that meant only one thing—Lily was getting worse. He watched their gloved hands on his daughter's tiny body, these strangers touching her, hurting her to save her. "She's not responding," someone said. "Need more dextrose. Stat." Their urgency confirmed his worst fear.

He clutched the bedrail, fingers digging into metal worn smooth by other parents who'd done the same under similar circumstances—watching their child fight to live. The cold steel steadied him as the room seemed to spin wildly around him.

God, it was happening again. Like Hannah—the same nightmare, the same smells, the same desperation. Nathan's throat closed as the memory crashed over him. Blue-clothed figures surrounded Lily's bed, blocking the view of her face. He needed to see her face. Voices rose and fell. Equipment rattled. Merciless machines kept beeping, beeping, beeping. *Please God, don't take her.*

Someone tugged at his arm. "Nathan. Let them work. Give them space." Rachel. But he couldn't move, couldn't breathe, his feet rooted to the hard flooring. "Mom," Rachel said. "Help me get him to settle before he collapses."

Another hand pressed against his back carrying decades of maternal comfort. "Sweetheart, you're not helping Lily by making yourself sick. Come sit with me."

His phone buzzed in his pocket...Grace's photo lit the screen. Another message. The fifth one since early morning —"Joseph's healing service starts at 6 PM. Victory Chapel. Bring Lily if you can. I'll be there." The timestamp read 5:42. Eighteen minutes. The church was fifteen minutes away in Sunday traffic. Nathan stood. "I have to go," he said, the decision crystallizing in his mind.

Rachel glanced up. "Go where? Nathan, what are you talking about?"

"That healing service Grace told me about. It's tonight. Joseph Freeman is there—the one who healed that football player." Nathan checked his watch. "If I leave now, I can make it."

His mother's eyes widened. "How will that help Lily? You surely can't bring her."

"Why not? She's dying here." Nathan moved to the bed. Dr. Montgomery stepped into his path.

"Nathan, we're preparing to transfer her to intensive dialysis. Her kidney function is critically compromised by the ketoacidosis. We must start treatment immediately."

"How long will that take?" Nathan asked, his mind racing.

"The transfer? Minutes." Her complexion soured. "But the treatment will take hours. *Meaning*...moving her could push her over the edge." She emphasized the last three words.

Nathan looked at his daughter's face, at the tubes and wires connecting her to machines that beeped with increasing urgency. "What are her chances if you start dialysis?"

Dr. Montgomery's expression tightened. "Her condition is extremely serious. The dialysis will buy us time, but with her glucose levels still unstable and the damage to her kidneys..." she paused. "We're doing everything medically possible."

Everything medically possible. Those words again.

"Nathan," Rachel said, coming to stand beside him. "I believe in prayer. I believe God can heal. But rushing Lily out of here right now—"

"I'm not asking you to understand," Nathan said, his voice rough. "I'm asking you to help me. Help me get her to that service."

She searched his face, then nodded slowly. "Then let's figure out how."

"I don't know what God wants anymore. But I know what I want—I want my daughter to live." Nathan turned to Dr. Montgomery. "Can she be transported safely? Just for an hour?"

The doctor's professional mask slipped, revealing

genuine concern. "Nathan, you can't move her. I won't allow it. Her condition is critical."

"If you can't bring Lily to Joseph," Nathan's mother, who'd been silent until now, interrupted with the proverbial Mohammad cliche, "why not bring Joseph here?"

Nathan exchanged glances with his sister. He grabbed his jacket from the chair. "Rachel, stay here. I'm going to grab that healer."

His mother nodded and reached for her phone. "I'll call the church."

"Nathan," Dr. Montgomery called after him. "We can't delay treatment while you—"

"Then don't delay. Do whatever you need to do. But I'm bringing that man here." Nathan paused at the door, looking back at his very sick daughter. Her small form seemed to be shrinking before his eyes, fading away like Hannah had. "I lost her mother. I can't lose her too."

The hospital walls blurred around him as he ran, dodging nurses and visitors. The elevator took an eternity, each second ticking away precious minutes of Lily's life. When the doors finally opened to the ground floor, Nathan sprinted to the parking garage, his phone already in his hand.

He pulled up Grace's text with the address, started the car, and accelerated the SUV out of the parking space.

For twelve years, he'd kept his distance from God, nursing his anger like a wound he refused to let heal. Now, racing through the streets of Biloxi with his daughter's life hanging in the balance, Nathan found himself doing something he hadn't done since Hannah died.

"Please," he whispered, gripping the steering wheel so tight his hands ached. "Please help her. I'll do anything. Just don't take her from me too."

A traffic light turned yellow. Nathan punched the gas, shooting through the intersection as the light changed. Six more minutes to Victory Chapel. Six minutes that might make the difference between life and death for his little girl.

His phone rang—Rachel's ringtone. His heart seized as he answered on the car's Bluetooth.

"Nathan," his sister's voice trembled. "You need to hurry. Her vitals are dropping. They're talking about—" She broke off, her breath hitching. "Just hurry."

JOSEPH COULDN'T BELIEVE how many people still waited. He'd been ministering for an hour. Could he get to them all?

His button down shirt clung to his back, damp with perspiration. He surveyed the discarded crutches, braces, and even an oxygen tank scattered across the stage like abandoned armor. A dozen or so people had been healed so far—but what about the dozens more who waited?

The tingling pulsed through Joseph's palms as the old woman shared her need in his ear. Seventy-three years old, joints twisted like ancient tree roots, tears streaming down weathered cheeks. Joseph placed his hands over hers.

"Lord Jesus," he whispered, his voice barely carrying beyond the first row.

Power surged through him—not like electricity, more like sunlight breaking through storm clouds. Warm. Gentle. Unstoppable. The woman gasped as her fingers straightened, her rheumatoid arthritis vanishing in seconds. She flexed her fingers, staring at them as though they belonged to someone else.

"I can feel my rings again," she sobbed.

The church erupted. Shouts of praise mixed with aston-ished murmurs. A chorus of singing erupted spontaneously in ragged harmony. His uncle approached him. "How you holding up?" He laid a steady hand on Joseph's shoulder.

"Okay," he answered, scanning the packed aisles and pews. Dozens of faces stared back—hope, desperation, and faith all swirling together in the river of humanity. Congre-gants leaned forward in their seats, some curious, some calculating their path to the altar. Others hung back, arms crossed, waiting to be convinced. A few recorded every-thing on phones—ammunition for skeptics or believers?

Standing sixth in line, Joseph caught sight of the woman he'd exchanged glances with earlier, leaning on an older lady with kind eyes. Something about the way they were huddled together got his attention. He didn't know them— had never seen either of them before. But something in the younger woman's eyes stood out, as if God was pointing him toward her, and the burden she bore.

An elderly man, nasal tubes dangling from his nose, shuffled forward with the help of two teenage boys. As Joseph reached toward him, a jolt ripped through his mind —blinding, unstoppable—a hospital room. The sharp beep of monitors slicing the silence. A little girl, fragile and still, tangled in IV lines. Her chest barely rising. Her small fingers limp against the sheets.

Beside her, a man—her father—bent over the bed, grief carved deep into his face, his hands gripping hers as if he could will her back to life.

Joseph blinked, momentarily disoriented. The vision vanished as quickly as it had appeared, leaving him staring at the old man who gasped for breath an arm's length away.

Focus, Joseph reminded himself, pushing the strange image aside.

He touched the man on his forehead, who breathed easier immediately. Decades of emphysema dissolved like dew on summer grass. The man inhaled and exhaled in a steady rhythm. "My first full breath in years." He stood straighter, breaking free of his grandsons' support.

"Give God the glory," Joseph said.

The man pulled the plastic tube from his nasal passages. "Thank you, Jesus," he shouted, lifting his hands in the air.

With each healing, Joseph felt not depletion but renewal. The divine energy coursing through him seemed to grow rather than diminish. This was nothing like the exhaustion of his seminary studies or the fatigue after football practice in his high school days. This was purpose. This was his ministry, his calling.

Uncle David gestured to the worship team, who transitioned to a slower melody as the next person approached—a teenage boy limping badly, supported by his parents.

"Torn ACL," the boy explained, pointing to his knee brace. "Basketball injury. Surgery didn't go as planned."

Joseph nodded. He knelt to place his hands on the boy's knee. "Let's pray."

The church security team had formed a loose semicircle around the stage now. The crowd's enthusiasm had been building with each miracle, people pressing forward eagerly, some calling out conditions and needs. Uncle David leaned in close.

"We should wrap up soon," he murmured. "You've been going for two hours."

Nodding but not stopping, Joseph aligned the boy's knee. The swelling subsided. The teenager put weight on it, then stepped to test it. His eyes widened in disbelief. "It's fixed. Mom, Dad—look." He bounced on the formerly injured leg, then sprinted across the stage to prove the miracle.

A commotion erupted near the side entrance. There was a sudden shift in the crowd's attention. Someone pushed against the flow of bodies. The security team moved toward the disruption.

Then Joseph saw him—the father from his vision of the sick girl. Tall, disheveled, eyes wild with desperation. The man fought through the mass of people, ignoring protests and security personnel attempting to intercept him.

"Let him through," Joseph called out, his voice carrying across the sanctuary. The security team hesitated, looking to his uncle, who nodded.

The crowd parted reluctantly, creating a narrow path. Joseph scanned the faces, sensing the importance of this moment. Stepping forward to meet the man, Uncle David guided him to the front whispering something in his ear.

The man didn't respond, his focus locked on Joseph as he climbed the steps to the stage. His breathing was uneven, barely contained panic. "My daughter," he managed. "She's dying at Merit Hospital. They're putting her on dialysis right now. I was told you could help her."

The burning in Joseph's palms flared, confirmation rising like the gulf at high tide. This wasn't an interruption. It was the reason for the vision—his presence in Biloxi, the appointment God had prepared all along.

Uncle David stepped forward, his face lined with quiet concern. "Joseph, we still have dozens waiting. Perhaps this gentleman could—"

"I need to go with him," Joseph said, with a certainty that left no room for debate. "God showed me this man's situation."

The father introduced himself as Nathan. He shifted

his weight from one foot to another. His eyes darted to the exit. A muscle twitched in his jaw. "Please." A fracture broke through his voice, spilling despair. "There's no time."

Joseph turned to the confused congregation, many of whom had risen to their feet. "I'm sorry, but I must leave now. The Lord is calling me to minister elsewhere tonight." He gestured to his uncle. "Pastor David will continue in prayer with anyone still seeking healing."

Murmurs spread through the crowd. Some nodded in understanding, others frowned in disappointment. The worship team, sensing the shift, began playing softly as Uncle David took the microphone. "The Holy Spirit moves as He wills. Let's pray together as Joseph follows His leading."

Not waiting to hear more, Joseph followed Nathan's brisk stride to the side exit. Church security created a path. Congregants reached out to touch Joseph as he passed.

"My car's right outside," Nathan said over his shoulder. "Merit Hospital is fifteen minutes away if we hurry."

They pushed through the heavy sanctuary doors into the warm Gulf Coast evening. They raced across the dimly lit asphalt to a silver SUV tilted awkwardly against the concrete curb. One wheel mounted on the grass, the driver's door was still open.

Joseph slid into the passenger seat as Nathan fumbled with his keys. The tingling in Joseph's hands hadn't subsided—but intensified. Something momentous was coming. Something beyond anything he'd ever experienced.

"Her name is Lily." His voice cracked open like a dam of anguish. "She's only twelve. Type 1 diabetes, like her mother. The doctors say her kidneys are failing and—" His phone rang. He grabbed it from the console, glancing at the screen. "Rachel? We're on our way. How is she?"

All color drained from Nathan's face. The phone slipped to his shoulder before he caught it.

"No," Nathan whispered, the single syllable containing a universe of grief. "No, that can't be right. We're coming. Tell them to keep trying. Tell them—"

His voice failed him. His eyes swam in tears that refused to fall. "She's gone," Nathan said, the words hollow. "Lily's heart stopped two minutes ago."

The burning in Joseph's palms flared like a supernova.

FORTY-ONE

The double doors at the back of Victory Chapel crashed open. Grace's heart lurched as Nathan burst through, his face stripped bare with desperation.

Where was Lily?

Grace's fingernails dug into her palms. She'd been sixth in line, so close to Joseph Freeman and the healing touch that had drawn hundreds to this evening service. Her arthritic joints had flared all week, as if her body knew how desperately she needed this miracle. But Nathan's arrival changed everything. His wide, pleading eyes locked onto Joseph, not straying for a second as he pushed through the crowd. He rushed forward with hands outstretched, palms up like a beggar. His shoulders caved inward, all pride and restraint abandoned.

"Please." The word boomed from Nathan's throat, barely above the congregation's murmurs. His brow lifted, mouth parted with unspoken words trembling on his lips as he leaned toward Joseph. "My daughter—"

The sanctuary fell silent under the vaulted beams of the Biloxi chapel. Dr. Winters squeezed Grace's elbow.

Joseph whispered something to his uncle, then nodded to Nathan. He and Joseph moved to the side exit together, steps quick and synchronized. The heavy door groaned open, spilling streetlight into the darkened corner of the sanctuary.

Grace's joints screamed as she lurched after them, each step sending daggers of pain through her inflamed hips. "They must be going to Lily at Merit." She couldn't stop them, not with Lily's condition so dire. But she couldn't let them disappear—not when healing was within her grasp.

"We'll follow them to the hospital." Dr. Winters pulled a key fob from her purse.

Grace nodded, relieved. Calling another Uber would leave her behind. Strapped in the passenger seat, she winced as Dr. Winters maneuvered through Biloxi's evening traffic.

Ahead, Nathan's truck wove between cars, tires squealing as it changed lanes. He wasn't stopping for anything.

"Still with me?" Dr. Winters asked, glancing Grace's way as they neared the hospital.

She blinked, fingers tight around the door handle as they pulled into Merit's parking lot, near the emergency entrance. Before the car had fully stopped, Nathan and Joseph vanished through the entrance.

"Go," Dr. Winters said with barely contained energy. "I'll find you inside."

Grace exhaled sharply, bracing herself as she stepped out. Her body resisted the movement, a dull ache locking her hips and knees. She ignored the discomfort as she half-walked, half-limped to the doorway. Cool air hit her as she entered the white lobby of the medical center. Nathan's crumpled blue shirt disappeared around a corner toward the elevators, Joseph keeping pace across polished floors. She pushed forward, biting back a groan as pain flared up her spine. She was moving too slowly.

The elevator door was sliding shut with Joseph and Nathan inside.

"Nathan," she called, her voice rough, breathless.

For a split second, Joseph turned with a furrowing brow. His eyes flickered—confusion? Recognition?—but then the doors sealed with a quiet thump, swallowing the two men whole.

A sharp breath hitched in Grace's throat. She jabbed the call button, her body sagging against the wall as she watched the red indicator light creep upward.

When another elevator finally arrived, she entered and pressed the fifth floor. In the mirrored walls, her reflection stared back—pale skin, damp hair sticking to her temples, dark circles under her eyes.

The numbers counted up at an agonizing pace. Third floor. Fourth floor. Fifth. The door opened to a wave of motion—nurses moving quickly, an intercom paging a doctor, the beeping of monitors blending into the background noise. Grace limped through the elevator past Dr. Winters' office, past the pediatric ward where she'd met Lily and Nathan.

There they stood, just outside the Pediatric ICU. Nathan punched a code into the security pad—once, twice. Red light. Denied. Joseph waited silently, the rear flap of his sports jacket hanging freely.

His jacket. If only she could touch some part of it. One touch. That should be enough after twelve years of medication and treatments and false hope. Twelve years since the morning she was unable to demonstrate a grand jeté to her advanced student, since she'd gripped the barre with white knuckles as pain like shattered glass filled her joints. Twelve years since Andrew had called off their wedding before she returned his precious ring.

Her knees wobbled, threatening to buckle. She pressed a palm against the corridor wall, the cool surface doing nothing to ground her. The air felt thick—sterile, suffocating with desperation.

Nathan swiped again. The red light blinked back. Still locked. She had time.

Twenty-five yards. The same distance she'd once crossed in a series of fouettés that had brought audiences to their feet. Now each step was a negotiation with pain. The seizure notice on her studio door flashed in her mind—trying to teach while medications that barely kept her mobile devoured what little income remained. "FINAL WARNING" stamped across her lifelong ambition. Twelve years of treatments, and all she had to show for it was a body that betrayed her and threatened to ruin her life again.

One touch of his jacket. Not to dance—she'd surrendered that dream years ago—but for the simple freedom of climbing stairs without counting every one, of holding a coffee mug without wincing, of waking without the stiffness that made every morning feel like rigor mortis setting in, of living happily ever after with Nathan and Lily.

Nathan fumbled with the keypad again. The security system beeped its rejection.

Her right knee locked, sending a spike of pain up her thigh. She hugged the wall for support, stumbling forward. The corridor stretched endlessly, warping like a funhouse mirror. The vein in her neck pulsed with each ragged heartbeat.

"Pediatric ICU entrance assistance needed," blared over the hospital's PA system.

Twenty yards.

Her hip seized. She moved too slowly. Security would help them through in seconds.

Heavy footsteps approached from behind. "Hold on, I'll get that door for you." A guard strode past, a security badge dangling from a lanyard.

Fifteen yards.

The wall wasn't enough. An empty wheelchair sat ahead—she grabbed it, rolling it alongside her for support. The wheels squeaked against the tile as she pushed forward.

Five yards.

Nathan and Joseph remained focused on the door, their backs to her. The hem of Joseph's jacket swayed, taunting her. Her fingers trembled with anticipation, with desperate hope.

"Grace? Is that you?" called a voice from behind her.

A guard stepped in front of her—Johnny, from weekday security. "I'm sorry, but you can't go in there without authorization." He blocked her path, his expression sympathetic but firm. "Even staff need proper clearance for this unit."

She veered left to slip around him, but her ankle rolled. The wheelchair clattered against the wall as she stumbled. Johnny caught her shoulders—steadying her, but also holding her back.

"Please," she rasped. "It's important."

"Protocol's protocol, especially for ICU patients," he said, not unkindly.

The first guard lifted his security card, ready to swipe. Joseph's jacket swayed just beyond her reach. One touch. One chance. Just a sleeve, just the seam—anything. Then the miracle would come. It had to. Then Joseph could move on. Then Lily could live.

A beep. A click. The lock released.

"I just need—"

Nathan shifted left, just a fraction. The first guard reached for the handle. Johnny's grip tightened—then loosened, just for a split second, as he instinctively turned to the sound.

Now.

Grace lunged. Her joints moved like rusty hinges, each tendon a violin string pulled too tight. Her fingers stretched —just one inch more, brushing the coarse fabric of the hem of Joseph's jacket.

He vanished through the doorway. The touch lasted less than a heartbeat.

A JOLT COURSED through Joseph's shoulders, stopping him mid-stride. His breath caught. Heat surged from his shoulder blade down to his backside—flowing outward like water rushing into a valley. His vision blurred for half a second. The sensation was unmistakable. Healing had left his body.

But it wasn't like before—the gradual, familiar tingle of restoration. This was an unrestrained flood. A force that left his skin humming—his body twitching, energy still burning within.

Somewhere ahead, Nathan called out. "This way. Hurry." But Joseph couldn't follow.

His hands clenched. He had healed dozens of times. But never like this. Never with him not directing. Never without knowing where the power had gone. His gift had always flowed through him in service. But this—this had been pulled from him, as if someone reached out and claimed it. Confusion and awe rippled through him. Was this even allowed? The gift wasn't his to control, he knew that—but this felt like spiritual trespassing.

And there she was. The woman he'd noticed earlier at the service—sixth in line. But she wasn't clutching her friend's shoulder for support. She stood tall. Her fingers hovered in the space between them. Her breath paused as if she, too, realized the power transfer.

Their eyes met. And in hers, he saw it—not surprise at being caught, but wonder. Wonder he had seen on the faces of others, that moment when their pain was replaced by a blessing. "You felt it," she whispered, barely audible through the security door.

Joseph nodded. The sensation lingered in his belly, a gentle aftershock.

"Hurry." Nathan's voice cracked with urgency. "We need to get to Lily. Now."

A code alarm had gone silent. The hallway behind Joseph was eerily quiet. A woman in blue scrubs approached, her face grave.

"Nathan," she began in a low tone. "I'm very sorry, but she didn't respond..." Her unfinished sentence landed like a death sentence.

"No." His face drained of color. "I brought him here to heal her." He motioned to Joseph. "Tell her. Tell her you can help my child."

The security door started to close, its automatic mechanism engaging. But Joseph caught it and held it open. "You're whole now—because you believed," he said to the woman who'd touched him, the words rising from somewhere beyond himself. "Now go give thanks to God in heaven for freeing you from your disease."

Her eyes widened. She straightened as if testing a newfound freedom, as if any doubt melted into joy.

But Nathan had moved down the hall, his shoulders hunched as if the weight of the world fell on him. The doctor followed, still speaking in that terrible, gentle tone. Though Joseph couldn't hear the conversation clearly, the grim expressions told a story of life slipping away—of medical science reaching its limits. Nathan's body seemed to collapse inward with each word.

A divine certainty settled over Joseph, warm and real like a gentle touch. It wasn't just a feeling—it was a word of knowledge, bone-deep and unshakable, that transcended the death pronouncement he'd heard in the corridor.

He turned back to the woman who'd touched him and winked. "Why all the commotion?" he called out over his shoulder. "The girl is sleeping. That's all."

GRACE CAUGHT the conversation between Nathan and Dr. Montgomery, drowning out everything else. Her heart seized at the announcement. Her back hit the wall. *Lily...dead.* "No, please God, no."

Then it came. Joseph's wink ignited a warmth soft as sunlight after rain. The gentle heat flowed up her arms, melting the familiar ache in her elbows, her shoulders, her heart. It cascaded down her spine, through her hips. Her knees unlocked. The pain—her constant companion these past twelve years—evaporated.

But Lily—no. She wasn't gone. She was only sleeping. The same power that now filled Grace's bones would fill her too. She pressed her palms to her cheeks to feel the tears streaming down her face. Her body was her own again.

Johnny reached for her arm. "Grace."

"Praise Jesus," she shouted. "Praise Jesus, my Lord and my Healer."

She wanted to sing. She wanted to shout. But without thinking, she kicked off her shoes. It was time to thank God for her healing. To worship Him.

To dance.

She rose on her toes, her feet naturally aligning with effortless precision. Her arms floated upward, gracefully extending outward. Movements that were impossible moments ago now flowed as smoothly as water. She spun in a flawless pirouette, her body remembering, rejoicing in each muscle's newfound freedom.

"Grace?" Johnny said, his eyes wide as car tires.

She couldn't contain herself. Her body remembered what her mind had long filed away as impossible. She spun once, twice, again and again, each turn feeding into the next as her leg whipped around her body, creating its own momentum. Tears continued, but not tears of pain, but pure joy breaking free.

With each rotation, memories flashed through her mind —the day she received her diagnosis, the day Andrew had abandoned her, the day she'd locked her studio door for what she thought was the last time. Spin after spin, she released them all. The hospital hallway became her stage, her audience unsuspecting visitors, staff, and stunned security guards. The overhead fixtures transformed into spotlights in her mind's eye, and for a heartbeat, she was back on Broadway, full of promise and possibility.

She gathered herself and then—release! She soared, her body twisting through the air in a perfect arc before landing softly on one foot, the other extended behind her like a bird's wing. Her arms stretched wide, trembling not with weakness but with the sheer electricity of movement. A laugh escaped her lips—when was the last time movement had brought laughter instead of dread?

Twelve years of imprisonment ended in a single touch. Twelve years of watching her students from the sidelines, of marking steps instead of dancing them, of living half a life—gone in an instant. The music that had been silent in her soul now played again, loud and clear and unstoppable.

Beyond the ICU doors, Nathan had vanished, unaware of what trailed in his wake.

But Grace knew. As she lowered her leg, every movement a symphony of restored grace, she whispered a prayer of gratitude. Not just for healing—but for the power that restored her health.

The power that could heal others, starting with Lily, who would experience a miracle greater than her own.

FORTY-TWO

Joseph bounded through the pediatric ICU with divine fire. Monitors beeped in erratic rhythms. Dim lights buzzed overhead, washing out small faces pressed against white pillows. Clear tubes snaked from tiny arms and noses, anchoring each child to towers of blinking lights. His lungs suddenly struggled to take in air.

A nurse's shoes squeaked past. The sharp bite of antiseptic burned his nose. The scent yanked him backward in time—to another place, another kind of suffocating air. The tunnel in Pakistan. His parents slaughtered in the schoolhouse.

But this would be different.

Nathan surged ahead, his untucked shirt flapping, shoulders rigid with desperation. Joseph followed, his hands tingling with anticipation and holy power. Warm. Ready. How marvelous it would be for God to work in this sterile room of science and medicine.

Lord, You brought me here. You showed me the way. These children. Lily. They all need You. You called me to

America for this. Give me Your compassion. Let them see You in me.

A woman's raw sob pierced through the mechanical symphony. Nathan broke into a run.

Joseph's heart kicked hard against his ribs. The sound carried too much grief, too much finality. It wasn't just sorrow. It was surrender.

Thank You, Lord, for bringing me here to show Your glory, even in death. Especially in death.

"No, no, no." Nathan's cry flooded the room. Joseph rounded the corner to find two women huddled over a small bed, their shoulders shaking. A doctor in a white coat stood nearby, her hand hovering over her clipboard, mouth pressed tight. Her jaw clenched. Her eyes flicked briefly to Nathan, routine brushing against something too human.

And there, swallowed in hospital sheets, lay Lily. No breath. No flutter of lashes. Only stillness.

Joseph froze. The fire inside him flared with purpose, even as sorrow passed through him—sharp, familiar, holy. The sorrow of a ten-year-old in Pakistan, in a tunnel listening to his parents being murdered. That same grief-stricken ache now bent Nathan's shoulders, and Joseph knew it too well.

The doctor scratched her pen against paper. "Time of death, 10:37 PM."

NATHAN'S FINGERS trembled against Lily's cold forehead. The stillness—so complete, so wrong—sucked all the air from his lungs. His whole world shrank to that single point of contact. First Hannah. Now Lily. Both gone. Both stolen by this merciless disease.

A voice—sharp, unwelcome—cut into the haze. Dr. Montgomery. She moved to block Joseph, her clipboard clutched like a shield. "Sir, please step back. The family needs to grieve."

Nathan barely registered her. He sagged against the bed rail, unable to hold himself up. "My baby girl. Oh God...my baby girl."

Warm arms wrapped around his shoulders—his mother. Somewhere beside him, Rachel sobbed into a tissue, sharp, staccato breaths like drowning. Then she turned on him. "Where were you?" She spewed all fury and betrayal. "We called and called."

Across the room, Joseph stood still—too still. Something fluttered in his eyes. Nathan didn't know what it was—grief, maybe. Or memory. Like he wasn't hearing them anymore, but someone else. His lips moved, barely audible. A whisper. "Remember your gift. Your purpose." Not loud. Not for Nathan, though he heard it. It was for Joseph. And more importantly, it was all over him.

Dr. Montgomery stepped in again, louder now. "Sir, you need to leave. This is a restricted area. Don't make me call security."

"He stays." Nathan didn't plan the words. They clawed their way out from his throat. What did protocol matter now? What did *anything* matter?

"I understand you're grieving, Nathan," Dr. Montgomery said tightly, "but this man has no right to be here. These faith healers prey on desperate people, making outlandish claims that only give false hope."

"Grieve for what?" Joseph said in a voice that didn't seem his own. It felt like it came from someone else entirely, deeper, ancient. "She's not dead. She's only sleeping."

Everything inside Nathan warred—logic and loss,

memory and miracle. Hannah had slipped away, and nothing had stopped it. Now Lily. His throat burned as he spoke. "Just...let him through."

The doctor laughed. Harsh. Disbelieving. "Nathan, your daughter needs dignity now. Not some charlatan's voodoo magic."

CHARLATAN.

The word struck Joseph harder than it should have. How many times had he heard it? At seminary. From critics. From his own doubts in the dark hours before dawn.

But this wasn't about him or what people thought of his gift. It was about Lily, about offering what little he had—his faith, his prayer, his obedience to go where God sent him. And because Joseph was here, God came with him.

This wasn't about him. It never had been. It was about Lily. About obedience. About offering what little he had—his faith, his voice, his presence. And because Joseph was here, God would be here too. He had to be.

The doctor's voice pressed on, insistent, outraged, irrelevant.

Joseph tuned it out. He looked at the child, at her still body, all too quiet beneath a tangle of wires and sterile sheets.

And he spoke—not with his own strength, but with the certainty that filled him like rushing waters.

"Little girl," he commanded, "get up."

THE DOCTOR'S words punched through Nathan's ribcage, hollowing him from within. Time froze. Breathe. Why couldn't he breathe? His mother's fingers dug into his shoulder—five points of pain anchoring him to a reality he couldn't bear to accept. Rachel's gasp sliced through the suffocating silence, the sound somehow both distant and deafening. The overhead lights suddenly burned too bright, the antiseptic smell too sharp. This couldn't be happening. Not again. Not with Lily.

"Get this man out of here immediately." Dr. Montgomery reached for her phone. "This is completely inappropriate, and I won't allow it."

Hannah's deathbed request exploded in Nathan's brain. "Keep taking Lily to church. Don't lose faith." He'd failed her. Failed them both. And now...

Black spots danced at the edges of his vision. Should he make Joseph leave? Or accept what science told him was final—irrevocable?

But he couldn't handle losing her. Not like this. Not to the same disease that—

A warm hand settled on his shoulder. Joseph. The touch steadied him, grounded him in this sterile room that reeked of misery and death.

"Nathan." Dr. Montgomery's voice softened to the practiced tone she'd used when Hannah had died. "Don't put yourself through this. Let us handle this."

"Please." Nathan wasn't sure who he was begging—Dr. Montgomery? Joseph? God? "Please."

Rachel's sob caught in her throat. His mother's muttered prayers filled the silence, the same desperate murmurs he'd heard throughout Hannah's illness. But now...

He stared at Lily's face. So still. So wrong. His vibrant

little girl who helped him prepare dinner for Grace just two days ago.

Grace. The dinner she and Lily had helped prepare... her quiet smile. Her lupus. Another unwinnable battle. Another failure.

JOSEPH WRAPPED his fingers around Lily's tiny hand. Cool. Lifeless. No spark remained.

He laid his other hand against her forehead. Cool, but not gone long. But gone.

The familiar fire of God's presence burned inside— eager, alive, pressing to get out like a river behind a dam. But the room held its breath. The soft beeping monitors. The hitched sobs of Lily's aunt. Her grandmother's whispered prayers. Her father's fists clenched tight, white-knuckled around the bed rail.

Nothing happened.

The silence stretched.

Rachel sniffled a fresh sob. Nathan buried his head near Lily's side. Dr. Montgomery exhaled through her nose. "Enough," she shouted. "Enough I said."

"Little girl." Joseph's voice was steady as stone. "Lily."

The air shifted. A weight pressed into the room, unseen but undeniable.

"I command you, again. Get up and live."

A beat. Another. Then—

The sheet covering Lily rose. A sharp, sudden gasp followed.

The room exploded into motion.

NATHAN FELT it before he saw it—Lily drawing in a breath, sudden and sharp. He lifted his eyes. Color bloomed in her cheeks.

His heart stopped. Started. Stopped again.

Lily's eyes fluttered open.

"Oh my God." Rachel stumbled backward into a chair.

"What..." His mother's prayers died on her lips.

But Lily was pushing herself up, her movements jerky but growing stronger with each passing second. Her eyes found Nathan's, clear and bright—no trace of the glazed confusion that had haunted her final hours.

"Impossible." Dr. Montgomery shoved past Joseph, stethoscope already in her ears. "This...I don't understand. It's not possible."

Nathan gathered Lily into his arms, her warm body alive against him. Her heart beat strong and steady through his shirt.

Real. *This was real.*

And this time, he hadn't lost her.

JOSEPH KEPT his hands in place, feeling God's healing power surge through every cell, every molecule of Lily's body. Not just reviving her—but restoring her. Whole. Perfect. Free from the disease that had claimed her life.

The familiar warmth of divine presence lingered in his bones as he stepped back, giving the family space.

"She's hungry," he said softly. "Give her something to eat."

The doctor jabbed at the monitors, her medical certainty crumbling beneath the weight of divine truth.

But Joseph's spirit tugged elsewhere. His gaze drifted

beyond the reunion, to the other beds lining the ICU. Machines beeped and hummed. Parents sat with desperate expressions. Children lay still or restless, each one a heartbeat away from despair or deliverance. The room was thick with need—rich with opportunities for God's mercy to reach those desperate for a miracle.

Joseph's palms began to tingle.

NATHAN KISSED LILY on her forehead, her cheeks, her neck. Tears ran freely now, but not from grief.

"Daddy, stop," she giggled, brushing his face with her fingers. "I'm hungry."

Rachel dropped into the chair behind her, hands over her mouth. "Oh my God."

Nathan's mother just stared, silent for once. The prayers had stopped—but an awestruck expression had taken their place.

Dr. Montgomery hovered near the monitors, tapping through the readings. Glucose. Ketones. Oxygen saturation. She blinked hard and checked again. "This doesn't happen," she murmured. "Diabetes doesn't just disappear. I have her blood work. Her charts. I saw her flatline."

She stepped back, shaking her head. Her arms hung useless at her sides, as if she had nothing left to offer. Her gaze lifted to Joseph, raw with disbelief. "How?"

"The disease is gone," he said steady as scripture. "Every trace of it."

Nathan held Lily tighter. Her skin was warm, her breath easy, her eyes full of life. His heart squeezed.

Grace. Her faith. Her insistence on healing. Her invitation to Victory Chapel. She had made this possible. "We must tell her," he murmured aimlessly. "We must tell Grace," he cried to Rachel.

Joseph turned from the adjacent bed where a child lay unconscious. "Grace?"

"A friend," Nathan said, voice thick with wonder. "She believed this could happen. She led me to the healing service."

After the child's eyes blinked open, Joseph offered a thumbs up. "You'll find her outside—celebrating her own miracle."

FORTY-THREE

Six Months Later

"Higher, Lily. Stretch through your fingertips." Grace paced around her student, her gaze tracing every angle, every line. The girl lifted her arm with intention, a flicker of determination tightening her twelve-year-old frame.

Better. Clean lines, engaged core. Grace nodded her approval. "Hold it there. Feel how the energy moves through your body?"

Lily's brow furrowed in concentration.

Autumn sunlight spilled through the east-facing windows, warming the freshly polished floors. Grace inhaled the scent of rosin and faint traces of lavender.

Six months ago, this studio had been slipping through her fingers—fading paint, dim lighting, an empty whiteboard. Now? The mirrors reflected something alive again. A space filled with students, music, and second chances.

"Can I try the fouettés now?" Lily lowered her leg with impeccable control, barely a wobble.

Grace smiled. "Let's see."

Lily moved to center floor, settling into her starting position. Grace watched with a critical eye—weight properly centered, shoulders aligned over hips. A breath, a push, a whip of motion—her first pirouette spun seamlessly into a développé à la seconde, her working leg unfolding skyward. Grace noted the stretch with a teacher's instinct—almost ninety degrees now. Not bad for a beginner finding her footing.

"Spot. Eyes forward," Grace reminded. Lily's rotation sharpened, her arms cutting precisely through first to third position.

Grace swelled with pride. At twelve, she would have given anything to have Lily's focus.

"My turn," Grace said, stepping beside her student. "Watch the transition from fouetté to grand jeté."

A familiar thrill coursed through her as she took position. Then—motion. A series of fouettés, precise and sharp, flowed into the next move, her body slicing through the air, legs extending in precise opposition. She landed with barely a sound, the floor accepting her weight as if it had always known her.

No stiffness. No deep-seated ache dragging at her limbs. No protest in her spine.

She breathed in, steadying herself. The ghost of pain remained only in memory, replaced by something else entirely. Freedom.

"That was amazing." Lily beamed. "Can I try the jeté too?"

Grace chuckled, tucking a stray wisp of hair into her bun. "One step at a time. Let's refine your adagio sequence first. Control over height, remember?"

As Lily moved through her next exercise, Grace's phone buzzed from her bag near the sound system. She glanced at the screen—Marissa, her wedding planner. "Keep working on that développé," she said, answering the call. "Hi, Marissa." She watched Lily's extension, noting the slight tremor in her supporting leg. Grace gestured silently to engage her core more firmly—the correction a ballet teacher makes a thousand times.

"Perfect timing! The florist confirmed the gardenias for the altar, but they're suggesting peonies instead of lilies for the bouquets. Supplier issues."

Grace's gaze flickered back to Lily, who bent into an arabesque penché, a bit wobbly but holding firm. "Peonies?" She considered this unexpected change while keeping her eyes on Lily's form. "That wasn't what we planned, but they would complement the bridesmaids' dresses nicely."

"Great. And David Freeman agreed to officiate. He said he'd be honored."

Warmth unfurled inside her. David Freeman. Joseph's uncle and now their pastor. A steady presence in their lives since Jesus healed them. "That's wonderful. I'll call to thank him this evening."

"Miss Grace." Lily's voice rang out. "Dad says you're gonna be the most stunning bride ever. Even prettier than the ladies in your bride magazines."

Grace turned, heat rushing to her cheeks. Lily bourréed across the floor, feet fluttering like hummingbird wings.

"Your dad is very biased."

"He said you could wear a paper bag and still be beautiful."

Grace laughed, twisting the engagement ring on her finger—sapphire, vintage, a promise Nathan had placed there five months ago at Pier 44. She lifted the phone back to her ear. "Sorry, Marissa. You were saying about the reception?"

The studio door creaked open. Nathan stepped inside,

khakis and a blue Oxford, sleeves rolled to his forearms, his Meridian Engineering badge still clipped to his front pocket. His gaze locked onto hers, and the slow, easy smile that followed sent warmth curling through her.

"Daddy." Lily bolted to him. "Did you see? I did three fouettés in a row."

"I caught the last one through the window," he said, patting her shoulder. "Looking more like a pro every day."

Grace held up a finger. "That all sounds great, Marissa," she said into the phone. "Let's touch base Monday on the final guest count."

Nathan leaned against the barre. Lily performed another sequence of fouettés.

As Grace swiped off the call, she gave an approving nod at the improved alignment. Nathan crossed the room, wrapping an arm around her waist and pressing a warm kiss to her lips.

"How was your day?" she asked, straightening his slightly crooked collar.

"Better now." His eyes crinkled. "Richard approved the Bayshore timeline—no travel until after the honeymoon."

Relief loosened the last bit of tension in her spine. "That's a blessing."

Nathan took in the studio. "This place looks more amazing every time I see it."

Grace followed his gaze, lingering on the framed newspaper article near the door—Merit Hospital Miracle-Multiple Children Healed. Next to it, a piece on the studio's reopening, preserved like a relic.

"Sometimes I still can't believe we pulled it off," she murmured. "Six months ago, this dream was all but lost."

Nathan's fingers brushed hers. "I'm just glad I could help with the financials while you worked your magic here."

She leaned into him briefly, conscious of Lily practicing her turns nearby. "The studio's thriving again," she said with a quick squeeze of his hand. Her deeper feelings could wait until they were alone.

He grinned, eyes dancing. "Best investment I ever made. And totally selfish—I get a full-time ballet instructor for my daughter."

Lily twirled to them. "After dinner, can we talk about my recital costume? Maybe blue sequins. And a sleepover at the studio for my birthday?"

Grace laughed. "Let's survive the wedding first, then plan your birthday extravaganza."

Nathan pressed a kiss to the side of her head. "Whatever the bride wants."

As she gathered her things, she caught him watching her with that look—the one that suggested he still couldn't quite believe she was real. She tilted her head. "What?"

His smile was soft. "Nothing. Just...happy."

The simple word said everything.

"MY CAR OR YOURS?" Nathan asked, keys already in hand.

As they stepped outside, the air carried a hint of Autumn coolness, a welcome relief after the humid summer. Grace locked the studio door, testing the handle twice—a habit she'd developed since reopening the business.

"Yours," Grace replied. "I need to keep my hands free for any calls about the wedding."

Lily climbed into the backseat, immediately buckling herself in.

Nathan settled behind the wheel, watching Grace in the passenger seat as she placed her dance bag at her feet. Sometimes he still couldn't believe how quickly everything had changed.

Six months ago, he'd sat beside Lily's hospital bed, watching helplessly as her glucose levels crashed and her kidneys failed—the same ruthless disease that had taken Hannah had threatened their daughter.

Fear had been a constant presence, gnawing at the edges of his sanity through sleepless nights and impossible choices, juggling a career that suddenly felt meaningless against the weight of what he stood to lose.

Then came that day—the day everything changed. Joseph's hands on Lily's forehead, the desperate prayer, the impossible miracle. One moment, she'd been slipping away. The next, she was whole. Test after test had confirmed what Nathan already knew—the diabetes was gone. Just like Grace's lupus. Two miracles, one after the other, rewriting the future he thought had been set in stone.

And now? Now, life felt almost unrecognizable. His career at Meridian had taken off, the project manager role falling into place without the crushing travel schedule that would have stolen these moments with Lily.

The same executive who had once doubted his commitment now praised his efficiency, unaware of the difference a full night's sleep made—no more 2 AM blood sugar crashes, no more waiting for the next emergency call.

Lily was living. Grace was thriving. And for the first time in years, Nathan was at peace.

"I got a text from Joseph this morning," Nathan said as he turned onto Beach Boulevard. "He's making the rounds with Pastor David—three churches this week alone."

"How's he doing?" Grace asked, her voice gentle with concern.

Nathan exhaled, watching the sun shimmer off the gulf. "Tired, but hopeful. He said the hardest part isn't talking about Pakistan. It's explaining why he wants to go back. To the place that took everything from him."

"That takes a different kind of faith," she murmured.

Nathan nodded. "He said it's not about forgetting what happened. It's about building something better from it. A mission. A school. A future."

From the backseat, Lily piped up. "Joseph showed me pictures! There's going to be classrooms and a garden. And he said I can visit someday, after the school is built."

"Did he now?" Nathan said, glancing at Grace with a smile.

"Yep! And I'm gonna help him. I want to be a doctor. Or maybe a ballet-dancing doctor. Or maybe I'll teach and help at the mission."

Grace laughed. "Well, I can't think of a better résumé than that."

"And when I grow up," Lily continued, "I'm going to help run the studio with Grace. We're going to have the biggest classes in all of Biloxi!"

"Is that so?" Nathan smiled, catching Grace's eye.

"Yep! Grace already said I can be her assistant teacher when I turn thirteen. And when you two get married next month, it'll be a family business!"

The innocent way Lily saw their future—so straightforward, so full of certainty—warmed Nathan's heart. She had embraced Grace completely, had celebrated when they converted the studio's storage room into a bedroom for her overnight stays.

The foreclosure that had nearly destroyed Grace's

dream had ultimately brought them closer together, forcing conversations about future and family that might have taken months longer otherwise.

As they drove along the coastline, the gulf stretched out beyond the sandy beach, its waters reflecting the late afternoon light. Grace rested her head against Nathan's shoulder, a gesture that still filled him with wonder.

Six months ago, their lives were wracked with disease and financial uncertainty.

And here they were—healed, whole, together.

From the backseat, Lily began humming "Make a Way," a song at the top of her playlist. The simple melody filled the car, wrapping around them like a blessing.

Images of Joseph flashed through Nathan's mind—his hands trembling as he'd prayed over the children at Merit Hospital, the quiet conviction in his eyes when he spoke about his calling.

After years of hiding his gift in plain sight, playing football and attending seminary like any normal young man, he was now traveling from church to church, sharing his story with strangers who would decide whether his dream was worth believing in. The same place that had taken everything from him would now become his mission field—if he could find enough people willing to send him back into the fire—for good this time.

A warmth spread through Nathan's chest as he inhaled deeply. God hadn't simply erased their suffering like it never happened. No. He'd taken each jagged shard of their brokenness and transformed it into something Nathan could never have imagined. Their pain hadn't disappeared —it had become the very foundation of who they were now. Every tear, every sleepless night, every moment of pain now strengthened what they were becoming.

He felt Grace's hand in his, solid and real. Heard Lily's innocent voice radiating impossible health. This was their new beginning. Built not despite their past, but because of it.

"What are you thinking about?" Grace asked softly, squeezing his hand.

Nathan smiled, watching Lily in the rearview mirror as the girl gazed out at the water, still humming her song.

"I'm thinking that sometimes the most unexpected journeys lead to exactly where we're meant to be."

Grace squeezed his hand, and in that simple gesture was everything he needed to know—that she understood, that she felt it too, that whatever came next, they would face it together.

As Patio 44 came into view, Lily's humming grew louder, more confident. Nathan recognized the final verse of the hymn, the one about promises and hope and home.

"We're here!" Lily announced as Nathan pulled into a parking space.

"So we are," Grace agreed, her heart full.

In more ways than one.

EPILOGUE

The mountain path crumbled beneath Hassan's weathered boots as he descended to the skeletal remains of what had once been his home and place of worship. Twelve years. The number carved itself deeper into his chest with each step, heavy as the silence that had replaced children's laughter.

Blackened timber jutted from the earth like broken bones. The administration building—where Pastor William's voice had once boomed across the courtyard in welcome—now gaped open to the sky, its walls reduced to jagged teeth. Hassan's throat constricted. The militants had been artists of destruction, leaving nothing but stone foundations and the ghosts that haunted them.

He pushed through the twisted remains of the gate, his fingers trailing along metal that still bore scorch marks. The courtyard stretched before him, empty as a held breath. Here, Joseph had kicked a soccer ball while his mother hung laundry. There, by the well, the boy had skinned his knee and Hassan had carried him, sobbing, to Lyla's gentle hands.

I'm going back someday. Joseph's ten-year-old voice echoed in the stillness, fierce with the kind of determination that could move mountains. *I'm gonna build it again. All of it.*

But promises were fragile things. America was far from this broken place, and the boy—now a man—had remained silent. Perhaps Joseph's remarkable gift had led him down paths that had no room for Pakistan—or for this broken place. Perhaps healing strangers in air-conditioned hospitals had replaced the memory of that dying child outside Islamabad, the one whose fever had broken beneath Joseph's miraculous fingers.

Hassan's chest ached. A flutter of wings drew his attention to the chapel ruins. Sparrows burst from what remained of the pulpit in an explosion of brown feathers. He could see Pastor William there with clear remembrance, his arms spread wide, speaking of resurrection to anyone who would listen.

"Your son spoke of returning," he whispered to the empty pulpit. "But Twelve years, William. Twelve years without a word."

The desert wind answered, whistling through broken stones with a sound like weeping.

Hassan forced his legs to carry him to the back of the compound, where Lyla's garden had once transformed dust into beauty. Nothing grew there now. Nothing had grown there since—

Wait a minute.

A flash of green pierced the monotony of brown earth, impossibly vivid against the lifeless soil. Hassan's breath caught. A cardamom plant, tender and new, pushed through the exact spot where Lyla had once knelt in prayer among her mint and jasmine.

His knees buckled.

The plant shouldn't exist. Nothing grew here. Nothing could survive here. Yet there it stood, alive and defiant, its leaves catching the afternoon light like small hands reaching for heaven.

The air around him stilled, heavy with an unseen presence. In the pause between heartbeats, in the weight of watching eyes, in the certainty that settled into his bones like warmth. Hassan's skin prickled with recognition. This feeling, this impossible knowing—he'd experienced it once before, watching a fever-bright child gasp back to life beneath Joseph's touch.

"A sign?" The words scraped his throat raw. "Is this real? Are You telling me something?"

Silence. Then, so softly he might have imagined it, a gust of wind sounded almost like an answer.

Hassan sank to his knees beside the plant, his weathered hands shaking as he uncapped his canteen, splashing water onto the struggling plant, darkening the surrounding soil to a rich brown. Then, driven by something deeper than thought, he pressed his palms into the dirt where Lyla had once labored with Joseph.

The earth felt alive beneath his fingers. Waiting. Pregnant with possibility.

Somewhere across an ocean, did Joseph feel it too? Did his hands ache with phantom soil? Did his dreams echo with the same new life of this tiny plant?

Hassan squeezed the moist dirt tight, the grit scratched between his fingers.

"Joseph," he breathed, his words directed beyond the distant mountains, beyond the farther shores, "your mother's garden remembers you and is calling you home."

PLEASE LEAVE A REVIEW

If you have enjoyed this book, it would be a tremendous help if your could leave a review.

Reviews help me gain visibility and bring my books to the attention of other readers who may enjoy them. You can leave a review on the Desperate Souls Amazon book page.

GET EXCLUSIVE WILL MARLER MATERIAL

Building a relationship with my readers is the best thing about writing. Join my Legacy Readers Club for more information on new books and deals plus:

A free copy of Eli Colt's adventure in Helmand Province, Afghanistan—"The Silver Star."

You can get your content for free by signing up on my website at www.willmarler.com.

ABOUT THE AUTHOR

Will Marler is a seasoned author specializing in Christian suspense novels, best known for his gripping Eli Colt series. His writing intertwines high-stakes drama with themes of faith, resilience, and redemption.

Marler draws inspiration from his roots in New Orleans and the Gulf South, which enrich the cultural and atmospheric elements of his novels. He resides on the Mississippi Gulf Coast with his wife Wendie.

For more information:
www.willmarler.com
will@willmarler.com

ALSO BY WILL MARLER

The Worst Kind of Evil

Evil on The Southern Border

Evil For Good